VANISHING POINT

Also by John Nichol

Fiction

Point of Impact

Non-fiction

Tornado Down (with John Peters)
Team Tornado (with John Peters)

VANISHING POINT

John Nichol

Hodder & Stoughton

First published in Great Britain in 1997
by Hodder and Stoughton
A division of Hodder Headline PLC

10 9 8 7 6 5 4 3 2 1

British Library Cataloguing in Publication Data

Nichol, John, 1963–
Vanishing Point
1. English fiction – 20th century
I. Title
823.9'14 [F]

ISBN 0 340 67183 1

Typeset by Hewer Text Composition Services, Edinburgh
Printed and bound in Great Britain by
Mackays of Chatham PLC

Hodder and Stoughton
A division of Hodder Headline PLC
338 Euston Road
London NW1 3BH

Dedication

During the Persian Gulf War of 1991, twenty-four British servicemen were killed in action.

Since the end of Operation Desert Storm in February 1991 it is estimated that some one hundred and thirty British veterans have died from Gulf War Syndrome. Their average age was twenty-eight. As many as four thousand others are now suffering from debilitating illnesses and many have irreparable damage to their systems.

This book is dedicated to all of these heroes, living and dead.

Acknowledgements

In researching the background for *Vanishing Point* I was assisted by many other people. I could not have completed the novel without the assistance of the various Gulf veterans' associations, especially the team at Newcastle who gave many hours of their time to recount their horrific stories.

The trade between the West and Iraq in the equipment and precursors needed to manufacture chemical and biological agents was, and is, labyrinthine and secretive. In guiding me through these mysteries I would like to thank Brian Johnson-Thomas for his encyclopaedic knowledge of the history of Iraq's chemical weapons and of UN investigative operations.

Dr Hugh Miller was a mine of information on the unpleasant effects of chemical and biological agents. Sadly, a number of those who provided advice have to remain anonymous. You know who you are and you have my gratitude.

Many thanks to Neil, Phil and the team at Hodder & Stoughton for helping put the whole thing together. Finally, to my agent Mark Lucas, without whom there would be no *Vanishing Point*, I send my heartfelt gratitude.

Prologue

There was no warning, just a pinpoint of white light streaking towards them, swallowing the distance in an instant. Even above the bellowing of the engines Mark heard a roar and saw a blinding flash. The stick went slack in his hands as the sirens began screaming out. Instinctively his eyes shot to the warning panel but the firestorm of lights told him there was no hope of saving the jet.

For a split second he hesitated, gulping down his fear as he looked out into the black void of the desert night. Then the canopy shattered above his head as straps tightened like steel bands around him, slicing into the flesh of his shoulders and thighs. He groaned aloud as the ejector seat blasted him upwards into the darkness.

The howl of the engines was replaced by the scream of the slipstream as a 600-mile-an-hour wind hit him with the force of a sledgehammer. The breakneck ascent faltered then turned into a downward plunge. He tumbled helplessly, then the chute opened, jerking him savagely upright.

He had little time for reflection. They had been at low level, barely thirty feet above the ground. Although the ejection had flung him high into the sky, the desert floor was already rushing up to meet him. He took a swift glance around, trying to orient himself.

Unbroken blackness lay to the east, south and west, but to the north a faint glow of light came from a distant town. In the middle distance, lines of blue, green and white anti-aircraft fire cut into the night. As he watched, they were answered by the dull red and orange flashes of bomb-bursts. The rest of his formation had got through to the target. Mark felt sick at the thought of the jets turning for home, heading south to safety.

His legs buckled as he hit desert floor. Sand and grit ground against his helmet as wind filled the chute and dragged him along. He fumbled with the release button on his chest, and as the parachute came free, he hauled it in, hand over hand. It was a pointless precaution; the flames from the burning Tornado were like a beacon in the darkness, visible miles across the desert, but he did it mechanically, still in shock.

At a burst of gunfire, he threw himself down, heart beating wildly as tracer ripped through the air around him. As the firing ceased he realised it had come from his own jet, rounds from the Tornado's guns blasting off in the furnace heat of the blaze engulfing it.

The shock brought Mark back to his senses, and he began searching the area around him, peering into the darkness. The moon, low in the sky, threw grey light over the sand, but the fierce fires raging around the Tornado seemed to cast everything into shade.

At last he saw a figure slumped near the blazing wreck. His navigator's eyes flickered open as Mark bent over him, scanning his face. 'Steve! Steve! Are you all right?'

Steve moved his arms and legs tentatively before replying. 'I think so.' He winced as he turned his head to look at Mark. 'Shit. I must have smacked my head. What happened?'

'I don't know. I didn't see it until the last minute. A SAM 14, I think.'

Steve raised his head and stared at the blazing wreck. 'How the hell did we get out of that?'

'You must have ejected us – I didn't. I saw the flash and the next thing I knew I was dangling from a parachute.'

Mark stood up and turned his back on the burning jet,

giving his eyes a few moments to become reaccustomed to the darkness. His breathing grew shallow and ragged, the vapour fogging in the cold night air.

In the electronic cocoon of the cockpit there was never time to feel fear. War was fought like a computer game and even when real physical danger presented itself – a fighter manoeuvring towards his killing zone or the white light of a missile streaking towards him out of the blackness of the sky – the high-speed, adrenalin-fuelled reactions to avert it allowed no time for reflection. Within a handful of seconds, either their lives were extinguished or the danger was past. Here on the ground, however, there was no comforting glow of electronic instruments, no metal-skinned cockpit to protect them.

He turned back to Steve and studied his face. 'You scared?'

Steve nodded. 'You?'

'Absolutely bloody petrified. Can you walk? Then let's get out of here. There's nowhere to hide in miles and there'll be Iraqis round here any minute like flies round shit.'

Without waiting for a reply, Mark ran over to the yellow survival box, lying in the sand a few yards away. He ripped it open and dumped out the contents. He picked up the rucksack full of water packs, food and survival aids, and slung it over his shoulder, then carried the inflatable dinghy and the empty survival box away from the jet and threw them both as far as he could in opposite directions.

Steve had propped himself up on his elbows and was staring at him. 'What are you doing? Let's just get the hell out of here.'

'I'm buying us a few extra minutes. The first Iraqis here aren't going to leave anything lying around for the next ones to nick. If we make it a treasure hunt it'll take them longer.' He sent the last few items from the box spinning away into the darkness, then stooped to gather the loose bundle of his parachute. He crammed it under one arm before hurrying back to Steve, who staggered to his feet.

Before they moved off, Mark checked his GPS and then activated the tacbe radio on his flying suit. It was set to the Guard frequency, the international distress channel.

'Mayday. Mayday. Falcon 2-1, two down aircrew, location Bullseye 200-10.'

He switched off the tacbe and began moving away across the desert, holding Steve's elbow to steady him.

'We're going the wrong way,' Steve said, panic edging his voice. 'This is north.'

'I know. We'll head this way for a few hundred yards to confuse the Iraqis, then we'll loop round to the south.'

'Why the parachute?'

'Don't worry, we're not carrying it far.'

He put an arm round Steve to support him, and they began to half-walk, half-jog away from the burning jet. Instinct made them crouch, but the terrain of bare rock, with a thin covering of coarse, grainy sand, gave virtually no cover.

Mark's flying boots gave him no purchase on the smooth, windworn rock. He slipped and stumbled constantly as they hurried away, his breath rasping with the tension and effort. After they had fallen twice, he gave up his attempts to support Steve and they walked in single file.

A few minutes later, Mark blundered into an area of soft sand, dumped by the wind in the lee of a low rock outcrop. The sand sucked at his boots, making each step an effort. He paused, bent down and scooped out a rough hole with his hands. He thrust the parachute into the hole and scraped a thin layer of sand back over it, but parts of the vivid orange fabric were still clearly visible in the moonlight.

'What's the point of that? You might as well have left it on the surface.'

'I want to make sure they find it. It'll be confirmation that they're heading in the right direction.'

They carried on heading north, their footprints scarring the sand, but as soon as he felt hard rock under his feet Mark began to make a long curving turn back towards the south. They passed within a few hundred yards of the crash site and headed on across the waste.

His eyes were never still, scanning the horizon for Iraqi troops. He kept glancing at his watch as the minute hand ticked ponderously towards the hour, holding his tacbe at the ready.

The search and rescue sequence was ingrained on his

memory. After the initial Mayday call, every half hour they would send out a thirty-second burst, followed by a pause of thirty seconds and then another thirty-second burst. A signal at any other time would be taken as a sign that they had been compromised. The response then would not be a rescue helicopter but a missile from an A10. He let the first hour come and go without activating the tacbe, wanting to put some distance between themselves and the crash site before he risked using it again.

They had been moving for another twenty minutes when they heard the faraway murmur of engines. Looking back, they saw headlight beams stabbing into the night as vehicles bumped across the desert towards the downed aircraft.

They redoubled their speed, and ran up a long, gradual slope, stumbling over a rockscape scoured and sculpted by the wind into strange ridges and patterns. As they crested the faint rise, they found a shallow, windworn depression in the ground between two boulders. They lay prone in the hollow, gasping for breath.

As Mark looked back towards the still-blazing Tornado, he saw the dark shapes of military vehicles outlined against the flames.

A wind was blowing from the north-east, keening over the plateau, and the sweat was already cold on him in the bitter desert night. He shivered and hunched down.

'What do you think will happen if they find us?' Steve said.

'They won't.'

'Mark, this is me you're talking to.'

'I don't know.' He paused. 'If they're smart, they'll realise we have a far higher value as hostages than we do as dead bodies. Let's hope they're regular troops rather than some local militia looking for revenge because we've just bombed the shit out of their town.'

'What do you reckon our chances are?'

After a long silence, Mark turned his head to look at Steve. 'Not good. The parachute and the tracks might hold them up for a while, but if they start a methodical search outwards from the wreck site, they'll pick us up pretty quickly. They'll probably wait for dawn – I would if I was them.' He glanced towards the east where there was already a faint glow in the sky. 'Not that that gives us long. We'll get a signal out on the half hour. We're as far from the crash site as we're ever going to get now.'

'The Iraqis'll direction-find the transmission.'

Mark nodded. 'That's the chance we take. If we don't do it they'll find us anyway within a couple of hours.'

'Mark.' Steve gripped his arm. 'What if they torture us?'

The same thought had been going through Mark's mind. He felt his heart thump and tasted sour bile at the back of his throat. 'I don't know. Let's hope we never have to find out how brave we really are.'

Precisely on the half hour, Mark turned on his tacbe. Even though the Iraqis were two miles away, he found himself lowering his voice as he spoke into the set. After he had finished transmitting, he switched to receive and waited.

There was a long silence, then a muffled-sounding American voice came up through a haze of static. 'Falcon 2-1, this is Magic on Guard. Authenticate.'

'Shit. Where's the code?' Mark fumbled in his flying suit and pulled out his code tables. He found the code for that exact minute of their mission time and was shocked to realise that less than an hour had passed since the missile strike.

'Number of the day,' AWACs challenged again.

'Nineteen.'

'That checks out,' AWACs said. 'Switch to alpha.' It was a safer frequency, but still not a hundred per cent secure.

'Mission 2-7 is in the area. He's—' The rest of the message was lost in a burst of static.

Mark gave Steve a nervous glance then thumbed the transmit button again. 'Magic, repeat please.'

'Mission 2-7 is in the area,' came the faint reply, barely audible above the background hiss and crackle, as if they were talking on a steam radio set instead of the most sophisticated electronic communications. 'He's twenty miles north-west of your position and could be with you in a few minutes. Hold on.' Mark listened as AWACs contacted the helicopter. 'Panther 0-1. Two down aircrew twenty miles south-east of you. Do you have fuel?'

'Affirmative,' an American voice replied. 'We're on our way.'

Steve grimaced. 'I'd be happier with a full-up rescue, rather than a solo Chinook on its way back from dropping special forces up country.'

'For Christ's sake, Steve. I don't care if it's a secondhand double-decker bus, just as long as it gets us out of here.' As Mark spoke, the Iraqi vehicles began to move away from the burning Tornado. 'Shit, they're not even waiting for dawn.'

The lorries and armoured cars fanned out, covering wide arcs as they pushed out into the desert, sweeping backwards and forwards like yachts tacking into the wind. Ground troops were visible from time to time, frozen for a moment in the headlights as the vehicles swung around for the next pass. Suddenly yells and a fusillade of gunfire could be heard a few hundred yards to the north of the crash site.

'I think they've found the parachute,' Mark said.

There was a crackle of static. 'Falcon 2-1, this is Panther 0-1.'

He grabbed at the tacbe. 'Panther, this is Falcon. Are we pleased to hear from you.'

'Glad to be able to help. What's your location?'

'Approximately two miles due south of the crash site. When we get you visual we'll talk you in.'

'Mark.' Steve was tugging at his sleeve.

Two Iraqi armoured troop carriers had broken away from the pack and were heading south fast, their lights rearing and dropping as they bounced over the rough ground. Mark could just make out figures clinging to the outside of the vehicles, gun barrels outlined against the sky.

'Panther, we're going to get visitors very shortly. How far are you?'

'Ninety seconds. Get ready.'

The harsh wind had dropped as dawn approached, but a bank of clouds had drifted over, obscuring the weak light from the setting moon. Above the growing noise of the armoured cars, Mark now heard the deafening metallic rattle of a Chinook helicopter's twin rotors grow rapidly louder.

'Panther, we hear you now.' Mark paused, straining his eyes into the darkness. He spotted a shape blacker than the night sky, to the north-west of their position. 'Visual, Panther, visual. We're in your eleven o'clock.'

'Okay, Falcon. I'll just keep the locals' heads down a bit.' The Chinook made a pass over the top of the Iraqi vehicles and the darkness was suddenly lit up by lines of red and yellow tracer stitching a pattern towards the troop carriers. As the lines intersected, the armoured car veered suddenly to the right and burst into flames. A soldier toppled from it, his uniform ablaze. He lay still where he fell, a smaller pyre alongside the blazing wreck of the vehicle. The other one ground to a halt and men spilled out as the Chinook passed over them, its guns still raining down fire.

Suddenly the hot white streak of a missile launch flashed across the sky towards the helicopter. Flares pumped out of the Chinook as it swivelled to mask the heat of its engines from the missile's infra-red seekers. Mark waited helplessly, dreading the sight of the flash and fireball as the missile struck home. Then it blasted past, wide of its target, streaking away across the sky and exploding over the empty desert.

Mark was already talking into the tacbe again. 'We're now in your one o'clock, Panther. Come right twenty. Steady ... steady ... We're on your nose now, about four hundred yards.'

Guns chattering, still pumping out flares, the Chinook roared overhead, but passed straight over them.

'You've overshot, make another pass.'

'Falcon, you'll have to use a flare.'

Mark exchanged a look with Steve, then pulled a distress flare from the rucksack. Fingers trembling, he fumbled with the cap and pulled out the firing pin. As it came free, gouts of red flame and smoke began belching up into the sky. The beat of the Chinook's rotors changed in pitch as the helicopter angled back in towards them.

The other Iraqi vehicles were now moving towards them, racing across the desert to encircle the shallow rise where Mark and Steve lay hidden.

Mark looked across at Steve for another long moment, then thumbed the radio. 'Panther, abort and we'll take our chances on our own.'

'Negative, Falcon, I've come this far, I might as well go the last fifty yards.'

The Chinook was now hovering above and slightly to

one side of them. The downwash lashed at them, raising stinging flurries of sand and grit. As the helicopter dropped steadily lower, an Iraqi gunner opened fire from the surviving armoured car. Mark watched, frozen, as the unseen gunner worked the tracer across the sky, the lines closing inexorably on the massive bulk of the Chinook. The first rounds hit the rotors, striking sparks like small explosions, the light glinting from the flashing steel.

For a moment the helicopter seemed unaffected, then the back end sagged towards the ground. The rotors began to tilt out of the horizontal and the steady beat was replaced by a new and terrible sound as the blades began hacking into the fuselage, as if the Chinook was being fed through a blender. The tailplane vapourised and what remained of the fuselage plummeted to the ground, still cutting itself to pieces as the rotors struck fountains of sparks from the rock.

The thundering rotors, roaring engines and staccato bursts of gunfire were all extinguished in the noise of the blast as fuel gushing from the broken tanks ignited in a massive explosion. Mark buried his face in the dirt, feeling the searing heat as the blast flashed over them.

As the shockwaves ebbed away, Mark stared slack jawed at the ruins of their only hope of rescue. The bodies of the two pilots lay in the dirt alongside the Chinook, thrown clear as it blew apart. There was no sign of the two crewmen, butchered by the flailing rotors or burned to cinders inside the blazing fuselage.

Mark and Steve began belly-crawling towards the wreckage, squirming along the ground like snakes. Mark went to the figure lying furthest away but as he put a hand on the man he felt a wet, dark hole where his chest should have been.

He flattened himself as the firing broke out again. Several shots splintered the rock and the body twitched twice as it was hit. A round plucked at the fabric of Mark's flying suit, like a hand tugging at his sleeve. He lay motionless for a moment, too frightened to move.

He took a deep breath, then began worming his way backwards, eyes closed like a child hiding his face from danger. His foot touched something soft. Steve was lying flat alongside the other pilot, partly screened from the Iraqis by the blazing wreck.

Together they began crawling back towards their refuge, dragging the burly figure away from the furnace heat of the blaze. They dropped him and fell to the ground as fresh bursts of small-arms fire spattered around them.

They were full in the open, with not even a rock for cover. Mark lay still, twitching at each near miss as rounds shattered the rock and ricocheted away with a sound like screaming. He shouted at Steve, trying to make himself heard above the gunfire. 'We have to get back to our cover.'

'No,' Steve yelled. 'We're dead if we move.'

'We're dead anyway. They'll just pick us off if we stay here.' He tried to take a series of deep breaths, but fear had made his breathing too fast and shallow to take in much oxygen. He closed his eyes for a second, wondering if it would be his last. 'Ready. One, two, three. *Go!*'

They sprinted the last few yards through the hail of fire, dragging the pilot between them, then threw themselves down in the hollow. The pilot's flying clothes were torn and scorched and there was the stink of singed hair. His thigh was sticky with blood. Mark ripped a field dressing from his first-aid pack and pressed it against the wound.

When the firing stopped, Mark lay motionless, flesh creeping, straining his ears for any sound. He gave Steve a questioning glance, then inched his way to the edge of the rock. He counted to twenty, trying to slow his pounding heart, then raised his head.

The firing began again instantly. He caught a glimpse of a line of troops advancing, before he dropped back into cover. Bullets whined and ripped at the rock around him, showering him with fragments.

'Look, Mark,' Steve said, 'I don't know about you, but I've no wish to die right now, and pistols aren't much use against automatic rifles. If we come out shooting we'll just be cut to pieces.'

Mark nodded, and Steve, his hand shaking, pulled a silver foil space blanket from the rucksack. He gingerly waved it above him, still keeping his face pressed down into the dirt.

There was no firing, no sound in reply, then a shout in Arabic. Mark raised his head. Forty Iraqis faced him from less than fifty yards away. Every gun barrel was pointing at his head. Mark and Steve got slowly to their feet, holding their hands above their heads. Mark looked from face to face around the hostile circle confronting them. Some stared back impassively but hatred blazed from the eyes of the rest.

Their commander fingered the belt holding in his bulging paunch. He shot a glance at Mark as brief as a snake's tongue tasting the air. 'American?'

Mark shook his head and turned his shoulder to show the Union Jack patch on his uniform. 'British.'

'You have gold or dollars. Give them to me.'

Mark hesitated for a second, then slowly undid his belt and handed over the bail money issued to every pilot before a combat mission. Two more soldiers stepped forward and took the money from Steve and the injured pilot.

The Iraqi smiled. He handed out one bundle of dollars to his men, but stuffed the other two into his pocket. There was a mutter of protest, at which the commander swung round and swiped his pistol across the dissenter's face.

He barked an order and rough hands seized Mark's wrists and ankles and bound them with electric flex. Mark winced as the wire bit into his flesh. As he was seized by the hair, he felt a clump rip out of his scalp. He was dragged and kicked down the slope, then thrown bodily into the back of a truck.

He lay winded on the cold metal floor as Steve and the helicopter pilot were pitched in with him. Some of the Iraqi soldiers clambered up into the truck and ranged themselves along the wooden benches at either side, their boots inches from their prisoners' faces. Every few minutes, as if reminding him of his helplessness, one of them ground Mark's face into the floor with his boot.

At another barked order, Mark's head was lifted from the floor. A coarse, black bag, stinking of diesel, was dragged over his head as a blindfold, and he fought down waves of panic as he struggled to breathe. He jerked his head to and fro, trying to work the cloth away from his face enough to create an airspace, but each movement he made earned him another kick from his captors. He lay still, forcing himself to breathe slowly, even though his lungs were clamouring for air.

A few moments later the engine started and the truck rumbled off, bouncing and jolting across the desert.

Mark had no idea how long they had been moving when he heard the driver changing down through the gears and felt the lorry bounce and sway as it turned off the road. There was the rattle of metal gates and the lorry nosed its way forward and stopped. The tailgate was thrown down and Mark was dragged out and hustled into a building.

Without warning, he was dropped on to a concrete floor, then a steel door clanged and there was silence, broken only by his own laboured breathing, although he knew that the Iraqis still surrounded him. He strained every nerve, panting with fear, and tensed his body for what he knew would come.

The silence erupted and blows began raining down on him. He heard the dull impact of each blow a fraction of a second before the stabbing pain that followed it, but gradually it merged into one continuous, pounding agony as the sounds of the blows eventually receded and the darkness engulfed him.

Mark lay motionless in the blackness of his cell, wondering what had woken him. Tiny chips of stone and concrete pressed into his face as he lay on the cold, hard floor and the fraying edge of the coarse, threadbare blanket scratched against his cheek.

For a moment the only noise was the scratching and scuttling of cockroaches across the bare concrete and the drowsy buzzing of flies, then he heard the sound of approaching footfalls, accompanied by a dragging sound.

The noises stopped, and further down the corridor a door was thrown open. Mark heard a thud like a side of meat thrown down on a butcher's slab. A low moan, so faint it was barely audible, was silenced by the slamming of the metal door, and then the footfalls moved on down the corridor. His muscles tensed as the footsteps became closer, sweat starting on his forehead. He gulped down waves of nausea as he strained his ears, waiting for the grating of a key in the lock.

No one ever entered his cell, except to drag him out for a fresh interrogation. A disembodied hand shoved stale bread and grey, greasy soup through the hatch once a day, which he wolfed down, eating on all fours like a dog, before it was smothered by the flies which swarmed in clouds around the filthy, stinking hole in the floor that served as a toilet. He lived in darkness and silence, barely able to keep track of the passing days, interrupted only by the pain of beatings under the glare of the interrogation lights and by the sounds of the others' sufferings. Their screams echoed from the cold, grey walls scratched with the pitiful graffiti of previous captives.

The footfalls stopped. Mark stiffened as the door rattled and faces peered in at him through the spyhole, then he let his pent-up breath escape as the tread of the men's boots receded.

He counted the steps, measuring their progress down the corridor. Five paces – a metallic clang as they kicked Steve's cell door. Ten paces – Marvyn, the American businessman. Fifteen – Dan, the helicopter pilot. Twenty – the American oil worker, Luther Young. The footfalls stopped and he heard the squeal of a metal bolt. As Mark heard the man being dragged back along the corridor, he could not prevent a guilty feeling of relief. This time it was not him.

A cry – part terror, part protest – was cut off by the hollow thud of boots. After a pause, Mark heard a thin, voice again, crying with panic. Another silence, a harsh shout, a broken mumbling, then an agonised, ululating scream.

Mark turned on to his side, away from the sound. The wire binding his wrists bit savagely into his flesh and fluid from the broken sores trickled down his hands on to the ground. He almost welcomed the pain, using it to drown out the screams.

As he lay there, a pale, intermittent light began breaking through the blackness of his cell, like the flickering of a neon sign through the window of a cheap motel. He rolled over again, sending fresh waves of pain coursing through his swollen wrists. Through the tiny slit-window high up in the wall, lines of white, green and blue anti-aircraft fire seared upwards, cutting arcs like welders' torches across the night sky.

The light played across the massive triumphal arch at the entrance to the site, decorated with leaden, social-realist images: Saddam the great leader, Saddam the peacemaker, Saddam the wise, Saddam the benevolent.

Mark closed his eyes, listening for the sound of the bombs. For the last few nights he had counted the seconds between the flash and the rumble of the explosions, just as he had lain awake in his bed as a child during summer storms, counting the interval between the lightning and the thunder. Tonight was different. Above the screams and sobs, Mark heard a moaning, rushing sound, faint at first, then growing louder, beyond the reach of natural sound.

Suddenly, there was a blinding flash of light. The floor of Mark's cell shook and dropped away as the blast wave picked him up and hurled him against the wall.

He lay trembling with fear, not daring to move, then after a moment's silence, the noise began again. It was louder still this time, starting higher and culminating in a banshee screech and a fresh explosion.

Again the blast wave battered him, and he curled into a foetal position. As the air was sucked from the cell, he gasped for breath. The wind rushed back, and a torrent of bricks and shards of concrete crashed around him, half-burying him in a mound of rubble.

Through the clouds of dust and debris, he could see the steel door of his cell hanging crazily from its hinges. A gaping hole had also been torn in the outer wall. There were shouts and screams, the sound of running feet, the smell of burning.

Mark hauled himself to his feet, and was staggering towards the doorway when he felt as much as heard the roar of another incoming bomb. He flung himself back to the ground as a third massive explosion shook the building.

The steel door toppled towards him, but smashed to a halt on a lump of rubble inches from his face. More chunks of concrete cascaded down on to the steel as gaping cracks snaked up the walls. Beneath the cries of fear and pain came the hissing sound of fractured pipes and the roar and crackle of flame.

The wall listed outwards, then stopped. One more direct

hit and the whole building would collapse. Even if Mark survived the blast, he would be buried alive.

During a brief pause, through the hole in his cell wall Mark watched four Iraqis sprinting across the compound. Another blinding flash of light and another explosion came, followed by another and another, but these were different: air-bursts detonating a couple of hundred feet above the ground. Outside, the four Iraqis simply disintegrated, cut apart by the hail of sharp steel shards.

These were anti-personnel weapons, deadly seed-pods opening to spill hundreds of tiny bomblets, each one capable of maiming and killing any living thing in its path. He pressed himself flat against the buckled concrete floor. The ground boiled with fire as the bomblets exploded with a noise like a machine-gun chorus. Shrapnel whined around him, gouging furrows out of the floor and walls and striking sparks from the steel door above him.

Silence fell again as a familiar smell filled his nostrils: the morning after Bonfire Night, the stale smell of fireworks hanging thick in the cold air. Hardly daring to breathe, Mark gently flexed his limbs. A sharp pain stabbed up his left leg and he cried out.

Steve's voice answered him. 'Mark? Are you all right?'

'My leg's trapped.' Mark turned his head as far as he could to look over his shoulder. A jagged hole had opened in the wall separating their cells and Steve's swollen face was framed in the gap. He limped across the ruins of Mark's cell, crouched down and began removing the lumps of concrete and rubble from on top of the steel door.

He was interrupted by shouts and the sound of running feet. Two Iraqis burst into the cell, and Steve got warily to his feet as one swung his gun to cover him. The other grabbed Mark by the shoulders and began trying to drag him out. He screamed in agony as the broken bones in his ankle grated together.

Steve yelled furiously, and hooked his fingers under the edge of the steel door, feeling for grip, then he braced himself and began lifting. The sinews stood out on Steve's neck and a vein throbbed in his forehead as he heaved the door off his leg. He stood motionless, arms locked, streaming with sweat, and jerked his head at the guard.

The Iraqi stared suspiciously at him for a moment but then took hold of Mark's shoulders again. This time Mark's foot came free. Steve let out a gasp of relief and dropped the door with a crash. Mark stumbled as he tried to keep the weight off his leg and threw out an arm to break his fall. His hand touched something soft and wet. In the half-light he made out a blood-soaked torso, stripped naked by the blast. As he reeled back, the guard jerked him upright by his hair and hustled him out of the building into the yard. The other prisoners were thrown into the dirt alongside him.

Petrol spurting from a ruptured fuel tank ignited with a roar, spraying fire across the compound, where massive blocks of torn concrete were strewn, steel reinforcing rods jutting from them like fractured bones. Thick, billowing clouds of black smoke rose from the ruins of the buildings as the fire advanced hungrily along the block that had been their gaol.

Mark looked up as a white streak flashed across the sky, the trail of a Scud burning overhead. It arced away over the desert and a moment later he saw the flash of a massive explosion. As the light began to fade, he glimpsed a yellow-brown cloud spreading outwards from the air-burst, carried on the desert wind.

The glare of the explosion also lit up the dirty yellow POW suit of Luther Young, who had escaped from the ruins of the interrogation cell and was hobbling away as fast as his battered body would carry him. At a roar from the Iraqi commander, two soldiers set off in pursuit, unslinging their weapons as they ran.

Just then the alarms began to sound. This was not the air-raid warning siren that Mark had heard every night. This was a different tone, a strident, repetitive, shrieking klaxon.

The effect on the Iraqis was instantaneous. His voice cracking, the commander began yelling orders, and Mark saw raw fear in his eyes.

The soldiers chasing Luther stood irresolute for a moment, then they abandoned their pursuit without even firing a shot and ran back, leaving him stumbling on across the desert.

A dozen or so undamaged trucks and armoured vehicles began to lumber out from beneath their camouflage nets, and a guard, his pupils dilated with terror, half-dragged, half-threw Mark into the back of one of them.

There was a series of cracks like pistol shots and parachute flares began drifting down, flooding the compound with harsh white light. Peering over the tailgate of the lorry, Mark saw a line of tanks advancing steadily across the desert. Infantry, moon-suited in chemical protection gear, followed in their wake. As he glimpsed Luther's yellow-clad figure stumbling towards them, his hands held high in the air, a soldier grabbed Mark by the hair and threw him down again on to the floor of the lorry.

A salvo of shells screamed in and fell just short, sending spumes of sand high into the air. As the next salvo landed, the lorries rumbled out of the compound in a storm of gears, swinging north, away from the advancing troops.

Mark's last sight of the place where he had been held was the solitary remaining fragment of the triumphal arch, a pillar capped with a few feet of frieze, from which the stone face of Saddam still glowered out across the desert.

As the Iraqi column bounced away over the rough road, Mark shuddered. In this blank terrain, helicopter gunships would pick off the lumbering lorries and armoured vehicles as easily as shooting rats in a barrel. As if echoing his thoughts, a lorry towards the front of the convoy disappeared in a fireball as a rocket struck home. A few seconds later an armoured car erupted, the impact of the rocket immediately followed by a second, even larger explosion as the fuel and ammunition detonated simultaneously.

Mark was thrown violently to one side as the driver swerved around the blazing wreckage and floored the accelerator. Two more lorries erupted in balls of flame. After a brief, frantic exchange between the driver and the Iraqi commander, the lorry made a savage turn off the road and plunged into the desert.

Juddering and jolting, it crested a slight rise and, barely under control, slid down a slope into the bed of a shallow wadi. The other vehicles were lost to sight, though their course was plotted by a series of massive explosions sending up pillars of flame and smoke as yet more salvos of rockets found their targets.

At another word from the commander, the driver cut his

engine. None of the Iraqis broke the ensuing silence. Mark huddled on the floor, his flesh creeping as he waited for the whining roar of an incoming rocket, but the only sound was the metallic clicking of the engine as it cooled. The commander waited for fifteen minutes after the last explosion, then nodded to the driver, who restarted the engine.

Straining his eyes into the darkness, the driver nosed the lorry slowly down the wadi, lurching around the huge boulders in its bed. After a few hundred yards, he spotted a slight break in the wall of the wadi and set the lorry grinding up through the gap. The wheels span and slid in a patch of soft sand, but as the lorry slewed sideways, they gripped again on rock and gravel. The lorry juddered, righted itself and crept over the rim of the wadi. The driver eased it back towards the road, the only moving thing in the vast, empty expanse of desert.

The road behind them was punctuated by charred, blackened wrecks like milestones, and ahead of them lay another, an armoured car surrounded by a corona of dead bodies. Its crew had dived out of their vehicle, fleeing for their lives as the rocket struck home, but the explosion had engulfed them all, burning each to a blackened shadow on the grey surface of the road.

The driver hesitated but the commander urged him on, his face a mask. The lorry inched past the wreck, its wheels crunching cinders, then accelerated away, following the faint grey luminescence of the road north across the desert.

Just after dawn the lorry slowed and turned off the road into a barbed-wire compound surrounding a series of low concrete blockhouses. As the soldiers fumbled with the lock of a rusting iron door, Mark felt Steve's reassuring hand rest on his shoulder. It was a fleeting moment of human warmth.

Then the Iraqis seized him and pushed him into a small, dank, windowless cell. The door clanged shut and he was once again alone.

Chapter 1

The taxi inched its way through the traffic choking High Street Kensington and pulled on to the sweeping forecourt of the Royal Lodge Hotel.

The size of his tip earned Mark a withering glance from the cab driver, who exchanged a look with the top-hatted doorman and then disappeared back into the traffic, leaving a cloud of blue diesel fumes hanging in the air.

The plate glass doors swung soundlessly open and the cool draught of air-conditioning met Mark as he entered the cavernous lobby. His footsteps echoed from the marble floor, emphasising his slight limp, a permanent reminder of Iraq.

He glanced around him looking for familiar faces, but saw none. Two sharp-suited businessmen stood in the middle of the lobby, greeting four white-robed Arabs with elaborate courtesy. Near by a group of American women sat surrounded by Harrods carrier bags, noisily comparing their purchases. Elsewhere a few lone individuals read newspapers and cast surreptitious glances at their watches.

Mark ran his eye down the gilt-framed board welcoming the day's visitors. Halfway down, sandwiched between a meeting of Infotech PLC in the Elizabethan Suite and a

Waterstones literary lunch in the Garden Room, was the legend: 'Tudor Suite: Gulf War POW Association, Sixth Annual Reunion'.

A stunningly beautiful, auburn-haired receptionist gave him a professional smile as he reached the desk.

'Mark Hunter, I'm with the Gulf POWs.'

Her smile grew noticeably warmer. 'We're delighted to have you here, Flight Lieutenant. If you could wait just one moment, our manager would like a word.' Mark smiled back every bit as warmly.

As he stood watching her walk across the lobby towards a discreet mahogany door, he felt a hand on his shoulder and heard Steve's West Country voice in his ear.

'Don't even think about it. This is the one night in the year when you're going to stick with your mates, whatever the temptations.'

Mark gave a rueful grin. 'A man can dream, can't he?'

'Of course, but yours have an annoying habit of coming true.'

He turned to look at his friend. 'Hell, Steve, never mind me, you look like shit. I didn't poison you with my fabulous home cooking, did I?'

Steve forced a smile. 'No. The meal was terrific. We both enjoyed it. Didn't we?'

Steve's wife had been standing to one side.

'Sorry, Jenny,' Mark said. 'I didn't see you. How are you – and how's the bulge?'

She gave a thin smile. 'We're both fine, thank you.'

'You haven't come to chaperone him, have you?'

'No, I'm just dropping him off. You needn't worry about me cramping your style. I'm just grateful for whatever's left when the Air Force and his precious squadron have finished with him.' There was an uncomfortable silence. 'Well, enjoy yourselves,' she said. 'I must go.'

Steve held her back for a second. He kissed her and whispered a few words in her ear. She gave a listless nod and walked away across the lobby.

Steve avoided Mark's eye.

'Ouch. Have you had a row?'

Steve shook his head. 'She's just a bit tense.'

'Is everything all right? With the baby, I mean.'

Steve exhaled before replying. 'As far as we know, yes. She's just anxious, that's all.'

Mark put an arm around his shoulder. 'That's natural enough, especially after last time, but you've only got two months to go now. You're through the real danger period for miscarriages, aren't you?'

'I suppose so.'

Mark waited but Steve did not elaborate.

The growing silence was broken by the return of the receptionist and the manager, immaculately dressed in a morning suit. He leaned forward slightly as he spoke. 'Flight Lieutenant, we're honoured to have been chosen to host your reunion.' He had the head waiter's gift of effortlessly combining servility with condescension. 'I trust you will find everything to your satisfaction. As a small gesture of our appreciation, you'll find some champagne on ice in the Tudor Suite. If you need anything, just let me or one of my staff know. Enjoy your stay and . . .' He gave a confidential smile. 'Good luck with your mission.'

Steve gazed blankly at him.

'Thank you very much. You've already been more than generous,' Mark said hurriedly. 'We really do appreciate it.'

The manager waved away Mark's thanks and walked back to his office.

'Okay,' Steve said. 'Who are we supposed to be this time?'

Mark glanced towards the receptionist and lowered his voice. 'I can't really divulge much, but we're expecting to be deployed overseas in the next few days – a secret mission. It's likely to be the last time that we'll all be together.' He grinned. 'It seemed to do the trick, he's given us the Tudor Suite for nothing and the rooms for about a third of the normal rate.'

'You crafty sod.' They both turned to face the slim, wiry South Londoner who had appeared behind them. 'Not that I'm not grateful, mind, I was thinking a hundred and fifty quid was a bit steep.'

Mark shook his head. 'No, Dexy, this is Kensington, not Kennington. That's the price after the discount. What's up, don't the SAS pay wages any more?'

'Jesus, I think I'm going into shock,' Dexy said. 'Let's

dump our bags and see if some of that champagne can revive me.'

The receptionist was watching them with amusement. Mark glanced at her as he picked up his key. 'Shall we save you some champagne?'

She held his gaze for a second. 'I wouldn't if I were you, it'll be warm and flat by the time I finish work tonight.'

'Not if I leave a bottle on ice.'

'Sorry,' Dexy said, putting an armlock on Mark and propelling him away from the desk. 'There's no ice to spare, we need to put it all down the front of his trousers.'

'Wait a minute,' Mark said. 'I haven't got my things.'

'It's all right,' the receptionist called after him. 'This is Kensington not Kennington. Your bag's already in your room.'

'I hope they haven't dropped it,' Mark muttered as Dexy steered him towards the lifts. 'It's got my Pentax in it.'

'Not your bloody camera again. If I'd known it was in your bag, I'd have thrown it around a bit myself.'

'Me too,' Steve said.

'You didn't complain when I did your wedding for nothing.'

'That was a bloody embarrassment; the only wedding in history where the bride was on time but the ceremony was delayed while the best man took a few more pictures.'

'Well, he's not taking mine,' Dexy growled.

'It's all right, Dexy. I'll put a little black box over your face before I show them to anyone who hasn't been positively vetted.'

'I can't see how you'll be able to take pictures anyway,' Dexy said. 'A glass of champagne in one hand and that receptionist in the other, where are you going to put the camera?' He broke off to give a low whistle as they came out of the lift and began walking along the corridor towards their rooms. 'The pile on this carpet must be at least six inches deep. If you dropped a pound coin, you'd never find it again.'

'*You* would.' Mark gave him a sideways look. 'Right, no playing with the toiletries, exploring the mini-bar or trying on the bathrobes. Let's get straight down to the Tudor Suite and see who else is here.'

They were almost the last to arrive. About a dozen other men stood around a damask-covered table which was already littered with empty bottles. Mark saw Steve almost every day, sharing the cockpit of their Tornado, but he had not seen most of the others since the last reunion a year before.

There were raucous greetings, jokes, handshakes and backslaps all round. They were an unlikely bunch – all shapes, ages and sizes – but the searching looks they exchanged, scanning each other's faces intently, showed the depth of the bond they had formed.

They had looked like a party of refugees from a famine as they boarded their flight to freedom six years before. Several had had to be carried on to the aircraft. Mark and Dexy had broken legs, others were simply too weak and sick to walk. All were gaunt, emaciated, hollow-cheeked and hollow-eyed, their POW suits flapping around them. There was nothing now to suggest the ordeal they had all shared, other than a certain guarded look behind their eyes.

Mark smiled to himself as he saw Dexy greeting the others distractedly whilst making straight for the table. His anxious look disappeared as he found several still unopened bottles of champagne. He walked over to Steve and Mark carrying three generous glassfuls in one hand and a spare bottle in the other.

Dexy drained his glass, refilled it, then took a more relaxed look around the room. 'They look in better shape than they did after those Iraqi bastards had finished with them, don't they?'

Mark nodded, and gave Dexy an appraising look. 'I heard a rumour that some of you had been back to pay your respects to the guys who looked after us.'

'You don't want to believe all the rumours you hear.' Dexy glanced around him and then dropped his voice. 'Though you'll be sorry to hear that their chief had an unfortunate accident. He choked to death on his own electric baton.'

Mark shuddered. 'He used that on me just before I broke. He told me they could use them internally and gave me a few minutes to think about it. Then he said, "Oh no, that's not the worst. If I put it in your mouth, it'll make every metal filling explode".'

Dexy nodded. 'He was right.'

'Jesus . . .'

'You did ask,' Dexy said, turning to greet one of his SAS mates.

'But how did you know where to find them?' Mark said. 'I couldn't even have told you where we were held.'

Dexy tapped his nose. 'Int. They knew where we were the whole time; which is why I was so pissed off that they bombed the shit out of the place. They even used anti-personnel weapons, the bastards.'

'But how did they know?'

Dexy raised an eyebrow. 'I *could* tell you . . .'

Mark smiled. 'But then you'd have to kill me.'

Steve had been studying the other faces. 'There are a couple of guys missing. Is Dan coming?'

'He should be. He's probably just late.'

'He's always bloody late,' Steve said. 'He was late with his helicopter in the desert, he's late for the reunion and now he's going to be too late for the champagne.' He raised his glass in a silent toast and knocked it back in one, then reached for the bottle.

'You're beasting that stuff a bit, aren't you?' Mark said.

'What's—' Steve broke off as the bottle slipped from his fingers. It toppled over, smashing two glasses. There were howls from the other end of the room.

Mark chuckled. 'There you are, that proves it. I haven't seen you shift it like that since your wedding day. Remember when I started my speech and you thought I was going to mention those twins, Ilse and Ella, that we met in Aalborg?'

Steve nodded distractedly, reaching for another glass.

'The look Jenny gave you when you knocked the ice bucket over and spilled champagne all over her wedding dress. I thought you were going to be divorced before the ink had dried on the marriage certificate.'

Steve smiled but did not join in the laughter.

Mark topped up their glasses with champagne. 'Now is everybody here – apart from Dan?'

Steve glanced around the room again. 'Raz isn't here. Where's my cellmate?'

Dexy looked up. 'Raz died a couple of months ago.'

'What happened?' Steve said.

Dexy shook his head. 'Now isn't the moment. Let's just get on with the party.'

Mark hesitated for a moment, then picked up his glass, banged on the table and raised his voice. 'Here's to us; we're still here, but we're the lucky ones. Twenty of us were held in Iraq; seventeen got out; only thirteen of us are here today. We're going to have a great night, but first let's remember the guys who couldn't or didn't make it.' He raised his glass. 'Absent friends, all badly missed.'

He drained his champagne in one gulp, then stood in silence. No one stirred.

Finally Marvyn, the American businessman who had shared their prison in Iraq, threw a well-upholstered arm around Mark's neck. 'Come on, guys, let's party. I'm only here for twenty-four hours.'

Mark gave him a grateful smile. 'I don't know who you are, buster, but you're obviously an impostor. The Marvyn King I remember was so thin his clothes were hanging off him. You look more like Burger King.'

Marvyn laughed and poked him in the ribs. 'You're not exactly wasting away yourself, buddy.'

'That's solid muscle,' Mark said, hastily breathing in.

'My ass. Now tell Uncle Marvyn what you've been up to – or is it all classified?'

'We've been preventing Argentina from invading the Falklands and the Soviet hordes from invading Britain. The Argentinians don't want to invade the Falklands at the moment and there aren't any Soviet hordes any more, but we've been out deterring them anyway, just in case. When we haven't been doing that, we've been frightening the sheep all over the North of England. In two days we're off to Nevada to frighten the USAF instead.'

'What's in Nevada, apart from a few thousand hookers and a few hundred thousand slot machines?'

'Nellis USAF base, surrounded by a few million acres of desert,' Mark said. 'It's where they hold Red Flag, the biggest battle this side of Gulf War Two. Steve and I are going out there to show your boys how to really fly fast-jets, aren't we?'

Steve gave a perfunctory nod.

Marvyn laughed. 'You must be Tom Cruise. Funny, you look a lot shorter on screen.'

'No, it's just the films that got small.' Mark smiled. 'After Red Flag, we're off to your favourite place again. We're being posted to Kuwait to take our turn patrolling the Iraqi exclusion zones.'

'You wouldn't get me near Kuwait again, never mind Iraq,' Marvyn said. 'I saw enough of it six years ago. I don't even want to fly over the Gulf, let alone land there.' He peered at Mark's uniform for a moment. 'I never could work out all this braid-and-button shit. Did you guys make it to general yet?'

'We're in the Air Force, Marvyn. We don't have generals.'

'Whatever. Just answer the question.'

'We're both still flight lieutenants,' Steve said, refilling their glasses. 'Mark just behaves like a squadron leader.'

The complimentary champagne lasted barely another twenty minutes, and after running room service ragged for a couple of hours, they decided to cut out the middlemen and adjourn to the bar. As the evening wore on and the decibels increased, the figure of the hotel manager could be seen from time to time, hovering indecisively in the middle distance.

Mark spotted him and nudged Steve. 'I think he's a bit worried about our mission.'

Mark stayed at the bar for a while, then stood up and reached for his camera. He shot a couple of rolls of film as he moved amongst the POWs. Some waved him irritably away, others did not even notice.

Two of the SAS men had flown in from an overseas mission that morning and were taking a catnap, having succumbed to the combination of jetlag and champagne. They sprawled across a sofa, heads together, snoring like an old married couple. Dexy was explaining to anyone within earshot how Millwall were really a Premier League football team that just hadn't had the breaks yet and Marvyn was hotly disputing the location of the best pastrami sandwich in New York with another American he had met at the bar.

Mark stood on a table to take a final series of photographs, group shots of all the POWs, their faces sidelit by the warm glow from the fake log fire blazing in the hearth. Then he put his camera down on the bar, perched on a stool next to Steve and lit a cigar. With a contented sigh, he tilted his head back and let a mouthful of smoke spiral away up to the ceiling.

Steve glanced up from a prolonged study of the bottom of his glass and focused on the glowing end of Mark's cigar. 'I thought you'd given up.'

'I have. I only smoke cigars now.'

'Then why are you inhaling?'

'Because otherwise it's like drinking alcohol-free lager or decaffeinated coffee – pointless.'

'Just like smoking, in other words.'

Mark groaned. 'If I'd wanted my mother to come I'd have brought her myself.' He glanced around the bar. 'Anyone got a spare shoulder for Jiminy Cricket here to sit on? I'm getting earache from his wholesome advice.'

'No thanks,' Dexy said. 'He's your mate, you listen to him.'

Steve downed his drink and signalled for a refill, then turned to look at Mark. 'Can I ask you something?'

'Of course you can. Everything I have is yours.'

'It's about me, not you.'

'Okay. Hang on one minute while I put my camera back in my room. I'm paranoid about forgetting it and leaving it lying on the bar.'

As Mark walked back through the lobby, the receptionist called out to him. 'There's a message for you.' She handed him a fax.

'Sorry. Couldn't make it. If you're coming over to Vegas for Red Flag look me up. Dan.'

'Las Vegas is obviously too strong a counter-attraction,' said the receptionist.'

Mark smiled. 'Not from where I'm standing. Anyway, don't you know it's rude to read other people's messages?'

Her own smile deepened. 'I know. Sad, isn't it, but I'm desperate for entertainment.' She paused. 'By the way, if the offer of champagne is still open, I'm off duty in five minutes.'

'Great . . .' He leaned across the counter to read the brass badge pinned to her lapel. ' . . . Sarah. I'll be in the bar', he said, and hurried back there.

'Steve? That chat, would it wait till tomorrow? The receptionist is off duty in five minutes and—'

Steve hesitated, then nodded wearily. 'Sure. I'm tired anyway.'

Something in his voice made Mark pause. 'Sorry, I'm being selfish. Let's talk now. I'll give her the elbow.'

Steve got to his feet. 'No, it doesn't matter. Enjoy your night.'

'Are you sure?' Mark said, but Steve was already on his way out.

Mark felt a pang of guilt, but it was forgotten as Sarah strolled into the bar. She smiled as she saw him and began picking her way around the tables.

Dexy looked up blearily from his empty glass and followed Mark's gaze. 'You lucky bastard,' he said. 'How the hell do you do it?'

Mark leaned closer to him. 'I could tell you. But then I'd have to kill you.'

Mark woke the next morning with a pounding headache. Unable to open his eyes, he stretched a hopeful arm across the other half of the bed, but his hand encountered no warm, soft flesh, only the cold metal of an empty beercan lying on the pillow.

He dragged himself wearily out of bed, drank some water and took a long, hot shower. He shaved, squinting into the steamy bathroom mirror, then raked his fingers through his short-cropped dark hair, frowning as he registered his bloodshot eyes and the dark shadows beneath them. He shook his head. 'You're getting too damn old for this.'

He forced himself to eat some breakfast in the nearly empty dining-room. Steve and the others were nowhere to be seen. They had either already left or were still lying comatose in their rooms. There was also no sign of Sarah when he went to check out.

The size of his bill increased his pallor still further. He pushed his credit card across the desk and was gazing into the middle distance when he realised that the desk clerk was staring expectantly at him.

'I'm sorry?' Mark said.

'The card, sir,' the clerk said, handing it back to him as if it were something particularly unpleasant that had been trodden into the carpet. 'I'm afraid there seems to be a problem with it; an administrative error, I'm sure.'

More in hope than expectation, Mark handed him his American Express card instead and heaved a private sigh of relief as the transaction went through.

He emerged blinking into the spring sunlight. 'Taxi, sir?' The doorman managed to convey a lifetime's world-weariness with the faintest arching of an eyebrow. He turned, let out a piercing whistle and raised an imperious arm above his head. A cab obediently swung in off the street. The doorman held the cab door as Mark rummaged in his pockets. He could only find a fifty-pence piece.

The doorman took it and inspected it, still holding open the door, then returned it. 'Thank you, sir. You obviously have more need of this than I do.'

Mark laughed, pulled the door closed and gave the cab driver an address in the East End. As the taxi nosed its way out into the traffic, he wound down the window and sat back, letting the cold breeze blow over him. He stared silently out of the window as the taxi made the long journey across London and out past the towers of Dockland, turning off into a narrow, curving street running down towards the river, a dark canyon between sheer warehouse walls.

He paid off the cab outside a five-storey converted tobacco warehouse, then let himself into the lobby and took the small, clanking lift to the top floor.

He unlocked a door marked 'Shoot 'n' Scoot Photography'. The building was zoned only for commercial use, one of the reasons why Mark had been able to afford to buy the lease on his loft. He had managed to live there for six years without arousing the curiosity of the caretaker or the other leaseholders. In truth even the most lyrical estate agent would have been hard pressed to describe the interior of his loft as domestic.

Mark liked it all the more for its unpretentiousness. He loved the feeling of air and space, and the rough brickwork, exposed steel beams and bleached wooden floor. Most of his friends shuddered and departed muttering about brutalism, but Mark had no intentions of softening the lines with fabrics and furniture. It reminded him of a Tornado – stripped down, spare and brutally functional – and he liked it that way.

He had bought the place in the depths of the property slump, intending all sorts of renovations and improvements, but six years later it was still a single huge space. Only the bathroom and his photographic darkroom were screened from the rest of the room.

Photography was somewhere between a hobby and a passion for Mark. An array of camera bodies, filters and lenses were stacked on the steel shelving by the darkroom and framed prints of fragments of industrial landscapes were dotted around the walls. Interspersed with these was a scattering of more conventional, personal photographs.

He put on the kettle, then stared out of the window as he waited for it to boil, watching the traffic on the river. The masts of white-hulled yachts bobbed in the more fashionable Dockland waters further up river, but the only boats tethered in the grey waters below his window were dredgers which rocked and strained against the ropes securing them as the incoming tide sent a scummy wash of water slapping against the ugly concrete wall of Balfour Dock.

A couple of hours later he emerged from the darkroom, carrying the barely dry prints from the films he had shot at the reunion. His glance lingered over one of the pictures on the wall, a shot of himself and Steve at their passing-out parade from officer training. Two impossibly young faces stared back at him, their eyes fixed on some distant horizon, their shoulders half-turned towards the camera to emphasise the shiny-bright new wings stitched on their uniforms. There were other photographs punctuating the eight years since that day. Almost all were work related – new squadrons, detachments, training camps and NATO exercises – and Steve featured in every shot.

Mark laid the photographs from the reunion down on the table, pausing as he glanced from a shot taken in the hotel bar to the pictures on the wall. Steve's once boyish, rounded face was now lean and lined. He stared at the photograph of Steve for a long time, tapping his thumbnail against his teeth, then he shrugged. None of them was getting any younger.

He shuffled the photographs back into a stack, glanced at the clock and then leaped up, swearing under his breath, as he began to pack. Red Flag, the exercise that could clinch his promotion, began in less than twenty-four hours.

The last thing to go into his bag was a mahogany shield emblazoned with his squadron crest. It was studded with inset silver plaques, most polished until their legends were almost indecipherable. The two most recent carried the inscription, 'Flight Lieutenants Mark Hunter and Steve Alderson'. He wrapped it in a T-shirt and laid it carefully on top of his clothes. Then he took a last look round his flat, banged the door and ran down the stairs.

RAF Coldchurch was a few miles south of Maldon, deep in the Essex flatlands. One of a necklace of Spitfire bases protecting London during the Second World War, it had limped on through the cold war and beyond, always on the brink of closure but somehow always earning a reprieve as the other bases around it were shut down one by one.

Now even Coldchurch's charmed life was at an end. The last defence review had pronounced sentence, both on the base and its resident squadron. Mark and his colleagues already knew that their tour of duty in Kuwait would be the last act in the long, but not particularly distinguished career of 21 Squadron. When they returned, 21 would be disbanded and its men dispersed amongst the dwindling number of surviving Tornado squadrons. Coldchurch's buildings and runways would be surrendered to the bulldozers, making way for another charmless London satellite town or industrial estate.

The runways, hardened aircraft shelters and pilot's briefing facility were still functional, but the peripheral facilities had all been allowed to deteriorate, and Mark for one would not be sorry to see Coldchurch go. As he slowed at the gates, his gaze flickered over the rusty, sagging barbed wire fencing and the rows of ancient Nissen huts, still occasionally pressed into service as accommodation for single men.

As he wound down the window to speak to the guard, he felt the blast of the cold, damp easterly blowing over the marshes from the North Sea. The guard sniffed and wiped his dripping nose on the back of his hand as he checked Mark's ID. Mark grabbed the card and hastily wound up the window again as the guard's face contorted in a sneeze.

He let in the clutch, and ignoring the road that ran straight towards the heart of the base, sent the Audi bumping and jolting along the potholed perimeter track. After a few hundred yards, he swung on to the end of the taxiway and gunned the car down the concrete towards the squadron crew-room, a single-storey, whitewashed brick building, like a seaside bungalow stranded by a freak wave.

Mark was the first to arrive. He made some coffee and began studying charts and briefing papers on the Red Flag operating area around Nellis. The rest of the squadron drifted in one by one. Their animated conversation showed that this was far from a routine day. Bobby was one of the squadron's newest recruits, round faced and always looking freshly scrubbed. He had never been to Nellis before and was unable to keep the excitement from his voice.

Steve was one of the last to come in. He helped himself to some tea and then sat down next to Mark.

'Everything all right?' Mark asked.

'Fine.'

'Sure?'

He nodded and took a mouthful of tea. 'Apart from a hangover. Everything all right with the receptionist?'

Mark smiled. 'As far as I know. She wasn't there to ask when I woke up.' He paused. 'What did you want to talk about when we were in the bar?'

Steve glanced around him, then shrugged. 'It doesn't matter. It wasn't important.'

'It sounded important.'

He shook his head. 'Forget it. Let's get our minds on Red Flag.'

A broad grin spread across Mark's face. 'Now you're talking.'

The squadron boss, Wing Commander James 'Grecian' Edwards, bustled in a few moments later. His suspiciously black hair gave him something of the look of a fading matinée idol; older women found him handsome, younger ones dismissed him as smooth. His expression appeared open and unguarded, but few of his squadron could say with any confidence that they knew the man behind it. If asked to describe him, they always floundered to a halt, lost for words after the most brief physical description.

'Morning, guys. The briefing-room ceiling is leaking – again – so we'll do the brief in here, if you don't mind.' His voice was soft and his accent a curious amalgam of East London and upper crust – an Essex boy made good or a public schoolboy trying to mask his origins. He glanced around, checking that everyone was present.

'Bobby, if there's any coffee left, I'd be willing to risk a cup.' Edwards was handed a battered mug emblazoned with the squadron crest, but after tasting a mouthful, he grimaced and put it down. 'The next person who buys instant coffee out of Mess funds gets to be guard commander for a month. Right. We're transiting to Nellis today by Tristar and we have to hit the ground running, because the first briefing for Red Flag is at 0600 tomorrow. Local time is eight hours behind UK time, so if we get a following wind, we'll be arriving shortly before we set off.' He paused for the ripple of polite laughter.

'Now I know it's expecting too much to ask you to give the fleshpots of Las Vegas a miss tonight, but go steady. There's plenty of time over the next fortnight to drink the town dry and lose your money, or your virginity for that matter.' His glance rested on Bobby for a moment, who blushed crimson under his thatch of blond hair. 'You don't have to do it all tonight. We're going to have a lot of fun out there, but let's remember why we're going. It's not a holiday, or at least not between sunrise and sundown it's not. We're there to work.

'First of all there's the matter of the Top Crew trophy to be decided. I'm sure I don't have to remind you that we're being disbanded in three months' time. Well, I'm buggered if I'm going to leave the trophy lying around for some Whitehall suit to dispose of.' There was a rumble of agreement from his men. 'So whoever wins the trophy this time will keep it in perpetuity. Mark and Steve were top crew last time. Let's see someone else take their title from them.'

'Like hell,' Mark said, holding up the shield. 'This is going nowhere. We only brought it back to remind you what it looks like.'

As the other crews began barracking, Edwards held up a

hand for silence. 'If you need any more help to keep your minds on the job, think about this. Red Flag is the most important exercise in our calendar, but that's all it is – an exercise. In just over three weeks from now we'll be flying for real, patrolling the no-fly zones over Iraq. We'll be in range of real enemies with real missiles that they'll be itching to use on us. Use Red Flag to perfect your skills and test the limits of yourselves and your equipment; it could save your life over Iraq.'

Chapter 2

The face confronting Natalie was unpleasantly familiar: heavy-lidded eyes, and a bristling black moustache above a cruel mouth, twisted in the caricature of a smile.

She dropped her gaze and walked down the steps from the plane. As she paused on the dusty, fly-blown concrete, she cast another glance up at the hoarding towering above her. Saddam was even less prepossessing from that angle.

Four members of her team hurried past her to the rear of the plane, where airport workers in dingy brown overalls were already beginning to unload the pallets of boxes and equipment, all stencilled with the UN crest. A three-ton truck stood waiting to receive them.

The rest of the inspection team, a dozen people in pale blue uniforms, followed Natalie into the building. Two security men checked her passport and visa. They made laborious longhand notes and paused frequently to confer in whispers with a gimlet-eyed plainclothes man lounging against a doorframe, whose gaze never left Natalie's face. She was used to stares from men – her looks attracted them – but there was only hostility in this man's eyes. As he finally waved her through, she flashed him a false smile. It was not returned.

The terminal was deserted save for a scattering of hard-faced men in shapeless suits or outdated casual clothes. Some were leafing through newspapers, others pretending to study the departures board, blank save for the daily flight to Amman.

Natalie glanced around her and smiled. 'Some familiar faces here, Lars.' Her many years working overseas had erased almost all trace of her American accent.

Her companion, a craggy-faced Norwegian some fifteen years her senior, followed her gaze. 'How can you tell? They all look the same to me – heavy moustaches and Crimplene casuals. They'd be better disguised having a shave or wearing a smile.'

She nodded and dropped her voice. 'No wonder no one's ever been able to assassinate Saddam: you'd have to sort him out from half a million lookalike wannabes before you could be sure it was him.'

The look on Lars' face suggested that such talk, even in jest, was dangerous.

They walked out of the terminal into the baking heat of the late afternoon. A line of four pale blue Toyota Landcruisers was drawn up at the kerb, the UN symbol picked out in white on the doors.

The driver of the first one smiled in recognition. 'Dr Kennedy, bet you're glad to be back.'

Natalie laughed and adopted a mock Noël Coward accent. 'My dear, glad just isn't the word.'

As they drove away from the terminal, a dust-covered Mercedes pulled out, settling in behind them as they turned out of the airport approach and began the long drive through the urban sprawl of southern Baghdad.

Amongst the ranks of shabby concrete buildings lay weed-strewn pockets of rubble and waste ground, and pock-marked, half-collapsed buildings, the detritus of the Allied bombing raids, still unrepaired six years after the war. The stern visage of Saddam stared out over the wastelands from yet more hoardings, punctuating the road as regularly as milestones.

Three times the convoy of vehicles was stopped by police or army roadblocks. Each time they were pulled from the Landcruiser at gunpoint and their papers minutely examined before they were allowed to proceed. Each time, as they pulled away, the Mercedes reappeared on their tail, waved through the roadblock without stopping.

Natalie acted as though the searches, the brooding hostility and the rough handling were happening to someone else. She kept herself remote, her face expressionless, indifferent both to the petty harassment of the Iraqis and to Lars' irritable protests.

It was almost dusk as they turned into a broad street running alongside an old irrigation canal and pulled up outside the Canal Hotel, a shabby two-storeyed building. The dust-covered Mercedes parked at the end of the street, and as she got out of the car Natalie saw its two shadowy occupants settling themselves for a long wait. Glancing up at the next-door building, she saw the faint outline of other figures staring down at them from behind the blinds. She smiled at Lars. 'The natives are restless tonight.'

'They'll be a lot more so by tomorrow.'

They hurried through the empty lobby and went straight to their offices on the first floor. A UN soldier stood guard at the door.

'Okay?' she asked.

'It's been swept for bugs again this morning. It's clean.'

'And the briefing room?'

He grinned. 'The Iraqi engineers did a very thorough overhaul of the air-conditioning.'

'You've left it in place and operational? Good.' She winked at Lars. 'Let's check the latest satellite pictures, then we'll put out the broadcast on Radio UN.'

The photographs of their target area were stacked on her desk. She spread them out and studied them as Lars leaned over her shoulder. They had been taken just after dawn and the low light threw everything into sharp relief. They showed detail down to three feet across. At first sight there was little to see, for the pictures covered an apparently barren area. Apart from a road slicing across the desert, the only other features were strange patterns incised in the sands like some ancient cuneiform script.

Natalie tapped the photograph. 'Anti-tank birms. You wouldn't bulldoze those out of the desert for nothing, would you? Notice anything else curious?'

Lars furrowed his brow, then smiled. 'The road. It doesn't go anywhere.'

She returned the smile. 'Nowhere we can see from aerial photographs anyway.' The road stopped dead in the middle of the desert, ending in a low, flat-topped sand mound. 'A Belgian company built four underground airfields for Iraq during the nineteen eighties,' she said. 'All you can see on the surface is a runway – everything else is buried deep underground. They also built two other underground structures. I think we're looking at one of them. According to the contract, it's a hospital.'

Lars gave a cold laugh. 'What they're making down there isn't going to help anyone get better, is it? Too much to hope we could have got a picture of a lorry coming in or out, I suppose.'

She shrugged. 'They know the times the satellites pass overhead, but you can bet the trucks are rolling the instant the satellites drop below the horizon. Now, what do you make of this? It covers an area beginning about a mile north-east of the main site.'

The other photograph was of a cluster of low, windowless buildings and two strangely symmetrical sand dunes near by. Natalie pointed to a maze of spidery markings leading to the dunes. 'Heavy vehicle tracks. If those dunes don't turn out to be storage dumps, my name's Saddam Hussein.' She paused and glanced at her watch. 'Briefing in ten minutes. Let's get a breath of air first.'

Natalie led the way up the stairs and out on to the roof. Heat was rising from the concrete beneath her feet, but the evening breeze was cool. She glanced around. The flat roof was pocked with dark patches where someone had tried to plug cracks in the concrete with tar. There were a handful of iron chairs, a table and a canvas-covered swing-seat. It reminded Natalie of childhood evenings on the stoop outside her Texas home, though in this setting it seemed as incongruous as a mosque in the Midwest.

She gave the concrete balustrade a dubious look and stopped a couple of feet short of the edge of the roof. As she glanced down into the street, she saw the red glow of a cigarette end in the shadows opposite the building. 'I wonder if I could spit that far,' she said.

Lars followed her gaze. 'You probably could, though I wouldn't recommend it. The secret police are going to be angry enough with us already tomorrow without any extra provocation.'

She laughed. 'Ever the voice of reason, Lars. Where would I be without you?'

'Probably over there.' He pointed towards the black hulk of the secret police headquarters.

Lars remained standing alongside her as they gazed out over the city. Patches of bright light illuminated the government buildings and a few of Saddam's innumerable residences, but whole swathes of Baghdad had been cast into darkness by the nightly round of power cuts. The domes and minarets of a dozen mosques were outlined against the night sky, and the only visible traces of the devastation rained on the city during the war were the jagged outlines of some buildings and the gaps in the city skyline where others had been reduced to rubble.

'It's better by night,' she said. 'The darkness hides a lot.'

Lars nodded. 'The same goes for most cities.'

She smiled. 'Except Paris, for one.'

Lars turned to look at her.

She met the look for a second, then stepped away from the balustrade. 'That was a long time ago, Lars. We're both a lot older and wiser now.' She glanced at her watch. 'Right, let's make the broadcast, then eat and get our heads down. We've an early start. It's Saddam's birthday tomorrow. I do hope we don't spoil the celebrations.'

They strolled down the stairs to the briefing room, where the rest of the team was already waiting, grouped around the conference table that dominated the room.

'Final briefing,' Natalie said. 'I've nothing much to add to what we discussed in New York, but let me remind you once more that there must be no careless talk about any aspect of our work, particularly tomorrow's inspection. Surprise is essential.'

The team members exchanged smiles.

'We're leaving for Ar Muzam at 0800 hours.' As she spoke, she held up her hand, palm outward, five fingers extended. 'It's forty miles north-west of Baghdad, so we should arrive on site no later than 0930.'

She paused. 'Now this is very important. Whatever the provocations from the Iraqis, stick to your brief, carry out your tasks, and above all, keep your cool.' She shot a sideways glance at Lars. He pretended not to notice but the tightening of his lips gave him away. 'Once we reach the site, speed is absolutely essential. We cannot afford the thirty minutes it will take to suit up on site, so though it will add to our discomfort, full NBC chemical protection gear must be worn on departure from here.' There were groans from around the room. The thick charcoal-lined suits would make the desert heat even more unbearable.

'NBC State Black will operate all the time we are on site. Check your own and your partner's protective gear thoroughly both before we set off and when arriving on site. We don't know what's down there.'

The smiles faded from her team's faces and they filed out of the room in silence.

Dawn was just streaking the sky as they assembled in the lobby the next morning, already clad in their cumbersome NBC suits. Natalie peered out of the window at the street. It was deserted save for two UN vehicles and the dusty Mercedes parked at the far end. The two figures inside it were slumped in their seats, apparently asleep.

'Everybody ready?' she said, her voice distorted by the respirator. 'Then let's give Saddam his birthday surprise. First team go!'

Eight of the hooded figures hurried out of the door and clambered into the two Landcruisers. Natalie again positioned herself at the window as she heard the engines fire. As the vehicles reached the end of the street, one of the figures in the Mercedes stirred and cast a bleary eye out of his window. He shook his companion frantically by the arm as the Landcruisers swept past and disappeared around the corner. A minute later the Mercedes pulled a frantic three-point turn and disappeared after the decoy in a cloud of dust. Natalie smiled as she imagined the fullscale panic about to erupt at the secret police headquarters.

She turned away from the window. 'We'll give them two minutes' start.'

'Natalie.' Lars pulled her to one side and dropped his voice. 'We should notify the Americans.'

She shook her head. 'This is a UN operation, Lars. It's nothing to do with them.'

'It will be if things turn ugly. They're the only ones who can force the Iraqis to toe the line.' He paused. 'We may need them. They're our lifeline.'

'If we do need them, I'll contact them. But not until then.'

Lars knew from long experience that there was no point in arguing. He exhaled slowly, then turned towards the door. 'Okay. Let's go.'

The team filed out of the building in silence as four Landcruisers and the three-ton truck rumbled out of the compound at the side of the building. The convoy moved off a few moments later, but instead of taking the road to the north-west, they turned due south, heading out of the city through Baghdad's decaying suburbs.

Natalie looked out at the men and women already setting up stalls at the roadside in the first light of dawn to sell their pitiful collections of secondhand goods – a threadbare cushion, a battered radio, a few plates and cups, anything that might bring in a few precious dinars.

'Where do they get that stuff?' Lars asked, following her gaze.

'Out of their own homes,' she said, watching an old woman carefully arrange three electric lightbulbs on a piece of cloth spread in the dust.

Once clear of Baghdad the convoy picked up speed. There was little traffic on the road. Most goods came and went on the highway west to Jordan. The route south towards the closed border with Kuwait was a ghost road, with only an occasional battered truck and a few military vehicles to break the monotony of the drive.

Lars was studying the map, and at his instructions, they swung off the main road on to an unsigned dirt track leading out into the desert. As they made the turn, Natalie glanced in her mirror and saw a Mercedes storming up behind them. 'We've got company,' she said. 'I suppose it was too much to hope they'd put everything on the decoy.'

She thumbed the radio. 'There's a Merc on your tail. Time for plan B.'

The truck at the rear of the convoy immediately stopped dead, blocking the way of the Iraqi Mercedes. Natalie heard an irate crescendo from its horn as the Landcruisers sped along the track, jolting in the deep ruts scored by heavy vehicles.

Only a hundred yards of the track was visible before it disappeared behind the shoulder of a ridge. As they rounded it, passing out of sight of the main road, the rough track gave way to a smooth tarmac road.

Ahead of them a barrier was flanked by a small gatehouse and two concrete pillboxes. To either side a barbed wire fence stretched away into the desert. At the sound of the vehicles a guard stepped from the gatehouse, rubbing the sleep from his eyes.

Natalie wound down the window and handed the guard a thick wad of papers in Arabic script. 'UNSCOM inspection team. In accordance with UN resolution 987, we are here to carry out an inspection of Multhana.'

He stared uncertainly from her to the papers, then muttered something in Arabic and moved back towards the gatehouse, where he gabbled into his radio.

'Go steady, Natalie,' Lars warned, but she was already reaching for her own set.

'Go! Go! Go!' she yelled.

The driver floored the accelerator and the Landcruiser leaped forward, splintering the barrier. The other cars piled through behind them.

Natalie reached for the radio again to call the crew of the truck. 'Okay, we're through. Come up behind us, but don't let the Merc pass until you're clear of the barrier yourself.'

She squinted into the sun, still low over the horizon. Looking ahead, she could see the point where the road ended in a long manmade sand mound rising from the desert floor. Two huge steel blast doors blocked the way, recessed into the face of the dune.

'We'll not crash through that in a hurry,' Lars said.

She shrugged. 'We didn't expect to find the welcome mat out, did we? Anyway that's not the way we're going in.' She pointed to a small hummock rising fifty yards to the side of the sand mound. A narrow opening was visible in the curving blast walls that surrounded it.

Again she stabbed the radio button. 'Teams C and D disembark. If persuasion fails, use sledgehammers. Once you're in, don't worry about the equipment at this stage. Just secure the documentation and then sit tight until we've completed the preliminary inspection of the other area. Meanwhile, nothing enters or leaves without our permission.'

Eight NBC-clothed figures jumped from the Landcruisers and moved towards the narrow entranceway. Natalie waited, listening on the net as the team leader argued with the Iraqi guarding the entrance. There were a few seconds of silence and then the sound of fractured wood and shattering glass as the sledgehammers went to work.

She nodded to the driver and the remaining cars moved off again, cutting across the desert following a track over the rough, rocky ground.

The huddle of buildings Natalie had spotted on the satellite pictures were dilapidated and near derelict. The door of one swung ajar, hanging from a single hinge. A collection of metal drums was roughly covered by a frayed camouflage tarpaulin, which flapped idly in the desert wind.

'This does make a refreshing change,' she said. 'I think we really caught them on the hop this time. No mounds of burned documents, no recent heavy vehicle tracks, no imprints in the sand from where containers and equipment used to stand. This time we've got them by the balls.'

They jumped out, checking the telltale contamination patches on their suits, and the team members began unloading their equipment. The scientists stayed in a huddle as the security teams moved around them carrying out initial tests.

Even with the sun still low, heat burned through Natalie's suit and sweat trickled down her neck. Each breath inside the stifling mask brought the smell of stale rubber and Fuller's Earth to her nostrils.

She looked around her, feeling a growing sense of unease. Something was wrong but she could not identify it. Then it hit her. Everywhere else they had travelled in Iraq, they had been pursued by hordes of flies. Swarming in thousands, maddening in their persistence, the flies crawled over their faces, into their hair, eyes, noses and mouths, or buzzed endlessly against the visors of their NBC suits. Yet here there was not a single fly to be seen.

Lars broke her chain of thought, touching her arm and pointing back across the desert. Two dark shapes, trailing clouds of dust, bounced over the sand towards them. 'Our three-tonner and some very bad-tempered Iraqis, if I'm not mistaken,' he said.

She waited, impassive, as the Mercedes slewed to a halt in the dust and two figures stumbled out. The passenger tugged at his crumpled uniform, then strode towards Natalie. 'This is a prohibited place. You are not permitted here.'

'On the contrary,' Natalie said. 'Under UN Resolution 987 we have every right to be here. We're a duly accredited UNSCOM inspection team carrying out our appointed task – to locate, identify and destroy Iraq's weapons of mass destruction.'

The uniformed man glared at Natalie's visor, but she knew he could see only the reflection of his own face. 'There are no weapons here. Multhana is a civilian area.'

'If that is so, you should have no objection to my team inspecting this storage area.' She gestured towards the tarpaulin. 'Presumably those drums contain only harmless products. Perhaps you'd like to help us inspect them?'

As he glanced towards the drums, the man blenched and took an involuntary step backwards. He began to argue again, but Natalie ignored him and raised her voice to call to the others. 'The alarm will have been raised the moment we left Baghdad. We may have as little as half an hour before reinforcements arrive and start making our job really difficult. Let's get on with it.'

Recovering his nerve, the Iraqi stepped in front of them and drew his gun. 'You will not be permitted to proceed further.'

Natalie laughed. 'We may be unarmed but we carry the full authority of the UN and the military backing of the United States. It would be extremely unwise for you to interfere. The consequences for you personally would be extreme.'

She left the threat hanging in the air, and as he hesitated, she waved the others past him. They split into groups of two or three and began moving towards the buildings and storage dumps, pausing every few steps to check readings on their detection equipment.

Lars led a group towards the building with the sagging door, and Natalie watched as they fed a long probe into the opening, sunlight flashing from the stainless steel. A moment later an electronic alarm could be heard.

The Iraqi had returned to his car and was speaking into the radio. After a few moments he fell silent, making only a few further halting attempts to interrupt the diatribe from the other end. Natalie could not hear what was being said, but the strident tone issuing from the tinny radio was unmistakable.

The man re-emerged, pasting an insincere smile to his face. 'There has been an unfortunate misunderstanding. Return with us to Baghdad so that we can sort out the paperwork and we will happily escort you back here tomorrow or the day after and show you everything you wish to see.'

Natalie laughed. 'By which time everything we wish to see will have been moved somewhere else. I don't think so, thank you. Now if you'll excuse me, we have work to do. Any attempt to remove any material or hinder us in the collection of documents or samples will be treated as a hostile act. I'm sure I don't have to spell out the consequences of that to you.'

They were interrupted by a shout from Lars, who was standing by one of the storage dumps.

Natalie tried to push past the Iraqi but he held her back. 'Your colleagues at the underground site are being detained at this moment. They are of course free to leave, but the documents they have collected must remain behind. Once the correct formalities have been observed, you will be allowed access to the site.'

She shrugged her shoulders, sending a fresh stream of sweat rolling down between her shoulderblades. 'The only correct formality is for you and your fellow hoods to get out of our way. If you fail to co-operate you'll find a few cruise missiles flying down the ventilation shafts.' She paused, trying to read his expression. 'It's a lot safer this way, believe me.'

She shook her arm free and strode over to Lars, who had pulled back the tattered tarpaulin covering a corner of one of the dumps.

'Look at this,' he said. 'If this isn't the most dangerous place on God's earth, I hope I never see it.' He gestured at a row of drums. Most were dented and scratched. 'None of them carries any identifying marks whatsoever. Look at this one.'

Natalie followed his gaze to a drum that had been heavily scored by the prong of a forklift truck. Black liquid had oozed from the wound and a pool of chemical had congealed in the sand, but a faint line of moisture still seeped down the side of the drum.

'What is it?'

'Blister agent.'

She shuddered.

'Now look at this.' He led her to the side of the dump, where row upon row of unmarked drums stood exposed in the open, in the direct heat of the sun. Most of them had ballooned from over-pressure.

'The other mound is composed of munitions, shells and bombs. They look like they've been there since the Gulf War. If so, they'll be deteriorating rapidly and may be very unstable.'

'Any more good news?'

'Plenty.' He pointed to the building behind them. 'The readings we got in there went right off the scale. There's a leaking bulk tank just inside the entrance. God knows what else is in there.'

Natalie had already reached her decision. 'All right. It's too dangerous here. Never mind the munitions – if one of those drums blows it'll shred our NBC suits like Kleenex. Get everyone back to the underground site. We'll gather every scrap of documentation from there, then pull out and evaluate it. Once we have a better idea of what's actually here, we'll send the destruction team in to begin clearing the site.' She shook her head, gazing at the score of buildings and the acreage of drums and canisters. 'I don't know how they'll do it safely though. They may just have to detonate it.'

'They can't,' Lars said. 'There'd be a toxic cloud that would make Chernobyl look harmless.'

'Let's hope Saddam is standing in its path.' Cold with fury, Natalie strode back to the Iraqi. 'This area is heavily contaminated with chemical agents. Without protective equipment you are at extreme risk. You may already be contaminated.' The man's face went white.

Lars and the others were already decontaminating their NBC suits with Fuller's Earth. He helped Natalie take the final safety readings and then clambered into the Toyota. As soon as the last of the equipment was loaded, they stormed off back to the main site.

She swore as they came within sight of the entrance. The blue UN lorry was parked by the blast doors, ready to receive the documents and computers. Facing it was a crescent of Iraqi lorries, troop-carriers and armoured cars. Armed soldiers swung their weapons to cover the Landcruiser as it came into view.

'I was hoping they'd have been tied up in Saddam's birthday parade long enough for us to get the stuff loaded and be out of here.'

'No such luck,' Lars said. 'These boys would as soon see us dead as leaving here with any of their secrets.'

She hesitated a moment, then nodded and reached for the radio. 'Now is definitely the time to call the Americans. Cobra Command, this is UNSCOM 2.'

After a few seconds of silence, an American voice came up through the fog of static. 'Read you, UNSCOM. What have you got for us this time, Natalie?'

'We're at Multhana, grid 295447. We've found major stockpiles of CBW agent in munitions and bulk. The Iraqis are holding some of my team with the documents they've collected. They're refusing to allow us to take them.'

'Why were we not notified of this operation?'

Natalie hesitated. 'Could we save the discussion of the protocol of this until my team members and the documents have been released, Jack?'

The static hissed for a few moments. 'I'll take the necessary steps to secure your free passage. Once that's achieved I'll expect an explanation. It had better be good.' He broke the connection before Natalie could reply.

For seven hours they stayed in the vehicle, sweltering in the heat, as the Iraqis brought up extra troops and even bussed in a rent-a-mob of demonstrators to ratchet up the tension.

As the stakes were raised, Natalie alternated between arguing with the Iraqis and talking on the net, reassuring her team members held underground and keeping in contact with Cobra Command.

Just before sunset the radio crackled back into life. 'UNSCOM, this is Cobra. I think we've solved your problem. The Iraqis have been told that if you aren't on the road by 1900 hours, with all your documents, the first air strikes will be going in on Saddam's new palace. Give it ten minutes for the good news to reach his boys on the ground there.'

'Thank you for your help, Cobra.'

'All in a day's work. Oh, and Natalie? Now the heat's off, that word about protocol. Think yourself goddamn lucky we were willing to bail you out this time. That pale blue uniform you're so proud of isn't worth shit. What protects you and your pantywaist crew is American muscle. So don't you ever – *ever* – think of going on an inspection without informing us again. You don't move without us knowing who, what, why, where and when. We saved your neck this time, but if you pull a stroke like this again, you're on your own.'

'Understood, Jack,' Natalie said, her voice even. 'But be grateful that we identified that site before you boys decided to use it for target practice. It could have wiped out half Kuwait and Saudi Arabia as well as most of Iraq.'

'Just keep us informed. We're on the same side, in case you hadn't noticed.'

As Natalie broke the connection, Iraqis began to stir. An officer barked orders, and the soldiers clambered back into their transports. The encircling ring of vehicles broke up, disappearing into the desert night in a cloud of blue diesel fumes. A few moments later the huge blast doors rolled back and the UN team appeared and began loading boxes of documents into the back of the lorry.

'What now?' Lars asked.

'Straight to the airport. There's a plane standing by to get ourselves and those documents safely on our way to Bahrain.'

'And after that?'

'We'll start on the paperchase for the next inspection, at As

Salman. That should be quite entertaining too, because the Brits are being even more obstructive than the Iraqis about it.' She paused. 'There's something very curious about it. It appears to be abandoned, and yet the Brits have it under constant surveillance.'

'How do you know?'

She tapped her nose. 'I've got my sources, Lars.'

He gave her a curious look, rubbing his hand across the grey stubble on his chin, then he shrugged and let it go. 'So where will you be till then – New York?'

She shook her head. 'Las Vegas. There's a symposium on genetically engineered viruses at the University of Nevada. We're interested in one of the scientists attending it. She travels on a Syrian passport, but we suspect she may be working for the Iraqis. We want to know which seminars she attends and which scientists she contacts.'

'Spying on scientists is a bit out of your normal line of work, isn't it?' Lars said. 'That's what we have spooks for.'

'I know. I wangled it because I need to be in Vegas anyway.' She paused. 'I have to see my brother.'

Lars reached across and squeezed her arm. 'The same problem?'

She nodded. 'Only much, much worse.'

Chapter 3

The Tristar swept in over the saw-toothed peaks of the Spring Mountains, rearing ten thousand feet into the sky. The air was gin-clear, but away to the west, beyond the mountains fringing the Mojave Desert, Mark could see the smog bank smothering Los Angeles as a smudge appeared on the horizon.

The jet rocked and lurched in the turbulence as it met the warm air rising from the desert floor up the barren flanks of the mountains, then it was out on to the plain, sweeping over the vastness of the desert, an endless expanse of red rock, sand and scrub.

As the Tristar dropped lower, a pencil-thin line bisecting the desert swelled into a strip of blacktop, along which a procession of cars and camper-vans streamed towards the distant pyramids, turrets and towers of Las Vegas.

There was a buzz of excitement at the sight of the Vegas skyline, glittering like a crystal city in the sunlight, then it disappeared from sight as the jet banked to make its final approach to Nellis, over the blinding white floor of a dry salt lake.

Suddenly the base came into view. Mark had seen Nellis many times before but was still staggered by the sheer scale of it. The younger aircrew had never seen anything like it.

The Tristar landed, slowed and turned off, barely one third of the way along the length of one of the two enormous runways. It taxied in past miles of concrete hard-standing and rank upon rank of military aircraft. In addition to a dozen squadrons of USAF F15s, F16s and F18s, there were two squadrons of British Tornados and clusters of Belgian, French, German, Norwegian, Dutch, Italian and Spanish aircraft.

'A fiver for the first one to spot an Aurora.'

'What's that?' Bobby blushed as Mitch, one of the older navs on the squadron, gave him a pitying look.

'Don't you guys know anything? It's the successor to the Stealth fighter. It does about three thousand miles an hour and doesn't leave a radar trace.'

'I'll be leaving one,' Bobby said. 'A trail of empty bottles, gambling chips and fallen women. What's up with you, Mitch? We're about to hit the streets of Sin City, USA and the base is full so sadly the Queen is paying for us to stay in a five star hotel but all you can talk about is some poxy aircraft.'

Mark smiled. 'Don't get too excited about Las Vegas. Before you can think about enjoying yourself there's the tasking for tonight's mission.'

Bobby's look was uncertain. 'What mission?'

'The most vital part of Red Flag: getting a few beers in at welcome drinks before the Belgians and Germans neck it all.'

Bobby glanced around as he was propelled towards the bar in the officers' club. 'Who are those guys? They look like they've been shopping at Soviets 'R' Us.'

Mark followed his gaze. A group of men dressed in rumpled and faded Soviet surplus gear with red stars pinned to their lapels stood aloof from the other aircrew. They were toasting each other loudly in Russian and knocking back shots of neat vodka.

'I know you've led a sheltered life, Bobby, but you must have seen *Top Gun*. That lot are Red Air – the aggressor squadron in the simulated air battles. They fly F16s painted with Russian markings. They can't shake the habit out of the cockpit, hence the vodka.'

Bobby drained his beer. 'They sound like a right bunch of wankers.'

Mark raised an eyebrow. 'If I were you I'd reserve judgment until you've flown against them.'

'Mark. Mark Hunter.' One of the Red Air pilots, a rangy Texan standing at the bar, was signalling to him.

Mark broke into a smile, hurried over and shook his hand. 'Jeff Rivers. Great to see you again.'

'Back for another go? What are you flying this time?'

'Still Tornados, but I'm with a different squadron.'

'Mark, some things don't change. You could fly lower than a rat's ass in this desert and I'd still find you.'

Mark knew he was probably right, but there was no way he was going to admit it. 'Just watch the screen at the debrief, Jeff. It'll be the only sight you'll get of us.'

Jeff laughed and slapped him on the back. 'Attaboy. The two things I like best about the Brits: crap equipment and unshakeable spirit. Nothing's changed since the *Titanic*. The ship's sinking but the band keeps playing.'

Mark gave a tolerant smile. 'The two things I like best about the Yanks: great equipment and unshakeable bullshit.'

'Let's drink to that.' Jeff signalled to the barman, glancing around to make sure his squadron was out of earshot. 'And let's make it a beer – I'm sick of vodka.'

Jeff came with them when they set off for Las Vegas an hour later. Mark paused on the way out of the Mess to call Dan from a payphone. A woman answered, her voice soft. 'Dan can't come to the phone right now. Can I take a message?'

'That's not Marie, is it?'

'No, I'm Dan's sister.'

'I'm Mark Hunter. I'm over from England with my squadron. We'll be in the bar at Bally's in an hour or so if he fancies joining us.' He paused, trying to imagine the woman behind the voice that held only a hint of a slow Southern drawl. 'Come along yourself, if you're free.'

'Some other time maybe.' There was a moment of silence. 'I'll pass the message.'

* * *

As their battered USAF bus passed the barrier and swung out on to the highway, Mark saw a group huddled outside the main gate. Their faces flared white in the harsh neon light and he caught a glimpse of a crudely hand-lettered placard as the bus accelerated away: 'Stop The Cover Up. Justice For GWS Victims Now!'

Steve swung around in his seat, looking back towards the protesters until the gathering darkness swallowed them up. No one else on the bus had given them more than a passing glance, too busy sharing out cans of beer.

Bobby took the seat behind the driver and leaned over to pinch his microphone. 'Anyone fancy a detour to the Chicken Ranch?'

'No thanks,' Mark said. 'I don't want to catch salmonella.'

Steve did not join the laughter, but stared out of the window into the night.

'I know,' Mark said. 'It's an old joke.'

Steve looked around. 'What?'

'What's up? We're getting a free holiday in a place people back home pay a fortune to visit.'

They were interrupted by a shout from Bobby. A glow had been visible through the windscreen for some time, but now the bus had climbed the last ridge and Las Vegas lay before them, the base of a billion-watt pillar of light burning into the night sky.

As they drove into the city, even the most ultra-cool aircrew were rubber-necking like tourists, at the MGM lion, the Pyramid of Luxor and the Camelot-meets-office-block architecture of the Excalibur. They pulled up outside Bally's, and there was a rush for the door.

'Right,' shouted Mitch. 'Twenty minutes to check in, shit, shower and shave, then it's straight down to the bar for the start of the Grand Tour – a drink in every casino on the Strip.'

A broad, plushly carpeted walkway stretched away to their left, flanked by a reception desk staffed by twenty or thirty people who were checking in an endless procession of new arrivals as a stream of bellboys wheeled away the luggage.

The reception area was the length of a football pitch, but it was dwarfed by the size of the casino, set a few feet below the level of the walkway. Looking down its length, Mark could not even see the far end, lost in a haze of movement and flashing lights. Rank upon rank of slot machines stretched away into the distance, surrounding the roulette, baccarat, craps and poker tables. A tide of people moved amongst them. Bobby had already started stuffing his loose change into the nearest one.

'I'll pass on the grand tour tonight, if you don't mind,' Steve said. 'I'm not really in the mood for it.'

Mark gave him a quizzical look. 'Suit yourself, but a night on the piss with the guys would probably be the best thing for you at the moment. It'd take your mind off things.' He paused, then lowered his voice as Bobby hurried past, gazing at his room card as if it was the key to the garden of earthly delights. 'Besides, Jeff says they've got a bit of new kit on the F16. If we get a few drinks down him he might let on what it can and can't do. It could give us an edge.'

'No, really,' Steve said, 'I'll just—'

Mark took him by the arm. 'Trust me, Steve. If I let you go up to your room in this mood they'll be cutting you down from the back of the bathroom door in the morning.'

Steve hesitated, then shrugged his shoulders. 'All right. But just a couple of quick ones.'

Mark slapped him on the back. 'Sure. Whatever you say.'

By the time they got to the bar, the rest of the squadron were already lined up and banging down tequila slammers. Steve hesitated but Mark steered him into a space between Mitch and Jeff. They watched the others for a moment. Bobby already looked drunk, his eyes unfocused.

'In deference to tomorrow's activities, perhaps we'll take the soft option and stick to margaritas,' Mark said.

Bobby looked round. 'Margaritas? Great idea.' Next minute he was lying back with his head resting on the bar, issuing instructions to the barman. 'Let's cut out the middle man. Put the salt on my lips and mix the drink in my mouth.' Deadpan, the barman did as he was told. Mitch shook his head in disbelief.

'They love drunks in Las Vegas,' Jeff said. 'They're easier to part from their money. As long as you don't put the gamblers off, you can do just about anything you want.'

Mark looked at Bobby. 'I knew a bloke like you when I was

at college, Bobby. He'd drink anything. A bunch of us went out together on New Year's Eve and we bet him fifty quid that he couldn't drink a gallon of beer in an hour.'

'For fifty quid, I'd do it in half an hour.'

Mark smiled. 'There were two conditions. He had to drink each pint a different way; the first was through a straw, the second was with a teaspoon, the third was out of a saucer, and so on.'

'What was the other catch?' Bobby said, half-raising his head.

'Every time he was sick we fined him five minutes.'

'Did he do it?'

'Oh, he won the bet, but he was so ill he had to go home at half past nine.'

There was a pause. 'So?'

Mitch laughed. 'Tell you what, Bobby, have another drink and think about it.'

Mark's smile faded as he glanced up and saw a stick-thin man in a wheelchair making his way towards them. By the time he reached the entrance, the loudest noise in the bar was the squeak of his wheels. He paused for a moment at the top of a double step, surveying the faces. As his eyes met Mark's his face twisted into something halfway between a smile and a frown, then he dropped his gaze and seemed to shrink into his chair.

Mark breathed, 'Fuck, it's Dan,' but Steve was already moving across the room, and he stopped a couple of feet from the wheelchair. The man's skin fitted him as badly as a crumpled linen suit, and his scalp showed through where his once-thick hair had fallen out in clumps.

Mark could not trust his voice, but went over and gripped Dan's shoulder, tears pricking his eyes. Steve stood motionless alongside him.

Dan looked from one to the other. 'Not pretty, is it?'

'It's not that. It's . . .' Mark did not know how to continue.

There was a long silence. The other men shifted uncomfortably. 'Look,' Mark said. 'You must be dying of thirst, let me get you a drink and then we can talk.' He paused. 'You are allowed to drink, aren't you? I mean, you're not on any drugs or . . .'

'I'm dying all right, but not of thirst.' Dan glanced around the bar. 'Look, I'm sorry I came. You guys carry on with the party.' They started to protest, but Dan held up his hand. 'Honestly, I shouldn't have come. I'm too tired anyway.' He turned his chair around and began to wheel himself back out into the lobby.

Mark moved after him. 'Dan, please come back.'

He shook his head. 'It was a mistake to have come.' He paused. 'Like I said, I'm really tired.'

Mark hesitated, searching his face. 'Can we come and see you tomorrow?'

Dan nodded. 'I'd like that. It's been too long. Come by about seven,' he said, then he wheeled himself out through the doors, leaving Mark alone in the middle of the lobby.

Mark walked slowly back to the bar. There was no sign of Steve, and the others were beginning to drift away. Bobby lurched off towards the lifts, using the slot machines for support.

Mitch held out a glass. 'I got you another margarita. You look like you could use one.' He took a pull on his own drink. 'So, who was that guy?'

'Dan Kennedy. He was flying the Chinook that got shot down trying to rescue Steve and me in Iraq.' Mark raised a hand to massage the hollow ache in his temples.

'How long's he been in a wheelchair?'

'I don't know. Not long. I haven't seen him since the POW reunion a year ago.' He paused, remembering their conversation. Dan had complained of not feeling too good, and Mark had clapped him on the shoulder and ordered some more drinks.

'Well, shit happens,' Mitch said draining his glass. 'Want another?'

Mark turned back to the bar. 'Just one,' he said. 'We've got some serious business to do tomorrow.'

The briefings for Red Flag began at six. Mark heard snatches of half a dozen different languages as he eased his way past the aircrew sprawled on the tiered benches.

Looking pale and tired, Steve just nodded a greeting, but Bobby showed near miraculous powers of recuperation, chatting animatedly as they waited for the start.

Finally a USAF colonel strode in, sporting a crew cut straight from the 1950s. He gripped the podium like the wheel of a twenty-ton truck and scanned the room. 'Welcome to Nellis. Those of you who've come for a holiday, this is the moment to get the hell out. Red Flag is the most serious flying you'll ever do this side of actual combat. We fly against real targets here, using real weapons. You'll have all the fighter cover and electronic warfare support you could ever wish for, but the defences you're taking on are state-of-the-art as well: surface-to-air missile and gun systems, Triple-A and associated fire-control radars, and the best – and I mean the best – air defenders.

'Red Flag is about testing yourself as an individual against the best there are, but it's also about learning to work together. There are twelve different nations represented in Red Flag, but you're all here to learn to fight as a single unit: a force disciplined and powerful enough to whip the ass of a Saddam Hussein or any other warmongering son of a bitch, anywhere on this planet.

'No one predicted the Gulf, Bosnia, Rwanda, Somalia. Nobody knows when or where the next war could break out. Train today as if you were going to war tomorrow.'

He gave a slow smile, knowing he had everyone's attention. 'One more thing. Right here we have the finest facilities you'll find anywhere in the world. Your job is to use these two weeks to make the best use you can of them.' He signalled to a technician at the back of the room.

The lights dimmed and Elvis's 'Viva Las Vegas' erupted from the loudspeakers. On the giant screen, jets could be seen skimming over the floor of the desert and soaring over precipitous mountain ridges. Aircraft flashed together in combat, twisting in ever tighter turns, their pilots urging their jets to the limit as they sought the kill-zone.

Mark glanced around the room, knowing what was coming next. The faces of Bobby and the other first timers at Red Flag were flushed with excitement, their eyes never leaving the screen. There were whistles of admiration.

'Yessir,' the colonel said, 'Red Flag is what you make it.'

As he spoke, two jets locked in combat flew into each other and vapourised. Bobby froze, his mouth hanging open. Another aircraft flashed up on screen, then went into a flat spin. It wobbled slowly around its own axis at first, accelerating as it spiralled down, hit the ground and burst into flames.

Next, an F15 traced a perfect, high-speed diagonal and impacted with the desert floor. The pilot did not even eject. Then a B52 tore off a wing as it brushed a ridge. The huge body of the aircraft was hurled into the side of the mountain, mowing down tall pines like straws, as a flashflood of fire swept ahead of it through the forest.

On and on went the trail of disasters: ten, fifteen, twenty aircraft. Some pilots misjudged their height and simply ploughed into the ground, others pushed too hard, turned too tight or simply lost track of one of the other elements knifing across the sky at close to a thousand miles an hour.

The viewpoint suddenly switched from the remoteness of distant, third-person shots to the first-person immediacy of an in-cockpit camera. The canopy of a Tornado streaking through an empty sky was suddenly filled by a civilian light aircraft appearing from nowhere. It near-missed by less than ten feet.

The nose camera of another jet picked out the sheer face of a looming ridgeline. The nose began to come up, but too slowly. The ridge zoomed into close-up, every crack and crevice in the sandstone etched across the screen. A scream on the voice track died as the image disintegrated and the screen went white.

The colonel left the silence unbroken as he gazed around the room, studying the shocked faces. He nodded slowly. 'Every one of those was real film of real people killing themselves during Red Flag exercises. Don't let any of you end up the same way. Fly to the limit, but don't fly beyond the limit. That's all. Let's do it.'

The silence continued well beyond the briefing room and there was little of the usual banter as the aircrew changed into their flying kit for their missions.

After the pre-flight ritual of checks and more checks, Mark led out his fourship of bombers. They inched forward in the queue of aircraft on the taxiway like commuters in a traffic jam.

The formation ahead wound up their engines, sending

tongues of flame and clouds of black fumes blasting out behind them. As they howled off down the runway, Mark swung his jet into position. His wingman, Bobby, lined up alongside him, with barely six feet between their wingtips. The other pair tucked in behind, offset to avoid the blast from the leading pair's afterburners.

The radio crackled. 'Shark 2-1. Cleared for take-off. Have a nice day.'

'Roger, tower,' Mark said. 'Okay, here we go.'

He glanced across at Bobby and gave a slow nod, easing the throttles forward. Even inside the cockpit the noise quadrupled, the engine notes rising to twin screams as the jet strained against the brakes, every part of the airframe vibrating like a tuning fork.

Mark's eyes flickered over the gauges and warning panel, then he gave another nod and released the brakes. The seat punched him in the small of his back as the Tornado blasted forwards, with Bobby on station alongside him and the other two jets in formation behind.

Steve called out their ascending speeds. 'A hundred knots. Cable. A hundred and thirty knots. EMBS. A hundred and sixty knots. Rotate. Engines good. Captions clear, rotating.'

As he spoke, Mark hauled back on the stick and the Tornado lifted into the sky.

'Gear travelling . . . and the flaps.'

There was a dull thud as the wheels retracted.

'Two hundred and fifty knots.'

'Out of reheat.' Mark eased the throttles back.

The four Tornados levelled out at ten thousand feet and joined a bank of bombers and fighters circling just north of Nellis, waiting for the last few formations.

The enemy were waiting for them beyond a steep cleft in the mountains to the north, the only break in the wall of rock that stretched away into the haze.

At 0800 hours precisely, the massive package of aircraft began flowing towards Student Gap. No command was issued, but every formation leader knew his allocated time, track and position.

Mark glanced around him. His breathing quickened. Even after ten years of flying, he was still excited by the awesome power ranged around him. Formations of fighters patrolled the skies above and behind them, while others flew ahead like the nose-tackle on a football team, blocking the enemy threat.

The fighters were spaced to maximise their ability to cross-cover, protecting each other as well as the bombers. The mud-movers were separated by the minimum distance, to allow the snowstorm of white-hot metal fragments from the lead aircraft's bombs to dissipate before the next one flew over the target.

As Mark's fourship approached Student Gap, he pushed the throttles forward to idle for a descent to low level. The other jets stayed in close formation as they flashed through, the rock walls looming high above them on either side.

As they emerged into the immensity of the desert, Mark armed his weapon systems, hearing the familiar warning growl of the Sidewinders. They took up battle formation, the lead pair in parallel track two miles apart, the other pair four miles in trail of them.

The airframe rattled and vibrated as they reached their low-level entry point, having dropped from ten thousand feet to a bare thirty. It was low enough for the jet-wash to shake the sagebrush and cacti, and stir plumes of red dust from the desert floor.

The reassuring signatures of the other bombers in the package winked out one by one as they hit low level and dropped out of radar vision, then Mark's formation was alone, but for the fighters patrolling high above them.

Mark caught a glimpse of a lone prairie dog loping into the shadow of a clump of rocks, the only moving thing in the heat-blasted landscape.

They flew on, hugging the ground. The wingtips flexed and dipped as the Tornado surfed the air pockets, the airframe juddering violently enough to make Mark's green head-up display drift in and out of focus. He held his concentration as they hurtled on towards the distant mountains, every sense now alert as they waited for the fighter attack.

High above them he caught a flash of sun on metal. Their top cover was wheeling to the north-west, the microscopic silver darts outlined against the sky aligning themselves as they sped away to meet a threat still invisible to Mark's radar.

Then came the first sign of danger, the first alarm from the radar warner.

'Bogies, one o'clock,' Steve said. 'Twenty miles.'

Steve kept up a commentary from his screen as their own fighters engaged the enemy, the radar traces circling and dodging each other, passing so close that the images often merged.

'Bogies, ten o'clock.' Four fighters had evaded the package's own air defenders and were closing fast on Mark's formation. The radar warner shrieked and a green bar of light slashed across Mark's screen.

'Spike! Spike! Buster! Break right.'

Mark rammed the throttles forward to max power. The engines howled and he felt himself plastered to his seat as he threw the jet into a screaming, seven-G turn.

'Screen clear.' Steve's voice was flat and unemotional but Mark knew the adrenalin would be pumping.

Twice more the formation twisted and broke to escape the probing radar of the hostile fighters, but each time they resumed their track the warning tone sounded and the green traces on the screen moved a little closer.

'Buster! Widen!'

'Split and widen!'

Mark watched the other jets in the formation spiralling away, afterburners blazing. He accelerated to maximum speed and threw the Tornado towards a narrow canyon, flanked by red stone cliffs.

The ground blurred below them. A distant ridge swelled until it filled his canopy and then disappeared beneath them as the jet bounced through the hot desert air.

Mark's eyes flickered to the green trace on the radar warner. The bandit was circling steadily around through the nine o'clock and eight o'clock.

'He's on your case.' Steve's warning was superfluous. Mark already knew he was the F16's chosen victim.

He forced the Tornado even closer to the valley floor, hugging the rock wall that rose sheer above them, trying to disappear from the F16's radar. They lurched left and right as Mark swung through a dogleg in the canyon.

Steve groaned as he was thrown around in his seat, his helmet banging against the canopy. 'Still closing.'

Mark grunted an acknowledgement, then cursed aloud as he saw the valley ending in a steep rock face. He gunned the jet into a climb, rolling inverted to reduce the time they would spend above the ridge, stark against the cloudless sky.

Still flying upside down, he forced the nose down ever lower as they climbed the ridge. A line of jagged rocks reached up for them then they were over and plunging for the floor of the next valley. As he rolled back upright, he plugged in the burners to regain the speed lost on the climb. They had been above the ridgeline for only fractions of a second, but he knew the F16 was close enough to have got them visual for the first time.

Mark risked quick looks right and left behind him, straining for a sight of the attacker. Blinding sunlight flared from the reflector strips on Steve's helmet as he too craned his head in the direction of the threat.

'Spotted him. He's six, maybe five miles in trail and closing.'

'Spike! Spike!'

'We'll let the jamming pod take care of that one,' Mark said, but the sirens kept shrieking and the green bar remained locked across the screen. 'He's still got us locked up, what's going—' He glanced down at the panel. 'Shit. The pod's failed.' He kicked in the burners again and threw the jet into a savage turn around an outcrop. The engines howled up through the octaves. 'Chaff. Flares.'

Steve groaned and swore as his head smacked against the side of the canopy, then began punching out chaff.

Mark pushed the jet to its limits, breaking right and left, stooping and soaring over the canyon walls, but still the enemy closed. Mark knew it was hopeless. The F16's top speed was over 150 knots faster than anything he could dredge from the Tornado.

'I'll try to throw a bomb in his face. It's our only hope. Let me know when he's in range.'

'Closing . . . closing . . . closing . . . now!'

Mark hauled back on the stick. At the top of the loop he thumbed the weapon release button, then he rammed the nose into a dive back towards the desert floor. 'Did he buy it?'

Before Steve could reply, Mark saw the answer for himself

as the F16 pulled up and away to the side, climbing to five thousand feet.

'Come left, zero-two-zero,' Steve said. 'Let's get in amongst the weeds before he comes back for us.'

Mark pulled the jet on to the new heading, aiming for a maze of rocky peaks and steep valleys, but the F16 spiralled back down on to their tail. Once more the cycle of spiking, chaffing, breaking and weaving began again, but this time there could only be one conclusion.

The sirens screamed again, then faltered and died. Sunlight glanced from the F16's wings as it banked to the west and then disappeared beyond the glowing walls of the canyon.

'He probably missed or ran out of fuel or something.' Steve's voice held little conviction.

'And my name's Doris Day.' Mark eased back out of combat power. 'Screen clear. Resume track.'

Mark pulled into a turn for home, still thirty feet above the desert floor. 'Student Gap,' he said. 'We'll be on the deck in five minutes.'

'Maybe less.' Steve winced as a spire of rock reached up like a claw towards the belly of the jet.

As they swept in towards the vast parallel runways, there were more jets circling and landing than at Orlando airport on a Labor Day weekend, but the controller sent them peeling off to land left and right with the rhythm and nonchalance of a caller in a barn dance.

'Eagle 2-1, break left; Cobra 0-1, break right; Hawk 2-2, break left.'

As each jet swung into the maze of taxiways, the next was already over the stanchions at the end of the runway, ready to touch down.

Once on the line outside the hangar, Mark raised the canopy, jumped out and ran across to the flight engineer. 'The jamming pod failed on us.'

Noel Smith was five years younger than Mark, but he had already cultivated the world-weariness of a flight engineer reaching pensionable age. 'They do that sometimes, don't they, sir? Not to worry, I'll have a look at it later on.'

'It's not just a minor fault, Noel. It's a complete wipe-out. We need it sorted or replaced double quick.'

As Noel sighed and started to reply, Steve grabbed Mark's arm and pulled him away to one side. 'Mark, it didn't fail. I . . . I forgot to switch it on.'

'You what? I don't fucking believe it.' He pulled off his helmet and wiped the sweat from his forehead. 'You forgot? If we'd been fighting for real, that little oversight would have got us killed. How could you forget?'

Steve said nothing, eyes downcast.

Mark tried and failed to control his anger. 'Well, don't fucking forget again. You've only got four things to do in a fight: jamming, chaffing, flares and keeping your eyes open. Even Gerald Ford could manage it.'

As Mark looked at him, he remembered his own cockpit errors in the past. Steve had corrected them without comment. He forced himself to take a deep breath. 'I'm sorry, but you know how important this is. If we do well here it'll mean promotions. At this rate I'll still be a flight lieutenant when I retire.'

He turned and walked off into the hangar. Still hot, sweaty and exhausted from the flight, he drank some water then grabbed a cup of coffee and walked through to the screening room. He sat down next to Mitch and waited for the debrief of the battle on the two vast computer screens. Steve came in a few moments later but sat on his own at the side of the room.

Two jargon-laden staff officers on a raised dais presided over the reruns like the hosts of a bad TV gameshow, but Mark still found himself swept up in the excitement as the two giant screens began replaying the battle, zeroing in from the overall picture to dissect each individual combat.

Every formation was identified by a different colour. Blue, green, red, purple, yellow, the dots marched across the screen, as red triangles and dotted lines representing missiles arced out from the attackers, answered by clouds of chaff.

The massive mission computers, powerful enough to run a city, held the power of life and death. If they decided that the chaffing and evasion had been successful, the threatened aircraft flew on as the missile symbol winked out. If a missile shot timed out, a coffin symbol encircled the doomed aircraft and it faded to white.

There was no place to hide and no room for doubt. Kills were greeted with whoops and yells, misses hooted and jeered. The bomber pilots were drowned in volume by the air defenders, who invariably had more to celebrate.

Mark forced a smile and waved his hand in acknowledgement of a whoop of Texan triumph from Jeff Rivers, who had hunted him down and scored a kill. Even the Tornado fighters fared little better against the swifter and more agile F15s and F16s.

'Just as well they're on our side,' Mark murmured.

Mitch nodded. 'And just as well the British taxpayers don't know how easy it is to shoot down an aircraft they've paid thirty million pounds for.'

As the screen dimmed, Mark hurried over to Steve. 'I'm sorry I bit your head off . . .'

Steve shrugged. 'Forget it.' He glanced at his watch. 'Look, it's nearly eleven back home. I'm going to phone Jenny before she goes to bed.'

'Okay. Don't forget we're due at Dan's at seven.'

As Mark watched him go, there was a tap on his shoulder. He turned to see Jeff's grin. 'Set 'em up, Mark. It's an old tradition we have here: you get shot down, you have to buy the drinks.'

Chapter 4

It was just after seven as Mark glanced towards the bar and caught a glimpse of Bobby holding court to a circle of tourists, then saw Steve waiting in the lobby.

Their taxi moved away from the glitter of the Strip, heading west, where the neat, near-identical suburbs seemed to stretch to the horizon.

Steve said little, responding in monosyllables to Mark's attempts to start a conversation. They turned off the main road into a street where pastel-coloured, mock-colonial houses, each with a swing-seat on the covered stoop, were surrounded by white picket fences and neat lawns.

In the silence after the taxi pulled up, Mark heard the hushed whisper of sprinklers. The grass ended abruptly a few yards beyond Dan's house, where a forest of surveyor's poles marched out into the desert.

They stepped out into the road, and Mark grinned. 'Look, no pavements. Even if you only want to go next door, you have to take the car.'

As he spoke, he caught a glimpse of a slim, dark-haired figure disappearing around the side of the house. 'Wow, I wonder if that's Dan's sister.'

Steve shrugged and said nothing.

Dan's wife Marie opened the door and stood back to let them enter. There were flecks of grey in her dark hair and deep pools of shadow beneath her eyes.

Mark hugged her. 'Marie, I—'

She nodded, holding up a hand. 'I know. Let's not talk about it. Dinner's in half an hour. Fix yourselves a drink. Dan's in the yard.'

They helped themselves to a beer, then walked out of the french doors on to the sun-deck. Dan was sitting in his wheelchair at a table, a newspaper spread in front of him. He glanced round as they walked towards him.

Mark shook his hand. 'Was that your sister I saw in the garage? Please tell me she's not married.'

'Forget it, Mark. You're at the end of a long line of admirers.'

They exchanged desultory small talk for a while, and gradually it petered out.

Mark took a deep breath. 'Come on, then, Dan, what's wrong?'

Dan shrugged his stooped shoulders, setting off a paroxysm of coughing. 'It depends who you want to believe,' he said, dabbing at his mouth with a handkerchief. 'The military doctors say it's Post Traumatic Stress Disorder or maybe ME.'

'And the others?'

Dan spread his hands wide and raised his eyebrows.

'Gulf War Syndrome?'

'Perhaps. Whatever, you won't catch anyone calling it that.'

There was an uncomfortable silence.

'I thought you guys might need some reinforcements.' Dan's sister had walked down the yard to join them, holding four bottles of beer. She was tall and slim with short, spiky, dark hair, and even in a T-shirt, jeans and a pair of Timberland boots, she looked stunning.

Dan smiled as she leaned over him and kissed him. 'Mark, Steve, this is my sister Natalie.'

There was the ghost of a smile on her lips. 'Mark, good to meet you.' She held the look a moment longer, then turned away. She put three of the beers down, took a long pull on the other, then perched on the edge of the table. 'Sorry, am I interrupting?'

Dan shook his head. 'No. You just came to the rescue.' She laid a hand on his arm.

After another silence, Steve said, 'But the doctors must be able to do something.' There was a tremor in his voice.

Dan shook his head. 'I'm afraid I've got them beat.' He paused. 'I've had some of the classic symptoms – acute fatigue, pains in my joints, headaches, memory loss – since I got back from the Gulf, but there's also this.'

He struggled to pull up his shirt, shaking off Steve's hand as he tried to help. Panting with the effort, he finally succeeded in exposing a series of ugly, purple lesions across his stomach, the surface bubbled and broken by white blisters.

Mark glanced at Steve, who was speechless and red eyed.

Dan looked at each of them. 'What you can't see is what's going on inside me. The doctors call it demyelination. What it means is that the coating of the brain and spinal cord is being destroyed. It's like having multiple sclerosis – but that's not what I've got. The end result will be the same though: incontinence, blindness, loss of motor ability and then . . .' He let the shirt fall again. 'No one can tell me what caused it or how to treat it. Even the doctors specialising in Gulf-related illnesses don't know. They say they've only ever seen one similar case. The only explanation they can come up with is a virus. That's like saying a bullet killed JFK.'

'They must be able to do better than that, surely,' Mark said.

'They say they have to know exactly what we were exposed to, and there's no way of knowing that. I've got my suspicions, but that's all they are.'

'Tell me,' Steve said.

'Well, put it like this: when those oil wells burned, they took with them the huts beside every drillhead and wellhead, where they stored the chemicals. Natalie and I come from oil country – Odessa, Texas – we know about that stuff. There was a fire at a plant that manufactures that shit when we were kids and they evacuated half the town.' He gave a hopeless smile. 'Nobody evacuated any of the troops in the desert: there was a war on. Every living thing was dying around there – dogs, rats, birds, ducks, camels – and not one had a bullet hole in it. We lived beside those wells for weeks. We breathed in the smoke and drank the water.'

'But it can't just be the burning oil wells,' Steve said. 'People who were never anywhere near them have got GWS.'

Dan shrugged. 'Then take your pick from a wagon-load of other possible cause: insecticides, diesel fumes, injections, tablets, or a cocktail of all of them. That place where—' He paused and looked at Natalie, who gave a near imperceptible shake of her head and reached forward to touch his shoulder. 'Anyway, no one knows for sure. I tell you what, though: I sure as hell have got something.' He stared past them, watching the leaves of a tall palm moving in the evening breeze.

The setting sun disappeared behind the mountains to the west, casting Dan's face into deeper shadow, but Mark could see tears in his eyes.

'I just want to know what's wrong with me. I want to be better. I want to be . . . not . . . not this.' He gestured at his body and began to sob soundlessly, his mouth opening like a wound.

Steve leaned over him and cradled his head to his chest.

After a few moments, Dan pushed him away. 'I have to go to the john.' He began wheeling himself back to the house, grimacing with the effort.

'Here, let me push you,' Mark said.

'No. I'll do it.' Dan's mouth was set in a thin line as he strained to turn the wheels, inching up the shallow ramp to the sun-deck. He paused in the doorway to catch his breath, then disappeared inside.

After a few minutes they walked back into the house. Marie was standing at the kitchen window. Natalie stood alongside her and slipped an arm round her shoulder. Marie started at the touch, then gave a distracted smile and pointed out of the window. They followed her gaze, along the twin ruts scored in the grass by the wheelchair, to a clump of palm trees at the bottom of the yard.

'Dan always said he could build a wonderful tree house in those palms. I kept telling him that this wasn't New England and that you could only build houses in trees that have branches, but he said he didn't care, no kid of his was going to grow up without a tree house.'

She paused, then began speaking again, so softly that they had to strain to catch the words. 'We'd always planned to have children, but Dan wanted to wait until he'd finished in the frontline. He said he didn't want to miss his kids growing up because he was always overseas, like his own father.' Her mouth twisted. 'He was doing one last tour after the Gulf. It's always "one more tour", isn't it?'

'You're both still young,' Mark said. 'There'll be plenty of time to start a family when Dan's better.'

'Perhaps,' she said, but the look in her eyes denied it.

A moment later Dan wheeled himself back into the room and they sat down to dinner. None of them had the stomach for small talk, and they ate much of the meal in silence.

Mark made an effort to lighten the mood. 'You were badly missed at the reunion, Dan. Marvyn was completely surrounded by Limeys this time.'

'Still no show from Luther Young, then?'

'No. The last time I saw him he was legging it across the Iraqi desert, running along in that yellow POW suit with his hands above his head.' He paused. 'I wrote to him a couple of times care of Aramco, but I never had a reply. He's probably got better things to do.'

'Sure,' Dan said. 'Or maybe he didn't make it.'

'He must have made it,' Mark said. 'When I saw him he was practically at the British lines. The Iraqis were flapping so much they weren't even firing at him.'

Dan shook his head. 'Something happened to him. Luther and I made a pact that first night in the interrogation centre: "If you get out and I don't, go and see my wife, tell her I died thinking of her." That sort of thing. He was still listed as missing when I got back to the States, so I went to see Cora. They – she – lives in Oxnard, a navy town just up the coast from LA. She looked about twenty, but they had three small kids. I told her what I could about Luther, which wasn't a heck of a lot. She heard me out and then started to cry like her heart was breaking. That made the kids cry too. It was the most godawful sound I ever heard.'

He paused. 'I should have gone to see her again, I know, but I had problems of my own to deal with by then. I send a Christmas card every year, hoping he'll reply. He never has.'

Dan sank lower in his wheelchair and Marie shifted her gaze to Natalie, who gave a faint nod and stood up. 'Listen, you guys, I have to go into town to get some stuff on the overnight to New York. I can drop you off at your hotel or someplace.'

Dan roused himself and wheeled his chair to the door. Steve turned to look at him and tried to say something, then hurried down the drive.

Mark gripped Dan's hand. 'When you're back in shape, we're going to come round here and take you out for the biggest meal even *you*'ve ever eaten, and then get you so drunk you'll need that wheelchair to get home.'

Dan gave a weary nod. 'Yeah. See you around, Mark.' He wheeled himself back inside and Mark heard the door shut with a soft click.

No one spoke for a few minutes as Natalie's red convertible sliced through the evening traffic. Mark watched her worrying her lip with her teeth.

'Dan will be okay, Natalie, you'll see. He won't just lie down and give up.'

She glanced across at him, then switched her gaze back to the road, narrowing her eyes against the glare of the Strip. 'There's no point in fooling ourselves. We all know he's not going to get better.' They drove the last half mile to the hotel in an even more oppressive silence

'Come on, Steve,' Mark said, as they watched Natalie drive off. 'Let's go and get a drink. That was pretty gruelling.'

'Especially for Dan.'

Mark put a hand on his shoulder. 'Seeing him like that hit you pretty hard, didn't it?'

He nodded. 'I—' He fell silent again as the overdressed occupants of a stretch limo swaggered past them into the hotel. 'I'll see you tomorrow.' He turned and walked into the hotel.

During the mission the next morning, Steve worked the screens without a superfluous word. This time they evaded the fighter cover and flew through the target right on schedule.

'That's more like it,' Mark said as he shut down the engines on the line outside the hangar. 'A milk run, maximum points.'

Steve grunted an acknowledgement but hurried away into the hangar before Mark had climbed down from the jet.

Mark peeled off his sweat-soaked flying gear and then wandered through to the crew-room. 'Anyone seen Steve?'

Mitch looked up. 'I think you've missed him. I heard him phoning for a taxi as I came through.'

As the bus disgorged them outside their hotel that afternoon, Bobby pulled out a thick wad of dollars. 'It's my birthday and this lot is getting spent tonight, starting at the Starlight Bar in thirty minutes. That all right with everybody?'

'Erm, yeah. Probably,' Mark said. 'I'll be a bit late though. There's something I want to do. I'll see you there.'

Bobby gave him a curious look. 'Not more bloody photographs of close-ups of bits of rusty metal and broken windows. Give me Pamela Anderson any day.'

Mark smiled. 'I'd love to debate aesthetics with you some time Bobby – or even teach you to spell it – but not right now.'

Steve was not in his room. Mark scribbled a note on a scrap of paper and pushed it under the door, then picked up his camera. He stood on the corner for a moment, gazing at the sizzling neon, the strolling crowds and cruising cars. As he glanced down the Strip, he caught a glimpse of a tall, T-shirted figure.

He ran across Flamingo Road, ignoring the blare of a horn, and pushed his way through the crowds. He had almost caught up with Natalie as she stepped off the sidewalk on to a moving walkway. A recorded voice welcomed them to Caesar's Palace. He stood behind and to one side of her, studying her profile, then stepped alongside her. 'Natalie. Fancy a drink?'

She regarded him coolly for a moment. 'Why not?'

The walkway spilled them out into the casino. It was jammed with people, including a convention of Shriners and a bunch of fight fans in town for a world title bout. A high proportion of the middle-aged men in fezes were seriously drunk, weaving unsteadily between the avenues of slot machines and high-fiving each other like teenagers every time they met up.

Natalie raised her voice to be heard above the drunken shouts and the endless cacophony of the slots. 'But not here, though. I'm not too keen on swapping stares with hoods or being trampled underfoot when the guys in the Egyptian hats realise they'd feel more at home at the Temple of Luxor. How about the Starlight Bar? It's pretty basic, but it's quiet by Vegas standards.'

He hesitated. 'My mates from the squadron will all be in there.'

'Is that a recommendation?'

'Not really, although I wouldn't mind making sure Steve's all right.'

'I doubt if you'll find him in the Starlight. He was out at Dan's place when I left.'

'What was he doing?'

She gave him a curious look. 'Talking to Dan, I guess.'

They strolled through the casino and eventually found the exit. 'No moving walkway on the way out, then,' Mark said.

Natalie shook her head. 'You only get the limo service when they've got a chance of getting some of your money. If you want to leave, you walk.'

They paused to watch the quarter-hourly eruption of the Mirage's volcano. Mark stared at the fifty-foot plastic mountain spewing flames and smoke into the evening sky, and Natalie caught his expression. 'I know, but you have to admire bad taste carried out on this scale.'

'No wonder they loved Liberace so much here.'

The Starlight Bar was at the less flamboyant end of the Strip, a rundown place awaiting its appointment with the jack-hammers in the city's continual drive to reinvent itself. As they walked into the bar, one of Las Vegas's army of Elvis impersonators was on stage, acknowledging a spattering of polite applause. He adjusted his star-spangled jumpsuit, wiped his brow with a red chiffon neckscarf and then tossed it to a fading sweetheart of the rodeo in the front row.

Most of the audience were facing the other way, their faces registering a mixture of disgust, amusement and amazement. Mark groaned as he followed their gaze and saw his crewmates beginning to form themselves into a drunken human pyramid.

'What's this, an old English folk custom?' Natalie said.

'Something like that. It's called "stop the ceiling fan". We—' He corrected himself. '*They* all get shitfaced and then draw straws. The loser has to stop the fan with his head.'

'Doesn't it hurt?'

'Only the next morning, but by then you're in no condition to tell if it was the fan or the alcohol.'

Mark led Natalie to the far end of the bar, where they sat down at a corner table. 'Dan's told me a lot about you,' Mark said, taking a sip from his drink.

'Don't believe everything you hear. Dan's got an embarrassing habit of singing my praises. What did he have to say this time?'

'That you're some sort of scientist.' He smiled. 'And that you're forceful, opinionated and have already caused one major diplomatic incident out in Iraq.'

She watched him over the rim of her glass. 'And did he tell you why?'

'Why don't you?'

'I'm with UNSCOM – the UN Special Commission.'

'I thought we were all supposed to believe the UN's the new evil empire, intent on subverting the US government.'

'With some of the governments we've had, that could only be an improvement.' She paused. 'UNSCOM's job is to find and destroy Saddam Hussein's weapons of mass destruction and the plants where they're manufactured or assembled. Dan probably told you about a chemical plant which was being used to produce mustard gas – the stuff Saddam uses on the Kurds and Shiites. The West apparently doesn't care what he does to them. Of course if he starts on the Kuwaitis, the Saudis or – God forbid – the Israelis, then that's something else.'

Bobby slumped down in a vacant chair at the table. There was a reddening indentation in the skin of his forehead. 'When you said you were going to take some photographs, Mark, I didn't realise you meant glamour shots.'

Mark narrowed his eyes. 'Natalie, this is Bobby. Bobby, this is a very good moment for you to piss off back to the bar and stick your head back in the fan.'

'Well, excuse me,' Bobby said, hauling himself to his feet. 'You've obviously got better things to do than spend time with your mates.' He swayed gently, then stalked off to the bar.

Mark met Natalie's amused glance. 'Look, if you don't mind, I'd rather leave the boys to it and go somewhere else.'

'Don't hold back on my account. Get over there and work up some bruises if that's what you enjoy.'

'I'm not really in that kind of mood. Let's go somewhere quieter.'

'"Las Vegas" and "quieter" aren't normally found in the same sentence.' She gave him an appraising look. 'But if you can survive for an hour or so without a drink in your hand, we can go somewhere really quiet.'

'Where?'

'Wait and see.'

They picked up Natalie's car from a parking lot at the back of the Mirage and she drove them out of town on West Charlestown Boulevard. Inside ten minutes Las Vegas had disappeared from view. The desert, flattened by the heat, was a landscape of horizontals, broken only by the yuccas, creosote bushes and Joshua trees. Mark watched her as she drove towards the hazy outline of the Spring Mountains, the hot wind ruffling her hair.

After half an hour, she pulled off the road and parked near the entrance to a vast natural amphitheatre. The sheer walls of the sandstone escarpments were the colour of fire – blood reds, oranges, yellows, purples and pinks. Near the rim of the canyon, the rock had weathered and faded to a sombre ash grey. Narrow clefts opened on to cool side-canyons, and massive sculpted boulders cast shade as deep and inviting as pools of water.

'Red Rock Canyon,' Natalie said. 'Every time I get too depressed about the way we're fucking up this planet, I come out here and reassure myself.'

Mark picked up his camera and began moving among the rocks. She leaned against the side of the car and watched him in silence for a few moments, the clicking of the shutter echoing in the canyon.

She smiled to herself. 'You're a lot happier out here, aren't you? A safe distance from all those unpredictable human beings.'

He grinned. 'You know where you are with a Joshua tree.'

'I guess photography's the perfect hobby for someone who'd prefer not to get involved.'

He stopped in mid-shot.

'You were the same last night. I could tell your friend Steve was really empathising with Dan; he was sharing his pain. You were keeping yourself detached.' She paused. 'Perhaps it goes with the job. At thirty thousand feet you never have to look anybody in the eye.'

'Sure,' he said. 'And you know what? I wanted to murder my father and marry my mother.'

She held his gaze for a moment. 'If you can tear yourself away from photographing the same three square millimetres of cactus from every conceivable angle, you'll just be in time for the best sunset you ever saw in your life.'

He leaned against the car next to her, very aware of his arm resting lightly against hers, and they watched in silence as the sunset painted the sky and deepened the colours of the canyon walls.

They stayed there until the glare of Vegas neon began to light up the sky to the south, then Natalie glanced at her watch, stretched and straightened up. 'I have to go. Dan and Marie are expecting me.'

They did not speak for much of the way back, content to take in the play of the fading light and the lengthening shadows across the rock.

As she pulled up outside his hotel, Mark turned to her and took her hand. 'Thank you.'

'For the lift?'

'No, for sharing your desert with me.'

She laughed. 'I didn't realise sharing was a big thing with you.'

There was a brief, brittle silence, then Mark said, 'Could I see you again?'

She hesitated, weighing up the idea. 'I don't know, Mark. I'm not really looking for a relationship at the moment.'

'Someone else?'

'There's my work, and there's Dan . . .'

'I'm not proposing marriage or anything. Nothing heavy, just a drink.'

She shrugged. 'Perhaps.'

'How about tomorrow?'

'I can't. There's an evening reception at the symposium I've been attending.'

'Sounds great. What time shall I be there?'

She shook her head. 'This is work.'

'You're a waitress as well as a psychologist?'

She gave a faint smile. 'I'm working, that's all.'

'I know,' Mark said. 'You could tell me—'

'But then I'd have to kill you.' Her smile deepened at his look of surprise. As he opened the door and made to get out, she laid a hand on his arm. 'I'm not working on Thursday though.'

He grinned. 'I'll call you.'

Chapter 5

As Mark entered the crew-room the next morning, Bobby turned his back and became very interested in the toaster. Mark smiled to himself, then walked over and dropped a hand on his shoulder. 'Morning, Bobby. Sorry I sounded off at you last night, but you were pissed and well out of order.'

Bobby brushed Mark's hand away. 'If anyone's out of order, it's you. It'd be nice if you could remember who your friends are.'

'Oh, for God's sake, this isn't the fourth-form outing.'

Bobby pushed past and stalked out of the room.

Mark glanced around. 'Anyone else got a problem?' No one moved. Mark helped himself to a cup of coffee and sat down next to Steve. 'How was Dan?'

Steve's face showed his surprise. 'How did you know I'd been to see him?'

'I saw Natalie. You should have told me. I'd have gone with you.'

'Why? To tell Dan being in a wheelchair can be a hell of a lot of fun?'

Mark swung round to stare at him. 'No. I like the guy.'

Steve glanced at the clock. 'I'd better get on. I haven't

finished the routeing for the mission yet. I wouldn't want to make you late for your promotion.'

'Come on, Steve, this isn't like you—' but he was already heading for the door.

Mark made several attempts to defrost the atmosphere between them as they went through the pre-flight checks, but eventually lost patience. 'Jesus, Steve, what is up with you? We're about to start flying thirty tons of steel at six hundred miles an hour about fifty feet above some very hard ground. Stop sulking and get your mind on the job.'

There was no reply from the back seat.

Mark exhaled slowly and counted to ten. 'Right,' he said, forcing down his anger. 'We'll sort this out when we get back. Until then, let's pretend we're a crew, shall we?'

The mission was a mirror image of the first day. The formation had been scattered by a bounce from the Red Air attackers, and once more Mark had the uneasy feeling that Jeff had targeted him and scored a hit. They turned for home, heading for their next RV point, a rock-stack a few miles north.

'Another day, another missile flying up our arse,' Mark said as he rolled the jet back into the horizontal after clearing the ridge at the head of the canyon. One wall of the rift was still in deep shadow, the other thrown into stark relief by the glare of the sun. He eased the throttles back a touch as he pushed the jet down towards the canyon floor, hugging the left-hand wall. 'If this keeps up we'll have a near perfect record: ten missions, nine kills. The only problem is the kills'll all be on us.' All the time Mark spoke, his eyes were flickering from his instruments to the narrow canyon framed in the cockpit, unfolding like a videotape on fast forward.

'You know your trouble, Mark?'

Steve never finished the sentence. Still hugging the rockface, the Tornado flashed past the point where the canyon merged with another, narrower one running in from the right. As it did, Mark caught a flash of silver in the corner of his eye. Reacting by instinct, even before his brain had processed the information, he rammed the throttles full forward and whipped the nose of the Tornado upwards.

There was a roar more deafening than thunder, and

another Tornado streaked towards him, filling his vision. There seemed no way that they could avoid a collision.

Mark ducked as he glimpsed two white frightened faces – Bobby and his nav Jim – then the jet flashed past, its wing slicing the air inches beneath his aircraft. The canopy rattled in the wash from Bobby's jet and Mark could almost feel the heat from its afterburners through the Perspex. His heart pounding, he pulled the throttles back and dropped the nose again, fighting to hold the Tornado steady. Then he let out a long, low groan.

In his frantic attempt to avoid them, Bobby had lost sight of another, greater danger. The rock-stack, a red spike rearing from the floor of the canyon, was one mile's – six seconds' – flying time from the point where the canyons merged, and by the time Bobby had regained control of his aircraft, he was almost on top of it. Mark saw the jet twitch as Bobby hauled on the stick. For a moment it looked as if he had saved himself, then the tip of his wing touched the rock. It did no more than brush against it, but it was enough.

As Mark watched, frozen, the wing crumpled and collapsed and the jet swung savagely around, smashing into the wall of the canyon. There was a burst of flame. Bits of blazing wreckage tumbled down the face of the rock and crashed to the canyon floor.

Mark swallowed hard and stared at the black smoke billowing up into the cloudless sky as the Tornado flashed past the crash site. He thumbed the radio. 'Mayday. Mayday. Tornado down. Map reference 365115. No 'chutes.'

The crash investigators interviewed them at Nellis the next morning. Two officers listened impassively as Mark gave a halting recitation of the events leading up to the crash.

When he had finished, the senior officer leaned forward, studying their faces. 'You do realise that we've pulled the voice tapes from the jet, don't you?'

Mark saw Steve stiffen. 'And you heard us arguing,' Mark said.

The officer nodded.

'I'm sure you'll be recommending that we're given a severe

reprimand for bickering like kids instead of focusing on our job. We certainly deserve it.' Mark paused. 'But we didn't cause Bobby's death. Bobby did. In my opinion, we reacted quickly and correctly to the threat of collision. Bobby was coming at us out of our five o'clock. We did well to spot him.'

Mark hurried on, knowing that Steve had not spotted him at all. 'We were in Bobby's eleven o'clock. He should have seen us first, far sooner than he did. He overcooked it as he tried to evade us. He was so busy fighting to recover his jet that he didn't see the rock-stack until it was too late.'

The officer continued to stare at Mark for a moment, then he gave a slow nod. 'The two ADRs would seem to bear out that version of events.'

Doubt and relief chased each other across Steve's face as the two officers exchanged glances. 'Thank you, Flight Lieutenants, that will be all for now. You'll be required to give a fuller interview at a later stage and you'll be stood down from flying for at least the rest of the week. Just make sure you stay by a phone.'

'And the forty-eight-hour signal on the accident?' Mark asked.

'Once it has been completed, your squadron commander will receive a copy in the normal way. Now, unless there's anything else?'

When Mark walked into the crew-room for a coffee, there was an unnatural silence. He glanced up from the coffee machine and caught several of his crewmates looking hurriedly away. He could guess what they were thinking. He thought about saying something, then shook his head and walked out, leaving his coffee untouched on the counter.

He found Jeff in the Mess. 'Is there any chance I could borrow your car for a couple of hours?'

'Sure.' Jeff held out the keys. 'You can keep it all night if you want. I'm duty officer tonight, so I sure as hell won't be needing it.'

The group of protestors, still huddled by the gates in the shade of a beach umbrella, gave Mark a desultory shake of their banners as he drove out of the base.

Instead of following the highway back to Las Vegas, he took himself off into the desert, picking dirt roads almost at random, and by mid-afternoon he found himself at the foot of a long, winding track, clinging to the side of the mountains. He paused at the bottom, realising that Jeff had brought him here three years ago, during his first visit to Nellis.

The track climbed the mountains to a point called Freedom Ridge, commanding a view right out across the bed of a dry salt lake. Beyond it, visible even through the heat haze, were the squat, ugly buildings and vast runway of Area 51, so clandestine that it did not even appear on US Air Force maps. The Stealth bomber had been developed and tested there, and the even more revolutionary Aurora was still being put through its paces.

Mark and Jeff had not been the only spectators that day. A group of UFO enthusiasts had gathered, staring towards the distant buildings as if they expected the second coming of Christ. Jeff had whispered, 'Welcome to Dreamland. If you thought Vegas was full of aliens, it's got nothing on what's supposed to go down in Area 51.'

Mark put the car into gear and began to drive up the track. He had gone barely a hundred yards when his way was blocked by a tall chainlink fence, topped with multiple strands of razor-wire. A warning sign hung from the fence. 'US Department of Defense. Top Secret. Entry prohibited. Deadly force authorised.'

He reversed back down the track. The UFO spotters now had fuel for a fresh conspiracy theory. The Pentagon had obviously put in a compulsory purchase order for another forty or fifty thousand acres of desert, to stop anyone so much as laying an eye on Dreamland, even from twenty miles away.

He found another dirt track leading up the other side of the ridge, and parked on the edge of a bluff, watching the line of shadow marching steadily out across the desert floor as the sun set.

He thought about Dan and Steve, about Bobby's death and the men huddled outside the gates at Nellis. The things that had been puzzling him suddenly dropped into place. He sat motionless for a few more moments, cursing himself for his stupidity, then turned the car back towards Las Vegas.

* * *

There was no sign of Steve at the hotel. Mark grabbed a sandwich, then went to the bar, positioning himself where he could see the lobby. As he waited, sipping at his drink, he thought back to the day he and Steve had passed out from Cranwell, and the elation he had felt when he discovered that they had been posted to the same Tornado squadron. He remembered evenings he had spent with Steve, watching him eat for two and drink for three, his laughter so infectious that the whole place was swept along with it.

He remembered too the night that Steve and Jenny had told him she was pregnant, their hands clasped on the tablecloth, Jenny's hand almost invisible inside Steve's fist. He pushed the thought away and stared straight ahead of him into the dark mirror behind the bar. He did not like what he saw there at all.

It was after twelve when Steve appeared in the lobby. Mark hurried to intercept him as he made his way to the lifts.

'Steve, we need to talk. I've been waiting for you. Where have you been?'

'At Dan's.' The strain showed in Steve's face. 'Then just walking around.' He looked hollow eyed, and fatigue was making one eyelid twitch. 'I'm really tired, Mark. Won't it wait?'

He shook his head. 'I'm sorry. I've finally realised what's wrong. If I hadn't been so obsessed with chasing trophies, I would have seen it sooner.'

Steve waited for Mark to continue.

'You've got it too, haven't you?'

Steve glanced around them. 'We can't talk here.'

'Let's go up to my room.'

They shared the lift with a gum-chewing blonde and her white-haired consort, a lifetime older and a head and shoulders shorter. He cast a small look of triumph in their direction.

Steve walked to the window of Mark's room and stood looking out along the Strip.

'I'm right, aren't I?' Mark said. 'You've got the same problems as Dan.'

Steve hesitated, then nodded.

'How bad is it?'

'I don't know. Not as bad as Dan, obviously. I'm not in a wheelchair, not yet anyway.'

'Is it that serious?'

'I suppose so.' He paused. 'I don't know.'

'Well, what does your doctor say? You have been to see your doctor, haven't you?'

'I've seen my own doctor.' Steve looked close to tears. 'I can't go to the military doctors, can I?'

'And? What did he say?'

'He couldn't be sure, but he said it could be connected to my time in the Gulf.'

'So he didn't say it was Gulf War Syndrome?'

'No, he didn't say that, but . . .' Steve fell silent, gazing out of the window.

'Then how can you be sure it's the same as Dan's illness? It could be any one of a hundred other things . . . temporary things.'

Steve shook his head. He moved away from the window and pulled his shirt up, exposing his midriff. A row of small purple lesions, the size of five-pence pieces, stretched across his stomach. One or two had faint white flecks on their surface. 'Dan says that his started the same way.'

Mark walked over and hugged him. 'Why didn't you tell me? Why haven't you said anything before?'

'I . . .' Even though they were alone, Steve lowered his voice. 'I didn't want anyone to know. If it got out that I was ill, I could be grounded.'

'Steve, if you're ill, you should ground yourself. We're flying fast-jets, not driving delivery vans.'

'I can't do that.' There was a note of pleading in his voice. 'I can't lose my job now. We're having a baby. What would I do?'

'You could still fly a desk.' As he said it, Mark knew how empty his words were. If aircrew were too ill to fly, they were probably too ill to stay in the Air Force at all. He scanned Steve's frightened face. 'Look, even if the worst happens, you'll survive – all three of you. You'll have an Air Force pension and you'll get a decent job, even if you can't do the *Top Gun* stuff.'

Steve started to interrupt but Mark held up a hand. 'You can't support your family if you've been killed in a crash. Think of Bobby, for Christ's sake. The first thing to do is to get you well again. After that you can start worrying about what job to do.'

Steve gnawed at his lower lip.

'There's something else, isn't there?'

He nodded. 'It's the baby.'

'What? There's nothing wrong, is there?'

'No. I mean I don't know. You hear all sorts of stories . . .' Steve's voice was now so low that Mark had to strain to hear him.

'But you've no reason to think there's anything wrong with the baby. Everyone feels like that. Everyone has nightmares about all the things that might be wrong with their kids. It'll be fine, just wait and see.'

Steve gave a distracted nod. There was a long silence, then he raised his eyes and held Mark's gaze. 'Don't say anything about this, please.'

'You can't keep flying if you're in less than A1 condition.' Mark cut off Steve's protest. 'Too many lives depend on you, not just mine.' He saw him wince. 'I'm not talking about Bobby and Jim. You know as well as I do, Bobby killed himself.'

Steve stared at the carpet for a few moments, then walked to the door and vanished down the corridor.

Mark braved the crew-room the next morning, even though the atmosphere remained as bleak as a Falklands winter. The strained silence was punctuated by the fleeting appearance of Steve's pale, brooding face, although he was gone again before Mark could react. He sat nursing a cup of coffee until the boss walked in.

'Mark, a word please.'

James Edwards led the way into his temporary office, where Steve was already waiting. He and Mark avoided each other's eyes as Edwards strolled round behind his desk and sat down.

He rolled a pen between his fingers for a moment, then raised his eyes. 'Two things. The forty-eight-hour signal on Bobby's crash blames pilot error.' A look of relief crossed Steve's face, and Edwards gave him a cold stare. 'However, your conduct – taking a personal argument into the air – was reprehensible. It was pure good luck that it didn't lead to a double tragedy. I will not tolerate this again from either of you. If you aren't capable of setting your differences aside, then one or both of you must leave the squadron.'

Mark remained expressionless but Steve looked as though he might cry. He started to speak but Edwards held up his hand.

'I'm not interested in the whys and wherefores. It's a simple choice: sort it out or leave.' He looked again from one to the other and his tone softened. 'I hope you do sort it out, because I'd hate to lose either of you.' He looked at Steve. 'One other thing.'

Steve had begun to relax, but he snapped back to full attention. 'Yes, Boss?'

'Why didn't you spot Bobby's jet?'

'Boss? I . . . I, erm . . .'

'He did,' Mark said.

'Not according to the voice tape. The only warning came from you, not the nav, who would be expected to be the first one to spot a threat from that area.'

'Steve had his head in the screen for a second, Boss, that's all. Bobby came at us out of a side-canyon. The rock wall screened him from us until the last moment. It was only luck that I spotted him.'

'Is that really what happened?' Edwards stared at Steve intently.

'Er, yes, that's right.'

Edwards let the silence stretch before he spoke again. 'I'll let it go at that this time, Steve, but learn the lesson. It isn't just what happened the other day. You used to be the best nav on the squadron, by a distance. That's no longer the case.' He gave him a measured look, then broke into a smile. 'Right, have a few quiet beers together and then get your minds back on the job. We're due in Kuwait in two weeks and I need everyone focused on the no-fly zones.'

'Thanks for bailing me out back there,' Steve said as they walked back to the crew-room. He bit his lip and glanced back towards Edwards' office. 'Did that sound like a final warning to you?'

'No. Just a friendly one.' Mark stopped in the corridor. 'But you have to come clean about this.'

Steve did not reply.

'I meant what I said last night. I won't fly with you again until you've had treatment and sorted out your problem. And I won't let anyone else—'

Steve cut him short. 'It doesn't make any difference anyway. I've got my annual medical when we get back. I'm not going to get through it.'

Mark held his gaze. 'Then at least take the credit for coming clean about it.'

Edwards appeared before Steve could reply. 'Steve, I've just had a call from Coldchurch. Jenny's been taken into hospital. They think she's in labour.'

Steve turned white. 'But it's not due for two months.'

Edwards put a soothing hand on his shoulder. 'It's probably a false alarm, but I'm shipping you home anyway, just in case. We've no military flights back today so we're booking you on a civilian jet. There's a flight in just over an hour, so you'll need to scramble. I've got a car waiting. Just pick up your toothbrush, I'll get someone to pack the rest of your gear and send it on.'

Mark gripped Steve's arm. 'Don't worry. Jenny and the baby are both going to be absolutely fine.'

'Of course they are.' Steve summoned up a smile. 'And Mark? That other thing? I will do it.'

Mark watched as his friend hurried off.

Edwards hung back. 'Anything you feel I ought to know?'

Mark shook his head. 'Just things I feel I ought to.'

'If there's something wrong with Steve, I need to know about it. Loyalty to your friends is all very well, but my overriding concern is the safety of members of this squadron. That should be your first priority too.'

Mark met his gaze but still said nothing, and after a brief pause Edwards walked away.

Mark caught the bus into Las Vegas and wandered the streets for a couple of hours, then went back to the hotel to collect his camera, hoping that the familiar rituals of photography would calm him. He paused as he picked it up from the desk, and stood weighing it in his hand for a few moments, then tossed it on to the bed and reached for the phone.

* * *

The taxi stopped on Decatur Boulevard, outside a long, low building dressed as a log-built Wild West saloon, even down to the hitching rail. A neon sign, modest by Las Vegas standards, read, 'The Lone Star Bar & Grill'.

Mark went inside and blinked in the gloom, then saw Natalie sitting at a corner table.

'I've ordered already,' she said. 'Are you sure you're not hungry? This is the real thing, not a tourist joint. Run by a Texan. The best steaks west of the Pecos.' She gave a brittle smile. 'Or that's what Dan told me anyway.'

She bought him a drink, then watched him, taking in the shadows under his eyes and the way he clenched his jaw as he stared into his glass. 'I don't think you'll find the answer to your problems in there.'

He gave an embarrassed look and pushed the glass away.

'So why did you want to see me?'

He dropped his gaze. 'I needed to talk to someone. I didn't know who else I could turn to.'

'What about Steve? Isn't that what friends are for?'

'It's about Steve.'

'But why me? You don't know anything about me. I'm a stranger.'

'You're a stranger with a brother who has the same problem as my best friend.'

Natalie waited for him to continue.

He looked up from the table. 'Did you know Steve has the same problem as Dan?'

Her eyes widened and she leaned over to take his hand. 'No. Dan never said anything. Is he sure?'

'He showed me the lesions on his stomach. They're the same as Dan's.'

She sat motionless, her brow furrowed. 'You've only just found out about this?'

He gave a slow nod. 'I should have realised ages ago. He tried to tell me once or twice, but I didn't even notice. If I had done, two guys might still have been alive.'

'What?'

'Bobby – one of the drunks who gatecrashed our conversation a few nights ago – and his nav Jim were killed the next morning.'

'Jesus.'

'I feel sick inside. The argument from the night before was still rumbling on and we all went into the air more focused on our anger with each other than the job in hand. My last words to Bobby were hostile ones. I'll never have the chance now to make amends.'

A waiter brought Natalie's steak, but she left it untouched, her gaze still on Mark's face. 'How did it happen?'

'They had a near miss with our aircraft, lost control and flew into a canyon wall. Steve never even saw them until it was too late.'

'Was it—' She hesitated. 'Was it his fault?'

'A little perhaps. It was mostly Bobby's.'

'And will Steve be blamed for it?'

He watched the bubbles rising in his glass. 'No. I covered for him. He'll probably never fly again anyway. He's got his annual medical next week and he thinks he's too ill to pass it.' He fell silent again. 'I want to do something to help him, Natalie. I don't want to see him go the same way as Dan.' He broke off, shamefaced. 'I'm sorry, I didn't mean—'

She held up a hand. 'It's all right, really. Go on.'

'I've thought about nothing else since I finally got the message that he was ill, and every time I think about it I feel guilty.' Natalie was about to speak, but he hurried on. 'I've known him since I joined the Air Force. We went through everything together – basic training, officer training – we even joined the same squadron. He's always been there for me, yet I let him down when he needed me.

'When we were in prison in Iraq, he was the strong one. He kept my spirits up when I was close to cracking.' He breathed deeply, remembering. 'And when I finally broke under the torture, he even told me he'd already broken himself. After we were released I found out he'd lied to spare my feelings. He saved my life when the prison was bombed. My leg was trapped under a steel door. The Iraqis were pulling out in a panic and would have left me to die. Steve had been beaten and starved for weeks, yet somehow he found the strength to lift that door off me.'

His voice cracked and he wiped his eyes. 'We were held in the same prison, survived the same air raids, ate the same food, breathed the same air. Yet he got sick and I didn't. The guy saved my life, but I've been no sort of friend to him. I've gone out for drinks with him, but when he really needed me, I was too busy thinking about winning some tinpot trophy and getting promoted.' He raised his eyes.

Natalie gave him a gentle smile and squeezed his hand. 'Where is he now?'

'On his way to England. His wife's gone into labour. She's two months early.'

'Jesus.'

'It's not been his week, has it?' He sighed. 'He's scared about that too – frightened the baby will have some defect.'

Her expression changed.

'What is it?' he asked.

She thought for a moment.

'Can you get away from the squadron for a while?'

'It should be okay as long as I check in regularly.'

'Good. Come to Los Angeles with me.'

Chapter 6

Natalie pulled up outside Bally's a couple of hours later. Mark threw his holdall into the back and jumped in. She glanced at the bag and raised an eyebrow. 'I'm not stopping while you take pictures.'

He shook his head. 'It's just a change of clothes.'

They set off down Interstate 95 and Mark felt his mood lifting as Natalie drove towards the distant line of the mountains, floating in the heat haze. The sun seemed to have bleached the colour from the desert. It stretched away on every side, grey as lead, stubbled with scrub and twisted, dust-laden cacti, raising their arms to the brass mirror of the sky.

At intervals, they passed long-abandoned cars, their bonnets gaping like alligator jaws in the heat. The wrecks had not rusted in the dry air, but the sun and wind had dulled their paintwork to the same flat grey as the desert floor. They had been stripped of everything usable – doors, tyres, engines, even seats – and the few remaining windows were starred with bullet holes.

Natalie followed his gaze. 'Don't worry, it's just trigger-happy good ol' boys getting in a little target practice.'

'I'm more worried by your driving.'

She smiled and put her foot down a little harder.

A battered mobile home lay on its side in the dirt, a scrap of tattered curtain still flapping from the broken window. Further on, a derelict oil-drilling rig lay abandoned near the breeze-block beginnings of a never-completed building.

'The boulevard of broken dreams,' Mark said.

'You're too late. Someone's already used it.' She frowned as she glanced in the mirror, accelerated to overtake a camper van, then slowed right down and checked the mirror again.

'What's up?'

'Maybe nothing. I thought someone might be following us.'

He swivelled in his seat. 'The Dodge?'

Through the glare of the sun on its windscreen, he could just make out two bulky figures in mirrored sunglasses. 'They look the part, but why should anyone be following us? They're probably just on their way to a Mafia convention.'

She smiled but her eyes remained watchful. 'I haven't made many friends in Baghdad recently.'

'Saddam won't follow you here, surely?'

'You're right. It's probably just paranoia.' Just the same, her eyes kept flickering to the mirror.

Mark watched her. 'Tell me some more about all that stuff. What do the Iraqis do while you poke around?'

'All the things you'd expect.' She shrugged. 'It's always the same. If they get any warning of where we're going, we tend to find nothing but empty buildings and mounds of ash from burned documents. But even though they bug our offices, our security's pretty tight and we usually manage to arrive unannounced. We seized a mountain of documents at the last place we raided, Multhana. So they barricaded us in, brought up extra troops and bussed in a whole bunch of demonstrators for good measure.'

'What happened?'

'Oh, we just sat tight and the Iraqis backed down after a few hours when the Coalition threatened air strikes. We've had worse – the Mexican stand-off at one site lasted four days.'

'What was that about?'

'The documentation on Iraq's nuclear weapons programme. For a country with no nuclear power stations at all, they were stockpiling a suspicious amount of fissile material. In some ways the nuclear programme is the least of our problems, because it's very hard to hide the evidence. Chemical and biological weapons are another story.

'Of course whatever Saddam does, we both know that the Allies have never had the slightest intention of getting rid of him: he's too important a part of the Middle East balancing act. They want him strong, but not strong enough to start another war or attack Israel. That's why we're concentrating on his weapons of mass destruction but leaving his conventional forces intact.'

Once more her eyes flickered to the mirror. Mark turned, but a truck blocked his view of the road behind.

'So there you are,' Natalie said. 'Once we've done all the detection work, all we have to do is destroy what we've found. We've demolished most of his plants but there's still a major suspect complex at As Salman. It's in the Southern Desert,' she said in reply to Mark's blank expression, 'equidistant from the Kuwait and Saudi borders. We're going in next week to see exactly what's there.' Her look darkened. 'I hope it's not like Multhana. You can't imagine how bad that place was.'

They left the desert behind them at Barstow and began the climb over the mountains. By the time they reached the summit the sun was sinking into the Pacific. The air was keen and clear, but a thick, brown blanket of smog lay across the whole of the coastal basin below them.

'Brown Windsor soup, my favourite.'

She gave him a sideways glance. 'Don't get too smug. The air I was breathing in London a few weeks ago wasn't exactly alpine-fresh.'

'Do you get to London often?' He paused, embarrassed by the eager note in his voice.

She gave him a faint smile. 'Now and then.' She pulled out to overtake a truck and floored the accelerator as the freeway dropped away in front of them on the long descent into Los Angeles. The dark line of the sunset came up the slopes to meet them, the flare of street lamps marking out the endless grids of streets like the landing lights of some vast airfield.

Natalie picked her way confidently through the mass of freeways and intersections, still heavy with early evening traffic, as she headed north towards the Hollywood Hills.

'Where are we going? Not Beverly Hills?'

She shook her head. 'Not even Burbank. We're heading a few miles up the coast.' Mark waited, but she offered no further explanation.

They turned off the freeway at Ventura and pulled up in a nondescript street of small, Spanish-style houses.

She switched off the engine. 'There's a guy I want you to meet. He's called Michael Ringwald and he was with 82nd Airborne in the Gulf.'

'What does he do now?'

'He runs a Gulf War Syndrome sufferers' association, though it's something of a temporary job.' Her expression was ironic.

'I'm really sorry,' Mark said. 'Were you – are you close?'

'Are we lovers, do you mean? No. We're friends.'

'I'm sorry. I didn't mean to pry. It's none of my business. I only meant . . .' His voice trailed away.

'It doesn't matter, really.' She studied him, as if unsure whether to continue. 'He has exactly the same symptoms as Dan. That's why I made contact with him originally. I'm glad I did, he's a hell of a guy, but don't get your hopes up too much. He's no more idea than you or I have what's wrong with him. He also has—' She paused, then shook her head. 'Never mind. He can tell you himself.'

Michael Ringwald met them at the door and hugged Natalie. He was stocky and running to flab, with skin the colour of candle wax, eyes buried in a lined, tired face. A few wisps of hair clung stubbornly to his bald pate. He turned to Mark, extending his hand. 'Mark, is it? Glad you could come.'

Michael led the way into the living room. A television flickered soundlessly in the corner, ignored by a cat grooming itself on the windowsill. Papers and files were stacked all over the table and chairs, and piled on the floor. 'There's an awful lot to do and not much time to do it in,' he said. 'Becky normally helps me keep the place in some sort of shape, but she's away for a few days. She's taken Sharon to see her grandparents.'

He made space for Mark on the threadbare sofa and took

the armchair opposite. The dry crackle of plastic came from under Michael's shirt as he sat down, and Mark glanced away, avoiding his gaze.

'It's a colostomy bag,' Michael said. 'Just one more treat I can thank the Gulf War for. Don't worry. It doesn't embarrass me – unless it leaks.' He gave Mark a broad smile. 'Now tell me about your friend. Give me everything, from where he served in the Gulf and what injections he had, right up to his symptoms now.'

As Mark talked, Natalie sat motionless at the side of the room, listening intently but saying nothing. Michael's gaze never left Mark's face. He asked a few terse questions and from time to time screwed up his eyes as if staring into the sun.

Mark paused. 'Steve's worried for himself, but he's even more worried about the baby his wife is about to have. She may even have done so by now. I . . .' His voice faltered and died.

Michael stared down into his lap, twisting his hands, then got up and walked to the window. He pulled it closed and stood staring out, his back to them.

When he turned round, his features were composed. He spoke rapidly. 'My daughter Sharon is six years old. She's like all kids – smart as paint and inquisitive about everything. She looks like a normal, happy child. So do her best friends, Sherry and Luke, but whenever they get together to play, their dolls always fall ill and die. Then they hold funeral services for them and sing hymns. All three of them had younger brothers. Now they don't. Sharon walks up to every baby she sees now and says, "What a nice little boy. Is he going to die?"'

Mark sat like stone as Michael paced the floor in front of him.

'Sharon was born on 16 January, 1991, the night the Gulf War began. I came back in May and we started trying for another baby soon after that.

'Every time we made love, Becky had a burning sensation. She talked to some of the other guys' wives and found they had the same experience. We called it "shooting fire"; we might have laughed about that once. When my semen touched my own skin, it caused swollen, burning blisters.

We went to the doctors again and again but they couldn't offer any explanation.

'Becky had her first miscarriage that December. She was three months pregnant. I remember thinking, this happens sometimes. She became pregnant again in February 1992. By this time we were pretty anxious and we asked our civilian doctor if he knew of any problems connected with the Gulf War. He laughed and said, "Oh no. If there really were any problems, we'd have heard about it from the Department of Defense or the medical journals by now." Three weeks later we lost that baby too.

'During the next few months Becky had severe depression. She was tired all the time and had constant infections and pain. Then she seemed to get better. We decided to try one more time for a baby. She became pregnant again, but at five months she haemorrhaged and was hospitalised for two weeks.

'Barry survived but was born two months premature. He had something called Goldenhar's Syndrome. We exhausted the lifetime limit of our health insurance in the first twelve weeks, by which time he'd already had seven operations. After that we had to pay for his treatment. The first hospital bill was $121,704.

'After six months and five more operations it seemed like Barry was getting better. He still clung to his mother more than Sharon had, didn't put on weight as fast and sweated more than most babies, but it had been a hot summer.' He fell silent and Mark watched, powerless, as he wrestled with his ghosts.

'About three in the morning of the first of October, Becky heard a whimper from his cot. She went in, picked him up and started rocking him, but he didn't react. I gave him some medicine, which came straight back up. Then I saw his eyes were closing. He wasn't going back to sleep, his eyes were rolling back under his lids. Becky started to scream.

'We began to drive to the hospital, but we hadn't got halfway up the street before Barry made a gurgling noise and stopped breathing. His head lolled forward and I knew straight away he was dead.' He fought back the tears. 'I never saw him sit up, smile, walk or talk, but I still think about him every day.'

'The next day the medical examiner called,' Natalie said. 'He'd discovered a structural defect in a valve in Barry's heart and a fibrous tissue growth in it.'

Michael nodded, trying to compose himself. 'At first we blamed ourselves, but over the next few weeks we began to hear of more and more cases. An army friend in Alabama called to say that two wives there had just lost babies the same way. Three of their neighbours had six miscarriages between them; two other women on our base lost their babies. All the men had served in the Gulf.

'It's been proved that men exposed to toxic chemicals can pass on genetic mutations through their sperm, yet the military doctors told me the stillbirths and infant deaths were "not statistically significant".' He fell silent, clenching his fists, his knuckles whitening.

'Could they be right? Is there any way all this could be a coincidence?' asked Mark.

Michael raised his head. 'An epidemiologist told me, "If a hundred people attend a banquet and one gets sick in the night, the cause isn't easy to determine. If twenty get sick, the source is very likely to be the banquet." As many as twenty per cent of some US units became ill after they returned from the war. Their wives got sick, and many lost babies. Gulf War Syndrome does exist and it's transmittable.'

'What's the cause?'

Michael rubbed his eyes. 'I don't know, Mark. You need to be talking to doctors, biologists, toxicologists and epidemiologist.' He smiled at Natalie. 'Even biochemists, but you still won't get a clear picture. No one has really been able to identify any single cause – or any single set of symptoms, for that matter. I don't know of anyone, for example, who has the same particular symptoms as myself and Dan . . . except your friend. We may be talking not about Gulf War Syndrome but Gulf War Syndromes – a range of conditions occurring individually or in combinations.'

He softened his tone as he took in Mark's expression. 'However, we do seem to be a little more knowledgeable about the problem here in the States than in Britain – probably because we have so many more cases. For what it's worth, they're looking hard at malathion, the active ingredient in the insecticide they sprayed over half of Saudi Arabia to keep the bugs down. I remember them doing it. They came in with smog machines and you couldn't breathe for minutes afterwards.'

'Then why did some people get sick while others didn't? Everyone was exposed to it.'

Michael looked weary. 'It just doesn't work like that. You remember thalidomide?'

Mark nodded. 'Of course.'

'Only twenty per cent of the people who took thalidomide had deformed babies.' He shrugged. 'It could be any one of a host of other causes – or any combination of them. Troops in the Gulf were exposed to at least twenty-one toxic substances, each of them capable of damaging an unborn child. It could have been the pollutants from the burning oil wells, the depleted uranium in armour piercing rounds, the NAPS tablets or the injections. It could even have been Iraqi chemical weapons.'

'Seriously?' Mark said.

Michael paused, studying the ends of his fingers as if searching for symptoms. 'Who knows?'

He left the silence hanging in the air as he walked over to the table and rummaged through his papers and collected a few pamphlets. 'I've about talked myself out, Mark. These may help your friend to feel a little better informed, a little less isolated. They round up what information the military has been persuaded into releasing.'

Michael's look held a challenge. 'The only way we're ever going to get to the bottom of this is by forcing the information out of them. They know GWS is genuine but they're running scared. All they can think of is the shitstorm of compensation claims. It's just like Agent Orange in Vietnam. The only real weapon we've got against them is the Freedom of Information Act, and even that doesn't get us more than a fraction of the documents we want.

'If you really want to help your friend, start working to make your government come clean and tell everything it knows about GWS. You can bet it knows a hell of a lot more than it's telling.' The fire in his eyes dimmed. 'Now I'm afraid you'll have to excuse me. I'm really very tired.'

Mark and Natalie let themselves out into the darkened

street and drove off in silence. Natalie was staring straight ahead, her lip between her teeth.

Mark glanced back. The glow from the living-room was extinguished and the house fell into darkness. 'I'm glad you brought me,' he said. 'He's a brave man.'

'He's had to be.' There was a catch in her voice. 'Like Dan.'

Mark reached out and touched her arm. 'Dan'll pull through this, Natalie, you'll see.'

'No he won't, Mark. He's dying. Why pretend otherwise?'

She nosed into the traffic on the freeway and headed south again, back towards LA. Mark gazed out of the window, paying little attention to his surroundings, until his eye was caught by a road sign. 'Oxnard, that's where Luther Young—' He paused. 'We can't pass up on an opportunity like this. Let's see if we can find him.'

Natalie signalled to pull off on to the sliproad as Mark reached behind him for his holdall and pulled out a battered Filofax. The POWs were all listed together. He ran down the list, pausing at the black line through Raz's name. He turned the page. 'Got it. Eleven Ocean Street, Oxnard.'

'I know.' She smiled. 'Dan told me the address. What do you know about this guy?'

'He was something to do with the oil industry. He ignored the warnings from the US Embassy and was still in Kuwait when Iraq invaded. He was taken north and held with us as part of the human shield. He took a hell of a hammering. He was the only black prisoner and the Iraqis treated him even worse than the rest of us.'

'How did he get away?'

'There was a bombing raid which just about blew the cell block apart. He just climbed out through a hole in the wall and took off across the desert.'

'Didn't they try to recapture him?'

'They were more interested in getting the hell out of there. The Coalition spearhead was in sight, and Luther was running straight towards it.'

Ocean Street was steep and narrow, lined with dingy rows of grey weatherboard houses. As they pulled up, Mark caught sight of a payphone. 'Shit, I haven't checked in for a while.'

'Who with?'

'The squadron. We're on standby to go to Iraq.'

'Even when you're at Nellis?

'Absolutely.'

He returned from the phone box a couple of minutes later. 'Panic over. No changes to the plan.'

They crossed the street and knocked at the door. A man shouted to silence the frenzied yapping of a dog. A moment later the door opened. The man's face was worn and lined with age and his hair was grey and thinning. Mark stepped back. 'I'm sorry. I was looking for Luther Young's house.'

The man stiffened. 'Luther used to live here.'

'Has he moved?'

'He died.' The man peered at him. 'I'm his father. Do I know you?'

'I was in prison with him in Iraq.'

The old man hesitated, blocking the doorway, then he stepped to one side. 'You'd better come in.'

They walked through the narrow hall into the kitchen. Three children were playing with the dog in the dusty yard outside. A woman in her mid-twenties looked up from the table where she was chopping vegetables. She waited, impassive, as Mark introduced himself.

'I only knew Luther a short time,' he said, 'but his strength and courage were an inspiration to us all.'

The old man inclined his head in grave acknowledgement of the tribute. The woman gave a sad smile. 'Is that the reason you're here?'

Mark struggled for the right phrase. 'I also wanted to ask you – I hope you'll forgive me – how Luther died.'

'We believe he was shot by the Iraqis while trying to escape.'

Mark was unable to keep the surprise from his face. The old man's gaze challenged him. 'That isn't what you expected to hear?'

'Not . . . not at all.' He paused. 'I watched him escape across the desert. He appeared to get clean away. The Iraqis were in such haste to get away themselves, they weren't even firing at him. The last I saw of him, he had almost reached the Allied lines.'

Luther's wife glanced out into the yard, then closed

the back door. She walked across to Mark, still holding the knife, and stood directly in front of him. 'You want to know what I think, mister? I think that son of a bitch is still out there alive and well and living it up somewhere. I think he saw his chance and thought to himself, "Why go back there to a wife and three children? Why not just disappear?" If I ever catch up with him, he'd better be dead. If he isn't, he'll wish he was.' She walked back to the table, sat down and began chopping the vegetables again, beating out an angry tattoo on the board. She did not even raise her eyes as Mark and Natalie left.

Luther's father followed them out into the street. 'Don't pay her any mind. It's been very hard for her.' He glanced back towards the house. 'Luther's body was never found, and for months, even years, I hoped against hope, praying to God that my son might be restored to us, that he might still be held somewhere in Iraq. Now there's no more hope in me.'

Mark and Natalie drove to the top of the street in silence. Two men stood on the corner, talking into mobile phones, but otherwise the place was deserted. 'Drug look-outs?' Mark said.

She shrugged. 'Or stockbrokers checking the closing prices.'

As they drove past a row of rundown shops with heavy steel shutters, a black car pulled out from the kerb and came up alongside them.

Mark had only time to register a blurred white face and a squat black shape. 'Look ou—'

Natalie stomped on the brakes and rammed the shift into reverse. A flash and a crack drowned the tortured squeal from the gearbox as the pillar at the edge of the windscreen crumpled and Mark felt the wind of the ricochet on his cheek. A crack snaked its way out across the glass from the corner of the screen. There were more shots and he hunched his shoulders in an absurd, instinctive attempt to make himself a smaller target.

The windscreen starred, but Natalie had floored the accelerator and the car was already hurtling backwards. They rocketed blind over the junction with Ocean Street, then she cranked the handbrake and span the wheel, sending the car spinning through 180 degrees.

Even before the nose had stopped slewing sideways, she had accelerated again, and they fishtailed down the street, scarring it with rubber as they flashed across the railroad tracks and over the brow of the hill.

Mark's heart was beating wildly and his face was wet with sweat. He swung round and stared behind them as Natalie kept the accelerator down, switching right and left as she worked them round towards the freeway. Only when they were in the traffic stream flowing south did she raise her foot and let the speed drop back to fifty.

She glanced across at Mark. 'You all right?'

He nodded. 'You?' There was a tremor in his voice, but Natalie's only sign of nerves was her tight grip on the wheel, the knuckles showing white through her tan. 'What the hell happened there? Was that a drive-by?'

She laughed. 'Two white guys in a Dodge follow us from Vegas for a drive-by shooting in Oxnard? I don't think so, Mark.'

'How do you know it was them? And why would someone want to kill us?'

'Not us, Mark, just me. I told you: not everyone's thrilled at what we're doing in Iraq.'

'They'd follow you here?' he asked, incredulous.

'Who else?'

They flashed past another exit from the freeway, still heading south towards Los Angeles.

'Shouldn't we be finding a police station?' Mark said. 'The longer we leave it, the more time they'll have to get away.'

'There's no point. What are they going to do? We can't even give them a description.'

'But we can't just let them get away with it.'

Her look was part amused, part impatient. 'What do you suggest? Get up a posse and chase them into the hills?' After a moment she stretched out a hand and touched his arm. 'Sorry, but there's no point in going to the cops. Trust me on this.'

Mark was still puzzled. 'Whatever you say. But what about the car?'

She smiled. 'It's hired.'

He glanced sideways at her. 'Where the hell did you learn to drive like that? I'm sure they don't teach J-turns at the UN.'

'You'd be surprised what you can learn at the UN.' She checked her mirror again. 'So what now?'

'Immediately? Several stiff drinks to settle my nerves.'

She smiled. 'I meant what were you going to do about the information you got from Mike?'

Mark gazed out at the palm trees as grey as ghosts in the thin mist drifting in from the sea. 'I'm not going to say anything to Steve about Mike's child. He's already worried enough. I'll give the other information to him and then start chasing people in the UK to see if I can get some action.'

She arched her eyebrows. 'Not a great career move.' It was her turn to study him. 'Mark, if you really do want to dig a bit deeper into this, I know a guy in England you could talk to.'

'You do? Who is he?'

'He's called David Isaacs. He used to work at your chemical weapons research centre at Porton Down. I'll have to dig for his number because I'm pretty sure he's moved since I last saw him.'

'I could contact him via Porton Down.'

'It doesn't really work like that. And he didn't leave under the happiest of circumstances.'

'How do you know him?'

'I worked at Porton on an exchange a few years ago.'

'What sort of exchange?'

'Tests on chemical agents, that sort of thing.'

Mark leaned forward. 'What were you testing these things on?'

'Who. British servicemen.' She caught Mark's expression. 'Volunteers.'

'Volunteers?'

'That's right. People are still used in tests on chemical and biological agents. You must have seen the notices. They put them up at every British military base. "Volunteers for studies at Chemical and Biological Defence Establishment." When I was there it used to be an extra thirteen pounds a day.'

'It still is, but I'd no idea they were looking for volunteers to be exposed to chemical weapons. We were always given the impression it was for testing flu vaccines.' He gave a wry smile. 'It doesn't sound a lot, does it? Thirteen pounds to let someone put nerve agent in your dinner.'

She shrugged. 'The dosage is very low. The worst you would suffer is some temporary discomfort. It hasn't always been as carefully controlled, though. There have been accidents. Some soldiers were once killed in a dosage mix-up. They were given ten times the normal dose.'

'That must have been a particularly valuable piece of research.'

'It's meant to save lives, developing vaccines to counter chemical and biological weapons. Or that's the theory anyway.' She paused. 'So where can I drop you?' She saw the disappointment in his face. 'I'm sorry, I'm due home for a family dinner this evening. If I took you, you'd be bored rigid and my parents would think I was going to marry you.'

'I'm not sure which would be worse.' He paused. 'All right, I'll head back to Vegas. Can you drop me at the bus station?'

'A pilot going by bus?'

'I've always wanted to travel by Greyhound.'

'Prepare to have your illusions shattered. You're probably in for a journey from hell with an assortment of bums, drunks, psychopaths and serial killers for company.'

'Great,' Mark said. 'It'll be just like a night out with the squadron.'

As she pulled up in the Greyhound depot, Mark touched her arm. 'Are you going to be okay?'

She nodded. 'I relaxed my guard back there. It won't happen again.'

He gave her a searching look.

'Don't worry, I'm not sticking around long. We're flying into London next week for a conference. We're there till we go back to Iraq. Maybe I'll call you.' She leaned across and her lips brushed against his.

Mark caught himself whistling as he walked into the depot and bought a ticket to Las Vegas.

He dozed as the bus ground its way up and over the Coastal Range and plunged into the desert. He was woken by excited chatter as they cleared the top of the pass through the Spring Mountains and the Vegas neon came into view. He gave a wistful look to the north, towards Red Rock Canyon, then settled back into his seat.

As soon as the bus halted, the other passengers hurried away. It was two in the morning, but the town without clocks showed no sign of slowing down. He followed slowly in their wake, pausing by a pawn shop just outside the transportation centre, the last stop for many people leaving Las Vegas. It also ran twenty-four hours a day. A woman came out as he stood there, and walked slowly into the transportation centre, grey faced in the pitiless glare of the neon lights.

Mark looked into the window. It was full of watches, jewellery and tray after tray of gold wedding rings. No one else spared a second glance as they hurried past, drawn by the empty promise of Glitter Gulch.

Natalie drove straight to the hire-car depot at the airport and swapped her convertible for an inconspicuous saloon. The clerk refused to be hurried with the paperwork and took another ten minutes to compile laborious notes of the damage to the windscreen and bodywork. Her attempts to pay the hundred-dollar excess in cash caused a further delay. 'They took cash in Las Vegas,' she said.

'Then take the car back there. That's a mafia town; they like cash. This is LA. We don't take cash, just credit cards.'

'They take American dollars everywhere from Mexico to Mongolia. Are you trying to tell me that the only place in the world I can't use US dollars is the USA?'

'Look, lady, after turning up with a car in that state, you're damn lucky I'll give you another one at all. Now, I don't make the rules. You want the manager, I'll get him on the phone. You want a hire car, give me a credit card.'

She drove back uptown at top speed, but was well over an hour late as she pulled up outside the restaurant. Lars was sitting at a window table, staring at a three-quarters-empty bottle of wine. 'You're late. Bloody late.'

'I know. I'm sorry.' She kissed his cheek and slid into the seat opposite him.

'Where the hell have you been?'

'With that English pilot I told you about.'

'You're spending a lot of time with him.'

'Hardly. I only met him a few days ago. Is there a problem?'

She tried to hold his gaze but he looked away. 'Only if it starts to interfere with your work.'

She leaned back in her chair and folded her arms. 'Come on, Lars, we both know this isn't about work.'

'You're wrong. That's exactly what it is about.' This time he met her gaze, but was betrayed by a slow blush. 'Well, mostly anyway.'

She smiled. 'That's better. For a moment there I thought you were going menopausal on me. And you above all people should know I don't let anything or anyone compromise my work.'

'I still have the footprints on my face to prove it.'

'Just so long as those are the only scars.' She held the look a moment longer, then reached for her briefcase. 'Now let's get down to business. We'll need a forward base at An Nasiriyah this time. One of those empty factories on the southern outskirts would do. Depending on what we find, we might need the place for up to three months. Get the guys in Canal Street on the case.'

'Won't being in An Nasiriyah give it away?'

She shrugged. 'They won't buy a decoy run again and they don't need to be rocket scientists to work out where we're heading this time. As Salman's just about the only site left worth looking at.'

'What about security? We're more vulnerable away from Baghdad.'

'Whatever you think we need – within reason.' She paused. 'To be honest, I'll feel safer there than I do here at the moment.'

He looked up at once. 'What's happened?'

'I got a little careless. A couple of spooks took a shot at me.'

'Shit. Are you all right?'

She nodded. 'Mark – the English guy – was with me.'

'And?'

'I told him I thought they were Iraqis.'

'And were they?'

She spread her hands. 'What do you think?'

'I think you ought to be a lot more careful. Especially around so-called English pilots.'

'That's what he is, Lars.'

'How can you be sure?'

'Apart from the fact they almost killed him as well? He was shot down in the Gulf War. He was in an Iraqi gaol with Dan. They didn't plant him there just in case they needed him to compromise me six years later.' She took a folder from her briefcase. 'Right, let's get back to the As Salman inspection.'

Lars nodded but his face remained troubled.

They spent another hour discussing their plans, then Natalie finished her drink and gathered her papers.

'So,' he said. 'Are you staying in LA tonight?'

'No. I'm going back to Vegas. I have to say goodbye to Dan.'

She passed the Spring Mountains just as dawn was breaking. The neon spires of Las Vegas dimmed and then vanished as the casino lights were extinguished one by one.

She turned off at the foot of the mountains and took the familiar road north. The canyon floor was still in darkness, the red line of the dawn inching down from the rim. She got out of the car and walked slowly towards a stand of Joshua trees, their arms raised to the brightening sky.

She stood motionless, her breath like strands of mist on the cold air. There was no sound, and no movement but the relentless advance of light down the canyon wall. She stayed there until she felt the warmth of the first rays of sunlight touching her face, then took a last look around the canyon, imprinting every facet on her memory as if she would never come there again. Then she drove on towards Las Vegas.

She walked round to the back of the house, expecting to find Dan in the yard, but there was no sign of him. She walked into the kitchen and called out.

A drowsy voice answered from the bedroom. Dan was lying there in the dark. He raised his head from the pillow. 'Hi, sis. Sorry, I'm not feeling so great this morning.'

'Where's Marie?'

He glanced at the collection of pill bottles on the bedside table. 'Apparently I need more drugs, so she's gone into town.'

'And now I've come and ruined your chance of a quiet sleep-in?'

He forced a smile.

'Mind if I have a look at you?' She opened the curtains a little and strong light spilled into the room. She kept her face neutral but her heart sank at the sight of him. His skin was almost translucent, and there was a sheen of sweat on his forehead. 'Anything I can get you?'

He shook his head. 'Just a new life. This one's about finished. You're looking good though. Mom always said you'd got the looks and the brains in the family. All I got was the muscles, and I don't have many of those left now.' He gave a rueful smile. 'Listen to me, will you? Have you ever seen a worse case of self-pity?'

She did not trust her voice enough to reply.

'What are you doing here anyway? You're supposed to be on your way east by now, aren't you?'

'I wanted to see you again.'

'The last goodbye?'

She nodded, her eyes bright with tears.

'It takes my sister to tell the truth. You don't know how tired I get of people telling me I'll soon be better. I can see in their eyes that they know I'm dying. Even Marie can't come out and say it openly.'

He turned his head to look out of the window towards the faint line of the mountains. 'We've had some good times together, haven't we? Remember the day we found Red Rock Canyon? Your boyfriend and my girlfriend were bored rigid within five minutes and wanted to go back to Vegas and play the slots.'

'So there was a big row and they took off together.'

'And it turned out we'd both been trying to find a way to finish with them anyway.' He smiled at the memory. 'We walked right to the far end of the canyon, lit a fire and sat up half the night talking, then slept out under the stars.'

'I stopped there this morning to watch the sun come up. I was thinking about that night.'

His smile turned into a grimace of pain, but he held up a hand as she moved towards him. 'It's all right.'

Natalie sat on the edge of the bed and took his hand. 'If . . . if I don't get back before—'

'I know. And you're the best little sister I ever had.'

Dan pulled himself upright and began rummaging in the cupboard next to the bed. 'I've got something for you.' He handed her a photograph. 'Remember me like that, not the way I am now.'

She hugged him close, rocking him in her arms like a child. They stayed like that, not talking, for a long time. Eventually she glanced at her watch and eased her arm from around him. She kissed his damp forehead and stood up. 'I have to go.' She paused in the doorway. 'You know what I'm going to do in Iraq, don't you?'

He nodded. 'Make those bastards pay for what they've done to me. Goodbye, sis.'

'Goodbye, big brother.'

She held back the tears until she reached the car, then the brave face cracked and she sobbed as if her heart would break.

Chapter 7

The Tristar descended towards Brize Norton. After the limitless expanses of Nevada, the patchwork of tiny Oxfordshire fields laid out below him made Mark feel as if he was returning to Lilliput.

Spring had burst over the landscape in a hundred vivid shades of green. Peering down through the scratched Perspex of the cabin window, he could see traces of mist still clinging to the water meadows, sidelit by the pale sun. Mark settled back as the jet banked to make its approach, glancing across at the giant teddy bear which sat on the seat beside him.

As the Tristar taxied in, Edwards rose from his seat and turned to face them. 'Right, guys, that's the end of the training. The next time we fly together it'll be in hostile territory. You've all got ten days off now, but don't lose sight of what we're going to be doing. And make sure you're at the end of a telephone in case we're called forward early.'

For once, even the queues in the cavernous arrivals hangar failed to irritate Mark. He gave a tolerant smile as an MP probed his bags and examined the teddy bear as if it was loaded with Semtex, then he hurried across to the car compound.

It was still only ten to eight when he pulled up outside Steve's house. It stood in a tree-lined Victorian street, so close to the Cricklewood Dairy that he could practically reach out and touch it. Mark smiled to himself. Steve always insisted that his address was West Hampstead.

Mark grabbed the teddy bear and the bundle of Michael's pamphlets. He paused for a moment at the gate, taking in the flaking paintwork and the overgrown patch of front garden. Steve had always kept the place immaculate. The curtains were still drawn, and for a moment he regretted he had not phoned from Las Vegas to let them know when he was coming, then he walked up to the door, rang the bell and waited.

It was some time before Steve opened the door, his face grey and haggard.

Mark held out the teddy bear. 'Congratulations. Present from Las Vegas. Guaranteed to bring good luck to all who touch it.' He smiled. 'Matthew's not letting you sleep much, by the look of you. Never mind, the first twenty-one years are the worst.' Steve's expression did not change. Mark looked at him more carefully. 'You've had the medical test, haven't you?'

He nodded. 'It's out of my hands now. I've had my last flight with you.'

'Shit, I'm sorry, Steve.' He paused, searching for the right words. 'Look, I made a really good contact in America. I've got a stack of information about Gulf War Syndrome and people we can contact, Gulf War Syndrome sufferers' organisations, that sort of thing. Let me have a quick look at my godson and then we'll sit down and talk it through.'

Steve started to say something, then swallowed and jerked his head towards the kitchen. He remained by the door as Mark walked down the hall.

Jenny was standing looking out of the window, cradling the baby in a blanket. One chubby pink fist rested on his mother's shoulder and his face was buried in her neck. All Mark could see was a halo of blond hair and the round curve of his cheek. Her own face was pale with dark shadows beneath her eyes.

'So this is Matthew,' Mark said. 'He looks gorgeous.'

The child started at the sound of the unfamiliar voice and

pulled away from his mother's shoulder. Mark froze, and the teddy bear fell to the cold, tiled floor. He struggled for words which would not come.

The other side of the baby's face looked like a crude child's drawing. The right eye was two inches below the level of the left and drooped at the corner. The side of the mouth was also pulled down, in a lopsided grin that showed his gums. He had no cheekbone or ear.

Mark tried to conceal his shock, but the look in Jenny's eyes showed that she had registered it. 'It's called Goldenhar's Syndrome. It's non-hereditary and extremely rare apparently. His face isn't the worst of it.' Her voice was a flat monotone. 'A few hours after he was born they also discovered that some of his internal organs, including the oesophagus, are either missing or not connected. He's attached to a feeding tube eighteen hours a day – it's the only thing keeping him alive. His colon doesn't work either, so I'm having to learn how to suction his body nine or ten times a day.'

'Can't they do anything?'

'They do what they can. There are lots of operations to come, if we decide to let him have them. I wonder if it's worth putting him through all this. What sort of life is he going to have at the end of it?' There was a tremor in her voice.

Mark stayed silent, knowing the truth of what she said.

Steve joined them in the kitchen and leaned against the dresser. He looked at Mark, then gave an abrupt, angry shake of his head, and walked through to the dining room, banging the door shut behind him.

'He'll get through this, Jenny. Steve's a fighter.'

She nodded wearily, too drained to speak. As Mark looked at her face, he noticed a faint yellowing bruise on her cheekbone.

She saw the direction of his gaze. 'He's changed, Mark, even before Matthew was born.' Her voice was a whisper. 'He's not the same man. He gets in such rages. He shouts and rants at me. Yes, sometimes he hits me. Afterwards he doesn't even remember doing it. That's what he says anyway.'

'What can I do?' Mark was unsure whether it was an offer of help or a rhetorical question.

Matthew gave a thin, mewling cry. Jenny stroked his misshapen face and rocked him gently in her arms, watching Mark over the top of her baby's head. 'I don't want to appear ungrateful, Mark, but—'

She gestured around her with her free hand. 'What exactly can you do? What I'd like most of all is just to turn the clock back six years and stop the Gulf War from ever happening, or stop Steve from going, but I think that's beyond even you.'

Mark stood helpless as her tone grew harsher. 'You can't tell me what caused Matthew to be born half-finished, or why our lives have been ruined. You can't cure him either, can you? Matthew needs twenty-four-hour care. How are we going to pay for it? What are we going to live on? What am I going to do if—' She glanced towards the closed door, her slim frame suddenly crushed.

Mark touched her tentatively on the arm. 'I can't do much, I know, but what I can do, I will.' He faltered, knowing how pitifully inadequate he sounded. He tried to marshal his thoughts. 'There are a lot of other families with the same problem, Jenny, the identical defor—' He stopped himself. 'The identical disability. There are organis—'

Jenny cut across him. 'A miracle might cure him. Nothing else will.' She turned away, her shoulders shaking.

Mark hugged her, but his touch disturbed the baby, who renewed his cries at the sight of the unfamiliar face so close to his own.

She pulled away and rubbed at her eyes with her free hand as she began to rock the baby, and looked over his shoulder at Mark. 'If you want to do something, ask them why Matthew had to be born.' Jenny looked at the baby with something close to hatred, then pressed his face into her neck again, clutching him tightly to her as her tears wet his blond hair. 'You'd better go.'

Mark barely registered her words, his thoughts on the empty future that faced her. He reached out a hand, then let it fall to his side. As he kissed her cold cheek, he glanced towards the dining room and then again at Matthew.

He turned to go, stepping over the teddy bear. The baby's weak, irritable crying began again. He could still hear the sound as he walked away down the street.

Mark sat in his car, tears streaming down his face. The

feeling of helplessness paralysed him, just as it had looking at his father in his wheelchair all those years. He closed his eyes and could still picture him on the day he died, holding his oxygen mask to a face the colour of putty as he fumbled with the other hand amongst the medicine bottles and pillboxes covering the table at his side.

Later he had held Mark's sleeve and spoken in a hoarse whisper about friends and benevolent organisations that might help his mother if ever she needed it. Mark knew his father was telling him that he was dying, yet though the knowledge hung over them like a shadow, neither referred to it. They sat throughout the dark winter afternoon, talking a little but often sitting in silence, just watching each other.

When he had risen to go, Mark had said, 'See you tomorrow, then,' and his father had nodded and smiled, though both of them knew that he would not. Mark had wanted to tell him that he loved him, that despite his illness he had always been a good father to him, but the words would not come. He had looked at him one last time and kissed his forehead, then closed the door and walked away. His father died that night.

There was a bang on the windscreen and Mark looked up to see two kids making faces at him through the glass, mimicking his tears. They ran off laughing down the street. Mark wiped his eyes on his sleeve, then dug his nails into his palms, forcing himself to concentrate. He thought for a long time.

Before he drove off, he adjusted the rearview mirror and studied his pale face. He saw as if for the first time the scattering of grey hairs, the fan of lines at the corners of his tired eyes.

Back at his flat, Mark made some coffee and drank it staring down into the dock. The grey water was filmed with a thin sheen of oil. He drained his cup and turned away from the window. As he looked around the room, he felt uneasy. Something was different. He looked again.

His Powerbook computer, its lid open, stood on the far end of the table. He had been working on it just before he left for Las Vegas and he was sure that he had left it closed. He sat down. As he leaned on the table it rocked to one side.

He peered underneath. One of the legs was shorter than the others and had been propped up with a folded beermat. The mat was now a couple of inches away from the leg. The table had been moved to one side and then replaced in a slightly different position.

He wedged the mat back under the leg, then got up and walked to the door. There were no scratches in the paintwork round the lock and it showed no signs of being forced. He moved around the flat for a few minutes but could find no other sign of anything wrong.

Chiding himself for his paranoia, he sat down at the table again and began working through the pamphlets and papers, making notes and recording contact numbers in his Powerbook as he read.

He was tired and jetlagged but unable to rest, haunted by the memory of Matthew's distorted face and the thought of Dan's cold body lying in some hospital morgue, while Jenny and Marie sat in their houses, staring at the ruins of their lives.

As he finished the last pamphlet, he pushed the pile aside, reached for the phone and began dialling numbers.

By three o'clock he was on his way to an address off Coldharbour Lane, a down-at-heel part of South London. He pulled up outside a building, once a cinema, now a ramshackle collection of garment warehouses and small offices. A minicab despatcher glanced up from his switchboard and gave Mark a curious glance as he checked the rough-lettered nameboard in the foyer.

He climbed to the second floor, easing his way past a line of cardboard boxes stacked along one side of the corridor. Visible through the frosted glass of a door at the end was a piece of card stencilled, 'GWS Sufferers' Association'.

He knocked and pushed the door open. The office had an air of cheerful chaos. Files and boxes of documents were stacked on every available surface and spilled on to the floor from the desks and shelves.

A grey-haired woman smiled and waved him towards a chair, as she spoke on the phone. A younger man stuck his head out of the neighbouring room. 'You're here to see Larry, yeah? He'll be with you in two minutes.'

A voice speaking on the phone in the back office grew

steadily louder and more irate. 'That's bullshit and you know it. Do me a favour, don't insult my intelligence. You've been feeding me the same crap for the last five years. I wasn't swallowing it then and I'm not about to start now.' There was a bang as the receiver went down, then the speaker strode into the room. To his surprise Mark saw that the man was in his sixties – the voice had sounded much younger. His handshake was firm and he met Mark's gaze with a confident smile.

'Mark? I'm Larry Rafferty, good to meet you.' He led him through to his office. 'I'm very sorry about your friend. I only wish he'd got in touch with us earlier.' He saw the question forming and shook his head. 'We couldn't have told him anything that would have helped his condition or prevented his child's deformities, but we might have helped him feel a little less alone.' He waved a hand at the overflowing shelves and filing cabinets around him. 'We have literally thousands of case histories here, some even more heartrending than your friend's.'

'What got you so closely involved?' Mark asked. 'Forgive me for saying so, but you're obviously too old to have served in the Gulf yourself.'

'You'd think so, wouldn't you? But I was there. I was a medic with the RAMC for twelve years, although by 1991 I'd been out of the Forces for sixteen years – I wasn't even a reservist.'

'So what happened? Did you volunteer?'

He smiled and shook his head. 'I was called up under the National Service Act.'

Mark was incredulous. 'But National Service was abolished forty years ago.'

'Correct, but the legislation was left on the Statute Book, ready to be picked up again at a moment's notice. Of course six years ago I didn't know that either. A policeman simply turned up on my doorstep in Newcastle one day and asked me to come down to the police station and speak to someone from the MoD. I thought there'd been a mistake, that they must want to talk to my son – he'd also been in the army, a lot more recently than me – so I left him talking to the policeman and went upstairs to have a shower. My son came up a few minutes later and said, "It's definitely you they want."

'I was very puzzled, but I went down to the police station and spoke on the phone to someone at the MoD, who asked me, "Where are you?" When I told him, he said, "Is there a policeman with you? Let me speak to him." The policeman kept staring at me while he was talking, as if he couldn't believe what he was hearing, then he handed the phone back to me. The MoD guy just said, "The constable will give you a rail warrant. There's a train leaving for London in eighteen minutes. Be on it."

'They took me down to the station in a squad car with the lights and siren going. I was met at King's Cross by four men in suits and put straight on a plane. I was in Saudi Arabia before dawn the next morning.'

'But why . . . ?'

'The MoD expected thousands of casualties in the Gulf War, and were calling up every medic from the Boer War onwards. I was lined up alongside the rest of the new arrivals – some even older than me – and given the standard speech about God, Queen and country and issued with our kit.

'We were then marched to a lab where some more medics were waiting to give us our jabs. They didn't ask any of us what jabs we'd had before and they didn't tell us what we were being given, they just stuck them in our arms, one after another. They didn't make any allowance for age or weight either: a man who was five foot and eight stone got the same dose as a six-foot, sixteen-stone man. We were also given NAPS tablets – the chemical warfare protection drug – and told to take two every six hours. After the war was over, I discovered that the correct dose is one every eight hours.'

Mark's face betrayed his amazement.

'It's true, Mark, but that's not the worst of it. As soon as we'd had our jabs, we were put to work. I was told to deliver supplies to the medical centre. There were long queues of trogs stretching back maybe a hundred yards from the centre. I walked in carrying a box and saw all these guys filing through between medics who held a needle linked to two syringes in either hand. It was like a production line. Some of the guys were being jabbed in both arms at once. I put a box down on the floor, and as I straightened up again, someone jabbed me in the arm. I said, "No, what are you doing?" As I did, someone pulled my other sleeve up and jabbed me in that arm as well.'

Mark shook his head in disbelief.

'I was asleep that night when someone unzipped my sleeping bag and gave me yet another jab. "What the hell was that?" I asked.

'The medic just said, "You don't want to know," and walked away. I'm pretty sure I ended up having four anthrax shots in one day.

'When I woke up again I was drenched in sweat. I felt sick and got out of bed. That's all I remember, because I collapsed and stopped breathing. They rushed me to the field hospital. There was a severe argument that morning between the doctor and the senior medical nurse. The nurse wanted me sent back to the UK, the doctor wanted to send me straight back to my unit. The doctor won the argument. My unit actually thought I was dead and had prepared a signal to be sent back to my wife.'

He paused, as if exhausted. 'Some people did die. A section commander said he wasn't feeling well, went to bed and never got up again. Two guys on the same squadron also died. It was only a six-week war, but twenty-four Brits died altogether. We had more casualties through inoculations than we did through enemy action.'

He rested his forehead on his hand and stared down at the desk. 'By the time I was sent home after the war, I was permanently ill. I suffered joint pains, memory loss, lack of bowel control and my eyesight has been steadily worsening. My immune system has been destroyed. When I got back from the Gulf, I felt really isolated. I thought I was the only one suffering these problems. Then I went to a meeting of Gulf War vets and was literally in tears of relief when I found I wasn't alone. They were all talking about their mood swings, lethargy, bad temper, lack of sex drive . . . and their tumours.'

As Larry looked up, Mark saw the determination in his eyes. 'That's when I resolved to do something to help others in the same plight. I'm an old man; I've had the best of my life, but some of the people with GWS were just eighteen or nineteen when they fell ill.' He gave a bitter laugh. 'We have something in common. They all say that they feel like old men too.

'Nature has its own way of helping out, though.' His jaw clenched as he pointed to a filing cabinet in the corner. It was marked 'Deceased'. 'We'll need a second cabinet soon. I told you we lost twenty-four during the fighting, but that's nothing to the death toll since then. At the last count we reckon about one hundred and thirty British Gulf veterans have died from Gulf War Syndrome in the six years since the war – about six times the number of battlefield casualties.'

Mark shuddered, staring at the cabinet as if it contained the corpses. 'Jesus Christ. I had no idea.'

Larry nodded. 'Nor does anyone else – the MoD tries to make sure of that. I went to see a doctor at the military hospital in Wroughton a few weeks ago. He's examining all the guys who say they're ill because of the Gulf War, to see if there's a connection . . . or that's the theory anyway.'

'And the practice?'

'The first words he said to me when I was wheeled in to see him were: "I'm here to disprove all your symptoms." They only did an X-ray and a blood test. After he'd talked to me and examined me, he told me I was suffering from acute fatigue and Post Traumatic Stress Disorder. I was on my way home again in less than two hours.'

'At least the military has got round to acknowledging PTSD these days – in the First World War they were just called cowards and shot.'

'I know that, Mark, but whatever I've got, it isn't PTSD.' He broke off as a fit of coughing racked his chest. Mark watched a thin dribble of blood-flecked spittle run down his chin. 'You wouldn't believe the stonewalling that's going on at every level, from the minister down to the lowliest records clerk.'

'Yes I would,' Mark said. 'My father had a lifetime's experience of that from the MoD.' He shook his head as he saw the question in Larry's eyes. 'It doesn't matter. Go on.'

'Well, Gulf veterans who try to obtain their medical records run into the same brick wall – and a set of excuses that would tax the credulity of a moron. Some meet a blank refusal, others are told their papers are missing or lost, or have been destroyed in a fire, or are just told they aren't entitled to see them. One guy eventually obtained a court order and got what he thought was his complete medical record. Then he discovered that the page covering his service in the Gulf had been removed.

'The civilian doctors say they have to know what inoculations were given in the Gulf before they can treat people. If they don't know, the drugs they prescribe could actually make things worse.'

'And?'

Larry's laugh rattled in his chest. 'The MoD won't tell them because it's "classified information which might be of use to an enemy". Doctors can have the details of every aspirin prescribed from the First World War to the start of the Gulf War, but after that they won't tell them anything.

'Despite that, we've now established most – but still not all – of the things the troops were inoculated against. It's quite a list: cholera, malaria, yellow fever, meningitis, hepatitis B, tetanus, polio, typhoid, botulism, bubonic plague, two types of anthrax and even whooping cough, which was apparently used as an accelerator for some of the other vaccines.

'Can you imagine the effects on your immune system of being given all that lot inside seventy-two hours? Then there were the NAPS and BATS chemical and biological pre-treatments, plus atropine and 2-Pam chloride if you were unlucky enough to use a COMBO Pen – the nerve agent antidote – as well.

'We've also heard talk of two other vaccines: the Porton Cocktail and something called Inoculation Scimitar. Porton Cocktail may or may not just be the name for all the vaccines I've already mentioned, but Inoculation Scimitar is definitely something else. It was given to British spearhead troops, but nobody knows – or at least nobody is saying – what it is or what it protects against.' He shrugged. 'Just one more mystery. I'm one of the few people who can actually prove what I was injected with. My jabs were recorded on a separate form, to be added to my medical record at a later stage. I've still got the form. I keep it hidden.'

He met Mark's questioning look. 'I know it sounds crazy and you'll think I'm paranoid, but it's my only proof of what they gave me. If I am paranoid, I'm not alone. Guys aren't even reporting their medical symptoms because they're scared they'll lose their jobs. I know a military policeman with GWS who has to wear incontinence pants all the time. If he tells anyone, he'll lose his job.'

Mark nodded, still staring at the filing cabinet. When he switched his gaze back to Larry, his expression had hardened. 'What can I do? How can I help? I've got ten days' leave before I'm posted to Kuwait. It's not much time, but it's a start. And who knows, I might even find out something useful in the Gulf; it's where the problem started, after all.'

Larry smiled. 'I don't think the answer's going to be lying buried in the sands like a Dead Sea scroll, and you're not going to find a cause or a cure for GWS. No disrespect, but an RAF pilot is rather unlikely to succeed where some very eminent scientists have failed. And ten days isn't a hell of a long time.'

Mark stiffened for a second, then relaxed and smiled. 'There must be something I can do.'

Larry was doubtful. 'We're always short of counsellors, but you seem more of a doer than a listener to me.' He thought for a moment. 'Do you have any science background?'

'Not unless a physics A-level counts, but I know a man who does. I made a couple of contacts while I was in the States. One of them knows an ex-Porton Down scientist.'

Larry leaned forward across the desk. 'Would he be willing to talk to you?'

'I don't know. Apparently he left Porton under pretty acrimonious circumstances, so he might.'

Chapter 8

It took Mark hours to get to sleep that night. As he lay in bed, long-buried images from the war kept returning to him.

He saw Dan's co-pilot sprawled in the sand with a bloody hole where his chest should have been, and the blackened corpses of Iraqi soldiers after the A10 attack on their convoy. And he saw with piercing clarity the boyish, almost childlike face of a young soldier hitching a lift to Brize Norton on the day they flew out to the Gulf.

He was just eighteen, the minimum age for a combat soldier. 'If I'd been born a week later, I wouldn't be going.' He had talked about the coming war as if it was a football match and he was a substitute waiting to take the field. 'I hope it isn't all over before I get my chance.'

Mark and Steve had exchanged a look. 'Don't worry,' Mark said, 'I'm sure they'll save some for you.'

After his release from Iraq, Mark had scanned the list of fatalities from the war. The boy's name was among them, killed by his own side, the first victim of friendly fire.

Mark turned over again, trying to clear his mind, but the thoughts kept crowding in on him. He saw his father in his wheelchair, his face half-hidden behind an oxygen mask, and heard the hiss of the gas and the rattle of the tube against the metal cylinder. As that image faded, it was replaced by the cruelly disfigured face of a baby, lifting his head from his mother's shoulder. The sequence recurred again and again. Mark woke with a start, his pillow damp with sweat. Sunlight was already streaming through the window.

He shocked himself awake with a cold shower, then caught the Tube into London, the carriages jammed with the last wave of the rush hour.

Colindale was well to the north of the city, two stops from the end of the Northern Line. He walked the short distance to the newspaper library, past a few pre-war semi-detached houses and a small parade of shops.

It was still a few minutes before ten and he found himself at the tail of a queue of people waiting for the doors of the library to open. There were a few students, but most were middle-aged men. Several wore raincoats despite the warmth of the day, and they clutched battered briefcases, Tupperwear sandwich boxes and Thermos flasks, as if they were spending the day at a cricket match, not turning the pages of yellowing newspapers.

The doors opened with military precision as the clock struck ten, and a uniformed attendant at a counter just inside the door dispossessed them of their coats and bags with all the charm of a concierge in a Soviet apartment block. 'Only notebooks and pencils allowed in the library,' he growled at Mark, not even bothering to look up. 'No pens.'

'I don't have a pencil,' Mark said.

The man gave an ostentatious sigh. 'There are some on the reservations desk on the second floor.' He took Mark's briefcase. 'Now, what's your reader number?'

'What?'

Once more there was an eye-rolling sigh. 'You have to have a reader number.'

'And where do I get one?' Mark imagined himself branding the number on the man's forehead with a red-hot iron.

He jerked his head towards the stairs. 'Reservations desk.'

'So I go up to the second floor, get a number, come back down here, tell you the number, then I can give you my bag and go back upstairs to the second floor?'

'Exactly.'

'And what do I do with my bag in the meantime?'

'You leave it here.'

'What, without a number? That's more than your job's worth, isn't it?'

The middle-aged men were already hard at work when he finally shook off the attendant and reached the library. The only sounds were the scratching of pencils, the squeak of microfilm rollers and the slap of leather-bound volumes of newspapers.

To his relief Mark found that the national newspaper files were held on CD Rom. He took a seat at one of the computers and typed in Gulf War Syndrome as the search term. An endless list of references began appearing on the screen.

He was still at his seat seven hours later, when a bell rang to signal that the library was closing. Mark frowned, then scrolled back to a piece that had caught his eye earlier. It had originally appeared in the *Dallas-Fort Worth Enquirer*, but had been reprinted in one of the English broadsheets.

The headline was tabloid lurid: 'MUTANT AIDS HITS CONS', but the text was more restrained, leavening its scare story with quotes from a professor at the department of tumour biology at the world's largest cancer centre in Houston, Texas. Mark scanned through it, ignoring the second ringing of the library bell.

> The type of mycoplasma we identified was highly unusual and almost certainly couldn't occur naturally. It has one gene from the HIV-1 virus, but only one. It was almost certainly an artificially modified microbe, deliberately altered by scientists, making it a much more severe infectious agent. We found evidence that mycoplasma vaccine testing had been carried out in a prison well before the Gulf War.
>
> We checked with the prison and learned that many of the prisoners involved – plus prison guards and family members – were currently ill with the same symptoms as Gulf War Syndrome.
>
> Dr Nicholson has published over four hundred scientific papers, edited thirteen books and served as an editor on thirteen scientific or medical journals.

> 'Yet since we have been working on this issue we have encountered many attempts to block papers and articles from publication, grant applications have been tampered with and our mail, phone and fax have been intercepted.'

'The library is closing. I'm afraid you'll have to leave now.'

Mark allowed himself to be shepherded out of the door and down the stairs. The jobsworth stood by the main doors, already holding Mark's briefcase in his thumb and forefinger, as if to avoid soiling any more of his hand with it.

Mark met the man's stare. 'If you're ever looking for another job, I can recommend the Indian railways. You'd fit right in.' The doors slammed shut behind him.

He walked slowly down the street, trying to drag some meaning from the mass of material he had read. If anything, Gulf War Syndrome now seemed even more elusive. The syndrome seemed to take at least a score of different forms and occurred, apparently at random, among hundreds of different groups. There were air crew, ground crew, special forces, infantry, gunners, tank crews, marines, cooks, nurses and civilians. Some had been in the frontline, others at bases well behind the lines; some had been inoculated, some had not.

Every hypothesis about the cause of their illness, from the most prosaic to the most fanciful, worked for some cases but not for all. The only common factor was their presence in the Gulf during the war. He had only nine days before leaving for Kuwait and was no nearer the answer; every lead seemed to end at a vanishing point, a blind alley where the trail went cold.

As he passed the parade of shops, Mark saw a café and realised he was ravenous. The café owner was just closing, but after a show of reluctance, he allowed Mark to buy a couple of curling sandwiches left over from lunchtime. He ate them as he waited for the Tube.

Tiredness was dragging at him when he got back to his flat. He made some coffee and had been wandering aimlessly around the room for some minutes before he realised that his answerphone was flashing. He stood lost in thought, only half listening to the message, until he realised who it was.

'Mark, this is Natalie. See, I told you I'd call you. I'm at Brown's Hotel surrounded by crushing bores of all nations. If you want to call me back, great; if you want to rescue me, I'll buy you a dinner in gratitude. Park the white charger out front.'

Natalie was lounging in a chair in reception as he walked into the hotel lobby. She stood up, smoothing imaginary creases from her long, figure-hugging black dress.

'Wow,' Mark said.

She smiled and inclined her head slightly. 'I thought I'd give the jeans and Timberlands the night off.' There was a pause as Mark continued to stare at her. 'Now, if you've seen everything you need to see, how about dinner? I'm starving.'

The restaurant she had chosen was fashionably vast, heaving with people and deafeningly noisy, sound rattling around the steel-lined walls. She gave a rueful smile. 'Not quite a candlelit dinner for two, is it? The food was highly recommended, but my friend neglected to mention we'd be eating inside an aircraft carrier during rehearsals for World War Three.' She sipped her drink. 'So. How's Steve?'

Mark's jaw clenched. 'Not good. I saw his baby for the first time yesterday. He was born with Goldenhar's Syndrome. Just like Michael's son.'

She reached across the table and laid her hand on his arm. 'Mark, I'm so sorry.'

He looked straight at her. 'I'm going to try and do something to help them.'

'But you're still in the Air Force: you'll be subject to the same pressures as every other serviceman. If you don't want to damage your career, keep your mouth shut.'

'I'm not worried about that kind of pressure.' As he spoke the words, he knew they were true. 'I still love flying fast-jets, and I'd miss it if I was kicked out of the Forces, but I've pretty much lost whatever respect I once had for the RAF.'

Her gaze was steady. 'Are you sure? If you stick your neck out, it could cost you your friends as well as your job and your future; your Ministry of Defence has long tentacles.'

'I'm sure. You were right about me. I was too much of an observer.' He paused and looked away. 'Do you know the worst thing? It suddenly came to me. If he were still alive, my own father would be ashamed of me.'

'That's rubbish.'

'No. It's true.'

She waited, her hand still resting on his arm, but he did not elaborate. 'So, what have you done so far?'

'I've been to the GWS Sufferers' Association and met a guy called Larry Rafferty. You'd like him. He's an old guy – in his sixties – and suffering from GWS, but he has so much energy and compassion in him. He's a real inspiration – just like Michael. He's given me a lot of information about the jabs given to troops out there and the NAPS tablets we all took. Some of his stories would make your hair stand on end. I've also ploughed through a mountain of press cuttings about GWS.'

'And?'

'And not much really. There was one about a deliberately altered version of the HIV virus. They'd been carrying out some sort of vaccine testing at a prison. Many of the prisoners had GWS symptoms.'

'I doubt if that's of much relevance, Mark, unless someone's developed a new way of transmitting HIV as well. The one thing we can be sure about all those troops in the Gulf is that, whatever else they were doing, they weren't having sex with each other. And whatever we might think about army medics, I do know they don't reuse needles.' She paused. 'I'm sorry. I'm not trashing you. I'm glad you're doing this.' She topped up their glasses. 'So have you found David Isaacs yet?'

'That's my next step.'

'You should do it straight away. The work he was doing at Porton Down was on antidotes to chemical and biological agents. He worked on developing the NAPS tablets.'

'How do you know?'

'I shared a lab with him.' She paused. 'Look. I'm not doing anything tomorrow. If you're free, why don't we see if we can track him down? I couldn't find that number, but he can't have disappeared.'

Mark looked doubtful. 'We can't exactly look in *Yellow Pages* under "Disgraced ex-Porton Down Scientist".'

'No, but we could try directory enquiries or the phone book. He's from Devon originally so we could start there.'

'Can you really spot a Devon accent? That's not bad for an American.'

She smiled. 'He told me he came from there.'

'So we'll check Devon, but if we don't find him there?'

'We'll check everywhere else. There can't be that many David Isaacs in Great Britain.'

'And if he's ex-directory?'

'We'll think of something else. Are you always this pessimistic?'

'No. By the way, I like the sound of "we", but it's not your battle, Natalie. You don't have to get involved.'

'Mark, the guy's a biochemist. Unless you've got talents I don't know about, you're going to need all the help you can get, both to ask the right questions and understand the answers.'

Mark was still finishing his breakfast when the phone rang the next morning. 'I've got the number,' Natalie said. 'A place called Totnes.'

'I've been there a couple of times. We used to go to Devon for our holidays every year when I was a kid.'

'Get your ass over here and we'll give him a ring.'

'Better still, be outside the hotel in twenty minutes. I'll never find a parking space at this time of day.'

'What if he's not there?'

He glanced out of the window; the sun was shining on the water. 'We'll go for a drive instead, it's too good a day to waste.'

Natalie was back in her trademark T-shirt and jeans when Mark pulled up outside the hotel. She was gazing the other way and he took a moment to study her before attracting her attention. As she jumped in, Mark set the phone to hands-free and she dialled the number.

It rang twice before an answerphone clicked on. A soft, diffident voice murmured, 'I'm not around to take the call, please leave a message.'

As Natalie started to speak, the voice cut in. 'Natalie, how are you? I haven't heard from you in ages. Sorry about the answerphone. I leave it on all the time to screen out unwanted calls. Not that I get many calls of any sort these days. So, how have you been?'

'Fine, fine,' Natalie said. 'Listen, David, can we catch up on the news later? I have a friend who needs to ask you some questions about—'

David interrupted immediately. 'If your friend's questions are in any way out of the ordinary, it would be better to have this conversation face to face.'

'Sure. Can we come and see you today?'

'I'd be upset if you didn't.'

'We're leaving London now, say two to three hours?' She looked at Mark, who nodded.

'All right. And Natalie? I'd prefer to talk in your car or in a pub somewhere. It may sound ridiculous, but you know how things are.'

She scribbled down the address David gave her, then broke the connection.

Mark cocked an eyebrow. 'He's paranoid.'

She did not return the smile. 'With good reason, but he can tell you more about that himself.'

As they sped along the motorway, Natalie steered the conversation away from Gulf War Syndrome. 'Okay, Mark, life story in a hundred words or less. You first or me?'

He laughed. 'You should be a TV interviewer. Go on, you first.'

'Army brat. One brother, no sisters. Mother devoted home-maker and child-rearer. Father a colonel in 82nd Airborne – that's how I knew Michael.' She smiled. 'That last bit wasn't part of the hundred words, by the way. Usual army life, a series of moves around dusty, godforsaken bases in places like Kansas and Oklahoma, and a few overseas postings, not including Vietnam. Dad did that one on his own. To the disgust of his more Neanderthal army friends, his daughter was something of a precocious pinko intellectual. To their even greater horror, she now works for the UN.'

'What does your dad think?'

'He doesn't mind. He's proud of me and never was one of

those gung-ho "God, Mom and apple pie" kind of officers. That's probably why he never made General: he's too civilised and straightforward for his own good.'

'That's enough about your dad. What about you?'

'Degree in chemistry at UCLA, Masters degree at Berkeley. A couple of years in industry, notable mainly for convincing me that I didn't want to spend even a couple of years in industry.'

'What were you doing?'

'Giving the world what it needed most – another kind of hairspray. In desperation I applied for a job with the UN and to my considerable surprise they took me on. Since then by naked ambition, ruthless backstabbing and sheer goddam talent, I've clawed my way into a senior position with UNSCOM.'

'I can't believe that,' Mark said. 'At least not the bit about the talent.'

She smiled. 'You won't know where and you won't know when, Mark, but you'll pay for that.'

'So is there any slightly more personal history to go with that impressive CV?'

'Not much. A few relationships, a disastrous affair with a married man, no husbands, no children.'

'And a trail of broken hearts scattered across five continents.'

'Four actually, I've never been to Australia.'

'Tell me about the married man.' Mark felt a stab of jealousy as he asked the question. The intensity of the feeling surprised him.

'It was a mess, that's all. He was a work colleague, which made it even more complicated.' She paused. 'Okay, that was rather more than a hundred words. See if you can do any better.'

'Right. Father retired – well, he was invalided out, actually – captain in the navy. My mother was his second wife. It was the classic cliché: she was a nurse on the ward where he spent six months fighting for his life.'

'What happened to him?'

He hesitated. 'It was during the war – the Second World War. His ship was bombed by the Germans as it was unloading munitions in Bari harbour in Italy. The munitions were shells filled with mustard gas, though nobody knew that at the time. He was thrown into the water, which was covered in a film of fuel oil and liquid mustard gas. Hundreds of men died, my father and a few others survived. When they were pulled out of the water, most of them could barely see or breathe and they were covered in blisters. Nobody knew what was wrong with them, but he was lucky enough to be treated by an older medic who had served in the First World War. He recognised the symptoms of mustard gas poisoning.

'My father lost the sight of one eye and his lungs were permanently damaged, but he lived. Most of the other rescued men died over the next few weeks. He was patched up and sent back to a hospital in the UK, where he met my mother. He was given a medical discharge from the navy but was refused compensation for his chest injuries. The MoD denied that the ship had been carrying mustard gas. My old man was very determined. It took him over twenty years of campaigning, but he finally won a disability pension, backdated to the end of the war.' Mark paused. 'It didn't do him much good though: he died the following year.'

Natalie was silent for a few moments. 'Is that part of the reason you're pushing so hard now?'

He nodded. 'I think I was trying to avoid the connection. I'd had enough of other people's pain. It was seeing Steve's son that really brought things home to me. I'm ashamed that's what it took to open my eyes.' He swallowed hard. 'I grew up surrounded by the paraphernalia of my father's illness. By the time I was old enough to notice, he needed oxygen several times a day. One of the first sounds I can really remember is the clank of the cylinders as they wheeled them up the path.' He fell silent again, staring at the road ahead, but aware of her eyes on him.

Natalie reached over and touched his arm. 'What you said last night about your father being ashamed of you.' She paused. 'You were wrong. He'd be very proud.' She watched his profile for a few moments. 'Did you have to deal with it on your own?'

'Yes. My parents tried and tried for a child, without success. My mother had three miscarriages and was advised not to become pregnant again, and as my father's health deteriorated, the chances grew smaller anyway. Finally, fifteen years after they married, they decided to adopt. I was the result.' He glanced at Natalie, checking her reaction.

She smiled. 'That explains it. I was beginning to think you were a very well-preserved sixty-year-old.' She wound down the window a fraction and took a breath of fresh air. 'Have you ever tried to find your real parents?'

He shook his head. 'They were my real parents. They brought me up.'

Natalie was about to say more, but saw the set of his jaw and changed the subject. 'One thing does puzzle me. Given your father's history, why would you have wanted to join the Forces yourself?'

'The flying bug. My uncle flew Spitfires in the War. I hero-worshipped him to a level which probably embarrassed us both. He gave me a spin for my tenth birthday. It was just a two-seater prop plane, but it was the most exciting thing that had ever happened to me. I can still remember the smell of the leather seats and the aviation fuel, the thrill of the take-off and the sight of everything shrinking in size as we soared upwards. Out towards the sea I could see cloudbanks piled up as high as mountain ranges. The earth was in shadow but a halo of sunlight illuminated the top of the clouds.' He broke off, embarrassed. 'Anyway, you get the picture. I was hooked.'

She smiled. 'You've already exceeded your word quota by about a thousand per cent, but don't worry.'

Mark looked rueful. 'I'll try to keep the rest of it short. School, university – Sussex – degree in history, spectacularly irrelevant to my chosen career, but it did get me out of three years marching around a parade ground and fiddling with screwdrivers and electric string.

'I realised around the age of twenty-five that attempting to improve on my uncle's flying career was a) impossible and b) pointless. Since then I've enjoyed my life a bit more and the Air Force a bit less.

'Shot down, captured and tortured in the Gulf, earning myself my fifteen minutes of fame. No permanent scars – physical or psychological – no regrets other than that I didn't ask Princess Diana for a date when we met at a reception for POWs. A few relationships, no wives, no children. No current partner, but applications from interested parties welcomed and treated in strictest confidence.' He glanced across at Natalie.

She held the look for a moment. 'I'll let you know.' Then she gave a slow smile and turned to glance out of the side window. 'But don't hold your breath.'

They reached Totnes just after twelve o'clock and threaded their way through a warren of tiny high-banked lanes to the village of Rattray. There was a cluster of thatched cottages around the church but David Isaacs' house was set apart, a grey, granite Victorian rectory at the end of a dark and overgrown driveway.

As they turned the corner, Mark braked. The road ahead of them was blocked by two police cars, their blue lights flashing. A young, pink-faced constable was manning a strip of blue and white plastic tape stretched across the lane.

'What's going on?' Mark asked.

'An accident, sir. I'm afraid we can't let you through for the moment.'

'We only want to go and pick someone up from that house there,' Natalie said. 'Okay if we go through on foot?' She gave him her warmest smile, but he was already turning away.

'D.I. Fuller?'

A balding man in a trench coat detached himself from a group of policemen standing twenty yards away. He gave the young constable an irritated look, then walked towards them. 'What is it now?'

'This lady and gentleman, sir. They're on their way to Mr Isaacs' house.'

The inspector scrutinised each of them in turn. 'What exactly was your business with Mr Isaacs?'

Natalie bridled at his tone. 'We're friends of his. Why?'

He gave her a cold look. 'I'm afraid Mr Isaacs has been involved in a hit-and-run accident.'

'What? You mean he ran someone over?'

'I'm afraid not.'

Natalie gave him a blank stare, and Mark took her arm. 'He means it was David who was hit.'

'Where is he? Is he badly hurt?'

The inspector stepped a little to one side, opening up their view of the lane. The other policemen were looking down at a chalk outline of a body. A dark stain discoloured the road around the outline of the head. Natalie's shocked gaze swung back to the inspector. He gave a slow nod. 'I'm very sorry.'

White faced and motionless, she stared past him.

'What happened?' Mark said.

'Apparently Mr Isaacs was in the habit of taking a walk up the lane here every morning. There's no shop in the village, so people get their newspapers and groceries from the petrol station up on the main road.' He broke off and gestured towards a knot of villagers standing beyond the tapes on the far side. 'According to an eye witness, he was on his way back when a car – a dark blue or black Range Rover – came speeding down the lane. Mr Isaacs tried to get out of the way by climbing the bank but he appears to have slipped and fallen back into the road.' He shook his head wearily. 'The witness wasn't entirely sure.' He spoke directly to Natalie. 'He wouldn't have felt anything. He was killed outright.'

The inspector waited for a moment before continuing. 'Now if you wouldn't mind just giving a few details to the constable here, in case we need to contact you.'

After giving their names and addresses, Natalie took a last look down the lane. She did not speak as Mark drove back through the maze of lanes.

'What now?' he asked.

'Let's find a pub. I need a drink and I need to stop and think.'

The Ring of Bells was set back from the road, a long, white-washed building under a weathered thatch. The interior was a low-ceilinged warren of small rooms, nooks and alcoves, and Mark had to duck to clear the smoke-blackened beams. A handful of customers were dotted around the bar.

Mark bought the drinks and led Natalie to a corner table. He glanced at a couple of men in business suits who sat down at a table a few feet away, then lowered his voice. 'You all right?'

She nodded. 'It's the shock, that's all. We were only speaking to him a couple of hours ago.'

'Tell me what you know.'

She stared at him for a moment. 'About David?'

'About what he was doing at Porton Down.'

She turned a beer mat over in her hands. 'I'll tell you what I can, but it's a few years out of date. I last worked at Porton Down—' She glanced around and dropped her voice even lower. 'Six years ago.'

'When did David leave?'

'A couple of months later. He's one of the best in his field, but he hasn't—' She checked herself. 'He hadn't worked since, as far as I know.'

'Why not?'

'Virtually all the work we do is government funded at some level. Journals that used to publish his work started to return it unread, and his job applications didn't even reach the shortlist.'

As she spoke, Mark glanced out of the window. A man was kneeling on the ground beside his car.

'Wait here.' He hurried out of the bar and sprinted across the car park. The man was just straightening up.

'What the fuck do you think you're doing?' Mark said.

'Is this your car, sir?'

'Yes it is. Not that it's any of your business. Now who the hell are you and what are you doing?'

Mark tensed as the man slipped a hand inside his coat, but he pulled out a plastic identication card. He glanced at it. 'Detective Sergeant Michael Tucker, Exeter CID. Very nice. But it only tells me who you are. It doesn't tell me what you were doing to my car.'

'Checking your tax disc, sir. Just routine.'

'On your hands and knees?'

'And making sure your tyres were legal. Everything seems to be in order.'

The man made to move past him, but Mark blocked his path. 'I don't know much about police procedure, but I do know that the CID don't waste their valuable time on routine vehicle checks. That's what your uniformed friends are for, isn't it?'

Tucker adopted a confidential tone. 'The truth is, sir, we're investigating a stolen-car ring. They specialise in high-performance cars like yours. We had reports of a dark blue Audi stolen from Paignton this morning. That's why I was checking your car.'

Mark gave him a doubtful look, then stepped aside to let him pass.

'Oh, and sir? If you keep leaving your doors unlocked, the next stolen car we'll be looking for will be yours. Good afternoon.'

Mark swung round. The locking buttons were raised and the passenger door was only half-closed. Puzzled, he reached for his keys. He heard an engine and turned round in time to see the policeman's Sierra disappearing out of the car park. He began searching the inside of the car, then stretched himself full length on the ground and examined the underside. He could see nothing wrong.

Mark went back into the pub, borrowed the phone book and then dialled a number from the payphone. 'CID, please . . . Good afternoon. I'm checking the identity of one of your officers. Could you confirm that you have a Detective Sergeant Michael Tucker based with you?'

'Please hold a moment,' a voice said in a thick Devon accent. Mark waited as the call was transferred. There was a clatter of relays and a faint hiss on the line, then, 'You're inquiring about D.S. Tucker?'

That's right.'

'What seems to be the problem?'

'No problem.' Mark put the phone down and rejoined Natalie. He told her what had happened, then gave a sheepish smile. 'Now I'm the one being paranoid.'

She did not return the smile. 'It didn't help David.'

'Natalie, what was he doing?'

'His contract at Porton Down was terminated because of concerns he expressed at some of his research findings. He'd been helping to develop the NAPS and BATS tablets used to counter chemical and biological agents. Many were new and practically untested on animals, let alone humans. There was pentavalent botulinum toxoid, used to fight botulism, and several anti-anthrax vaccines, including one using a live, recombinant DNA process.'

She paused. 'NAPS tablets also contained a new and barely tested drug called pyridostigmine bromide. An overdose causes a state of profound weakness, muscle cramps, diarrhoea, sweating and hyperventilation, the very symptoms that many Gulf veterans complain of. The Americans actually lost more men from the field – six hundred of them – because of adverse reaction to NAPS tablets than through enemy action.

'NAPS tablets were introduced in 1981, yet the MoD only applied for a licence in 1993 – two years after the Gulf War. I'm sure the only reason they applied at all was because of all the speculation about the origins of GWS. The MoD swore PB was perfectly safe because it had been used by civilians for years. They neglected to mention that it had been used only on a restricted, named-patient-only basis, and solely for the treatment of a serious nerve disorder, myasthenia gravis.

'One of your defence ministers was also wheeled out to claim that the safety and effectiveness of PB against chemical warfare agents was "internationally medically recognised", yet a report by the US Senate Committee on Veterans' Affairs said the drug was unsafe "for repeated use by healthy persons under any circumstances". It also stated that only in the event of an attack with one nerve agent – Soman – could there be any conceivable benefit. Men taking the drug would actually be rendered more vulnerable to other chemical agents.'

'How the hell do you know all this?'

'It's my job to know, Mark. David raised the strongest possible objections to the blanket use of NAPS without any regard to individual age, sex, health, weight, allergies or general medical history and without informing the recipients of potentially harmful side effects. He was told that vaccines and NAPS would only be administered under the principles of "voluntary informed consent". In other words, every soldier would be told exactly what he was about to swallow or be injected with, informed of the possible risks and then asked if he consented to the treatment. From your own experience of the military, Mark, would you describe that as a plausible scenario?'

'Of course not.'

'Exactly. When David persisted in his criticisms, he was removed from sensitive work and his contract was not renewed.' She paused. 'One other thing you should know, which illustrates their priorities. There was a shortage of human anthrax vaccine. They simply hadn't produced enough. The solution was simple. They used two hundred thousand ampoules of commercial veterinary vaccine instead – for use on animals.'

Mark's jaw dropped. 'So are NAPS tablets or inoculations the cause of Gulf War Syndrome?'

She put the tips of her fingers together and thought for a moment. 'I'm not qualified to give a scientific opinion. I've made no study of GWS victims or their symptoms.'

'However . . .'

'However. There is no single distinctive syndrome presenting itself. The only reason thalidomide was discovered was because it produced a very characteristic and limited set of defects. If thalidomide had caused fifteen or sixteen kinds of defects, as Gulf War Syndrome appears to do, we still wouldn't have a clue.'

'But just the same,' Mark said. 'You've already said the symptoms produced by an overdose of PB are the same as those suffered by many GWS victims.'

She inclined her head. 'Just so. Speaking as a scientist I can offer only tentative hypotheses, but speaking as a human being, the only way you can explain GWS is by exposure to chemical or biological agents. That exposure can only have been caused by the inoculations and the NAPS tablets.' She paused. 'Or by low-level exposure to chemical or biological weapons.'

'But there's no evidence of chemical attacks.'

'Perhaps. Anyway, the Coalition bombed several Iraqi chemical weapons plants. Toxic vapour could certainly have caused death and illness to those unfortunate enough to have been downwind.'

She paused to sip her drink. 'Gulf War Syndrome is like a needle in a particularly messy haystack; except it's not that simple. There may be one needle, there may be twenty. I'll tell you something else. The fog of uncertainty about GWS may also be concealing other things. If a serviceman – like Dan, like Michael, like Steve – who was involved in the Gulf develops unusual symptoms, doctors now tend to assume that he's got GWS.'

Mark searched her face. 'So the general confusion about GWS could be masking another disease?'

'Exactly. Dan, Michael and Steve's symptoms are virtually unique. As far as we know, no other GWS sufferers have them. Michael Ringwald's platoon was on the right flank of British spearhead forces protected by Inoculation Scimitar. Michael had no such protection.'

Mark nodded absently. 'I guess if we knew what Inoculation Scimitar was designed to counter, we might be nearer an answer to what's wrong with Dan, Michael and Steve.' He paused. 'But Dan and Steve weren't part of any spearhead force. They were in an Iraqi gaol with me.'

'And where was the gaol?'

He gave a helpless shrug. 'I don't know. When we were taken there, we were held face down on the floor of a lorry with hoods over our heads. The same thing happened on the way out. It could have been anywhere in Iraq. None of us knew where we were, or at least . . .'

After a few minutes he stood up. 'Let's go. I need to make a phone call.' As they left the bar he looked back. The two businessmen were engaged in an animated conversation and did not look up.

Once in the car, Mark picked up the phone.

'Ops room, please . . . Dexy? It's Mark. Listen, are you free later on today? I need to see you about something . . . What we were talking about at the reunion. Sure . . . yes, I know it. Six o'clock? See you then.'

'What was that about?' Natalie asked as he hung up.

'Someone I need to see.' He watched for a gap in the traffic before accelerating away up the road. 'You don't mind extending the tour of the English countryside to include Hereford, do you? We could find somewhere to stay if you like and go back to London tomorrow.'

He looked across at her and she coloured a little, then pointed through the windscreen. 'Sorry, Mark, eye contact at seventy miles a hour always makes me nervous.'

He switched his attention back to the road and pulled out sharply to overtake the lorry looming in his windscreen. 'So how about it?'

'I can't, I'm afraid. I need to get back. My conference opens tomorrow and I've a paper to deliver. I'm sorry.'

'So am I.' He changed gear. 'Do you mind if I drop you at Exeter or Bristol, then? It's a fast line, only a couple of hours to London.'

He drove along a ridge and gazed around him at the patchwork of fields, woods and scattered hamlets below them. 'I don't know about you, but I don't care if I never see another desert in my life.'

'I know the feeling. I've spent more time in Iraq in the last two years than I have in the US.'

'So how do you set about investigating a site?'

'Do you really want to know, or are you just making polite conversation?'

He smiled. 'Both.'

'Just for that, I'll give you the full unexpurgated version. Finding that GWS needle in a haystack is a breeze compared to what we're trying to do. Toxins like anthrax and botulism can be freeze-dried and put in a powdered milk tin or a plastic bag. They're not neatly stored in containers labelled "CBW weapons, please destroy".

'We work in teams of ten to fifteen people, a third of whom are simply monitoring and protecting us against possible contamination. The rest of us all have specialities: chemists, biologists, chemical engineers, experts in manufacturing processes, academics and theoreticians.

'The engineers might tell us that a particular centrifuge can be used to produce Sarin, say. The manufacturing specialist will calculate that it can produce X tons a week, and the theoretician will work out the amount of precursor needed to produce that quantity. We then compare that with the quantities of precursor that Iraq has imported over the years.'

'Back up a minute. What's a precursor?'

'Didn't you do chemistry at school? It's the base chemical used to manufacture the weapon.' She paused. 'The documentation will inevitably be hidden or falsified and the paperchase to trace the shipments can take us all over the world – including the UK.' She shot him a glance. 'I don't want to hurt your national pride, Mark, but Britain was the country that indirectly taught the Iraqis how to manufacture the stuff we're now trying to destroy.'

She waited in vain for him to rise to the bait. 'The Nazis originally developed nerve agents based on organophosphates.' She nodded. 'That's right, the same base as the insecticides. At the end of the War, teams of American, British and Russian investigators swept through the Reich, collecting every scrap of scientific or industrial material they could lay their hands on. The British were lucky enough – if that's the right word – to discover some undestroyed files relating to nerve gas experiments carried out on prisoners at Natzweiler concentration camp by Professor Karl Wimmer.

'When Wimmer was located he was taken into custody and was never heard of again.' She studied Mark's expression. 'He never appeared before any war crimes tribunal, despite the atrocities he committed, so either he escaped or he was given a new identity and taken to Porton Down to give Britain the benefit of his knowledge. I know which explanation my money's on.

'Britain decided that chemical weapons would be their number one deterrent, so huge production facilities were set up, turning out fifty tons of Sarin a week. The stockpile was enough to cover the RAF's estimated requirement in the event of an all-out war – nine thousand tons per year.

'By the 1960s, however, the strategic thinking had shifted. Nuclear weapons were seen as a sufficient deterrent and though Porton Down still carried on with research and development, the big nerve-agent production facilities were decommissioned.'

Mark found it hard to concentrate on what she was saying, distracted by her closeness. He gave an exaggerated yawn. 'Thanks for the history lesson, but what does all this have to do with Iraq?'

She gave him a look of mock severity. 'I'm just getting to that. International observers were brought in to watch the decommissioning process. The problem was that if you show someone how to decommission a plant, you also teach them how to commission one.

'Among the observers was a Yugoslav general, Vladimir Voivodich, who just happened to be head of the Yugoslav army's chemical weapons programme. Two months after he came back from Britain, work began on a plant at Potoci, just outside Mostar. The Yugoslavs also earned themselves some foreign currency by building replica plants in Iraq and Libya.

'Of course once you've got the plant, you need the precursor chemicals to manufacture the nerve agents. The British were very helpful there too. An export licence was issued in 1983 for fifteen tons of methyl phosphoric dichloride for Iraq. That's enough to produce ten tons of Sarin. '

'What?' Mark was torn between disbelief and outrage.

'Don't look so shocked, Mark, it's the way of the world. And we can't put all the blame on the Brits, because if they hadn't agreed to supply it, a dozen other nations including the good old US of A were falling over themselves to sell the stuff.

'The US government approved sales of toxic agents like anthrax and botulinum toxin to Iraq between 1985 and 1989 just in time for the Gulf War. They were capable of being cultured or grown for a biological weapons programme. We've found fifteen thousand litres of anthrax in Iraq so far, supplied by Britain and the US. Iraq claimed to need it for animal research. Virtually every member of the Security Council was doing similar business with Iraq, and the list of companies involved reads like the Fortune 500.'

Mark shook his head. 'I just can't believe the British government allowed it.'

'Why so shocked? After all, you guys were still training his pilots a few years before the Gulf War broke out.'

'That's different.'

'Perhaps. Tell me, did you know that your guys also trained Saddam's interrogators?'

Mark fell silent, remembering the perfect English of his own captors and the British-made electric batons they had used on him.

'Anyway, as you said, that's all history. Our job now is to trace every microgram and millilitre and find out what happened to it. We test what we know from our research against what the Iraqis tell us.

'So we carry out this game of hide and seek with them and piece together the most insignificant-looking pieces of information to build the picture. Lots of detection work is done in New York, on the seventeenth floor of the UN Secretariat.' She paused as he pulled into the station. 'We monitor which scientists attend which seminars and trace the backgrounds of unknown people involved in them. One of the major players in the Iraqi development of anthrax weapons is a woman with dual nationality. She has a Syrian father and uses a Syrian passport when travelling abroad. We knew nothing about her until she booked herself into a scientific symposium and identified herself as an anthrax expert.'

'The symposium in Las Vegas?'

'You're learning fast.' She jumped out of the car. 'See you back in London.'

Chapter 9

Mark stopped at the bridge. The floodlit outline of the cathedral dominated the Hereford skyline. The Saracen's Head was on the other side of the river. He eased past a group of early-season tourists on the terrace and went inside.

Two stocky figures were standing at the bar, both wearing blue jeans, check shirts and bomber jackets. Mark smiled to himself. SAS men were nothing like the seven-foot mountains of popular imagination, but if you knew what to look for, you could spot them a mile off.

Dexy's handshake was as firm as ever. 'I brought Stumps along too.' He gave no further explanation. Stumps smiled a greeting, baring the uneven teeth that had earned him his nickname.

They exchanged idle chat for a few minutes, then Dexy led the way to a quiet table. 'So what's up, mate? You didn't come all this way just to buy us a pint.'

Mark shook his head. 'I need some information.'

Stumps raised an eyebrow.

'You remember Dan, don't you?'

'The Chinook pilot?' Dexy said. 'Of course I do.'

'I saw him in Las Vegas. He's in a wheelchair. He's dying of GWS – or something like it.'

'Poor bastard.'

'Steve's sick too. He's failed his annual medical. He's got the same symptoms.'

'So what do you want from us?'

'I want to know about Raz.'

It was the first time Mark had seen Dexy look uncomfortable. 'He'd been ill ever since we got back from the Gulf. It was like he wasn't the same person any more. He'd always been ultra cool, ultra controlled, but he started letting rip at people for no apparent reason. We covered it up as well as we could, but then he hung one on an officer.' He shook his head at the memory. 'We were debriefing a training exercise. The Rupert was a bit of a fuckwit, but nothing we hadn't seen before. Raz just lost it completely. He started yelling at him and then decked him before we could get in the way. He couldn't even remember doing it. He was RTU'd immediately.

'We were in the jungle for three months after that. When we got back he was already pretty far gone. I couldn't believe how fast it all happened. He'd been going along for four or five years not getting better, but not getting that much worse either, and then suddenly it was like he'd got full-blown AIDS.'

'Could it have been AIDS?'

'Don't be fucking stupid. Of course it wasn't AIDS. He had Gulf War Syndrome.'

'Is that what the doctors said it was?' Mark asked.

'Of course not.'

'Then how can you be sure?'

'Because he went out to the Gulf healthy, one of the fittest men in the regiment. And that is pretty fucking fit. When he came back, he couldn't even run a hundred yards without coughing his lungs up.' He hesitated. 'There are another four guys in my troop with the same symptoms: pains in the joints, constant fatigue, memory loss, blinding headaches, unpredictable violent behaviour. Five out of the twelve in my troop, pretty bad odds.' He glanced at Stumps. There was a pause.

'One of them is me,' Stumps said.

'Jesus, Stumps, I'm sorry,' Mark said, overcome once more with the inadequacy of the word. No one spoke for a few moments.

'Dan and Steve also have another distinctive symptom,' Mark said. 'Purple sores on their chest and stomach.'

'Like these?' Stumps undid a couple of buttons on his shirt and Mark saw the familiar lesions. He nodded.

'Raz had the same thing,' Stumps said. 'What about it?'

'I'm not sure.' Mark paused. 'You weren't with Dexy's patrol in the Gulf, were you?'

'No.' He hesitated.

'Come on, Stumps,' Dexy said. 'It was six years ago, it's ancient history.'

'I was attached to the 54th Chemical Troop as a—' He glanced at Dexy. 'Well, you really don't need to know what I'd been tasked to do, but the 54th was driving north and east towards As Salman through Al Badiyah Al Janubiyah – the Southern Desert – to cut off the Iraqi retreat from Kuwait. One night – I remember the date well, because of what happened—'

Mark interrupted. 'Was it the twenty-fourth of February?'

'How did you know that?'

'I'll tell you later. Finish the story.'

'It was a couple of hours before dawn. We'd been awake all night, listening to the air raids going in as we waited for the order to advance. There'd been virtually nothing in reply, only an odd Scud.

'Don't laugh, but I was in the latrines, taking a crap, when there was another Scud warning. There'd been a few false alarms already so I decided to finish my crap in peace. Suddenly there was a hell of a blast directly in front of our position, not more than half a mile from us. There was a huge double flash and in the light of it I saw a yellowish-brown cloud forming. Then it all went dark again. A few seconds later every chemical alarm we had tuned up. I came out of the bog like Linford Christie off the starting blocks. There was a mass panic. People were scrambling over each other to get into their NBC suits. All the time the alarms were screaming.

'The other spearhead troops were ordered forward immediately. They were told to leave all their personal possessions behind. The camp was like the *Marie Celeste* – food still lying on the tables, books and magazines open at the pages that were being read. They disappeared into the night, leaving us behind.

'I organised a team to carry out residual vapour tests. We did loads of tests, using NAIADS, CAMS and FOX chemical detection vans. I did four of them myself. They were all positive.' He broke off, studying Mark's face. 'I know what I'm talking about. I'm a graduate of the JagerKaserne chemical school in Germany. I had the knowledge and the equipment to detect what I did: nerve agent.'

'I believe you,' Mark said. 'I believe you.'

Stumps nodded, satisfied. 'Twenty minutes later we were told it was a false alarm and stood down to all-clear, but a few minutes after that we were again put into NBC Black, the highest alert state, only used when chemical weapons have been detected.

'We were stuck in our NBC suits for another eight hours. Just after the all-clear was given, this unmarked Blackhawk helicopter landed, no warning. These guys came out of nowhere, dressed in unmarked desert fatigues, no names, no rank, nothing, just a patch with a yellow scorpion on it. They ordered out the troop commander and told him not to ask any questions, then two of them came over to our vehicle and took all our samples, the computer print-outs and all the testing devices. They didn't say why, they just said, "Hand them over." All our protective gear was collected and replaced.

'When we advanced we had to leave all our personal kit behind. We were never allowed to go back for it. There was no real opposition. The Iraqi ground troops had either fled or were dead. There were plenty of bodies. The helicopter gunships and A10s shot up fleeing Iraqi columns, but I don't think anyone in the spearhead so much as fired a shot in anger. It was like invading a ghost town.

'When we had a break to regroup, the boss warned us that the previous night's incident was to be regarded as top secret – UK Eyes Alpha. He told us that the explosion was just a sonic boom. The incident never happened. No chemical agents were found. All the tests were faulty. The experts – including me – were mistaken.

'I said, "If all these tests were faulty, what caused all the false alarms?" I was given a list including unburned jet fuel from aircraft take-offs, diesel fumes, cigarette smoke and even nurses' hairspray. The fact that the nearest nurse was several miles away didn't seem to matter.'

Mark leaned forward. 'So what really caused the alarms?'

Stumps spread his hands. 'What do you think? The Czechs had the best detection equipment of any country. They reported so many suspected chemical events that we were told to disregard any further reports from them.' He paused. 'Do you want to know what's really scary? The best detectors we had were only able to recognise some types of nerve gas at concentrations one thousand times above their hazard level, and we had no detectors at all for biological agents. If they were out there, we wouldn't have known it.'

'Am I missing something here?' Mark said. 'If there was an Iraqi chemical attack, why the hell would the brass want to cover it up rather than expose it for our propaganda?'

'Beats me,' Stumps said, 'but that's what they did, and not very well either. The NBC logs from eighty per cent of the units involved in the fighting have gone missing. But the citations for some decorated soldiers with the 101st Airborne were for bravery in dealing with chemical incidents. Incidents which never happened.' He coughed, his chest rattling. 'They're all full of shit. There's the mother of all cover-ups. That's bad enough, but it's being done to protect that murdering bastard in Baghdad.' He banged his fist on the table, slopping beer from their glasses. The anger brought a brief flush to his sallow cheeks.

Mark was still for a few moments. 'What jabs did you have?'

'I didn't have any. The grunts all meekly lined up for them, but I said, "Bollocks. This anthrax is so dangerous that there's a Scottish island you still can't fucking walk on, half a century after it was contaminated, and you want to stick it in my arm? You can sod off."'

'Do you know anything about Inoculation Scimitar?'

Stumps shook his head. 'Nobody knew what the hell it was for. I saw the boxes: "For Spearhead Troops Only", but the US had spearhead troops and they weren't given it. I never took any NAPS tablets either. I reckoned I was safer taking my chances with the Iraqis. Ironic, isn't it? The only thing I did use was a COMBO pen. I wasn't wearing my NBC suit while I was sitting on the bog, so when the alarms started going off I whipped out a pen and jammed it in my thigh. It hurt like hell.' He paused. 'You know how they always told us to be very sure we'd been contaminated with chemical agent before we used a COMBO pen, because if we hadn't, the cure could make us seriously ill?'

Mark nodded.

'I didn't get ill at all.'

Stumps pulled a battered packet of cigarettes from his pocket and offered them to Mark, who reached forward for one, then stopped himself. 'Thanks – I mean no thanks. I've given up.'

Stumps smiled as he lit his own. 'Fairly recently I'd say.'

Mark shook his head. 'It just seems that way.'

'So . . .' Stumps blew out a cloud of smoke and settled back in his chair. 'Are you any the wiser?'

'Not much,' Mark said. 'I feel like I'm trying to wade through quicksand. Every answer I get seems to raise more questions.'

'Well, if there's anything else we can do, get in touch.'

Mark turned to Dexy. 'One last question. Where were we held in Iraq?'

Dexy grinned. 'I don't know, Mark. You're not really cut out for revenge raids. Why not leave it to the big boys?'

'Please, Dexy. I'm serious.'

'It's about fifty miles north-east of the Kuwaiti border. A couple of miles north of a place called As Salman.'

Dexy gave Mark a penetrating look and then glanced across at Stumps. 'I don't know about you, mate, but something tells me Biggles here is about to do something fucking stupid.'

There was a long silence.

'So?' Dexy said.

'I'm going to go somewhere I can get some real answers.'

'As Salman?'

'Not yet.' Mark lowered his voice. 'Porton Down.'

'Do you mind telling me how?'

'I'm not really sure. I just know I've got to get in there.'

'Brilliant,' Stumps said. 'Now all you need is a way to get out again.'

Dexy shook his head. 'Stick with the flying and the photographs, Mark. You're good at that. Leave the breaking and entering to me.'

'This isn't your battle, Dexy.'

'It is now,' he said, clapping Stumps on the shoulder. He paused. 'Listen, rush into this without the right skills and equipment, and you won't just fail, you'll be dead. We're talking about Porton Down, for God's sake. They don't have to shoot you, they don't even have to leave a needle mark on your arm.

'If you're going to do the job right, you've got to do surveillance first, day and night, on the perimeter and the target. You've got to do it long enough to establish the patterns and routines of the guards. You've got to know what locks, alarms and security systems you'll have to defeat and what patrols are operating. You watch them long enough to find their weak points. Do they check the doors after they've closed them or do they just let them bang shut? Do they always patrol along the same route at the same intervals, or do they vary it? If the guard needs to take a leak, does he always do it in the same place? Does he keep his rifle with him or prop it against a tree?

'When you've got your Int., that's when you select your equipment and go in to do the job.' He grinned. 'Give me a week and I'll find what you want . . . if it's there to be found.'

'Dexy, this is getting too big for me, and I'm off to Kuwait next Monday,' Mark said. 'I don't have a week. I need some help now.'

'Well, what the fuck are we doing sitting here?' Dexy said.

It was after midnight when Mark got back to London. He closed his front door quietly behind him and stood without moving, allowing his eyes to become accustomed to the darkness, as he strained his ears for any sound. Small patterns of light moved across the ceiling, reflected off the river. Nothing was out of place, as far as he could tell, but again he had the feeling that someone had been there. For the first time since he had lived there, he slid home both the bolts on the front door before he went to bed.

Mark was up early the next morning. The face that stared back at him from the bathroom mirror had shed its cocky self-assurance.

He ate his breakfast, watching a line of barges as they

made their way upriver. Something kept nagging at him, some half-seen, half-remembered incident that he knew was significant. Try as he might, he could not raise it to the surface of his mind.

He got up abruptly, left his plate and coffee cup on the table and headed for his car.

The weeds had taken an even stronger hold on Steve's front garden. Mark walked up the path, a smile pasted to his face. He rang the bell and heard the shuffle of footsteps along the hall. The door opened a crack, then swung wider. Jenny looked at him without a flicker of recognition.

Mark's smile faded. 'I'm sorry to turn up without . . .' His voice tailed away.

Jenny's face remained blank. She stepped to one side and Mark eased past her into the hall.

'How's Matthew?'

She still did not react.

'Jenny, what is it?'

She shut the door with a dull thud. 'Matthew's dead,' she said, her voice flat. 'He died last night. Pneumonia, they said.' The line of her jaw tightened as she fought back the tears. She shook her head and walked through to the kitchen.

He followed and found her standing by the dresser. 'Where's Steve?'

'Upstairs. The doctor sedated him.' She began straightening the crockery with small, nervous movements of her hands.

He stood watching her, struggling to find words of comfort. 'Jenny—'

She gave an almost imperceptible nod but held up her hand, standing motionless, as if listening for a particular sound.

'Is there anything . . .' Once more his voice trailed away into silence.

'Nothing.'

The doorbell rang. 'I'll get it,' he said, glad of something to do. A funeral director stood on the step, his features already composed into an expression of sober, professional regret.

Mark showed him into the kitchen. 'Jenny, do you want me to stay with you?'

Her gaze flickered towards him, then away again. 'My parents are coming. There's no need. Thanks.'

The funeral director had been standing to one side, as discreet as a butler waiting at table. Mark and Jenny both glanced at him in mute appeal for some way out of the silence that enveloped them. He cleared his throat. 'I wonder if we might have a cup of tea, Mrs Alderson?'

She moved to the sink and tried to lose herself in the gush of the tap and the rattle of the kettle.

Mark walked across to her. Once more she stiffened as he kissed her cheek. 'Anything at all, Jenny, just ask.' He hesitated for a few more seconds, then stepped back. 'I'll call you later.' She nodded, her expression still blank and withdrawn.

He closed the front door silently. As he walked to his car he saw her parents hurrying along the pavement. He hoped that they would not recognise him. He had no words to say, no hope to offer. They passed him without a glance, their pale, frightened faces fixed on the house at the end of the street. There was a brief, muttered exchange of words on the doorstep, then they went inside.

Mark drove back into London, parked off the Bayswater Road and spent an hour wandering through Hyde Park. Lost in thought and barely aware of his surroundings, he eventually found himself by the banks of the Serpentine. A group of children were chasing each other in and out of the trees. Two of them held toy aeroplanes above their heads, locked in mortal combat. He stopped to watch, then strode away.

Back at Coldchurch, he scanned the Station Standing Orders pinned to the noticeboard twice before he found what he was looking for. 'Volunteers for studies at chemical and biological defence establishment, Porton Down. Volunteers receive a £13 a day bonus, plus additional leave entitlements. Next induction of volunteers: 5 May 1997.' The fifth of May was the next day; six days before the squadron had to leave for Kuwait.

He hung around in the corridor until the warrant officer, Ron Stamper, appeared. He was in the last year of his career, but his appetite for the rigorous enforcement of even the most minor Air Force regulations showed no sign of abating. Ramrod straight, uniform immaculate, boots gleaming, he strode across the lobby as if it were a parade ground.

Mark intercepted him and spent five minutes flattering him about the standard of discipline among the airmen, then he paused and glanced casually at the noticeboard. 'They don't really get anyone to volunteer for that, do they, Mr Stamper?'

Stamper followed his gaze. 'Not often.' He winked. 'We do send volunteers, sir, although they don't exactly go voluntarily, if you take my meaning.'

Mark played dumb.

'Well, sometimes we have to give them a bit of encouragement. Smith from your ground crew jumped night duty to go and play for his pub darts team last week. So I gave him a choice: three months on permanent guard duty or a week at Porton Down.'

'Which did he go for?'

Stamper cracked a smile. 'Let's just say he's taking his holidays in Wiltshire this year.'

Mark let him talk for another couple of minutes, then looked at his watch. 'I must go, Mr Stamper, I've got a briefing.'

He watched Stamper disappear towards the sergeants' Mess, then hurried out to the hangars, where he found Noel Smith up to his elbows in a Tornado engine inlet.

Mark shinned up the ladder and peered into the engine. 'How's it going, Noel?' His glance rested for a moment on the plastic ID card clipped to the crewman's overalls.

Smith gave him a suspicious look. 'Well, all in all life could be better at the moment, sir. On a professional level, we've currently got two working jets out of a supposed strength of thirteen. On a personal one, I'm supposed to be going away for a couple of days, but I'm going to have to cancel it and lose my deposit because the Fuhrer nabbed me for going AWOL for all of two hours.'

'Stamper?'

'Who else?'

Mark waited while Smith poured out his tale of woe.

'Listen, Noel, I can't guarantee anything, but if you like,

I'll have a word with Stamper and see if I can get him to give you a break.'

'Would you, sir?' Smith's face lit up momentarily. 'But he'll never do it.' He mimicked Stamper's nasal tone. '"I didn't get to be warrant officer by letting airmen who are still wet behind the ears break every rule in the book." He probably puts his wife on a charge if she forgets to salute him.'

'Well, for what it's worth, I'll give it a try. Don't cancel the holiday just yet.' As Mark hurried out of the hangar, he scribbled a sequence of numbers on a piece of paper.

Half an hour later he found Smith still working on the jet. 'Don't faint, but I've had a word with Herr Hitler and he's relented. You've got your holiday.'

Smith gave a whoop and jumped down from the wing of the jet to pump his hand.

'There's one condition though.'

'Which is?' Smith was instantly suspicious.

'That you don't tell anyone. He wasn't going to do it at first because he didn't want to be seen to be backing down. I persuaded him that if you left the base as though you were going off to do your porridge at Porton Down, but then went on holiday instead, no one would be any the wiser. He says if it gets out that he let you off, he'll have you castrated. So don't talk about it to anyone – even him. If he asks you if you had a nice time at Porton Down, tell him it was just like a holiday.'

'Thanks, sir. I owe you one for this.'

Mark walked over to the office where Sandra, the operations assistant, presided over the mail for the squadron. She was slim and attractive, and Mark flirted shamelessly with her.

She looked up from her desk and smiled. 'Hello, Mr Hunter, how's it going?' Even the civilian staff did not use the officers' first names, at least while they were in uniform, though if crew-room gossip was to be believed, Sandra had seen enough officers out of uniform to be on first-name terms with most of them.

'All right, Sandra, how about you?' Mark said.

'Okay, sir, apart from a hangover. There was a hen night for a friend of mine from the village last night.'

'Any outrageous behaviour?'

'Only by me.'

They both laughed. Sandra was uninhibited at the best of times, and with three or four drinks inside her, she was perfectly capable of debagging an Air Vice-Marshal at a Remembrance Sunday parade, if the fancy took her.

'So what can I do for you, sir? Is this business or pleasure?'

'Business, I'm afraid. I've left my wallet at home and it's got my ID in it. Can you give me a temporary one?'

She pretended to think about it, then reached for a pad of forms. 'All right then, but it'll cost you. Temporary Certificate of Service Identity, that's the one.' She began filling it in, the tip of her tongue protruding from her lips as she concentrated. 'Colour of eyes . . .' She held his gaze and took her time about deciding. 'Dark brown. Colour of hair . . .' She raised an eyebrow. 'Shall I put dark brown or grey? Now I need your service number, date of birth and blood group as well . . . Right, I'll just get this signed.'

To his frustration, Sandra picked up the pad and disappeared through a connecting door. She was back a few seconds later and pushed it across the counter to him. 'Your turn now.'

He signed the form with a flourish, then detached it from the pad.

'Oi, that's my job,' she said.

'Sorry, just trying to spare you any unnecessary exertion in your present delicate state.' He blew her a kiss and turned to go.

'Any chance you might be around to buy me a drink after work tonight?' she said. 'It might be the only thing that can cure my hangover.'

'In that case, I'm afraid you're going to have to suffer. Another time?'

Once in his car, he peeled back the top form. The second sheet he had removed with it was blank. He pulled the scrap of paper from his pocket and copied down the numbers. Then he filled in the rest, copying the scrawled signature of the commanding officer. He read it through, then folded it carefully and slipped it into his wallet.

Chapter 10

Mark found a parking space a hundred yards short of his apartment. A knot of dark-suited men clustered around the door of the building, making no attempt to enter or leave. Two of them had mobile phones pressed to their ears. A man wearing blue jeans, trainers and a windcheater walked out of the building and joined them. The fastidious way he adjusted the cuffs suggested it was not his usual choice of clothing. He looked to be in his early thirties, with thinning, sandy hair and piercing-blue eyes. Mark had the feeling that he'd seen him before, but could not place him. The man exchanged a few more words and then crossed the street to a dark saloon.

As it drove away, Mark hunched down in his seat. He waited a few moments, then restarted the engine and drove off. He drove east, not stopping until he reached the coast. He pulled off the road and parked facing out across the mudflats towards the distant grey line of the North Sea.

He started when the car phone rang.

'You got out alive, then?'

'What?' His mind whirled. 'Natalie, how did you know?'

'What are you talking about? I meant Hereford.'

'Oh that. No. I mean yes.'

'Are you all right?'

'Yes. I'm sorry. I was a bit thrown. A few things have been happening. Can I see you? Are you free?'

'I am after six tonight.'

He picked her up at exactly six and headed towards the West End. 'I thought we'd have a drink in Covent Garden and then eat in Chinatown. Okay by you?'

She heard the flat note in his voice. 'Sounds great. Something's happened, hasn't it?'

'Plenty.' He stared at the traffic clogging the road. 'Matthew – Steve's little boy – died last night.'

'I'm so sorry.'

'So am I.' He paused. 'But I'm going to make sure that his death isn't just another statistic. I'm going to find out why he died.'

Her voice was gentle. 'Mark, it'll take years for us to understand GWS—'

'I'm not trying to. You were right. There's something else here, something that GWS is concealing. I want to know what Inoculation Scimitar is and I want to know what happened at As Salman.' Although there was a tremor in his voice, he was hard eyed. 'One of the guys I saw in Hereford told me about an explosion in his sector on the night they began the advance into Iraq.' He told her about the meeting with Stumps. When he had finished, she frowned.

'There's a cover-up all right, Mark, but you don't need an Iraqi chemical attack to explain it. If the British government is forced to admit that the injections and NAPS tablets caused illness, birth defects and deaths, the compensation would run to billions. Why look beyond that?'

'You don't believe the chemical attack?'

'I didn't say that. Iraq's used that stuff often enough in the past, and it certainly had – and to some extent still has – the manufacturing capacity. But if the Iraqis had launched a full-scale chemical attack, why would the Coalition conceal it? Especially as they'd threatened to nuke one of Saddam's cities if he used chemical weapons.'

She paused. 'Hold on. If there was a chemical attack, Saddam knows that the threat of nuclear retaliation was an empty one. If other despots and terrorists around the world find out, it'll blow a gaping hole in the West's nuclear deterrent. You're getting into very dangerous waters with this, Mark.'

'Only if it is true. All I know is that something happened. What Stumps said about not having jabs or taking NAPS tablets started me thinking. The human shields didn't take NAPS tablets either, and a lot of them didn't have any jabs. Yet eight out of twenty have already got GWS . . . or something else.' He held her arm, his fingers tightening. 'Don't you see? Michael and Larry both told me that the worst-affected units in the whole of the Gulf theatre had casualty rates of twenty per cent. The illness rate amongst the POWs and the SAS troops in the sector around As Salman is at least twice that.'

She was still sceptical. 'Maybe so, but a weapon that only kills enemy soldiers one to five years after the war has ended isn't much of a weapon. Why cover that up?'

'I don't know. There are only two places where I might find that out: either As Salman—'

'Which is fifty miles inside Iraq.'

'Or Porton Down.'

'Which might as well be, for all the chance there is of getting access to it.'

'Not quite. I'm going there.'

'What?'

'I volunteered for one of those thirteen-quid-a-day sessions.'

'When?'

'There's a new intake of volunteers tomorrow, and luckily – if that's the word – they were a man short because someone had dropped out.'

'Why?'

He smiled. 'All we need is who and where for a full set.'

'I'm serious, Mark. What the hell do you think you're doing?'

'I told you. I'm trying to find out about Inoculation Scimitar. Everything that Dan, Michael, Larry and you have said to me is pointing in exactly the same direction – Porton Down.'

'Jesus, when you get down off the fence you get down off the fence.' She paused. 'Mark, Porton Down's one of the most secure sites in the business. You can't just wander around it till you find what you want. Hell, I was practically strip-searched every time I went to the john when I was working there.'

'Natalie, it may sound ridiculous, but trust me on this. I've never been to Porton Down, but I know when it was built and I bet it looks just like every other British military establishment – a collection of brick-built, one- or two-storey buildings with leaky roofs, rotting windowframes and creaking floors. The labs will be newer and much more secure, but the administration blocks will be practically antique.'

He smiled as he saw in her face that he was right. 'All our bases are top secret – we store nukes at some of them. The security at the perimeter is tight, but I can waltz past just about any internal security with nothing more than an ID card and an air of total confidence. I once walked into a nuclear bunker on a base in Germany, showing my hotel card as ID.'

'And?'

'The guard saluted me.'

'All right, I accept that you can walk on water, but what if you do get past the guards? You can't search every building. There are hundreds of them.'

He touched her cheek. 'Quite right. You're going to tell me where to look.'

She stared at him. 'How the hell do you think I'm going to be able to do that?'

'You worked with David for two years. So you know where the labs are and where the records are kept.'

'You're not going to break into the labs?'

'Of course not, they're far too dangerous. I'm going to break into the offices and look through some files.'

'And it's that easy?'

'Probably not, but I'm certainly not going to learn anything useful out here. I don't have a bunch of skeleton keys or A-levels in breaking and entering, but I know a man who does.' His voice softened. 'Natalie, I've got to at least try.'

He parked the car and they strolled towards Covent Garden hand in hand, but the feeling of uneasiness returned. He glanced back over his shoulder but could see nothing unusual. He walked a few more paces, then eased Natalie into a shop doorway and waited, scanning the faces passing them.

She glanced around. 'I've been looking too. I don't think we're being followed.'

'You can't be sure,' he said, his eyes still flickering over the passers-by. 'They tried to get you in LA, why not here?'

She nodded. 'Let's set both our minds at rest, then we'll talk about this.'

They began walking along Long Acre. Mark started to turn his head again but she tightened her grip on his arm. 'Don't look back, use the reflections in shop windows and car wing mirrors.'

He gave her a curious look, but did as she said. She turned into the entrance to a bookshop, then paused, holding the door open for a man coming in behind them. She watched him carefully before stepping back out on to the street. Twice more she moved into shop doorways, pointing to the window displays and talking animatedly to Mark, but her eyes never left the street.

'I think we're clear,' she said, 'but let's make absolutely sure.'

She steered him into the underground station. They waited until the lift doors were closing before stepping inside. When they reached the bottom, they hung back until the other passengers had disappeared along the passage leading to the platform, then doubled back and took the same lift up to the surface.

They walked back along Long Acre to a wine bar. She bought a bottle and chose a corner table, facing the door. 'Right,' she said, pouring him a glass of wine. 'Have you anything tangible to go on, or is it just a feeling?'

'Nothing I could put my finger on. A few times I've felt that someone's been in my flat while I've been out, but it could just be paranoia.'

'Anything missing?'

'No, a couple of things not quite the way I'd left them. Then today I had a visit. Some guys were hanging around outside my apartment.'

Mark poured himself some more wine, but Natalie shook her head and covered her glass with her hand. She took a deep breath. 'I'll be in Iraq by the time you get back from Porton Down. Be careful, won't you?'

His face fell. 'I thought you weren't going till next week.'

She hesitated. 'So did they. Going in a couple of days early helps to keep the opposition off balance.'

'In that case, why don't we make the Chinese meal a takeaway? I've got some champagne back at my flat.'

She thought about it as she finished her drink. 'I'd like that. You can show me your etchings or photographs or whatever.' She watched as he tried to hide his pleasure at the idea. 'And why don't we just forget about the meal?'

When they reached the car, he held out the keys. 'Do you mind driving? I had most of that bottle of wine.'

Chapter 11

The traffic began to thin as they left the West End behind and started to cut through the near-deserted City. She put her foot down, crowding the car ahead as she waited for room to overtake. She glanced in the mirror. A Vauxhall Cavalier was right on her back bumper, the driver flashing his lights and gesticulating furiously at her to move over. When she ignored him, she was rewarded with a prolonged blast on the horn.

'What's his problem?' Mark said.

'Who cares? He can work it out on someone else.'

She signalled and started to pull over, but the car hurtled through on the inside and then pulled in front of them so violently that she had to stamp on the brakes to avoid running into the back of it. There was another angry blast on the horn from a car behind her. The Vauxhall driver shook his fist and waved two fingers, then remained directly in front of them.

Natalie slowed, peering at the road signs.

'Sorry,' Mark said. 'I'm not used to being the navigator. Take the right fork and then follow the yellow brick road.' He pointed at the beacon of Canary Wharf dominating the skyline.

The road ahead was well lit and virtually deserted. The Vauxhall slowed, signalling right. She eased left a little, aiming the car at the gap on the inside. They were only a few yards from it when the Vauxhall suddenly began to swerve back across the road. She swore and hammered the horn as she stamped on the brakes.

'That does it,' Mark said. 'Stop the car and I'll sort this bastard out.'

She fought the skid, holding the Audi on line as the tyres squealed and the Vauxhall loomed in her windscreen. They stopped with inches to spare, rocking on the suspension. There was a squeal of tyres from behind them, followed by a sudden violent impact. Natalie was hurled forward and then whipped back into the headrest as the seatbelt bit into her shoulder. She shook her head to clear it. Mark undid his seatbelt and was reaching for the door handle when she glanced in the mirror. Two powerfully built men were moving down either side of the Audi.

'Mark! No!' she yelled, and fell on the locking button of the door as one of the men seized the handle, a claw hammer in his other hand. As he swung it at the window, she jammed the car into gear. The glass shattered as they shot forward, breaking the man's hold.

The Audi came free of the car behind with a screech of metal, but the Vauxhall still blocked the way. As she rammed into it, she was already selecting reverse.

Without his seatbelt, Mark was hurled forwards. He threw up an arm to protect himself, but his forehead slammed into the windscreen. He felt a searing pain and blood began to trickle down the corner of his eye. As the car sped backwards, he grabbed at the door handle and braced his feet against the dashboard as he struggled to refasten his seatbelt.

Natalie sent the car hurtling forwards again to batter its way out of the trap. Each forward charge shifted the Vauxhall a few more inches. She hurtled back once more, then punched her way clear and stamped on the accelerator.

Mark swung round in his seat and gave her a running commentary. 'They're in the car. It's starting to move.' He dabbed at the blood trickling down his forehead. 'They're past the Vauxhall.'

She held her foot down to the floor, crashing the gears, but at once the car began to slew sideways. The offside front tyre had been ripped to shreds. It hung from the rim, slapping against the road. Natalie fought to right the car, streaming with cold sweat. The car was now barely driveable. A few hundred yards ahead of them, the road took a sharp left turn. She could see the glow of approaching headlights, and glanced in the mirror.

'Get ready to jump.'

'What?'

'Just do it.'

She put her foot down again, piling on speed despite the deafening clamour from the wheel. The vibration threatened to snatch the steering wheel from her hands, but Natalie gripped it more firmly. Her eyes again flickered from the mirror to the oncoming car. She held it steady for one last fraction of a second, then rammed the wheel hard over, gunning the accelerator as she yanked on the handbrake.

As the Audi spun, their pursuers shot past, braking fiercely. The other car slid towards her, the white, frightened face of the driver framed in the windscreen.

Even before the Audi had skidded to a halt, Natalie was out and running towards the other car. Mark dived into the back of it as she threw herself into the passenger seat. The plump middle-aged driver froze, a look of incredulity on his face.

'They're trying to kill us. Drive!'

The man jerked upright as if he'd been hit with a cattle-prod. He let in the clutch, almost stalling in his haste, and the car shot forward. 'Where to?'

'Anywhere. But fast.'

As they pulled away, Mark turned to look behind. The other car had stopped in mid-turn, half-blocking the road. It remained motionless for a few more seconds, then swung away from them and disappeared into the darkness.

'Don't relax yet,' Natalie said. 'You don't organise an attack like that with just two vehicles.'

Mark swung back to stare through the rear window. Headlights were following them, but it was impossible to know if they offered any threat.

They sped back in towards the City, and the driver began to signal a turn.

'Where are you going?' she said.

'To the police station.'

'No police. Please.' She forced a smile. 'Just drop us where we can get a taxi or a Tube.'

'But if those men were attacking you, you should report it to the police.'

She shook her head. 'No police.'

As he pulled up at a traffic light, she caught sight of an underground station. 'Come on.' They yanked the doors open and jumped out.

'Hey!'

They ran across the road and disappeared into the station, then vaulted the turnstiles, ignoring a shout from a ticket inspector, and ran towards the escalator.

'Where to?' Mark said.

'Who cares? Anywhere.'

At the clatter of an approaching train, they sprinted down the rest of the escalator and took the stairs to the platform two at a time. They jumped into an empty carriage near the front.

Mark kept his eyes fixed on the stairs until the doors closed and the train pulled away, then he turned to Natalie and crushed her in his arms. She winced in pain and gently disengaged herself. He held her at arm's length. Her face was deathly pale, with a small gash at the corner of her mouth and a purpling bruise on the side of her head.

'You all right?'

'Just a few bruised ribs. You don't look too great.'

He winced as she touched the swelling on his forehead. Her fingers came away sticky with blood. He put his arm around her shoulders and they slumped down on a seat. Neither of them spoke for a while.

The train clattered into another station. 'What are we going to do?' Mark said.

'Tonight? I don't think we should go to your flat – or my hotel for that matter. I think it's pretty safe to say that we're not being paranoid: someone really is out to get us.'

'Who?'

'Take your pick: the CIA, MI6, the Iraqis. Maybe they think

you know something important. Perhaps you do and haven't realised.'

'I used to know who the good guys were.' His voice trailed away.

She looked into his eyes, then gave him a lingering kiss. They pulled apart as the train halted again and a party of noisy drunks got on, nudging each other and sniggering at the sight of their bruised faces.

'A bit of a domestic, love?' one said. 'Take a tip from me, mate. Next time just do as she says.'

Mark gave him a rueful grin.

'So where are we going?' he said when they had moved on down the carriage. 'Or are we spending the night on the Circle Line?'

'You tell me,' she said. 'It's your town not mine. Let's just find a place where no one knows who we are.'

'I know somewhere in Bayswater,' he said.

'A hotel?'

He nodded. 'Anonymous, clean and cheap.'

Queensway was busy with people, but there was no one in sight as they turned into Moscow Road. Still Mark could not stop himself from looking behind them every few yards. As he slipped his arm around her waist he heard footsteps and saw two figures walking up the street behind them. He gripped her tighter and quickened his pace.

'We can't have been followed,' she said.

The footsteps echoed from the pavement behind them, growing steadily louder. Mark was about to break into a run when he looked back to see two men disappearing into the bright glow of a pub doorway.

The dome of the Greek Orthodox cathedral loomed up in the darkness. They turned down the side of it into a quiet square lined with plane trees, their trunks glowing white in the light cast by the street lamps. The only sound was the faint noise of traffic on Bayswater Road.

The hotel was in the middle of a Georgian terrace. Mark paused in the entrance and glanced back the way they had come. The street was deserted. The receptionist booked them in with practised indifference, showing no more surprise at their lack of luggage than their battered faces. 'Double or twin?' she asked.

Mark hesitated.

Natalie said, 'Double. High up and at the back.'

She filled in the registration form, giving a false name and address, and paid for the room in advance, in cash.

'Morning newspaper?'

'No thanks, but we'll need a call at six o'clock.'

'So early?' Mark said.

She nodded. 'Work.'

They took the tiny lift to the fourth floor, their bodies close, her shoulder brushing against his chest. She took his hand as they walked down the corridor to the room.

Mark locked and chained the door then turned to face her. She had thrown off her jacket and was standing by the table holding up a cellophane pack of biscuits. 'Hungry?' She smiled and tossed them aside. 'Then come here.'

They stood in the centre of the room, clinging to each other like the survivors of a wreck. She held his face in her hands, her gaze locked on him, then closed her eyes as her lips searched for his.

She stroked his neck with her fingertips, feeling the tension ebbing away, then eased his jacket from his shoulders and undid the first few buttons of his shirt, running her hands over his chest. She pulled back for a moment, a smile playing around the corners of her mouth, then hooked her fingers in his belt and pulled him slowly towards her. She felt him responding, heard his breathing grow faster and saw his eyes lose their focus.

He slid his hands under her T-shirt, exploring the contrasts of her body, then pulled the shirt over her head, leaving her wrists tangled in it as he stooped to kiss her neck and breasts. They sank to the bed, and he gasped as their naked bodies touched for the first time. He moaned with pleasure and buried his hand between her thighs, stroking her gently.

As he slid into her, she closed her eyes and gave a long shuddering sigh, then wrapped her legs around him as he held her wrists, pinning her to the bed. She arched her back and turned him over, taking control. They moved together with a frenzied, desperate urgency as he tried to lose himself in her. At last she threw back her head and gave a soft cry, then they lay spent, sprawled in each other's arms, the aftershocks fading like echoes.

Mark stroked her damp hair from her forehead and tasted the salt sweat with his tongue. He raised himself to look at her. 'Natalie—'

She silenced him with a finger to the lips. 'I know. Not now.'

Later, she watched him as he slept. At first he twisted and turned in the bed. As he quietened and drifted into a deeper sleep, years seemed to fall from his face. She studied him for a long time before she too lay down and slept.

When she woke, she was alone in the bed. She sat up and looked around. Mark was standing at the window, framed by the sunlight.

She draped a sheet over her shoulders and stood alongside him gazing down into the empty street. 'Peaceful, isn't it?'

He nodded and slipped an arm around her. 'If only it would stay that way. I feel like I'm staring over the edge of a precipice. Am I doing the right thing, Natalie?'

'I think so, but only you can know that for sure.'

His voice trailed into silence and they stood motionless, arms locked around each other.

Natalie kissed him and pulled away. He reached for her but she shook her head. 'We've got to go.'

He smiled. 'We? I'm not due at Porton for hours yet.'

'Is there any point in trying to talk you out of going there?'

'Is there any point in trying to talk you out of going to Iraq?'

On their way out of the hotel, Natalie stopped to use the payphone in the foyer. 'Lars, it's me . . . Yes I do, it's just after six. I had a little more trouble last night. Like LA. Exactly. Can you bring some security and meet me at the usual RV? Thanks, I owe you one. You're a regular Norwegian prince.' She laughed. 'No, if I do that you'll turn into a toad.'

Lars and four burly men in casual clothes were waiting on the steps of Broadcasting House when they climbed out of their taxi.

'The BBC?' Mark said.

She smiled. 'Can you think of a safer place to RV? No spook in the world is going to try a hit in front of a couple of thousand journalists.'

Mark nodded to the UN soldiers and shook hands with Lars. The Norwegian stared pointedly at Mark and there was no friendliness in his eyes. He turned to Natalie. 'We have to get going.'

'I know. Just give me a minute.'

'That's the married man, isn't it?' Mark murmured.

'Is it so obvious?'

'He doesn't know whether to punch out my lights or give me one of those "If you harm a hair on her head, I'll kill you" speeches.'

'He's very protective.' She glanced over his shoulder and raised a hand. 'All right, Lars, I'm just coming.' She took Mark's hand. 'Look after yourself. And don't talk to any strange men.'

She tried to smile but he could see a tremor in her lip. She had to swallow before she could speak again. 'Be careful . . . please.'

'We're not just going to leave it like this?'

'We have to.'

'But it'll be months before you're back. Can't I see you out there?'

'I'm not sure.' She saw his expression. 'Don't get me wrong. If I can get to Kuwait I will.' This time she managed a smile. 'There's a better chance of that than of you dropping in on me in Iraq. I don't imagine they'd welcome you back.'

Mark gripped her hand. 'I can ring you.'

She scribbled a number on a piece of paper. 'It's Baghdad, the Canal Hotel. They tape all our calls, of course.'

She stood looking at him for a moment, then took his face in her hands and kissed him. Her eyes were shining as she pulled back and stroked the back of her hand along his chin, then she walked away.

Chapter 12

Mark approached his apartment building like a thief. He rang the bell for the caretaker at the side door. 'I've left my keys behind, could you let me in?'

The man eyed the yellowing bruise on Mark's forehead, then nodded slowly.

Mark hung back at the top of the stairs as the caretaker unlocked the door, but the flat was as he had left it. When he saw that the answerphone was flashing, he hesitated before pressing the message button.

'Mark.' In his disappointment that it was not Natalie, it was a moment before he recognised Jenny's dull, lifeless voice. 'Matthew's funeral is on Friday. It's at two o'clock at the parish church in Avedon. We'd like you to do the oration – or whatever they call it.'

He walked to the window and stared out over the river, watching the murky water of the rising tide inching up the concrete ramparts of the dock.

He picked up the phone and called Coldchurch. 'Twenty-one Squadron please . . . Mitch? Hi, it's Mark. Anything happening?'

'Only the Kuwait detachment. Why, are you planning to leave the country?'

'No, just checking in like a conscientious pilot should.'

'You must have the wrong number, we don't have any conscientious pilots here.'

'But seriously though—'

'Seriously, there's no change. We're all wound up and ready to go.'

'Good, see you Monday then.'

Mark hung up and picked up his bag, but then dropped it back on the table. He had six days to unearth an answer and the thought of what he was about to do scared him more than he was willing to admit. He made himself think of Dan, Steve and Matthew, and of his father.

He reported the Audi stolen, then headed for Waterloo station. A minicab took him from Salisbury through the network of old drove roads over the top of the downs. A few miles from the city the driver paused to check his map, then turned off into a narrow, tree-lined lane that twisted and dipped through the rich pastureland.

Sheep and lambs dotted the fields. Clouds of butterflies lifted from the wildflowers studding the verges and hedgerows, the sunlight stippling their wings. The lane climbed higher out of the valley, and larks rose, shrinking to specks, then disappeared altogether in the vastness of the sky.

As he dropped his gaze, he found himself staring at a sign, 'Chemical and Biological Defence Establishment, Porton Down. This is a protected place within the meaning of the Official Secrets Act.'

Just over the brow of the hill, a high and recently reinforced double steel fence sliced through the landscape. A rabbit was grazing the close-cropped turf at the roadside, and as the car approached, it flattened itself against the ground for a moment, then sped away, wriggling under the wire between two arc-light stanchions and below a sign warning that the gap between the fences was patrolled by guard dogs and that. 'The use of lethal force is authorised.'

The lane ran alongside the fence for several hundred yards, and as it curved away, Mark saw the entrance, a guardhouse presiding over a steel-ringed compound between double gates. Concrete crash barriers blocked the way, forcing vehicles to slow and weave, and closed-circuit cameras scanned every arrival. Shadowy faces and the dull glint of blue steel could be glimpsed through the embrasures of the concrete pillboxes flanking the gates. The cab driver raised an eyebrow and slowed to a crawl.

A guard cast a curious glance in their direction, then emerged from the guardhouse, gun at hip. He stepped forward as the outer gates clanged shut. Two more guards ran mirrors on poles along the underside of the cab and gestured for the boot and bonnet to be opened.

Mark handed over his ID certificate. 'I'm expected.'

He tried very hard not to look as the sergeant turned it over in his hands. 'What happened to your proper ID?'

'I lost it on my mate's stag night.'

The man clicked his tongue and took the form back into the guardhouse with him. Mark could hear him reciting Smith's name, rank and number into the mouthpiece of the radio. After a moment he re-emerged. 'That's fine. Would you like me to hang it on a string round your neck so you don't lose this one as well?'

'No. Would you like me to put you on a char—' Mark fell silent, remembering he was now outranked.

The sergeant waited. 'I think you'd better walk from here, Airman Smith.' Mark stayed silent, and the sergeant smirked. He pointed to a handful of cars on a tarmac area fifty yards away. 'Now if you can manage to find your way over there without getting yourself lost, we'll arrange to have you more formally greeted.'

Mark got out of the car clutching his overnight bag. As he reached the parking area, a minibus pulled up. The driver nodded to him to get in. Mark unzipped his bag and held it out for inspection, but the man gave it only a cursory look.

He sat in silence as they crossed the down. A side road branched off towards a cluster of barrack blocks and married quarters for the guards, surrounded by yet more chainlink fencing. There were no children playing on the brightly coloured swings and slides in the small playground just inside the wire.

He thought back to a weekend he had spent in the Lake District the previous summer. He had walked along a broad, flat, empty beach. He looked from the sunlight dancing on the wavetops to the profile of the nuclear reprocessing plant at Sellafield, just up the coast. Around half of the local labour force worked there, yet on one of the hottest days of the summer, not one of their children had been playing on the sand.

There was a broad sweep of downland beyond the last of the residential quarters. Observation towers on spindly legs looked out over a series of firing ranges punctuated by black and white targets. The dark earth was speckled with shell craters. In places where the topsoil had been blown away, the underlying chalk showed through, white as bone. The red flags were flying, stiff in the breeze, and Mark heard the crash of artillery and saw patches of ground erupt.

Beyond the ranges, thickets of birch trees and brambles smothered ruined buildings, locked away behind rusting fences. Only the warning signs were new. Mark was too far away to read their message. 'What's in there?' he asked.

The driver looked round. 'Mustard gas pots,' he said. 'Lead-lined containers. They stored liquid mustard gas in them during the Second World War. It was all burned or buried at the end of the war, but the root action of the vegetation kept bringing it up to the surface again. People were blistered just by brushing against the brambles. They say it's safe enough now though, unless you disturb the topsoil.'

The road crossed a ridge and began to descend towards a group of buildings the size of a small town. They passed ranks of decaying red-brick blocks. The grim, utilitarian architecture was the same on every military base, but these blocks were interspersed with other, less familiar structures.

A windowless concrete tower stood over a warren of narrow passageways between high brick walls. A low blockhouse with a single bulbous window so thick that it looked to be carved from obsidian looked out towards a curved steel ramp jutting up into the sky. A featureless concrete block like a sarcophagus, guarded by a triple fence, stood at the centre of an expanse of waste ground. Mark glanced across at the driver, but this time he offered no explanations.

A few hundred yards further on, the driver braked the van to a halt. A low-loader was blocking the road while a broken-down lorry, unmarked but bristling with antennae and sensors, was winched on to it. The driver pulled out his cigarettes. Just one, Mark thought, to settle my nerves, but the driver did not offer. He lit up, breathed in a lungful of smoke and threw the crumpled packet on to the floor.

As they waited, Mark noticed a structure not much bigger than a telephone box, standing alone in the middle of a field. 'What's that? A tardis?'

The driver's smile was getting more perfunctory.

A uniformed figure was fumbling with the lock set in the steel door of the building. He swung it open, revealing a glimpse of a bulkhead light and a flight of steep steps disappearing into the ground, before the door slammed shut.

The low-loader revved up and moved off, belching black smoke. They followed in its wake, inhaling diesel fumes, until it pulled off into a compound where a dozen similar lorries were already parked.

They came to a roundabout, and Mark found its sheer normality even more unsettling than the miles of barbed wire. A tall office block surrounded by neat lawns stood near by. Its windows were veiled by blinds. Beyond it, set back from the road within its own defensive perimeter, was a huge grey concrete edifice with a discreet sign: 'Containment Building'. The only break in its monolithic exterior was a doorway sunk below ground level, flanked by massive concrete blast walls. The minibus slowed and pulled up in front of it.

'This is new.'

The driver glanced over his shoulder. 'It needed to be: two of the buildings it replaced were built in the First World War.'

'When was it built?'

'Last year.'

'And what's it for?'

He gave Mark a brief, cool look. 'Take my tip: just do what you've come to do then fuck off out of here. That's all there is to it.'

As he led Mark into the building, they passed from bright sunlight to nocturnal gloom. The entrance was an airlock identical to the one in the pilots' briefing facility at Coldchurch. The only difference was that, except in times of emergency, the one at Coldchurch stood open and unguarded. This one was closed. An armed guard was just visible through the smoked glass. Mark again showed the ID.

'Step into the airlock,' a tinny voice on the intercom commanded.

He stepped forward. There was a dull click and whir behind him. Mark looked back through the thick glass and saw the minibus drive off.

There was a pause as the extractors whined. When the inner door swung open, Mark felt the rush of pressurised air. Any leaks would be from inside out, not outside in. It was not a reassuring thought.

A fresh-faced, white-coated young woman was waiting to greet him. 'Airman Smith? Welcome to Porton Down.' She gave him a brief smile and checked her watch. 'Professor Leary will explain everything about the tests you'll be helping us with at an eleven o'clock briefing. As we've got a couple of minutes to spare, let me show you the canteen and your quarters.'

She nodded to the guard, who let them out again through the airlock, then led Mark round the corner and across the road towards a two-storey brick building. She unlocked the door and stood aside. A warning of prohibitions within the meaning of the Official Secrets Act was fixed to every door.

'The others are already here,' she said. 'You're the only RAF man, I'm afraid. I must say we don't get many volunteers from the Air Force.'

She showed him into a ground-floor canteen, where five other men, all army, gave him an indifferent glance and then went back to their newspapers.

The noticeboard was dominated by yet more security warnings, Batemanesque cartoons of flapping mouths and listening ears. There was also a fixture list for the Porton Down cricket team and a poster advertising a concert by the Gilbert and Sullivan Society.

'The canteen's open from seven a.m. to seven p.m.,' she said. 'After that there's a vending machine in the corridor. When not required for tests, you're free to go anywhere inside the building – there's a TV room and a small gym. You're also welcome to make use of the bar in the social club at the end of the block. You can walk around the immediate area of these buildings during daylight, but you are not permitted to enter any restricted areas nor wander outside unescorted after dark.'

'And to make sure, you keep the outside doors locked,' Mark said. 'What happens if there's a fire? Do we assemble by the door and start praying that someone will come and unlock it before we get cooked?'

The woman's expression didn't change. 'There are fire doors with crash-bars,' she said, 'but only for use in a genuine emergency. As soon as you open them they trigger an alarm.'

The sleeping accommodation was on the first floor, a series of small cubicles opening off a long corridor, each furnished with a single bed, wardrobe and chair. 'No locks here, I notice,' Mark said as he put his bag on the end of the bed.

'Let's go and get the others,' the woman said. 'Professor Leary should be ready to introduce himself.'

'Morning, gentlemen,' the professor said, striding to the front of the small lecture room. 'Abandon all hope, all ye who enter here.'

Leary was a bluff, florid-faced man in his late fifties. His voice was loud, and his tweed jacket and cavalry twill trousers gave him the look of a gamekeeper rather than a scientist. Mark found his laugh even more grating than his tone.

Leary glanced around the circle of faces. 'I must say it's a pleasant change to have the RAF here,' he said. 'We don't get too many volunteers from above the salt.' He tried to give the five soldiers a conspiratorial smile, but they stared back, bored and stony-faced, impatient to get the ordeal over with. 'What persuaded you to join us?'

Mark shifted in his seat, wondering how much Leary knew of the circumstances under which his victims were induced to volunteer. 'I . . . I have a very persuasive warrant officer.' There was a snigger from one of the soldiers. 'I've also seen film of the Kurds in Iraq after they were hit with mustard gas. I wanted to do my bit to help.'

Leary's smile froze for a moment. 'I assure you no one will be exposed to anything like that,' he said. 'You're here to help us with the study of various protective measures and antidotes. We'll start with a routine medical examination. And don't worry,' he added, his air of joviality back in place. 'I've been here twenty years and I've never lost a patient yet.'

'Did you mean that stuff about the Kurds?' one of the soldiers asked as they waited in line for the medical. He had a boxer's nose and dark hair cut so short it was little more than a five o'clock shadow on his scalp.

'Not really. I thought it might impress him. What about you, did you volunteer?'

He shook his head. 'I applied to go on a course I need in order to get promotion. They turned me down, but told me my application would be reconsidered if I did a stint here.' He glanced around him. 'I'd be surprised if anyone actually wants to be here. Two of the guys I was talking to this morning said they'd been threatened with a posting to the Falklands if they didn't volunteer.' He held out his hand. 'I'm Rob, by the way.'

'Ma—' He froze, realising his mistake. 'My name's Noel.'

Rob looked at him, puzzled. 'Terry, Mick.' He beckoned another two of the volunteers over. 'This is Noel.'

The medical was as rudimentary as the one Mark remembered from basic training. 'Any physical problems? Eye problems?' The orderly didn't even bother to glance up from the forms in front of him. He took Mark's ID certificate, scanned it and was about to move on when he stopped, peered at the ID again, then checked it against his monitor.

Mark felt his heart begin to thump.

'Dr Reichman,' the orderly called. 'Look at this.'

The doctor examined the screen, then frowned and looked up at Mark. 'There's something wrong. How tall are you?'

Mark hesitated, trying to picture Noel, then deducted a couple of inches from his true height. 'About five ten, I think.'

'You're five foot eight, according to this, and a hell of a lot heavier than your last medical.'

Mark said nothing.

Reichman stared at him, then turned to the orderly. 'Take all his details again and get his file up to date.'

As Reichman walked back to the other side of the room,

Mark could still feel his eyes on him as the orderly began recording his details. Mark gave up trying to guess Noel's height, weight and age, and used his own statistics.

'I can't believe this,' the orderly said. 'The only thing they got right about you was your sex. At least I think they did; you are a woman, aren't you?'

Mark forced a smile.

'I've seen stricter medicals in a morgue,' Rob murmured as they were shepherded through into the next room. 'Why were they giving you such a hard time?'

Mark spread his hands, palms upwards.

Professor Leary was waiting for them, surrounded by a number of white-coated assistants. 'The first test is what we call a patch test. We're looking at various compounds of rubber and synthetic materials for protective clothing. You'll each have three patches fixed to your arm. They will be left on for twenty-four hours. We'll also be testing you with an antidote today, and after that you're free to sample the lavish nightlife of Porton Down.'

The volunteers were separated, and Mark found himself in a small room, containing a metal table and a seat that resembled the electric chair. There was a viewing window in one wall, and a recessed doorway like a submarine hatch with a locking wheel at its centre.

Four of the staff strapped Mark into the chair and taped three inch-square patches of black rubber to his arm, then they applied liquids to them from three different phials. Mark could feel his pulse racing. His forehead was clammy with sweat.

'Don't worry,' one of the white coats said. 'The doses are absolutely minute. They wouldn't hurt a mouse.'

Mark felt a jab in his other arm and saw another man withdrawing a syringe. 'That's the antidote,' he said. Stumps's warning sounded in Mark's head: 'They wouldn't even need to leave a needlemark in you . . .'

The white-coated men filed out and the door shut with a thud. As they reappeared at the viewing window, Mark heard an amplified voice. 'Beginning the test, breathe normally.'

There was a faint hiss and immediately he felt his throat and chest tighten. His mouth, lips and face went numb, as if they'd been injected with anaesthetic. He struggled to draw breath, feeling the first waves of panic.

The faces at the observation window remained impassive. Their mouths moved, but no sound reached him. One of the men made notes, glancing from Mark to a stopwatch in his hand. The others merely stared. One of them said something and there was silent laughter.

He tried to calm himself, to take slow, even breaths, but his straining lungs could not drag enough oxygen from the air. At last he heard the roar of a fan and felt a rush of air circulating through the chamber, then the door swung open.

He was subjected to another, much more thorough examination by the team of white coats, who paid close attention to his pupils as well as his chest. They also took a blood sample and then sent him back to the accommodation block.

He found the other volunteers comparing notes in the canteen. All were still short of breath, grey faced and red eyed.

'What the fuck was that stuff?' Mick said. 'I thought I was dying.'

'Don't ask,' Terry said. 'With some things it's better not to know.'

Rob glanced across at Mark. 'Did you have a jab first?'

He nodded. 'They said it was the antidote.'

'So did I. But these two weren't given anything. They were just sprayed with the shit.'

Mark sat with them for a few more minutes, then glanced at his watch and stood up. 'I need some fresh air.'

The sky was overcast and a cold breeze stirred the dust at the edge of the road. He pulled his jacket closer around him and stood facing the back of the containment building. Beyond the chainlink fence a sloping concrete ramp led to a loading bay. Empty steel cages and dump-bins were stacked at one side, next to a long row of steel refuse containers. Mark counted more than thirty of them. The breeze carried the stench of decaying meat.

A group of men in blue overalls were using a hoist to empty the bins into the back of an articulated lorry. Other bins, painted a lurid yellow, were wheeled around the corner towards a low building dwarfed by a towering metal smoke stack.

The containment centre had been built since Natalie's time there, but he recognised the other buildings from her description. He made out the administration block, a square two-storeyed building. Beneath it would be the basement store, repository for millions of low-grade Porton secrets.

Groups of people moved to and fro between the buildings. As Mark walked slowly across the road towards the administration block, watchful eyes glanced at him, then looked away. He heard the muttered conversations falter at his approach, then resume when he had passed.

When he reached the administration block, he took a few deep breaths to calm himself, then walked inside. A double staircase faced him, with a corridor leading off to either side. Despite the low voices and the click of computer keyboards from behind closed doors, the lobby was empty.

Mark glanced at the carved wooden plaque on the wall, inscribed with the Porton Down motto: 'Secrecy In All We Do'. He consulted the scrap of paper Natalie had given him, then walked down the corridor to his left.

A door opened and a uniformed man appeared. He checked when he saw Mark, and began to form a challenge.

'Afternoon, sir,' Mark said, flicking a salute. 'Good to see you again.'

The man hesitated, then returned the greeting.

Mark gave a broad smile and strode on. He kept moving purposefully, not daring to slow or look back, until he heard the man's footsteps receding.

Mark stopped outside the fourth door from the end of the corridor. He read the nameplate: 'Director: Dr B.W. Livesey', then rapped on the door and walked in.

A woman sat at a large desk in front of the barred window. She was in her fifties, with dyed black hair and a matching suit. The wall to her right was lined with grey steel filing cabinets. To her left a connecting door stood ajar and Mark could hear a man speaking on the telephone. The paintwork, carpet and curtains were all in shades of grey, but the woman had done her best to soften the military rigour of her workspace with a bunch of flowers and a family portrait on her desk.

She glanced up as Mark stepped into the room. 'Yes? Can I help you?'

He put on his most boyish smile. 'I certainly hope so. I'm helping out with some tests and I wondered if you could do me a favour. A friend of mine worked here a couple of years ago, an American scientist. Natalie – Dr Natalie – Kennedy. We lost touch. I just wondered if she was still working here, or if there was a forwarding address.' He paused. 'I know how busy you must be . . .'

'I'm afraid we can't give out details of past or present employees.' She gave him a smile that set his teeth on edge. 'You know our motto here.'

He smiled back, holding her gaze. 'Of course I understand that, it's just—' He leaned forward and lowered his voice. 'The truth is . . . oh, I'm sure I can trust you. We were romantically involved. I was posted overseas with my squadron at very short notice and wasn't able to see her before I left.' He gave a helpless shrug. 'I tried to write of course, but my letters weren't answered. I just don't know whether she didn't want to see me any more or had left England thinking that's how I felt.'

She put down her pen, glanced towards the connecting door, then flushed slightly and her tone became conspiratorial. 'I really shouldn't do this and I certainly can't give you an address, but I can check our personnel records for you. I'm pretty sure she doesn't work here now. I pride myself on knowing the names of all our permanent staff, even though there are several hundred of them. But we may have an address—'

'And you'd see the letter was forwarded?' Mark said. 'I can't tell you how grateful I'd be.'

She flushed again, casting another nervous look towards the connecting door, then stood up. 'Natalie Kennedy, you said?' She walked over to the filing cabinets and began leafing through one of the drawers.

As she did so, Mark slid round the edge of her desk. He examined the door and frame, and glanced into the other room. The director was in profile, still on the phone. Mark pulled back out of sight and was back in his original position before the woman turned around, a buff folder in her hand.

'As I suspected, she's no longer with us, I'm afraid. She was only here on a temporary contract. According to our records she's returned to the United States.' Mark allowed himself to look suitably crestfallen. 'However,' she added, her face bright, 'there is a contact address in the file, so if you want to write to her here, care of me – Dorothy Jackson – I'll make sure it's forwarded.'

Mark smiled. 'I can't tell you how grateful I am.' He opened the door, then looked back over his shoulder. 'Goodbye, Dorothy, and thanks again.'

He scanned the frame for any sign of contact alarms, then walked back down the corridor. He had just paused outside the main entrance when a hand gripped his shoulder. He jumped and whipped round.

Rob laughed. 'I'd take something for those nerves if I was you.'

Mark gave a weak smile. 'Sorry. I was miles away.'

'So what are you up to?'

'Nothing much. Just going for a walk.'

'Mind if I come along?'

Heavy machinery could be heard somewhere beyond the containment building, and they began to walk in that direction, passing another patrolling guard. As they reached the far end, Rob let out a low whistle. A construction site the size of several city blocks stretched away from them. It was ring-fenced, with rows of Portakabins lined up inside a smaller compound within the main site.

'All it needs is some Gestapo,' Mark said, 'and a bunch of us vaulting over a wooden horse.'

Rob pointed to the armed guards at the entrance. 'The Gestapo are already here.'

Jack-hammers pounded and riggers swarmed over a steel skeleton rising from the centre of the site, bolting each new girder in place as fast as the cranes could deliver them. A succession of concrete mixers were guided into position by a site foreman waving his arms like the flight controller on the deck of an aircraft carrier. As each one released a thick tide of grey concrete, an army of men sprang forward to work it into the steel grid which covered an area the size of two football pitches.

'No cutbacks here, then,' Rob said. He glanced at his watch. 'And they're all on overtime.'

A Land-rover pulled out of the site entrance gates and growled to a halt alongside them. 'What are you men doing here? Let's see your ID.'

'Sorry, are we off limits?' Mark said. 'We're volunteers on the testing programme. We were just having a stroll around.'

The guard checked their papers. 'Well, just stroll straight back again. This area's restricted.' The Land-rover waited as they turned and retraced their steps.

Rob went back to the accommodation block, but Mark walked down to the social club. He hesitated for a moment, watching the setting sun reddening the sky, then he pushed open the door and looked around.

The atmosphere was as sterile and subdued as a funeral parlour. The tables seemed to have been deliberately widely spaced, leaving echoing areas of empty floor between them. Small groups of people huddled at the tables, talking in low monotones or staring silently at the television flickering in the corner above the bar. Once more, muttered conversations tailed away at his approach and then resumed as he moved past, and a few heads swivelled to inspect him. He walked to the bar and ordered a beer.

Two other men leaning against the bar gave him incurious looks, then picked up their own desultory conversation, sliding from one neutral topic to another. Mark tried to establish eye contact and join them, just to kill a little of the evening that now stretched ahead of him, but they stared at him without interest and after a few minutes took their drinks to a table.

The door banged and Leary made his way to the bar and bought a drink. He scanned the room but no one caught his eye. Mark stared straight ahead at the optics behind the bar, but from the corner of his eye he could see Leary moving towards him.

'Smith, isn't it? How did you find today's test?'

'Unpleasant.'

'It's supposed to be,' Leary said. 'That's the whole bloody point.'

'I guess I was one of the lucky ones. It must have been even more unpleasant for the poor sods who didn't get the antidote first.'

'Of course some of those who believe they've been injected with the antidote have actually been given a placebo.'

Mark did not return the smile. 'Do these tests go on all the time, Professor, or just when you've some new agent to test?'

Leary paused. 'Afraid I can't tell you that. Nothing personal, you understand.' He assembled his sentences like scientific instruments, eliminating all inessentials.

'Naturally.' Mark picked up his beer.

'Professor Leary. There's something very—' They both turned. Still wearing his white coat, Dr Reichman had walked into the bar. When he saw Mark, he stopped in mid-sentence. 'Could I have a private word with you, Professor?'

The two men walked to the end of the room. Mark kept his face neutral as he sipped his drink, but strained his ears to overhear their conversation. He could make out virtually none of it, though he thought he heard the word 'Coldchurch'. When he glanced along the bar, both men's eyes were fixed on him.

Leary returned to drain his drink a moment later. 'Enjoyed our chat,' he said, 'but I'm afraid something's come up. I'm sure I'll see you again.' He hurried back to join Reichman, who was now in intense conversation with another man.

Chapter 13

'Bloody hell, Mark, you look half-dead and they haven't even started on you.'

Mark forced a smile. 'What's breakfast like?'

'Greasy and lukewarm but just about bearable if you use plenty of the antidote,' Rob said, reaching for the tomato ketchup.

'I think I'll stick to toast and coffee.'

'Suit yourself. It'll all look the same once we get another faceful of shit from Leary and his boys.'

'What time's the first test?'

'Nine thirty, come as you are.'

As Mark was finishing his breakfast, he heard the rumble of a lorry outside.

'That's us.' Rob drained his cup.

The others sauntered outside but Mark hung back and took a cautious look around before stepping out of the doorway into the sunlight. There was no sign of Leary or Reichman, but that did nothing to dispel his fears. They were hustled into the back of the truck and driven out to one of the ranges.

Reichman was among a group waiting for them. Mark met his gaze. He held the look for a moment then turned away to busy himself with a medical tray. 'Roll your left sleeves up.'

Mark felt a chill inside him. He craned his neck to see what was lying on the tray. There were six apparently identical syringes. He took his place at the rear of the queue as the men filed past, each receiving a jab in the upper arm. There were two syringes left. As Reichman picked up one of them, Mark tapped Terry on the shoulder. 'Your lace is undone, mate.'

Terry glanced down. 'No it isn—' but Mark had already stepped ahead of him and offered his arm to Reichman, who gave him the jab without any change of expression. He used the last one on Terry.

Mark's heart sank again as he saw the orderlies sorting through a pile of NBC suits. He hung back as the others began to put on the cumbersome gear, grumbling and complaining, then felt a push in his back.

'You too, Biggles. For once you can't leave all the dirty work to the army.' The sergeant who had been at the entrance gate when he arrived was standing behind him.

Mark began to clamber into the NBC suit. There was a foul stink of rubber and stale sweat as he pulled the hood over his head. 'Don't you wash these things?'

'What's the matter? Not used to a bit of honest sweat?'

Mark checked the contamination strips on the shoulder of the suit and took a few experimental breaths. He heard the thwack of the respirator and tasted charcoal from the filter.

The six volunteers stood like Michelin men as the orderlies tested the seals and then adjusted their own NBC suits.

'Morning, gentlemen.' Even through the distortion of a respirator, Mark recognised Leary's voice. 'A nice simple task for you today. We just want you to run a mile in full NBC kit. Anyone who manages it in less than four minutes will get a free ticket to the next Olympics.'

They were shepherded into a rough line and then sent off on the blast of a whistle. It was impossible to do more than stumble over the rough ground and Mark's speed barely rose above walking pace. As they struggled along, explosions were detonated around them and live ammunition was fired over their heads. Each unexpected blast set Mark's heart jumping wildly, his breath coming in ragged spurts, sweat rolling from his forehead and misting the visor of his suit.

They had covered about half the distance when another canister was suddenly detonated in front of them. It leaked a yellow-grey fog which hung heavy in the windless air. Mark faltered and stopped. There were shouts and whistles, fresh explosions behind him and he heard a voice shouting, 'Get on! Get on!'

The bank of sickly yellow gas rolled slowly towards him. He took in an instinctive lungful of air, ducked his head and began to stumble through it. Once more, he felt his throat and chest tighten and his breath start to rasp. This time his vision dimmed too.

He struggled on for a few more paces, then slowed to a halt. All the other volunteers had stopped as well. Some sank to their knees and Mark could hear Rob vomiting inside his mask. Terry staggered a few more paces, then fell to the ground, clutching at his throat. They crouched or lay where they were as the cloud gradually dispersed. No one moved to help them.

After several minutes Mark struggled back to his feet. 'Rob,' he said. 'Are you all right, mate?'

There was a pause, then a rasping voice. 'I will be when they get this frigging hood off my head. Some sod's filled it with puke.'

A loudhailer whined, 'Complete the course. Complete the course.'

Rob dragged himself to his feet. 'I'm going to come back here one night and kill that bastard, but first I'm going to make him do this. Without an NBC suit.'

The others hauled themselves upright, but Terry remained on the ground. 'He needs attention,' Mark yelled.

'Complete the course,' was the only reply.

A lorry waited for them at the top end of the range. Mark leaned against it, chest heaving, eyes and nose streaming mucus. Rob knelt near by, coughing and retching. He fumbled with the hood of his NBC suit, which brought an instant rebuke over the loudhailer.

'NBC State Black is still operative. Do not tamper with your NBC suits until the all-clear is given.'

After a few minutes, the burning in Mark's lungs began

to ease. He pulled himself upright and looked back down the range, shaking his head from side to side as he tried to clear his stinging eyes. Mark glanced down at the test strips on his NBC suit. They had changed to a vivid red.

Terry was still lying on the ground. An NBC-clad stretcher party made slow progress towards him, pausing to test the air with probes.

As the stretcher party collected Terry, Mark walked round the lorry and glanced over the other side of the rise. He stopped and stared. The downland turf ended abruptly in a stretch of grey and gritty tarmac, blistered with scorch marks and strewn with glass fragments. Beyond it lay rows of grimy terraced houses and a dilapidated block of flats, its concrete façade cracked, split and stained with damp. Some of the doors and windows were boarded up, others were starred by bullet holes or blackened by fire. The wrecks of burned-out cars littered the street corners.

Rob came up alongside him. 'We've got a site like this at our firing ranges,' he said. 'We use it to practise street-fighting drills and securing areas for house to house searches, but what the hell do the mad scientists need one for?'

'Working out how much CS gas you need to incapacitate a block of flats or a housing estate, I suppose,' Mark said. 'Though I'm sure they use something much nastier than CS gas.'

'Tell me about it. I just got a fucking faceful.'

Mark shifted his gaze. Beyond the Belfast set lay another series of test sites. He recognised the familiar hump-backed profile of a hardened aircraft shelter, alongside bunkers, ventilation shafts, bomb stores, pillboxes and even a cluster of slit trenches.

The stretcher party made its way up the slope towards them. The figure on the stretcher lay motionless, one arm dangling over the side. Rob began to run down the hill towards them but two guards intercepted him and pulled him away.

A field ambulance bucketed up the range, its tyres scoring dark furrows in the turf. It swung around the stretcher party and came to a halt facing back down the hill. They slid the stretcher into the back and the ambulance sped away, its siren howling.

* * *

In the changing rooms back at the Containment Centre they were all decontaminated by staff still wearing protective gear. They were sprayed with Fuller's Earth as they were stripped gradually of their NBC suits, which were loaded into a steel bin and taken away. Stark naked, they were then put through a series of airlocks. Jets of air pummelled them like water-cannon, and extractors roared like turbines.

Mark's vision was still blurred, and when he stepped dripping from the conventional shower which was the last stage of decontamination, he peered into a mirror. His pupils had contracted to pinpricks.

In the changing room, Rob had one of the orderlies pinned against the wall. 'What's happened to Terry? Where is he?'

'I don't know. Just be patient. He'll be okay.'

Mark took Rob's arm. 'Leave it, Rob. This guy's just a message boy.'

One of the volunteers was groaning and rubbing at his eyes. 'What's the fucking point of wearing NBC kit and a respirator, if the gas goes straight through it?'

'This is the army, isn't it?' Rob said. 'There's no fucking point to any of it.'

The post-test medical was even more thorough than the day before, and Mark could barely contain his impatience. Finally he stood up. 'I have to go.'

'What do you mean you have to go? We'll tell you when you can go.'

'I'm going to be sick. I need some fresh air.'

The orderly gave an audible sigh. 'All right, all right. Just hold on to your lunch while I take your blood pressure again.'

The door opened and Leary appeared. The room went quiet. The professor cleared his throat. 'After today's unfortunate incident on the ranges, we're naturally taking every precaution. We're suspending the current programme, so the volunteers will not be required for any further tests.' He paused.

'What's happened to him?' Mark said.

'We're still evaluating the incident.'

'But is he okay?'

'I'm afraid I can't discuss it with you.'

Leary strolled to the window and stood with his back to them. 'My assistant will give you all a telephone number that can you can ring in the extremely unlikely event of any further problems. I know I don't have to remind you that our work is covered by the Official Secrets Act. No aspect of it should be discussed with anyone, and that includes your civilian doctor. As I said, if there are any recurring problems – and the prospect of that is absolutely negligible – our medical staff here are willing and able to advise you.' He turned to face the room, his expression cold. 'Goodbye.'

Mark packed quickly and arranged a cab to take him to Salisbury station. He bought a ticket to London, made one phone call, then waited for half an hour on the platform. After satisfying himself that he was not being watched, he made his way through the side streets to a venerable, half-timbered pub. He sat at a table with his back to the wall, his eyes on the door.

Dexy arrived ten minutes later. He had a few days' growth of beard, his hair was tousled and his clothes were stained with mud. The landlord gave him a hostile look as he slid into the seat next to Mark.

'Well?' Dexy said.

'I think the stuff I need is in the director's office. I can't get back in. They've cancelled the rest of the test programme.'

Dexy shrugged. 'Nothing lost.'

Mark hesitated. 'There may be a problem. I'm sure they sussed I wasn't who I was claiming to be.'

'Don't worry, we won't be making an appointment. Now, how about a bite to eat?'

As Dexy shovelled down his food, Mark went over everything he'd seen at Porton Down. Dexy listened intently, interrupting to clarify details. 'What about the locks? I'll bet they're Yales. Every military base is the same, all the security is round the perimeter. Once you get inside all they have are Yales.'

'Not here,' Mark said. 'They've got deadlocks on both doors.'

'That makes a change. They must have something worth hiding, then. Are the doors normal size? How about contact alarms?'

'None that I could see.'

When Dexy was satisfied that Mark had told him everything that could be of use, he drained his drink and pushed his glass away. 'Right. I'll talk you through it when we get to the hide.'

They stopped four miles short of Porton Down, pulling into a pub car park. 'Don't get excited,' Dexy said. 'We're not stopping for another drink. It's a good place to leave the car.'

He led Mark past the side of the pub and on to a footpath leading into a wood. They climbed steadily higher and came out of the trees near the top of a hill. Dexy circled around the hillside keeping just below the skyline, then led Mark towards a clump of gorse. Even from a yard away, it was impossible to detect that it was a hide. Dexy took a long look around, then crawled in under the bushes, motioning Mark to follow. The hide consisted of a hollow under the gorse, the bare earth covered by a thick black plastic sheet. The front of the hide was screened by chicken-wire studded with gorse branches.

Dexy handed Mark some binoculars and pointed across the valley. 'Look just beyond the perimeter fence. See those posts at different heights? They're microwave masts. Break the signal and the alarm goes off.'

'So how do we get past them?'

'Count the stanchions moving east from the main gate. Just past the twenty-third, there's a rabbit track.'

Mark peered through the binoculars. In the low, reddening light cast by the setting sun, he could see a faint line, no more than a discolouration of the grass, running up to and through the fence at an angle of about forty-five degrees.

'The microwaves must be set high enough at that point for the rabbits to pass without triggering the alarms. We're going in the same way.'

'And how do we get into the building?'

Dexy smiled. 'We do that with a Trojan Horse.' He checked his watch. 'Dusk in half an hour. Let's get ourselves cammed up.' He tossed Mark some camouflage gear. 'It's not quite your size but it'll do the job. When you've got it on, dirty up your boots and then I'll do your face.'

Mark watched as Dexy streaked his own face with a fat crayon. 'What's that?'

'Theatrical make-up.'

When he'd finished their faces, Dexy pulled two bundles of rags from his rucksack, torn strips of fabric in dull greys, browns and greens. He gave one to Mark and pulled the other one over his head. The trailing strands hung down around his chest and shoulders. As he leaned forward, they obscured his face.

Dexy laid out his kit on the ground and checked off each item, then packed it into a small rucksack. As well as night-vision goggles, there was some much less high-tech equipment: wire-cutters, a strip of foam rubber, a small drill, two thick wooden blocks and a car-jack.

'What's that for?'

'You'll see when we get there.' He then armed himself with two flash-bang grenades and a pistol.

'Jesus, Dexy, they're supposed to be on our side. We're not going in there shooting, are we?'

'Only as a last resort.' Dexy fixed him with a level stare. 'You've chosen your side, Mark; you've come off the fence. But you've got to accept where it could lead. If you haven't got the stomach for it, then this is the moment to pull out. There's no turning back from here on in.'

Mark glanced away, looking out towards Porton Down, then he nodded. 'All right, let's do it.'

They cleared the hide, rolling up the plastic sheet and chicken-wire. Dexy packed everything into his rucksack, then stowed it under the bushes. 'Okay, here are the ground rules. Do as I say at all times, without hesitation. We communicate by hand signal or whisper. We move separately, so that one's always watching and listening while the other is moving. If we're tapped or split up, we RV at the points we'll establish on the way in. First RV on the hour. If there's no show, the back-up RV on the next hour. After that, you're on your own. If we are tapped by guards, leave any actions to me, but respond instantly to any commands or signals. Any questions? Then let's go.'

Dexy pulled on his NVGs and motioned Mark to do the same. There was a faint electronic whine and the familiar green flecks flickered before Mark's eyes. They waited a few minutes to accustom their eyes, then set off down the hillside.

The sunset had faded to a blood-red glow in the darkening sky and the evening chorus of birdsong was stilled. Only the call of a cock pheasant and the plaintive bleat of a sheep broke the silence as they crossed the floor of the wooded valley and began climbing the other side.

Twice they used the culverts of streams to pass underneath roads crossing their track. Dexy moved from cover to cover, using trees, rocks, bushes and patches of shade. Even knowing that he was there, Mark often lost sight of him as he blended into the undergrowth.

It was fully dark by the time they arrived at the edge of a scrubby pine wood. Beyond it lay the road and the perimeter fence. There was a glow from the guardhouse by the gates to their right and smaller pools of yellow light from the arc-lights punctuating the fence.

Dexy scanned the roadside until he saw his marker. 'I'll go first. As soon as I stop moving, double after me. Follow me exactly. Do everything I do, the way I do it. And keep your face within an inch of my boot as we go under the wire. That way, you stop when I do.'

Dexy inched forward and raked the length of the fence with his eyes. Satisfied, he nodded to Mark and then was gone, sprinting across the road, stooping low to the ground. Mark watched him reach the fence and drop from sight, then licked his dry lips, shot a look towards the main gates and raced after him. He threw himself down, his breathing fast and shallow.

Dexy severed the bottom strand of wire with his cutters, and began to worm his way forward, pushing the rucksack ahead of him, the sound of his movements as faint as the wind stirring the grass. Mark hesitated for a second before following him. He took a deep breath, then began to work his way under the wire. A strand of wire scraped along his back, then his head banged into the sole of Dexy's boot.

Dexy clicked his tongue softly to attract his attention. Mark raised his eyes and saw him pointing at a small rectangular shape, the size of a matchbox, on the wire above his head. 'Tremblers,' he whispered. 'They pick up vibrations. Keep your head down or we're fucked.'

It took half an hour to crawl just ten yards. There was another dry click as Dexy broke the inner fence. They wormed their way through, then paused as he checked the ground ahead.

The faint line of the rabbit track still glowed pale green in Mark's goggles, but at either side was a solid green bar, the posts of the microwave alarms.

Flattening himself against the ground, he worked his way forward behind Dexy, the hairs on his neck rising at the thought of breaking the beam. He kept his face turned to the side to lower his profile and stayed flat to the ground until he was well past the danger. Dexy was already crouching ahead of him, searching the next stage of their route.

Their progress over the down seemed unbearably slow. Mark felt conspicuous and exposed even in the deepest cover, and each unexpected movement or sound set his heart thumping and brought sweat to his brow. Bats flickered through his field of vision like green sparks, their sonar niggling in his ears as they hunted down moths. A rustling from a hedgerow sent him diving for cover, only to see the thorny outline of a hedgehog rummaging among the dry leaves. Nerves still jangling, he started as a hunting barn owl, ghost grey in the dim light, swept across the down in front of him.

As they neared the top of a low rise, Dexy flattened himself against the ground. Mark peered past him and made out the outline of an angular shape, even darker than the night sky. It was a Land Rover. He stared hard at the windscreen and saw two pale faces beyond it.

Dexy motioned to the right with his hand and they began to belly-crawl around the vehicle. Mark inched his way forward, using his elbows and toes to push himself over the ground. He recoiled, stifling a grunt of pain as the spikes of a thistle stung his face, then crawled on, trying to keep the dark shape of Dexy in sight. His flesh was creeping, but there was no sound, no challenge from the Land-rover. His muscles ached from the effort of belly-crawling but he forced himself on until they reached the shelter of a patch of scrub. He paused for breath, but Dexy was already moving on. He had to hurry before he lost him.

Lower on the slopes Mark glimpsed the dark, block-like

shape of a building. As they began to work their way around it, a dog barked. A moment later a door opened and light spilled into the darkness. Mark dropped and lay still. The dog's profile was silhouetted against the light, its nose raised, sniffing the air. It gave a low growl, then began to bark again. Covered by the noise, Mark heard the faint scrape of steel. He glanced sideways at Dexy and saw a combat knife in his fist.

A voice shouted at the dog. It barked its defiance once more, then fell silent. A dark figure paced around the yard, testing the doors of the outbuildings, and a few moments later the door of the house slammed shut.

Mark released his pent-up breath. They lay motionless for another minute, then crawled away back up the slope the way they had come. Soon they were circling the building on the downwind side, keeping a good four hundred yards' distance from it.

It was almost midnight when the Containment Centre came into view, its white concrete walls a faint grey in the starlight. Mark moved up to the hollow where Dexy was crouching in the shadow of a small bush.

Dexy glanced to his right, then stiffened. He made no sound, but the fierce pressure of his fingers on Mark's arm conveyed its own message. Mark followed his gaze but for a moment could see nothing. Then there was a slight movement and he saw a guard standing no more than twenty feet to their right.

Dexy's hand moved a few inches, signalling back and left. Mark worked his way back up the hollow, feet first, his eyes fixed on the profile of the guard. He had gone a few yards when his foot snapped a twig.

He dropped his face to the ground, feeling the torn strips of his camouflage settle around him, and lay still. The guard turned and moved towards him, stopping a couple of paces away, so close that Mark caught a faint trace of his aftershave on the breeze.

Every heartbeat sounded like thunder. Mark opened one eye a fraction and saw his breath misting in the cool night air, coating the grass stems like dew. The guard was outlined against the sky, so close that it seemed impossible he could not see Mark lying at his feet. The guard remained motionless, staring into the darkness. Minutes passed, then he hawked and spat, and turned away.

Mark raised his head a fraction of an inch at a time. The guard stood with his back to him now, looking down the slope towards the Containment Centre. His gun was pointing down.

Mark worked his way around and began inching away, feeling with his fingers for sticks or other giveaways before moving his body further from the guard. He worked his way round behind a low rock and waited.

He did not even hear Dexy approach. He materialised out of the darkness at his elbow, then led the way down towards the administration block. A few minutes later they crouched in the bushes a few feet from the doors.

'Now we wait for the guard,' Dexy said. He glanced at his watch. 'He's due in forty minutes.'

Mark hunched deeper into the shadows and settled himself. The night cold seeped into his bones, and he had to change position slightly every few minutes, easing the cramp from his limbs. Every faint sound above the rustle of the wind in the trees made him stiffen, his eyes flickering from shadow to shadow. At his side Dexy remained motionless.

Just as Mark thought his aching muscles would seize, he heard a heel striking against gravel, and a moment later saw the glow of a torch. A guard came into view, walking slowly towards the building, his head moving through an arc as he scanned the ground in front of him. There was the jingle of keys, then the door swung open, and closed again with a thud.

Dexy scanned every inch of the area, listening intently, then pulled the thin strip of dark-stained foam rubber from his rucksack and sprinted to the door. He pinned the strip to the frame, leaving it hanging down an inch or so over the top of the door.

A moment later he was back alongside Mark. They waited as the guard made his rounds, seeing the dull glow of his torch through the windows as he moved down the corridors inside. The main door swung open again, and the guard stood framed in the light for a moment, then he let the door bang shut behind him and moved off along the road.

Dexy gave him less than a minute to get clear. 'Wait here,' he said, then disappeared without waiting for a reply.

Dexy was soon silhouetted against the door. He paused, listening, then signalled to Mark. The thin strip of light broadened as Dexy eased the door open and removed the rubber strip, then they were both inside. The lock clicked as Mark shut the door. 'What about the alarms?' he asked.

'The security console will just show the door has been unlocked, then locked again. As far as they're concerned, the guard went in, had a look and then came out again. Now come on, which door?'

The lobby was brightly lit, but the corridors beyond were in darkness. Mark led the way past Dorothy's office to the door of the director's office. Dexy examined the door carefully then slipped the pack from his shoulder. He pulled out the wood blocks and gave them to Mark. 'Hold these against the door frame.'

Dexy placed the jack between them and began tightening it. The frame creaked. Dexy paused to test the door then gave the jack a few more turns. There was a metallic click as the tongue of the lock came free and the door swung open. Mark smiled to himself. It had taken two minutes. Dexy stooped under the jack and moved into the office.

'What about the jack?' Mark asked. 'What if the guard comes back?'

'I hope he does: he's our way out of here. But we've at least fifty minutes and that should be time enough.'

The director's office was very different from that of his personal assistant. The wood-panelled walls were crowded with photographs of visiting dignitaries, and there was a framed letter from the Prime Minister thanking the director and his staff for their 'Herculean efforts. When the history books come to tell the full story of this era, the contribution of Porton Down to the preservation of Her Majesty's peace and the protection of the interests of Her Nation will receive its due recognition.'

They dropped to their knees and crawled across the carpet, past the barred window, to the far corner of the office, where the filing cabinet stood against the wall, next to a mahogany drinks stand. The filing cabinet was locked. Mark smiled to himself. If it had not been locked it would not have been worth opening. They worked it away from the wall, then turned it towards the window and crouched behind it.

Dexy drilled a small hole in the corner of the cabinet, then pulled out the cutters he had used on the fence. They began to bite through the steel as if it was cardboard.

Twice Mark thought he heard noises and laid a warning hand on Dexy's arm. Each time, Dexy paused for over a minute, listening hard, then shook his head. 'Just the wind, Mark.' He winked and went back to work.

He cut across the top and down both sides of the cabinet to within six inches of the bottom, then peeled back the flap. Beginning with the top drawer, he lifted out each file in turn, standing them on top of each other.

Mark took the reading light from the director's desk and stood it on the floor behind the cabinet. Shrouded in his jacket, it threw a narrow strip of light on to the files. He picked each one up, scanned the contents, then replaced it in the correct order.

Much of the material in the first drawer concerned budget strategies and negotiating tactics for protecting Porton Down from defence cuts. Mark flicked through the files impatiently.

The next two drawers contained reports and evaluations of agents identified only by letter and number codes. Mark scanned them more carefully, looking for anything that would link the reports to the Gulf, but he found nothing.

Halfway through the bottom drawer he found a bulky file titled 'Vw'. He scanned the first page, then began flicking through the others. As he turned a page a phrase leaped out at him. He turned back and read it again: 'Inoculation Scimitar'. He grabbed his camera.

'Not here,' Dexy said. 'In the corridor.'

Mark carried the file through the office and out into the corridor, then pulled the door closed. He laid the file on the floor, against the wall at the side of the door, and began photographing the documents, the flash on his compact camera clicking like a metronome as he flicked through the pages.

When he had finished, they hurried back into the office, loaded the files into the drawer and pushed the steel flap back into place. Dexy squirted superglue at intervals around the cut edge, then pushed the cabinet back against the wall. Even the most cursory examination of the back would show it had been tampered with, but without removing all the files or shifting the cabinet away from the wall, there was no outward sign of anything amiss.

'All set? Let's go.' Dexy pulled the door closed and then lowered the jack. The door frame contracted to its normal position. The only signs of tampering were the faint cracks in the paintwork.

They moved back along the corridor to the lobby. Dexy took a careful look around, then led Mark up the stairs to the first floor. The fifth and twelfth stairs creaked.

'Stay off those on the way down.'

They stood on the landing at the head of the stairs. 'The guard's a creature of habit,' Dexy said. 'He checked the ground floor first last time, so he'll do it again this time.'

'What if he doesn't?'

'He will . . . but if he doesn't, we'll have to take him out and then leg it.'

They heard the sound of footsteps on the gravel. There was the rattle of a key and the door swung open. They drew back into the shadows.

Mark stiffened as the guard moved towards the stairs, but he passed straight by and began checking the rooms on the ground floor. The door of the gents banged, and then the guard's footsteps moved off along the corridor.

'Come on,' Dexy said.

Mark followed him down the stairs. They ran across the lobby and stood just inside the gents. The guard returned a few moments later and disappeared upstairs.

Dexy held the door open a crack. Peering over Dexy's shoulder, Mark saw the guard reach the foot of the stairs and walk to the door. As he opened it, Dexy was already moving across the lobby. He flattened himself against the wall at the side of the door and slid the rubber strip across the lock as the guard let it close behind him.

Dexy waved Mark forward as soon as the guard's footsteps had faded. He peered out into the darkness, then they slipped outside and closed the door.

There was still no moon and the stars visible through the

patches of broken cloud gave only the most feeble light, but the NVGs let them pick their way around the darkened buildings and into the shelter of the trees.

Mark felt the tension ebbing from him a little as they moved up the down. He trailed Dexy, still marvelling at his soundless, barely visible progress, using every scrap of cover to mask his movements.

By two in the morning they were within sight of the fence. Dexy had crossed a patch of open ground and was waiting in cover as Mark followed him. As he ran forward at a crouch, he heard a shout. 'Halt! Military police. Stand still!'

He froze, ice in his veins. Through his goggles he saw a figure to his right, light glinting like green fire from the barrel of his gun.

'Raise your arms.'

Mark uncurled and straightened up slowly. He moved his hands away from his sides and then raised his arms, his eyes fixed on the mouth of the gun-barrel, a black hole at the centre of his green-tinted field of vision.

Keeping his gun trained on Mark's chest, the guard brought his other hand up towards his lapel, reaching for his radio mike. Before he could touch it, however, he gave a muffled groan and crumpled to the ground.

Dexy's shadow stood over him for a second, then ran towards the fence. Mark followed, dropping into cover alongside him, his breath rasping.

Dexy glanced at him. 'We're still all right, we've probably got somewhere between ten and thirty minutes before he's missed. Keep calm and we'll make it easily.'

He moved parallel to the fence until he picked up his marker, then lay down and began to worm his way forward along the rabbit track, under the microwaves and through the first line of chainlink fencing. Mark followed him, his head inches from Dexy's boots. He worked his way forward, conscious of nothing but the eternity it was taking to cross these last few yards of hostile ground.

At last he saw Dexy rise to a crouching position and knew he was clear of the fence. He pushed himself forward and his own head and shoulders emerged into the open. Even the night air tasted sweeter outside.

Mark heaved himself forward again, but was jerked to a

halt as his combat jacket snagged on the wire. Fear seized him. He wriggled on to one side, reaching behind his back to free himself. His groping fingers closed on a square metallic shape. He dropped the trembler alarm as if scalded, but it was too late. The faint glow from the guardhouse suddenly erupted with light and noise.

'Come on,' Dexy said. 'Just get out.'

Mark hauled himself free, ripping the jacket, and they sprinted across the road and into the trees.

'Can you find the hide?'

Mark hesitated.

'Then wait near the bridge on the road at the bottom of the valley. Give me twenty minutes from now. If there's no sign of me by then, take off.'

As Mark turned to go, Dexy gripped his arm, holding him still. 'Wait.'

Mark heard the roar of an engine and the beams of headlights flared in his goggles. A Land Rover came pounding along the road and screeched to a halt.

There was the slam of doors, the sound of running footsteps on tarmac and then a shout. 'There's a break in the fence.' A moment later sirens wailed as the alarm went up.

'Go!'

Mark froze for a moment and Dexy pushed him in the back.

'Go!'

Mark blundered down the hillside, crashing through the undergrowth, then he forced himself to slow, using the cover and pausing to look and listen for signs of pursuit.

After a while he heard the murmur of water and a moment later the line of the road in the bottom of the valley glowed in his goggles. He followed it up to the steep, single-arched packhorse bridge straddling the river. He pushed his way into the heart of a hazel thicket close to the water and settled down to wait.

Just as his ragged breathing began to calm, the faraway barking of dogs set his heart pounding again. He peered at his watch. Ten minutes. If he waited the full twenty, the dogs might be on him.

He was beginning to move out of his cover when he heard

a faint noise behind him and whirled around. Dexy was standing there.

'They've got dogs.'

'I know,' Dexy said. 'I've left a diversion for them, but we'll still need to move fast.'

Dexy waded through the river and started up the far bank.

Mark grabbed at his arm. 'Shouldn't we wade down it for a while and hide our scent?'

'It's an old wives' tale; it doesn't work. They can pick up traces of the scent from the bank.'

As Mark still hesitated, Dexy pulled him up on to the bank. 'Look, tracker dogs or attack dogs are no problem. We'll just go straight up the hillside. Their handlers won't be keen to follow because they don't know what's waiting at the top. They usually pretend the dogs have lost the scent and call them off. If they do send the dogs up, I'll deal with them.'

An explosion lit the night sky behind them. 'That's the diversion. Now let's move it.'

The relentless pace that he set up the hill left Mark gasping in his wake. Dexy paused often, scanning the way they had come as he waited for Mark to catch up. Each time he urged him on. 'Come on, just a few more yards.'

At last they reached the summit. Dexy paused at the hide long enough to gather his rucksack, then they ran down the far side of the hill, moving faster over the open ground.

The car was now alone in the car park of the darkened pub. Dexy had the engine running and the car moving before Mark had even closed his door. He passed Mark a packet of wipes. 'Strip off your gear and get that shit off your face and boots. Get your street clothes back on, then take over driving while I do the same. If we hit a roadblock, let me do the talking.'

He flicked open the glove box and switched on a concealed radio, eavesdropping on the police frequencies as they sped northwards, changing direction a couple of times to skirt roadblocks.

They kept to the minor roads until they had passed under the motorway, and only when they had put forty miles between themselves and Porton Down did Dexy's concentration relax. He glanced across at Mark and cracked a smile. 'You'd never pass Selection.'

'Jesus Christ, Dexy.' Mark raised his shaking hands. 'Right now I wouldn't even pass the medical.'

Dexy's smile faded. 'But you've passed the point of no return.'

Mark didn't reply, staring out of the windscreen.

Chapter 14

It was late afternoon when Mark got back to the flat. It appeared untouched, a thin layer of dust on every surface. The answerphone was flashing. 'Hi, Mark. Greetings from Baghdad. It's hot as hell here.' Natalie's voice was almost obscured by the static on the line. 'Hope you're okay, I just wanted to say—' There was a pause. 'Well, just look after yourself anyway.'

Mark touched the machine, locked and double-bolted the door, and closed the blinds, then rummaged through the kitchen cupboards, unearthing a can of beans and a few stale crackers. When he had eaten, he clicked on the red light and shut himself in his darkroom.

After a couple of hours, he brought the first batch of prints out. He pored over them for an hour, but the reports were couched in such impenetrable scientific jargon that he struggled to make sense of them.

The only document in plain English was a clipping from an American newspaper. Mark began scanning through it: 'The type of mycoplasma we identified was highly unusual and almost certainly couldn't occur naturally. It has one gene from the HIV-1 virus, but only one . . .'

He realised that he had seen the story before, in the

newspaper library at Colindale. The only annotations on the report were a single word: 'Action?' and in another hand, 'Refer Group w for evaluation'. Mark read it again, then let it fall back on to the table.

He went back to the darkroom for the rest of the prints and began working through them, making occasional notes as he read. He returned to two particular documents.

The first was an incident report from a spearhead unit. It was dated 24 February, 1991. The only location was a map reference. Mark pulled an atlas from the bookshelves and turned to Iraq. The reference was for an area just to the south of As Salman.

The incident report was terse in the extreme: '0417 hours: Scud incoming. 0418 hours: Warhead detonated. 0440 hours: Spearhead advance.'

Mark sat motionless, staring at the page, then pushed it aside and reached for the next document. It was marked 'UK Eyes Only', the highest level of security classification, so secret that even the Americans were excluded. It was a casualty evaluation report, running to twenty pages, detailing the concentration and dispersal rate of an agent only identified by the initials Vw.

Fatalities and casualties were tabulated in two columns headed 'Inoculation Scimitar (IS)' and 'Controls'. The casualty rates declined as a factor of distance from point G, the epicentre of the blast. On the next page a pie chart reproduced the same figures. The estimated casualties amongst the control group ranged up to ninety per cent within a one-mile radius of the blast. Of these, over seventy per cent were fatalities. The rates dropped steeply as the rings moved out from the site of the blast. The effect of Inoculation Scimitar was dramatic. Less than ten per cent of the inoculated soldiers had been casualties, even within the innermost ring of exposure.

Mark read on through a dispassionate recital of injury and death. There were pages of autopsy reports, analyses of human and animal tissue, fabric and protective gear. It was obvious from the reports that the vast majority of casualties had been among Iraqi troops. His attention was caught by a footnote.

> Insufficient data is available to make any realistic assessment of the longer-term consequences of low-level exposure to agent Vw. Based on the closest comparable studies, an attrition rate amongst those with low to moderate exposure in the range of twenty to forty per cent might be expected over a five- to ten-year period. The casualty rate and symptoms presented should not vary significantly from the normal reactions to the inoculations and other prophylactics.

Mark rubbed his eyes. The last page of the report was an appendix headed 'Sanitisation'. It made even more chilling reading.

> The use of a thickening agent, concentrating dispersal within a closely circumscribed area, has led to contamination levels in excess of 500 ppm. Decontamination of the area is not a viable option. To some extent the site is self-policing, but in any event, it is recommended that the area be treated as highly toxic – Category w – for a minimum of ten years. Only IS-protected personnel should be permitted on site in this period. NBC protection alone is of uncertain value.

He stopped reading. Natalie was going into As Salman, protected only by an NBC suit. He pushed the last page aside and reached for the phone. He was unsure what he could say to her on an open line if he did manage to get through to her, but he had to try and give her some sort of warning.

It took him a dozen attempts to get through to Baghdad. As he waited, he forced himself to think. There was no longer any room for doubt. An Iraqi chemical weapon had been detonated at or near As Salman. Before the war, the Coalition leaders had warned Saddam of nuclear retaliation to any chemical attack, but when it came to the point they lacked the ruthlessness to carry out the threat.

The chemical weapon had caused massive fatalities amongst Iraq's own troops, but the British spearhead, protected by Inoculation Scimitar, had escaped with only minor casualties.

Unprotected forces, including Stumps and Michael, had been close enough to the site to be contaminated by low-level exposure. The moderate south-west wind recorded in the incident report would have blown the toxic cloud almost directly over the prison where the POWs were held. How had he avoided contamination when Dan and Steve had both succumbed to it?

Why had only British spearhead troops been inoculated against a weapon that Saddam could presumably have used in any part of the theatre of war? What about the Americans? And what was it about the incident report that rang a warning bell in his mind?

A voice down the phone interrupted his thoughts. 'Canal Hotel.' He could barely hear through the haze of static.

'Natalie Kennedy, please.' He wondered how many other people were listening in.

'Just a minute.'

There was a long silence, then a strongly accented man's voice. 'Natalie Kennedy is not here.'

'I must speak to her urgently. Where can I reach her?'

'I'm sorry. I'm not permitted to reveal her whereabouts. I can take a message, that is all.'

Mark tightened his grip on the receiver. 'It's very, very important.'

'I'm sorry.'

'Then tell her . . . tell her . . .' He searched for the words. 'Tell her she must contact Mark before she goes to—' He hesitated again. 'Where she's planning to go. Tell her that her life is at risk.' He hung up and stared out into the darkness.

He fetched a box of matches from the kitchen and began setting fire to the prints. One by one he held them till they were all but consumed, then let them go, watching as the blazing embers spiralled down into the scummy waters of the dock. When the last one had flickered and died, he closed the window and switched out the lights.

When sleep came, it brought back the old nightmares, images of his father, hollow cheeked and wheelchair bound. The old man's face became Matthew's, distorted, peering out from the shelter of his mother's arms at the world that had betrayed him. Then the flesh on the arms burned and blackened, and they weren't Jenny's but Natalie's and Mark saw her lying dead in the desert, her sightless eyes staring at him in reproach, her mouth frozen in a silent scream.

He sat suddenly upright, struggling to escape. Damp with sweat, his heart pumping, he swept the tangled bedclothes on to the floor, then got up and tuned the television to a blank channel. He lay back down, using the hiss of white noise like the rush of the sea, drowning the ghosts that crowded in on him.

Avedon church stood on a low rise, separated from the village by a stream. Mark crossed the ancient, arched footbridge, built from the same honeyed Cotswold stone as the church, and stopped by the lychgate.

The hearse was already parked at the side of the road behind him and he could hear the undertaker rehearsing the bearers in their task. He walked up the broad path, paved with the gravestones of long-dead villagers. Three men in RAF uniform stood at the side of the church porch, smoking a last cigarette before going inside.

'Mark!' James Edwards beckoned to him. He introduced him to the two other men, staff officers up from London to show the flag, and then took him to one side, out of earshot. 'Where the hell have you been?'

'I, er . . . away. I had a few things to wrap up before Kuwait.'

'You've been in the Air Force long enough to know that you never go anywhere without leaving a viable contact number. There was no reply from your flat, your mobile was permanently switched off—'

'It was in my car, Boss. It was stolen, then wrecked in a crash. I'm sorry.'

'It isn't good enough, Mark. We're a quick-reaction force. Another twenty-four hours out of touch and you'd have been too late.'

Mark waited. 'For what?'

'The deployment to Kuwait.'

'But that's not till Monday.'

'The whole thing's been brought forward forty-eight hours. Don't ask me why, but all hell broke loose yesterday morning. There's something going on in Iraq.'

'I'm sorry, Boss. It won't happen again.'

Edwards nodded, satisfied. 'All right, end of bollocking. As a matter of fact, you're not the only one. One of the ground crew was at Porton Down this week as a volunteer. Rather him than me, I must say.'

Mark didn't move.

'We phoned to recall him when the balloon went up, but they'd discharged him early,' Edwards said. 'We phoned his house and his mother-in-law said he's on holiday in Spain, so he's got some explaining to do when he finally condescends to join us.'

Edwards led Mark back towards the other two men. 'Sorry about that, a bit of squadron gossip to catch up on. Mark's giving the oration at the funeral. He and the boy's father have shared a Tornado cockpit for years.'

'Tragic business, tragic business.' The senior man, a group captain, nodded as he spoke. 'But then of course we're used to tragedy in the Air Force, aren't we? It's a fact of life on the cutting edge.'

Mark eyed him with distaste. His jowls flopped on to his collar, he had a corned-beef complexion and his bulbous nose was speckled with gin-blossoms. Mark suspected the closest the group captain had been to the cutting edge in his recent career had been while shaving himself.

'This is a little different from aircrew deaths, though, isn't it? We don't normally expect our wives and children to be put in the line of fire.'

'I'm afraid I don't quite get your drift.'

'Mark—'

He ignored Edwards' warning. 'Then let me put it more simply: Gulf War Syndrome.'

The group captain's smile was back in place. 'No such thing, Flight Lieutenant. Just a group of malingerers who think they've found a way to get some easy money out of the government. They'll discover their mistake soon enough.'

Mark's fists clenched. Edwards made to step forward, putting himself between them, but Mark was already turning away, white with anger.

The church was barely a quarter full. Steve's and Jenny's families sat huddled together in the pews as if for warmth.

The only other mourners were a handful of Avedon villagers, a few members of the squadron, and the staff officers.

The small pine coffin was carried through the church, crowned with a single wreath of white lilies. The congregation mumbled their way through a hymn, drowned by the vicar's penetrating tenor. As the last chord died away, the vicar glanced at his notes and began a halting address.

'Sadly I never had the privilege of knowing Matthew, or his parents, Steve and Janet, before this tragedy.' There were a few nervous coughs and one or two people glanced at Jenny, but the vicar ploughed on, unaware of his gaffe. 'Mark Hunter, who has shared some of their darkest days as well as their happiest times, will now give his testament to the all too brief life of Matthew Alderson.'

Mark stood up and walked towards the lectern, his footsteps echoing on the flagstones. The vicar gestured to the pulpit steps, but Mark shook his head. He stood in the centre of the nave, with his back to the altar rail. He glanced across at Steve and Jenny, who gave him strained smiles of encouragement.

'I never knew Matthew Alderson either, although I know how much Steve and Jenny wanted this child. But all the love they had to give wasn't enough to save this young life. His death was a tragedy, but the tragedy doesn't stop there.

'I never knew Matthew, but I know Steve. Steve Alderson is my friend. He was an inspiration to me and all the other POWs held in Iraq. He even risked his own life to save mine, but wanted no thanks, no mention of it. Nothing the Iraqis could do to him could break his body or his spirit. That task has been accomplished by an illness that officially does not exist, but which has now taken the life of his only child.

'Like Matthew's death, Steve's illness will never be explained, unless the truth can be forced from those who pretend that Gulf War Syndrome is a fiction.' He looked pointedly at the group captain. 'The conspiracy of silence shames us all.'

The vicar had been nervously shuffling his notes, and as Mark paused, he cleared his throat and took a hurried step forward, but Mark ignored him.

'Gulf veterans just want Britain to keep its part of the

bargain: to protect them and their families as they protected us. They're not asking for charity. They're not dole scroungers or tax evaders. They're decent, honest people who want nothing more than to know what is wrong with them and how it can be treated. The MoD is hoping that if it stalls long enough, the problem will solve itself. All those who are now sick will – like Matthew Alderson – be dead. And the dead do not dispute the official version of events, the dead do not require disability pensions, the dead do not sue for compensation.'

At the end of the service Steve sought out Mark and gripped his hand, but the staff officers looked at him with unconcealed fury.

The mourners picked their way over the muddy grass to the graveyard behind the church, where a piece of artificial turf had been laid over a mound of newly dug earth.

Soft rain had begun to fall and mist swirled around them, shrouding the trees and deadening the noise of the outside world. As the vicar intoned the committal, every sound at the graveside seemed amplified: the scrape and creak of the ropes as the coffin was lowered into the grave, the muffled clap as he closed his prayer book and the dull rattle, like a funeral drum, as the first handfuls of earth were scattered on the tiny coffin.

As Jenny stepped back from the graveside, she gave Mark a sad, resigned smile, then turned away, leaning heavily on Steve's arm.

Mark stood looking into the grave for a moment, not feeling the rain.

Steve's parents' house was on the other side of the village. They stood at the door to greet the mourners, observing the proper English rituals of politeness, though their faces were stricken.

Steve was in the dining room, handing round cups of tea and sandwiches. Mark pulled him to one side. 'I know this isn't the moment, but it's the only one I've got before I go to Kuwait. I need to talk to you about Iraq, the night the prison was bombed. I need to know exactly what happened.'

Steve gave him a dull stare. 'You were there yourself.'

'I know, but I'm missing something, something important.' He paused. 'I wouldn't ask, especially now, if I didn't think it was really vital.'

'Wait until they've gone and we'll talk.'

As the last guest drifted away, Steve's mask of self-control dissolved. With a visible effort he walked across to Jenny, who was sitting on the sofa gazing at the floor. As he sat down and slipped an arm round her waist, she started at his touch.

Steve turned to look at Mark, his face hollow and ravaged. 'So what do you want to know?'

'Tell me exactly what you remember about that night.'

As Steve began to talk, Mark closed his eyes, replaying the events of that long-ago night in his mind. He saw himself lying in the blackness of his cell, heard the whistle of bombs, saw the walls disintegrate and felt the agony in his ankle. He saw the ruins of the compound, the hot streak of a Scud missile across the night sky, the explosion and the billowing yellow cloud. Mark was no longer listening. He could still picture the trail of the Scud, but the explosion was a couple of miles to the south-east.

'The explosion. It wasn't a Scud.'

Steve stopped. 'Then what was it?'

'I don't know. That's what I'm going to find out.'

'But it's connected to this.' He raised his shirt to show the purple blisters.

Mark nodded. 'Shit, I'm so wrapped up in all this, I haven't even remembered to ask how you are.'

'The same as Dan, but not so far down the road. I've still got a job, though for how long I don't know. I've lost my child, I'm going to lose my livelihood. I'm shit scared, Mark. I don't know what's going to happen to me.'

'You've still got Jenny, that's the most important thing.'

'I wouldn't blame her if she left.' He paused. 'If she goes I don't think I could carry on.'

Mark was unable to find a reply. He stood and clasped his friend's hand. 'I'll call you as soon as I'm back from Kuwait.' He looked into his pain-wracked face. 'And Steve? I'm sorry – about everything.' He turned away before Steve could see the tears in his eyes.

Chapter 15

The briefing was at seven. Mark arrived at Brize Norton half an hour early, but Mitch was already waiting. 'Do you want the good news or the bad news?'

'I'll take the bad.'

'Wise choice. There isn't any good news. The moderately bad news is that I'm your new navigator and the really bad news is that the boss is hunting for you.'

'I've already had a bollocking from him. Yesterday, at the funeral.'

'Well, it looks like you're in for another.'

As the briefing ended, the boss appeared in the doorway. 'My office. Now.'

Edwards sat behind his desk. 'Shut the door.' He waved him to a seat and lit a cigarette. Mark resisted the temptation to reach for the packet. Edwards studied him through the smoke. 'I've had two incandescent staff officers and enough MoD desk jockeys on my back in the last couple of hours to keep British Telecom in profit for the next twelve months. Those that don't want you beheaded want you castrated. You're bloody lucky the press wasn't at the funeral, otherwise you'd be in even deeper shit.

'Just the same, I've been told to make the remainder of

your career as unpleasant as I can. And if I can come up with any grounds for cutting short that career, I imagine it will go some way to repairing the damage to my own prospects.'

He walked round to the front of the desk and perched on its edge. 'Of course I shall do no such thing. Group Captain Sykes is a toerag of the first order and I think this situation is an absolute bloody disgrace. I'm afraid I can't say as much in public, otherwise we'll both be looking for jobs, but I want you to know I'm a hundred per cent behind you. I'll keep the brass off your neck as far as I can.'

Mark felt a flood of relief.

'Group told me they wanted you yanked off the Kuwaiti detachment. I convinced them we'd just be creating a martyr, so you're clear to go. In fact Kuwait is probably the safest place for you at the moment.' He paused. 'You haven't got any more stunts lined up, have you?'

'I wish I did. I haven't been much help to Steve and Jenny or any of the others, but I don't know what else I can do.'

'The best hope would be for de la Billière or Norman Schwarzkopf to come down with Gulf War Syndrome. I don't think we'd be hearing too many more MoD denials after that.'

As Mark stood up to leave, Edwards said, 'Do me a favour, will you? When you get back to the crew-room tell the boys I gave you the mother of all bollockings.' He paused. 'There's nothing else, is there? This is your first time back over Iraq since the war.'

Mark said nothing.

'I know you've had a rough time, what with Bobby's accident, Steve's illness and now his son's death, but I get the feeling there's something more . . . Tell me it's none of my bloody business, if you like.'

Mark hesitated, uncertain.

'Well, I'm here if you want to talk.'

'I . . . You're right, Boss, there is something.' Mark made an abrupt decision. 'Have you ever heard of Inoculation Scimitar?'

'I can't say I have.'

'It was given to British spearhead troops during the Gulf War, but only in one sector, near a place called As Salman. No other troops were given it, not even the American spearhead.

'There was a suspected chemical incident early in the morning of the twenty-fourth of February. The alarms all went off and the NAIADS and CAMS registered chemical agents. The operators were later told it was a false alarm. All the test results, NBC suits and other equipment were collected by soldiers in unmarked fatigues and replaced with new kit.

'A number of soldiers later developed a very specific set of symptoms, quite unlike those of other GWS sufferers. All of them were men who had been in that sector, unprotected by Inoculation Scimitar. As far as we know, no one who had the inoculation has fallen ill.'

'Who's we?' Edwards asked.

'It's . . . it was a figure of speech.'

Edwards let it go. 'But I don't see the relevance of all this to Steve.'

'That sector was just to the south of where Steve and I were held with the other POWs. Steve has the same symptoms, so does an American Chinook pilot who was held with us.'

Edwards paused, tapping his pen against his teeth. 'So you think it could have been an Iraqi chemical attack which for some reason the brass are covering up?'

'That's one possibility, although there is another . . .'

Edwards gave Mark a penetrating look. 'How do you know all this?'

'Partly through a member of an UNSCOM inspection team in Iraq.'

'And the rest?'

Mark shook his head. 'Sorry, Boss, I can't tell you that.'

'You can trust me, Mark.' He waited, but Mark did not reply. 'So . . . apart from rattling staff officers' cages, what else are you doing?'

'I'm trying to find out what really happened at As Salman that night and exactly what Inoculation Scimitar is designed to protect against. So far without much success.'

Edwards was silent. 'There's one thing we can do quite easily, though after all this time I don't know whether it'll tell us anything useful.'

'What's that?'

'We can't access the satellite imagery of that area without raising suspicions, but we do have camera pods on the

Tornados patrolling the no-fly zones. I can arrange the routeing of your first mission to overfly As Salman. We can see if there's anything there.'

Something made Mark pause in the doorway and glance back. Edwards seemed to be staring straight through him, then the ready smile was back in place.

Ali al Salem lay just to the west of Kuwait City. The last time Mark had seen it, the sky had been as black as midnight, smothered in a pall of smoke from the burning oilfields.

Six years later, the clean-up was almost complete. The fires had long since been blasted out and the wells capped. Millions of tons of polluted sand had been scraped up by road graders and dumped miles out in the desert. The beaches had been cleared and the bomb-damaged buildings repaired or demolished.

The city skyline to the east was still busy with cranes, but the reconstruction work on the airbase was complete. The parallel runways had been lengthened and new areas of concrete hard-standing added. Batteries of Patriot missiles ringed the perimeter, jutting towards the north. Hardened aircraft shelters studded the scrubby ground surrounding the taxiways and massive anti-tank berms had been gouged out of the desert beyond the fence.

Mark stepped out of the aircraft into a wall of heat. Sweat drenched his shirt and he struggled to breathe the dense, humid air. He looked around and saw a member of 21's ground crew checking over a jet on the line. 'Kev!'

An oil-streaked face appeared from under an inspection cover. 'Yes, sir?'

'Is Noel out here yet?'

'Bloody hell, not you as well. Half the squadron's on his case.' He wiped the sweat from his brow. 'No he's not. He's turned up back home, but he's not due out here until the day after tomorrow.'

'Will you tell him to come and see me, the moment his feet touch the ground?'

'You'll have to join the queue. The boss wants first crack at him.'

'Kev, this is really, really important. Tell him he has to talk to me before he speaks to anyone else, especially the boss.'

Kev gave him a curious look. 'Shall I tell him what it's about?'

'No. I'll do that.'

Mark pushed open the heavy door to the changing rooms, goose-pimples forming on his arms in the blast of air-conditioning. He strolled through to the crew-room and introduced himself to a group of Kuwaiti officers. He broke off as he recognised a man reading in a corner. 'Sharif?'

Sharif al Said looked up from his paper, then broke into a broad smile.

Mark strode over and shook his hand. 'You haven't changed a bit.' It wasn't entirely true: the Kuwaiti's black hair and moustache were flecked with grey and he had put on a few pounds since they had served on a squadron together.

'Except for this,' Mark said, tapping the shoulder of Sharif's uniform. 'A squadron leader now, congratulations.'

'I have been very fortunate,' Sharif said. He clicked his fingers at the Pakistani behind the counter of the bar. 'Coffee for my friend.'

The coffee was as thick and sweet as treacle, but Mark gulped it down, smacked his lips with approval and accepted the obligatory refill with a smile.

The two men exchanged small talk for a few minutes, then Sharif leaned forward. 'So, my friend, I know what happened to you in the interrogation centre. Let's hope you get a chance of revenge. Now, while you're here in Kuwait, my house is yours. Will you eat with my family tonight?' There was no possibility of refusal. 'Are you flying tomorrow? Then let's eat early. Please. You helped us win back our country, and now you return. You must allow me this small indulgence.'

Mark smiled and bowed his head. 'It would give me great pleasure.'

'You'll need a little time to unpack. I'll wait for you here at five o'clock.'

Mark looked at his watch. 'Can you point me towards the communications room, Sharif? I'm expecting a signal.'

They walked along the dark corridor. Mark glanced into the offices they passed. Edwards sat at a desk in one, talking on the telephone. He smiled and raised a hand in greeting.

The communications room was down a steep flight of stairs at the far end of the corridor. Sharif produced a bunch of keys from his pocket and unlocked the door.

There were no windows in the concrete walls, and the room was flooded with harsh fluorescent light. Unlike Coldchurch, the banks of computers, fax, phone and radio links and secure communications equipment were all brand new, and were operated only by men. Three looked up from their work as they entered. Sharif spoke to one in Arabic, then turned to Mark. 'There's been nothing for you.'

Mark looked puzzled. 'I'll have to contact my base.'

'Of course.' Sharif spoke to the man again, then gestured Mark towards a desk. 'I've told them to give you every co-operation. Now, will you excuse me? I'll have to contact my wife and tell her we're expecting an honoured guest.'

As soon as the door closed, Mark grabbed the phone and began dialling. After a long delay he heard a man's voice. 'Canal Hotel.'

'Natalie Kennedy please.'

'Ms Kennedy is unavailable.'

'But is she in Baghdad?'

'I'm sorry, I have no information on that.'

'My name is Mark Hunter. I left a very important message for Ms Kennedy a couple of days ago. It is imperative that I speak to her.'

'I'm sorry. Ms Kennedy is not available. All I can do is pass on your message.'

Mark took a deep breath. 'When Ms Kennedy is operating away from her base, you must have some form of direct and secure communication with her. Please contact her now, and with her approval, patch me through . . .'

He cradled the receiver to his chest and looked across at the Kuwaitis. All of them had their backs to him. He drummed his fingers on the desk, waiting as the minutes ticked by with no sound on the line.

'Mr Hunter? I'm going to try to connect you.' There was the chatter of relays, a flat, metallic rattle and then a hiss. Through it he heard the faint sound of a woman's voice. 'Mark?'

The door opened and Edwards made his way across the communications room. 'Mark, are you there? Mark?'

Edwards was already in earshot. Mark's mind raced. 'Steve? No, promise me. Don't do a thing until I see you. Do you understand? Not a thing.'

Natalie was immediately cautious. 'You can't talk, can you?'

'That's right,' Mark said, longing to reach out and touch her. 'The boss is with me right now, we're at Ali al Salem. He'd say exactly the same thing. That's right. Exactly. Okay.'

He wanted to stay on the line, just for the sound of her voice, but Edwards was standing right by him. He broke the connection and turned to face Edwards. 'I know it's frowned upon, sir, but I thought you wouldn't mind. Steve's very low; I don't want him to do anything stupid.' He paused. 'Er . . . did you want me for anything?'

'No, not really,' Edwards said. 'I just wanted to say that I've made the arrangements for tomorrow's mission.'

Mark replayed in his mind the conversation with Natalie as he walked back across the airfield. Whether she had realised his warning related to As Salman, he could not say.

The afternoon was taken up with a stream of briefings. Mark forced his mind away from As Salman, back to the reality of combat flying. He tried not to think about his last mission over Iraq and what tomorrow might bring.

The accommodation block was new since Mark's last visit. His apartment was cool and airy, with marble floors, thick outside walls and heavy shutters repelling the heat. It had a balcony overlooking the central courtyard, where a group of palm trees surrounded a tall fountain. He tossed his bag into a corner and lay down on the bed, closing his eyes.

Sharif parked his Mercedes in a no-waiting zone near the old quarter of Kuwait City and steered Mark into a crowded alleyway leading into the souk. Vivid colours, scents and sounds vied with each other amongst the jostling throng of people. Bolts of cloth and mounds of food and spices – saffron, chilli, turmeric, cardamom and many that Mark could not even name – were stacked high on tables, worn stone steps and windowsills, or simply piled in the dust. The smell of burning charcoal mingled with the aroma of coffee, roasting almonds and the sickly perfume of rose-scented sweets.

Metalworkers tapped at copper bowls, watched by old men squatting cross-legged in the dust, sipping tiny cups of coffee as they clustered round their hookahs. Goats tethered to the stalls bleated as butchers in blood-soaked aprons hacked at slabs of fly-covered meat.

The al Saids' apartment was on the ground floor of a shabby building in a narrow street leading off the souk. Sharif rapped on the door to announce their arrival, then led Mark through the house and into a cool and shaded courtyard. In a country where every drop of water was precious, the fountain at its centre was more of a status symbol than Sharif's Mercedes.

The two men sat at a low table while Sharif's wife and sisters laid out salvers of food. Taking his cue from his host, Mark ate with his fingers. Their eyes downcast, the women sat to one side, remaining silent and eating nothing themselves until the men had finished. When the women had served them with coffee, they rose and disappeared into an inner room, leaving the two men alone.

Mark asked his host if he could use his phone to call a friend in Baghdad. He dialled the number of the Canal Hotel three times but got no answer.

'Well, my friend, I hope you haven't come to Kuwait expecting action,' Sharif said when he returned. He offered Mark a cigarette, then lit his own with a gold lighter. 'Even Saddam Hussein seems reluctant to make provocations at the moment.'

Mark was puzzled. 'It can't be that quiet, can it? I thought we came out here two days early for a reason.'

Sharif's face was blank. 'You must be mistaken. There hasn't been a violation of any sort in months.'

In the silence, Mark heard the steady drip of water into the fountain and the song of a caged bird, lit by a tiny band of sunlight penetrating the shadows.

After Sharif dropped him off back at the base, Mark found a quiet table in a corner of the Mess and sat alone with a bottle of wine, staring at the wall. Something linked Dan's, Steve's and Matthew's illness to the deaths of Luther Young and David Isaacs. But what could be the connection between a POW last seen escaping across the Iraqi desert and an ex-Porton Down scientist run over in a Devon lane? If As Salman couldn't provide the answer, he didn't know what he would do.

He was jerked from his reverie by Mitch. 'I'm off to bed. Don't sit up all night, I don't want you dropping off over Iraq tomorrow.'

'Don't worry, I've no intention of taking any more walking tours of the Southern Desert.'

Mitch glanced at him. 'You are going to be all right here, aren't you? You've got no problems about tomorrow?'

Mark forced a smile. 'None I can't handle.' He drained the last of his wine and stood up. 'What time's the alarm call?'

'We've got a lie-in. Not until three thirty.'

Mark winced. 'Breakfast at four, then, if you can face it.'

Mitch was already attacking a plateful of fried eggs when Mark walked into the canteen the next morning. He helped himself to some cereal and toast, then slid into the seat facing him. 'The low-cholesterol breakfast, I see.'

'I'd have had bacon and sausage too, if there was any.'

Mark smiled. 'If this was Saudi I could have you flogged for even thinking about it.'

'If this was Saudi, that'd be the least of my worries.'

Mark glanced at his watch, then picked up another couple of slices of toast and refilled his coffee. 'Come on, I'll finish breakfast on the hoof. The briefing's in five minutes.'

Six other aircrew were slumped on the benches in the lecture room. The boss took the briefing himself. 'Morning, everyone. This is a recap on yesterday's briefing. Today's sortie is a recce and show of presence mission in the southern no-fly zone, below the 32nd parallel, carrying out photo-reconnaissance of Shia encampments and Iraqi troop movements.

'Rules of engagement: calls go back to AWACS, codename Shepherd, who will contact COC, codename Storm, for authority to engage.' He paused. 'If you're locked up from the ground you'll be pleased to know that American F18 HARM-shooters are on CAP with authority to engage and destroy missile sites without further reference.

'Aircraft entering or leaving hostile airspace must do so through the designated entry gates and corridors. You will be using Gate Three, Drop Four at twenty thousand feet. Variations are only permitted in emergency and must be cleared with AWACS.

'We're flying with live weapons, flares and chaff. Make them safe every time you go to the tanker – codename Shell – or exit the area. Diversions are Al Jaber and Al Qaysumah, make sure you have fuel.

'We're flying as singletons.' He gave a thin smile. 'Yes, it's another part of the great economy drive, I expect, so there's even greater need for constant vigilance. There's no one to provide cross-cover, so keep your heads up. Take-off is 0600 hours. Time is 0435 . . . now! That's all. Good luck.' He paused. 'Intelligence brief.'

The intelligence officer stood up, fumbling with her sheaf of papers. 'No reported changes in missile sites. Those we know are marked on your maps with blue and red circles designating their effective range; red circles are for mobile launchers. There are also suggestions that the Iraqis may have completed rebuilding the site at Ar Ruiaytha, but we have no confirmation of this. There are reports of troop movements on the road north of An Nasiriyah, otherwise all is quiet at the moment. It's over four weeks since the last jet was locked up by an acquisition radar, but don't let that lull you at all. Saddam's record amply demonstrates a fondness for sudden, unpredictable action.' She sat down.

'Met brief.'

'The shortest one on record,' a Welsh voice promised. 'High pressure over the whole area, virtually nil cloud cover, a little thin cirrus at most. Winds light and variable. Have a nice day.'

'Combat survival brief.'

A stocky pilot stood up. 'Word of the day, Rattlesnake, letter of the day, V-Victor, number of the day, seventeen. Heat is – obviously – the main survival problem – apart from Iraqi missiles, that is. Keep topping up on fluids before your sortie; better a few uses of the pee-bottle than dehydration. If you are forced to bang out, remember the principles to preserve moisture: shade and stillness. Get out of the direct sun, then don't move. If you have to, move at night when the exercise will keep you warm. Having said that, we're confident of picking you up within two hours if you're unfortunate enough to have to eject. Any questions?'

The only answer was the shuffle of feet as the men headed for the changing rooms. After they had dressed, they filed past the ops desk, collecting their code tables, pistols and ammunition, plus the wad of US dollars that might bribe a path to freedom from Iraq.

They walked out through the hangar into the stifling heat of the morning. Mark glanced towards his Tornado. The desert camouflage glowed a deeper pink in the glare of the rising sun. A newly fitted camera pod hung from a stanchion, but it was the weapons bristling from the fuselage that drew his gaze.

A few of the ground crew walked out with them. Mark dropped back a couple of paces, letting Mitch move ahead, then edged alongside Kevin. 'Kev, don't forget what I said. If he lands before I get back—'

'I know, I know. I'll wrap him in brown paper and hide him under your bed.'

Two crewmen were still working on their jet. They shut the inspection covers and strolled away as Mark approached.

'Who are those guys, Kev, are they new on squadron?'

'No idea. They're not with 21.'

Mark broke into a run. 'Hey!'

They stopped and looked back at him.

'Who the hell are you?' Mark said.

They looked at each other. 'Who were you expecting, the Royal Ballet?'

'Don't get smart with me. You're not with 21 Squadron. What were you doing to that jet?'

'They were making some adjustments at my request.' Edwards walked over to them. 'It's all right, men, thank you.' The two saluted him and walked away. 'Sorry, Mark,' Edwards said. 'I should have let you know. They're on secondment to a Kuwaiti squadron here.' He lowered his voice. 'I managed to get hold of a piece of American kit, new high-resolution film. It gives much greater detail. I thought it would be more discreet if they fitted it, rather than our existing crew. Just in case questions get asked later on. Once you're back, it'll take a couple of hours to get the film processed. Drop by my office about twelve and we'll have a closer look at As Salman. Good luck out there.'

Mark checked the jet and signed for it, then climbed the ladder and strapped himself in. Sweat was streaming from him and he waited nervously while Mitch loaded and then reloaded the mission data into the computer.

When he at last pronounced himself satisfied, Mark rattled through the pre-flight checks and began the sequence to fire up the two massive engines. The calm of the morning was rent as the jet-wash fried the air behind the aircraft and sent flurries of dust and sand squalling away across the airfield.

He checked the gauges. The engine temperature had climbed four hundred degrees Celsius in the space of a few seconds. The warning siren sounded. The thunder of the jets was muted as the canopy locked into place.

Mark felt cooler air circulating around him. He radioed the tower for permission to taxi, then gave the thumbs-up to the sergeant in charge of the ground crew, who tipped his hand in salute and stepped away to the side, blocking his ears as the jet began to move forward.

They rumbled out along the taxiway, waiting in line as two Kuwaiti F18s took off in a cloud of smoke and dust and swung out towards the Gulf.

Despite the air-conditioning, sweat soaked Mark's flying gloves as he eased the throttles forward and rolled the Tornado on to the runway. After a final cross-check with Mitch, he wound up the power. Tongues of blue-amber flame flashed out behind them and the chainlink fence swayed and rattled in the jet-wash.

He released the brakes and pushed the throttles all the way forward. The airfield buildings blurred as the jet catapulted forward and the G force pinioned Mark to his seat. His eyes flickered over the warning panel as Mitch called the mantra of rising speeds.

'Captions clear, rotating.'

Mark eased the stick back. The nose lifted and a fraction of a second later the rear wheels left the ground with a clunk.

'Gear travelling . . . and the flaps.'

He caught a glimpse of the skyline of Kuwait City away to

the east, the white buildings still tinged pink by the rising sun, then he was hauling the jet west, holding their climb into the cloudless sky.

As they hit 250 knots, Mark adjusted the throttles and then thumbed the radio. 'Shepherd, this is Shark 2-1, Gate Three, Drop Four, mission as briefed for sector Blue Three.'

'Roger, Shark, this is Shepherd. Confirming Gate Three, Drop Four.' The accent through the static from the Saudi AWACS was impeccable English public school. 'No change to mission, Shark 2-1. Rocket 2-2 leaving the area at one-four-zero.'

Mark acknowledged and pointed their nose due north, and crossed into Iraqi airspace for the first time in six years. He reached down to touch the ejection handle. It was a pointless superstition but one shared by many aircrew.

The symbols of friendly radar tracking them from Saudi Arabia, Kuwait and the US ships in the Gulf faded one by one, leaving the screen almost empty. As he banked to take up track twenty miles below the 32nd parallel, hostile symbols began to flash, each raising a brief gong-like tone from the radar warner.

As his heart beat faster, Mitch instantly diagnosed them. 'SAM 3, four o'clock, outside lethal range. Triple-A, two o'clock, outside lethal range. SAM 3, one o'clock, just outside lethal range.'

A few weeks of routine patrols would render these monotonous, but now Mark was tense and alert, scanning the sky and the ground as restlessly as the beam of a lighthouse. There was an edge of tension in Mitch's voice as he kept up the recitation of missile sites. They lit the radar warner like Christmas lights as they swept round the arc of Iraqi airfields south and west of Basrah. No military jet had taken off or landed at any of them in six years, but their aircraft and their defences remained at readiness.

Far ahead, Mark saw the glimmer of water. The canal was a straight line ruled across the landscape. The oil tanks and towers of Abadan lay in the distance beyond the Shatt al Arab, and the superstructures of a couple of ships ploughed up the water towards Basrah. He banked the jet, keeping a safe margin from Iranian airspace.

Storks speckled the trees and the roofs of the houses, and

the low sunlight glinted on the domes and minarets of the city of Basrah. Few ships were berthed in the once bustling port, but the vast groves of date palms surrounding it were exactly as Mark remembered. A belt of them, up to three miles wide in places, flanked the Shatt al Arab north of Basrah, punctured by the smoke stacks of a giant, oil-fuelled power station.

Clear of the city, Mark drew a deep breath and took the Tornado down to low level. The jet-wash stirred the feather-fronds of the last of the date palms, then they were out over the marshlands, skimming over beds of reed reaching twenty feet into the sky.

Groups of Marsh Arabs stopped their reed-cutting, shading their eyes to peer up as the jet flashed overhead. The squat black shapes of water-buffalo browsed among the reeds. Clusters of dwellings stood on spits of sand and mud above the waters, and the sharp, curved prows of canoes reflected in the water.

'Bloody hell,' Mitch said, pointing down to an arid plain of dry mud and dust. 'Look at this, there must be a hell of a drought.'

'That's Saddam's new canal. If you can't control the Marsh Arabs, you just drain the marshes.'

Six years before, the marshes had extended in a vast triangle north of Basrah, covering thousands of square miles of land between the Tigris and Euphrates. Lake Hammar alone had been fifty miles long. Now the wilderness of reeds and streams had been reduced to pockets of stubborn marsh, surrounded by vast reaches of sunbaked mud. The tangle of decaying reed beds and the abandoned skeletons of dwellings stood like driftwood abandoned by a retreating tide. Even from the air they could see cracks crazing the surface as the chocolate colour of the exposed mud faded to grey dust.

The west bank of the Euphrates marked an abrupt transition to the stony desert that spread before them to the horizon. They flew on, tracking the 32nd parallel.

There were flickers from the radar warner as they came within range of fresh Triple-A and missile sites, but they saw no sign of air activity, no movement of ground troops, nothing but a few drifting herds of goats and camels, and an occasional truck grinding over the dusty roads. The warning gongs became monotonous, the sense of threat and danger lessening with each false alarm.

Mark's nerves had calmed a little as they refuelled from the tanker. They were on the eastbound leg of their circuit over the wilderness of the Southern Desert, about fifty miles from As Salman, when the radio crackled into life.

'Shark 2-1, this is Shepherd. We're going unserviceable and returning home. Magic 2-1 will be replacing us. Complete your mission.'

'Roger, Shepherd.'

'What's up with them?' Mitch said as Mark broke the contact.

'Something serious, I'm sure. They've probably run out of teabags.'

The Tornado skimmed over the desert. Ahead, a grey outline shimmered in the heat haze, and resolved into a ghost town, a sprawl of ruined buildings surrounded by bent and broken wire fencing. A concrete pillar, once part of a triumphal arch, reared up from the sand.

'Shit, that's the place, Mitch. Look, this is where we were held during the war. Just south of here is—'

A siren interrupted him and the warning panel lit up from top to bottom. He felt the jet lurch and the nose began to dip. 'Shit! Hydraulics failure!' He stabbed at the radio button. 'Mayday. May—' He broke off and thumbed the radio again. There was no familiar background hiss and crackle. 'The radio's dead.'

'That does it,' Mitch said. 'Let's get the hell out of here.'

The jet rocked again. Mark hauled back on the stick, but the nose dropped even further. 'Fuck! It's no good, Mitch. The back-up hydraulics are out too.'

'We've got to get out of here.' Mitch's voice rose as the stricken jet dipped again.

'No.' Mark froze, staring at the stony desert framed in the canopy.

'Come on!'

As Mark still hesitated, Mitch made the decision for him. 'Eject! Eject!'

There was a brief, heart-stopping pause, then Mark was hurled upwards into the sky. His parachute snapped open as the Tornado's dive steepened. It plummeted towards the sands, but before it impacted, there was a blinding flash from under the wings. The shockwaves of the explosion buffeted him as he dangled helpless below the 'chute.

Mark stared at the receding fireball in confusion, knowing that he had not armed the weapon system. As the desert rushed up to meet him, he remembered Edwards and the strange ground crew.

A thin, tinny rattle, like grains of rice dropping in a pan, brought him to consciousness. He lay still for a moment, his eyes closed. The heat was blistering and sweat trickled steadily down his face and neck. He rolled on to his side, turning his face away from the blinding light, and felt waves of pain from his hip, arm and shoulder. He groaned and opened his eyes a crack. The rattle continued as the wind blew grains of sand against the visor of his flying helmet.

He pushed himself up on one elbow, but the desert rolled and swam before his eyes. He lay down until the wave of nausea had passed, then propped himself up again and looked around.

The nightmare that had haunted him for six years had returned: a bleak vista of sand and red rock, the smouldering wreckage of a Tornado. The only difference was that instead of the cold darkness of the desert night, this time the nightmare was being played out in the blinding glare of the sun.

Mark sat up, still dazed, and pulled off his flying helmet. The heat made his head pound. He rubbed his eyes with his gloved hand, trying to clear his vision as he looked for some shade. There was little to be had. The sun was now high in the sky.

He heard a low groan. Mitch was lying in the sand away to his right, his leg folded back under him at an impossible angle.

'Mitch! Mitch!' Mark shouted, as he dragged himself to his feet and walked unsteadily towards him. A dark stain covered the leg of Mitch's flying suit from the waist down to the knee. 'It's all right,' Mark called, ripping open the survival box.

Mark knelt alongside Mitch, pulled off his helmet and raised his head, cupping it in the crook of his arm as he held a water bottle to his lips.

Mitch's eyes flickered open as he drank, then closed again.

'I'm going to have to move you a little, just to check your leg.' As Mark eased him on to his side and tried to straighten the leg, he heard the scrape of bone on bone.

Mitch screamed, the veins standing out on his forehead.

'Shit, I'm sorry.' Mark pulled an ampoule of morphine from the medical kit and injected him, then propped the survival box up behind his head, trying to screen him from the sun.

He tried to extend the sunshade with a survival blanket, but he could find nothing to anchor the thin kevlar and it fluttered and broke free. It sailed away on the breeze, sparkling as the reflective side caught the sun. The wind brought no comfort, just a hot, gritty blast, sucking the moisture from them.

Mark sat with Mitch, waiting for the morphine to take effect. 'That hydraulics failure saved our lives. If we'd stayed in the jet another ten seconds, we'd be history.' The only reply was a drowsy murmur.

When Mitch's pain had been replaced by a morphine-fuelled euphoria, Mark bound his fractured leg with the flexi-splints from the medical kit. He stood the survival box directly over him, like a hard plastic tent. He tried to heap sand on it, to cool it and hold it steady in the wind, but there was only a thin covering over the bedrock and he soon gave up.

'Mitch? Can you hear me? I'm going to scout around for better cover. We need some shade. I'll leave you some water. You'll be all right, I'll only be a few minutes.'

Mitch giggled.

To the south and east, belts of dusty scrub stretched away as far as Mark could see. An escarpment rose from the desert floor to the west, but he couldn't tell whether it was two or twenty miles away.

Mark divided the water, leaving two thirds of it and all the food for Mitch, then he packed the remaining sachets back into the rucksack and slipped it on to his shoulders. He draped his flying jacket over his head and shoulders, then began walking towards the west.

The ground was rough and undulating. He stumbled

frequently, losing sight of Mitch. He rested by a sheet of burned and twisted metal lying in the sand, the Tornado's wing, ripped from the fuselage by the blast, then he walked on. A number of shallow wadis crossed his path, running from south-west to north-east, but none were deep or steep enough to afford any shelter from the sun.

He walked for twenty minutes, the heat pounding at him as he crossed broad expanses of bare rock and sand-filled gullies. The high ground shimmered like a mirage, seeming no nearer than when he'd started out. This is crazy, he thought, stopping to drink from his water bottle. Get back, get whatever shade you can and wait for dark. If you keep moving now, you'll both die.

As he turned back, a movement caught his eye. He saw a figure and heard a faint tinkling on the wind. A flock of goats gradually emerged from the heat haze. The figure was side-on to Mark, the thin black outline of a long-barrelled rifle in his hands, standing on a slight rise, looking down towards the place where Mitch lay, Mark watched, torn between the instinct to cry out and the desire to stay hidden.

He heard another sound above the goat bells. A low murmur at first, then a menacing rumble. Shards of light cut across the desert to the south. Sun glinted on glass and metal as a line of vehicles, black against the sand and rock, moved fast towards them. A trail of dust drifted away like smoke on the wind.

Mark began to stumble towards the crash site, then checked and crouched down, watching and waiting.

The column of vehicles bore down on the figure with the rifle still crooked in his arms. They fanned out around him then stopped in a rough circle. As the sound of the engines died, there was a fusillade of slamming doors. Anonymous, hooded figures walked towards the man, who dropped his rifle. After a brief, staccato burst of fire, he crumpled to the ground.

Mark pressed himself flat amongst the scrub. The soldiers moved out of sight, towards the place where he had left Mitch. There was a long silence, then a series of barely human screams. He had not heard such noises since he had lain awake in his cell in Iraq, listening to the sounds from the interrogation chamber. The screams continued for several minutes and the silences that punctuated them were almost as oppressive. A last agonised cry was cut short by a burst of gunfire.

Mark whipped his head around, searching for cover, but there was only sand, rock and thin scrub. He spotted the twisted wing of the Tornado, and dropped to the ground, knotting the arms of his flying jacket around his ankles. He began to belly-crawl towards it, forcing himself to move slowly and carefully, though every inch of the journey seemed to promise a bullet in the back.

There was a narrow gap between the centre of the wing and the ground. Mark looked behind him, satisfying himself that the flying jacket and the wind stirring the sand had covered his tracks, then he began to scoop away the sand, widening the gap. He prayed that the layer below the surface would not be darker, as it had been on the beach where he had played as a child. He scraped until he reached hard rock, then twisted himself around and worked his body in under the wing.

Jagged metal caught on the back of his flying suit, and he wriggled and twisted like a caterpillar pinned to a thorn until his suit tore and he came free. The metal clawed at his back as he wormed his way further in. He reached out with his arms and pulled the rucksack in beside him, then swept the mounds of sand back towards him, leaving only a small airhole. He had no way of knowing if he had left a trail.

The heat under the wing was suffocating and the metal burned his shoulders and heels where it touched. He lay for what seemed like hours, watching the single shaft of light that penetrated his lair. All he could hear was the rasp of his own breathing and the steady drip of sweat from his brow on to the rock.

Without warning there was the dull thud of a boot on the metal above him. He felt the wing bow, pressing down on his back, as his unseen pursuer stepped up on to the wing. Mark gave an involuntary grunt as the air was squeezed from his lungs. The soldier dropped the butt of his rifle on to the metal, then Mark heard the rasp of a match, a muffled curse, and another. Mark lay paralysed, feeling the man's weight pressing down on him and hearing the scrape of his boots as he shifted his position.

The minutes crawled by. Mark's eyes were fixed on the tiny landscape of red sand and blue sky framed by his airhole. The soldier's boots shifted again, and the weight on Mark's back eased as the soldier jumped down, but the flexing of the wing sent a minute avalanche of sand down the slope of his hollow. Mark watched, helpless, as his ventilation hole grew to the size of a fist.

A cigarette butt dropped six inches from Mark's face. Smoke drifted into the airhole and he felt his eyes sting. A sneeze began to build. He wrinkled his nose and ground his teeth until he thought his jaw would break. He forced his face into the grit beneath him, using the pain, until a boot ground the cigarette end into the dirt.

At a crackle of static and a muffled, unintelligible burst of noise over the soldier's radio, the feet shifted. Suddenly a vehicle arrived. Brakes squealed and Mark saw the soldier disappear in a cloud of choking dust.

He let his pent-up breath escape as the vehicle stormed away. He felt himself trembling and could hear his boot-heels rattling against the underside of the wing. Slowly his breathing became more even.

His mouth was dry. He listened briefly for other sounds, but his thirst was so strong that he had to drink. He twisted to one side, as far as the cramped space would allow, and fumbled with the rucksack. He held the water bottle to his lips. The water was the temperature of hot tea and tasted metallic, but he drank greedily. Unable to tilt the bottle, he struggled to swallow and felt some of the precious liquid running out of the side of his mouth and down his cheek. He forced himself to stop, saving the rest, even though the little he had drunk served only to increase his thirst.

His head ached and sweat still poured off him as he laid his head down in the sand and closed his eyes.

Chapter 16

Natalie smiled to herself as the Iraqi border guards walked round the Landcruiser, kicking the tyres and banging each door panel.

Her companion gave her a suspicious look. 'I don't see what's so funny. We've been stuck at this bloody border point for two hours already.'

Her smile deepened. 'Sorry, Lars, I was just picturing the look on Mark's face when I turn up.'

'He doesn't know you're coming?'

'Not a clue.'

'Let's hope he's not in bed with an Arab boy at the time, then.'

'You've been watching too much *Lawrence of Arabia*.'

His look was suspicious. 'You're sure this isn't just a social call?'

'You saw the message. There was obviously someone in the room with him yesterday, so he couldn't say what he wanted. He knows something.'

Lars curled his lip. 'What would he know?'

'He's been in a place where he just might have got some answers to questions that have been troubling us for quite a while.'

One of the Iraqis, a tired-looking country boy in an ill-fitting uniform, reluctantly handed back their passports and exit papers and signalled for the barrier to be raised.

Lars jumped back into the Landcruiser with a theatrical sigh and eased it forward across the border. The road, little better than a dirt track on the Iraqi side, became a smooth, metalled road.

The border guards a couple of hundred yards away gave their papers a cursory glance, then waved them through. Lars gunned the Toyota on to the highway, heading due east towards Kuwait. The UN pennant flying from the radio aerial whipped and cracked in the wind as they picked up speed, leaving a trail of dust hanging in the air behind them.

An hour later they pulled up at the gates of the base at Ali al Salem. 'Thank God for that,' Lars said. 'I don't know about you, but my first priority is lunch. I had breakfast so long ago, I can only remember it in black and white.'

'There's something going on,' Natalie said.

Lorries, tanks and armoured cars were grinding their way round the perimeter track, helicopters clattered up into the sky and wheeled away to the north, and a formation of aircraft lined up and blasted off down the runway.

'What's happening?' she shouted.

The guard turned to look at her but did not respond. His companion, who had been talking into his radio, slid it back into his waistband and then gave a curt gesture of his hand, waving them away from the gates.

'For God's sake,' Lars said. 'What now? It's bad enough being buggered about by the Iraqis, but the Kuwaitis are supposed to be on our side.'

The guard gave him a black stare then unslung his rifle from his shoulder and gestured with the barrel.

'Do as he says, Lars.' Natalie laid a restraining hand on his arm.

Red faced with anger, he shoved the gear lever into reverse and sent the Landcruiser bumping back on to the gravel verge.

'Judging by the number of cigarette butts lying around, we're not the first to have got the five-star treatment,' Natalie said.

The two guards raised the barrier and heaved at the heavy steel mesh gates. As they swung open, the first of the convoy of armoured vehicles roared out and pounded away towards the north.

'Mad dogs and Englishmen,' Lars muttered.

They heard the sound of distant explosions and saw pillars of black smoke rising into the sky.

'That's no exercise,' Natalie said. 'Those explosions are coming from inside Iraq.' She was already reaching for the radio. After a long delay, she heard the voice of her commander. 'What's happening?' she asked. 'What are the British doing?'

'What do you mean?'

'We're at Ali al Salem, just over the Kuwaiti border. It looks like they're staging a solo invasion of Iraq. Armoured vehicles and helicopters are going north and strike aircraft are attacking targets inside the border.'

'What the hell are you talking about? There's been no UN authorisation for any military activity. Contact the base commander, make the strongest possible protest and find out what the hell they're doing. I'll speak to New York and try to get action from there.'

When the last vehicles in the convoy – two massive, heavily armoured bulldozers – had rumbled out of the camp, the guard gave a perfunctory wave and held the barriers raised. Lars powered the Landcruiser through the entrance, giving a string of Norwegian curses under his breath. He drove straight to the command centre, a squat, windowless block of massively reinforced concrete.

Natalie ran from the Toyota but had to stand fuming in the heat for ten minutes while a stone-faced Kuwaiti guard tried to reach the British commander.

When she was at last admitted to the tomb-like lobby of the building, she found an adjutant waiting for her. 'I'm afraid the commander's unavailable,' he said. 'What exactly is the problem?'

Her voice was cold with fury. 'The UN commander – to whose authority every British officer in this region is supposedly subordinate – would like to know exactly what the hell British forces are doing violating Iraq's borders, without any UN mandate, without even informing the UN of their actions.'

'I'm afraid I have no authority to discuss operational matters with you,' he said, his eyes fixed on the wall above her head. 'I suggest your commander takes the matter up through the appropriate channels.'

'I'll tell you what's appropriate,' Natalie said, taking hold of his arm. 'You get your commanding officer out from wherever he's hiding, to explain to me – the duly accredited UN representative – what the fuck he thinks he's doing. If he's trying to start another Gulf War, he's doing a pretty good job.' She released his arm. 'Now where is he?'

'Wait here.' The adjutant hurried away into the bowels of the building, and returned a few minutes later. 'He can't see you now.' He held up a hand as Natalie threatened to explode. 'But if you'd like to wait in the Mess, he'll try to find time to talk to you in the next hour.'

'That's not good enough.'

'I'm afraid it'll have to be.'

She shook him off as he tried to take her arm and steer her towards the exit. She strode outside and slammed the car door.

'Well?' Lars said.

'The Mess.'

He broke into a smile. 'At last, a voice of sanity.'

As they entered the Mess, Natalie spotted a US army major talking to a group of Kuwaitis. 'What the hell is going on out there?'

'Beats me,' the American said. 'It usually takes the Brits three weeks to get permission to unwrap a Hershey bar, yet they have a fullscale retaliatory raid moving within thirty minutes of one aircraft being shot down. It's almost as if they were expecting it.'

There was a discreet cough behind her. 'Ms Kennedy? I'm James Edwards, commander of 21 Squadron.' He gave her a warm smile. 'I'm sorry you've had such a wait, but I hope I can answer your questions. Shall we go somewhere a little less public?'

He led her to a deserted side room and closed the door. He motioned her towards a chair but she shook her head and remained standing.

'If I can just bring you up to date with the situation?' Edwards said. 'A British aircraft has been shot down over southern Iraq this morning. We are engaged in tracing and destroying the Iraqi missile battery responsible. The operation has been cleared at the very highest levels. It is limited in scope and finite in its aims. When it has been achieved, British forces will withdraw.'

'It has not been cleared with the UN. Your forces are in breach of international law.'

'International law recognises the right of legitimate self-defence. Two of our aircrew have been killed this morning.'

Her eyes widened. 'Which aircrew?'

'The next of kin have not yet been informed, but—' He hesitated. 'Please sit down.'

She shook her head. 'Which aircrew?' Her voice was low but insistent.

'I'm very sorry. Flight Lieutenants Mark Hunter and Mitch Thomson.'

Her face drained of colour. She swayed and caught at the edge of the table.

'You don't know how sorry I am to have to tell you this. I know that you and Mark were close.'

She gave no sign of having heard him. 'They could have ejected. You can't know he's dead.'

'The last sound from the radio was an explosion. The radar trace disappeared instantly. We had other aircraft in the area, and they reported seeing no parachutes. The automatic rescue beacon's not been activated and there's been no radio contact of any sort. I'm afraid there is just no possibility of either of them being alive.'

Natalie said nothing, her knuckles white as they gripped the table. His voice seemed to be reaching her down a long, dark tunnel.

'I'm very sorry.' He paused. 'Would you like some water?'

She shook her head and continued to stare down at her hands. At length she straightened up and raised her eyes. 'Did . . . did he leave anything for me: a note, a message?'

'I'm afraid not.' He waited for a few moments. 'My dear, if there's anything, any help or advice I can give . . .'

'I think what I need right now is a little time on my own.'

'Of course, but please keep the offer in mind. I counted

Mark as a friend and I know how much he thought of you. I really am very, very sorry.'

Natalie nodded and hurried out of the room. She found Lars sitting contemplating a pot of coffee and a slice of cake. 'Come on, we're leaving.'

'In a minute, Natalie. This is important.'

She looked behind her. Edwards was on the far side of the room, talking to another officer, but his eyes never left her.

'No, Lars. We've got to get out of here now.'

He heard the urgency in her voice and was on his feet before she had completed the sentence. 'What about Mark?'

'Mark's dead.'

Natalie said virtually nothing on the two-hour drive back to An Nasiriyah, staring out of the window at the monotonous landscape and ignoring Lars' attempts to start a conversation. As soon as they arrived, she went to her office and shut the door.

She worked late into the night but was at her desk again by seven the next morning.

Lars appeared two hours later. 'You all right?'

She nodded, not raising her gaze from the papers in front of her.

He put a hand on her shoulder. 'You didn't sleep much from the look of you.'

'It's better if I work.'

'We can postpone the inspection for a few days. I don't know how much there'll be to inspect anyway by the time the Brits finish dropping bombs and driving tanks all over the area. To be honest, I don't even know why we're going there at all. There's been no trace of Iraqi activity since we started monitoring the site. Whatever they might have been doing once, they're not doing it now.'

Natalie's mouth was set in a stubborn line. 'The inspection goes ahead as planned. I want to know exactly what's going on there and why they've been so anxious to keep us away.' She turned to a map on the wall behind her, hoping that Lars would not notice the tears in her eyes. 'I've arranged a brief at twelve thirty. We'll need the latest satellite pictures.'

* * *

A technician was still spreading the last few photographs on the conference table that dominated the briefing room.

'When were these taken?' Natalie asked.

'Eleven ten yesterday. Perfect visibility. You could see which side the Iraqis parted their hair, if there were any Iraqis there. I've been staring at these damn pictures every day for three months and I've never seen any trace of anyone inside that wire fence, but here's something.' He tapped one of the images. 'We picked this up yesterday. It looks like the Brit jet that got shot down.'

Natalie was already reaching for a magnifying glass. 'How do you know this is new? It could be a crashed jet left over from the Gulf War.'

'Easy.' He walked over to a plan chest and pulled out a drawer. He picked through the contents then pulled out another photograph and handed it to her. 'Same sector: ZA-1471. Taken two weeks ago. There's no wreckage in this one.' It fell from Natalie's fingers as she turned back to the other picture. She stared at it, focusing on every detail.

'Natalie?' Lars said. 'We need to get on.'

She nodded distractedly, then turned back to the technician. 'Can you blow this up for me?'

He gave her a curious look, but took the picture from her and walked over to the plan copier.

Lars leaned over the enlargement with her. The jet was scarred and blackened and both wings were missing, but the front section around the cockpit appeared relatively undamaged. The fuselage was canted to one side and she could see part of a symbol. 'That's a British marking, isn't it?'

Lars nodded.

She looked more closely, then snatched it up. 'Look at this.'

Lars followed her finger as it traced two thin white lines.

There was excitement in her eyes. 'Those are the ejection rails, Lars.'

He laid a hand gently on her arm. 'Don't get your hopes up. The rails don't prove anything. The impact of the crash could have knocked them out.'

'But there's no sign of any crew in the cockpit. They must have ejected.'

'They could have been thrown clear as it hit the ground.' He held on to her as she tried to twist away from him. 'He's dead, Natalie, you have to accept that.'

She ignored him. 'Blow this up again,' she said to the technician. 'And do the same to the ones covering the surrounding area.'

She paced up and down as he fed them into the copier, almost tearing the enlargements from the machine in her haste to get her hands on them. She scanned and discarded four of them and was about to do the same to the fifth when her eye was caught by a dark patch, near the corner of the image. She bent over it with her magnifying glass, then straightened up with an air of triumph.

Lars studied the image. Something had been roughly buried in the sand. Its outline was indistinct, but regular bands of light and dark grey marked its surface. Trailing away to one side of it was a pattern of thin black lines at right angles to each other.

'It's a parachute harness,' Natalie said, smiling. 'And look down to the right. There. That rectangle. It's a survival box.'

Lars held up a hand. 'It still doesn't prove he's alive.'

'The parachute didn't bury itself.'

'The wind could have blown sand over it.'

Her smile didn't even flicker. 'Horseshit, Lars. Do you think the wind opened the survival box as well?'

'Some passing Bedouin could have scavenged it.'

Natalie wasn't listening. 'There's no sign of figures . . . unless . . .' She pointed to a blurred outline, a dark shape half-hidden by the survival box. 'What do you think that is?' She peered at it again, scribbled down the co-ordinates of the crash site in her notebook, then turned and hurried towards the door.

Chapter 17

Mark woke with a shiver and banged his head against the metal. The pain reminded him where he was. At first he could see nothing, then he made out a faint glow and the flicker of a star in the tiny patch of sky.

He stretched out his hand and began to enlarge the hole, pausing after each movement of his hand to look and listen. After ten minutes he had scraped away enough sand to allow himself to inch his way forward, turning his head to fit through the narrow gap.

There was nothing visible to one side. He turned awkwardly to face the other way, the metal digging into his neck. Again, nothing. He took a deep breath and began worming his way out. As he did so, his leg locked. He stifled a grunt of pain as he pulled himself forward with his hands and elbows. His feet came clear of the wing and he rolled on to his back. He grabbed the toe of his boot, forcing it towards him to ease the cramp. The pain ebbed and he lay still for a moment, listening, then he got on to all fours, his gaze flickering, searching for any trace of movement. He sniffed the air like a prairie dog.

He raised himself to his feet, took several deep breaths and drank a few mouthfuls of water, then began to make his way across the sand towards the crash site. Moving a few paces, then stopping and listening, it took him over an hour to cover the ground.

The goatherd was lying face down. Mark turned the body over with the toe of his boot. Two neat round holes were drilled in the centre of the man's face. The back of his skull had been blown off.

Mark walked down the slope to where Mitch lay. His eyes were wide open, staring at the sky, his mouth framing a scream. A halo of dark blood stained the sand around his head. Mark reached down and closed Mitch's eyes, then sat motionless on a nearby rock.

Something had puzzled him about the bodies. It took him a few minutes to realise what. Wherever he had been in the Middle East there were flies, clustered over the bloody cuts of meat on butchers' stalls in the market, crawling around the eyes of the deformed children who begged at every corner. Yet there were no flies here.

The survival box that he had used to shelter Mitch lay empty a few feet away, but the one that had been attached to his parachute remained where it had fallen.

A three-quarter moon rose over the horizon, and Mark felt suddenly conspicuous in its soft glow. He hurried across to the survival box, undid the catch and was about to throw open the lid when he hesitated and stepped away.

He walked back up the slope to the body of the goatherd. He pulled the man's robe from one arm and then rolled the body over, yanking the rest free, then he began to rip the worn fabric into strips.

After a few minutes he had a ragged rope about thirty feet long, one end of which he tied to the handle of the survival box. He paid the rope out hand over hand, then lay down behind the goatherd's body, pressing himself flat into the sand.

As he jerked the rope there was a massive explosion. A tongue of flame flashed up into the sky and there was the screech of shrapnel.

Mark leaped to his feet. He reached for the goatskin water-bottle lying by the body, then thought again. He looked up at the stars and decided to head north.

He had been walking for an hour when he saw a faint,

dark line stretching across the horizon in front of him. He moved forward slowly, scanning the desert to either side of him. A few minutes later he stood inside a high chainlink fence, topped with an endless, snaking coil of razor-wire. A series of warning signs had been fixed along it, but they were facing outwards and he could see only a fragment of Arabic script on one that was bent towards him.

He stared at the fence for a few moments, then dropped to his knees and began tearing at the sand with his hands. He had dug down only a few inches when he tore his finger on something sharp. Scraping away more, he found that the chainlink extended horizontally several feet. He could see no way of digging under it.

Then he remembered the goatherd. There had to be a break somewhere. He turned and began to walk parallel to the fence. He had travelled a few hundred yards when he saw a glow in the darkness and heard an engine.

He turned and ran blindly away, back into the wilderness of rock, towards the one place he could think to hide. He ran until he felt his lungs would burst, then threw himself down into the sand and lay still, the blood pounding in his ears, drowning any sound of pursuit.

Chapter 18

The convoy of four Landcruisers, pale blue with the UN symbol picked out in white on the doors, pulled out of the compound at An Nasiriyah at dawn.

Natalie glanced behind and saw the familiar dusty Mercedes take up station behind them. 'The boys are along for the ride. Stand by for another few days of prevarication, obstruction and intimidation.'

'And that's just the British,' Lars said. 'Imagine what the Iraqis are going to be like.'

Natalie grinned.

After half an hour, the convoy slowed and turned due south towards As Salman on to a rough road pointing straight into the heart of the Southern Desert.

'That's strange,' Lars said, glancing in the wing mirror. 'Our escort's not following us.'

Natalie turned and looked through the rear windscreen. The Mercedes had stopped at the junction. As she watched, it performed a laboured U-turn, then sped back the way it had come. 'They've never willingly let us out of their sight before,' she said. 'What's going on?'

'I don't know. Either the reception committee is already in position up ahead. Or there's nothing here for us to find . . .'

He glanced across at her. 'Or maybe they know something we don't.'

She looked ahead. There was no sign of humanity in the desert waste, apart from a scattering of black Bedouin tents. A camel tethered close to the road curled its lip as the Landcruisers sped past, then disappeared in the dustcloud trailing behind them.

A few miles further on they reached a fork in the track. Natalie consulted her map, cross-checked it with her GPS, then pointed to the right-hand fork. The road was narrow and rough, little more than a cart track, following the contours of a ridge rising a few feet above the desert floor. A few stunted scrub bushes grew out of the centre of the track, their branches scraping the underside of the Toyota as it bounced and bucketed over the potholes. Low drifts of sand lay across the track like spindrift blown over a mountain road.

'Not much sign of recent traffic here,' Lars said. 'And it's the only road in.' He paused. 'Come on, Natalie, admit it, this is a wild goose chase.'

She shook her head. 'There's something here. I'm sure of it.'

The ridge petered out and the track turned to the south-east, towards a thin black line dancing above the heat haze. The only break in the monotonous horizontal line of the fence was a pair of high steel gates. She glanced up at the razor-wire and the signs posted every couple of hundred yards. Although the text was in Arabic, there was no mistaking the warning in the death's-head symbol above it.

The convoy ground to a halt in front of the gates. Natalie jumped down from the Landcruiser and called her team together. 'It seems that for once the Iraqis aren't going to get in our way. That may mean there's nothing to be found here, or they may be up to something. As ever, carry out your work calmly and methodically, whatever the obstructions and provocations, and think safety above all else. Right, let's get suited up and get to work.'

They changed into their NBC suits, checking each other at every stage, testing the seals and their breathing equipment. Natalie smelled the familiar blend of sweat, rubber and Fuller's Earth as she pulled her mask over her face.

She got the thumbs-up from each team leader, then nodded to Lars, who pulled the bolt-cutters out from under the seat of the Landcruiser. He sheared the chain locking the gates and began to swing them open.

The noise of engines rose above the protest of the hinges. Two long-wheelbase Land-rovers appeared in front of them. Soldiers in black NBC suits spilled out and advanced towards the UN teams. One stood at the back of each Land-rover, manning a heavy machine-gun.

'We weren't an Iraqi-free zone for long, were we?' Lars said.

Natalie narrowed her eyes and shook her head. 'They're not Iraqis, they're Brits.' She stepped forward to meet them.

'This is a restricted area.' The officer's voice was distorted by his respirator.

'On the contrary,' Natalie said. 'This area has been designated for an UNSCOM inspection. No one has the right to impede duly accredited UN personnel carrying out their duties in accordance with UN resolution 987.'

'The complex you intend to inspect has been destroyed.' His tone was almost robotic. 'This area is a free-fire zone. No one is permitted to enter or leave until it has been sanitised.'

'Spare me the euphemisms,' Natalie said.

The man's face was invisible, and she could only see a reflection of the desert in his visor, but there was anger in his reply. 'In layman's terms, then. Until we are satisfied that every Iraqi mobile launcher and every other military installation in this area has been located and destroyed, you can turn around and piss off back to Baghdad, or wherever it is you've come from.'

Natalie stood her ground. 'We are tasked to locate and destroy Iraq's weapons of mass destruction, weapons that might very well be used on British soldiers. Why are you obstructing us?'

'I've given you all the reasons you need. Now get back into your vehicles and leave the area. Anyone attempting to proceed further will be fired on.'

She stared at him, incredulous. 'You wouldn't dare fire on civilian members of a UN inspection team.'

'My orders do not specify any exceptions.'

Lars stepped forward and took her arm. 'Come on, Natalie, there's nothing to be gained from arguing with the errand boys. We'll have to take it further up the chain.'

'Just a minute,' she called as the soldier began to turn away. 'We're entitled to your name, rank and number, I believe.'

He swung back to face her. 'You're entitled to fuck all. You have five minutes to leave the area. After that you'll be treated as hostiles.'

Natalie allowed Lars to draw her back, but she was boiling with fury. She reached for her personal radio, but Lars stopped her. 'Save your batteries.' He lowered his voice. 'Let's wait till we're safely out of range of these trigger-happy grunts. We'll use the one in the car.'

As the soldiers began forcing the gates shut, Lars pulled off his NBC hood, then sent the Landcruiser in a wide turn across the desert, circling back on to the track. He led the convoy back over the ridge to the north as Natalie vented her anger on the radio link to her superior in Baghdad.

As she broke the connection, Natalie glanced behind her. The fence had disappeared from sight behind the ridge. Scanning the track ahead, she spotted a place where it curved around an outcrop of rock, shielding it from view.

'Pull in there, Lars.'

'What?'

'Don't argue, just do it.'

He swung the Landcruiser off the track and the others followed. He turned to look at her. 'Well?'

'I'm going in there.'

'Don't be insane. There are teams of well-organised, heavily armed psychopaths on patrol. They've just told you: if they find you, they'll shoot you.'

'Then I'll just have to make sure they don't find me.' She smiled, hoping she sounded more confident than she felt. 'They're bluffing. They wouldn't dare shoot UN personnel.'

'But even if you do get into As Salman, what can you possibly achieve on your own?'

'I can find out two things: why the Brits are really so anxious to keep us out, and what's happened to Mark.'

'But if he survived the crash, the Brits will have found him.'

She met his gaze. 'I hope not.'

'And even if he is alive, you can't search a hundred square miles of desert for him.'

'If he's alive, I'll find him in one of three places: at the crash site, the prison where he was held or at As Salman itself.'

'And if you don't?'

She didn't answer.

'If you're set on going in, I'm coming with you.'

She put a hand on his arm. 'No, Lars, I need you out here in case anything does go wrong.'

He banged the steering wheel. 'This is crazy. How the hell do you think you're going to get in there anyway? They'll be watching the gates.'

She smiled. 'Then I'll just have to find another way in, won't I? Right,' she said, cutting him off before he could protest again. 'You go with the others. Pull back to An Nasiriyah.'

She glanced at the clock on the dashboard. 'Give me twenty-four hours from now. If there's been no contact by then, feel free to contact the Secretary General or the 7th Cavalry.'

He did not smile. 'I supported you all the way when you broke the rules last time and found that mustard-gas plant, but this is different. This is just plain stupid.'

'There are no answers out here, Lars. I won't find out what the Brits are trying to hide by meekly going back to Baghdad when a few soldiers tell me to.' She gave a gentle smile. 'I hear what you're saying and I understand why you're saying it, but please don't try to persuade me any more. My mind's made up.'

He let out a long, slow sigh. 'All right. Be careful.'

Natalie waited for fifteen minutes after the other three vehicles had driven off, swallowed by their own dust cloud as they disappeared to the north, then she began to drive back towards As Salman.

She stopped just short of the crest of the ridge. There was no sign of vehicles or soldiers, just the fence stretching away into the distance. She drove down to it and stopped in a slight dip, then got to work with the bolt-cutters. She had to nose the Toyota up close and stand on the bonnet to cut through the coil of razor-wire. The strands sprang and snapped back, one ripping into her sleeve and gashing her arm. Sweat pouring from her, it took her twenty minutes to cut through the fence.

She put the Landcruiser into gear and inched through the gap. The squeal of the broken links along the flanks of the vehicle was like chalk on a blackboard. Once through the fence, she got out and pushed the section of fence roughly back into place, but she could do nothing to mask the severed coil of razor-wire dangling down its face.

She pulled her NBC hood over her head and checked the seals before getting back into the Landcruiser, then drove south, picking her way around the sand dunes, bouncing and jolting over the broken rock.

She slowed before each patch of high ground, inching forward to check the desert ahead before driving on. Whenever she stopped, she also checked her GPS, comparing the co-ordinates with one of three sets on a scrap of paper she had stuck to the dashboard.

At the sight of a dark shape on the track ahead she braked to a sudden halt. She sat motionless, blood pounding in her ears, then she got out of the Landcruiser and began to walk up the slope, her eyes watchful.

She stopped dead. The shape was a body, burned black by the sun. It had been stripped of most of its clothes, and a ragged, knotted rope lay across its chest. Hardly daring to look, she took another step forward. The face had been shattered by gunfire, but the hook nose and lank black hair were enough to show her it wasn't Mark.

She breathed deeply, her hunched shoulders relaxing. As she turned away from the body she caught a glimpse of the Tornado's fuselage. Nearer to her was some sort of crater, surrounded by debris.

Another body lay in the sand fifty yards from where she stood. Even from that distance she could see the flying suit. 'Please don't let it be Mark,' she murmured. She began to walk slowly towards it, repeating the silent prayer to herself.

The corpse lay on its back, arms flung wide. There was a dark stain across one thigh and a corona of dried blood around the head. The uniform carried a Union Jack patch.

Tears started down her cheeks, misting her visor. She heard her breath rasping through the respirator as she moved closer, then stooped over the body. Two holes had been blown in the face, which was so blackened by the sun that she could not make out its features.

She gave a strangled sob, then half turned as she heard a faint sound behind her. Pain exploded in her head.

When she came to, she lay still for a moment, feeling hot sand against her cheek, then she groaned and opened her eyes, wincing in the glare. The figure above her swam into focus.

'Natalie! Natalie!'

She put a hand to her eyes, trying to shade them. She gradually made out a face burned red, lips cracked and split. 'Mark?'

'Natalie. Thank God you're all right. I thought I'd killed you. I thought you were one of the soldiers.' His words rasped. 'Do you have any water?'

She nodded. 'Over . . . over . . .' She propped herself on one elbow, fighting down a wave of nausea. 'Over there.'

'Can you stand?'

'Give me a moment.' She took a deep breath and stumbled to her feet, leaning heavily on his arm. He helped her back to the Landcruiser, where she gestured to two five-gallon drums in the back.

Mark could not even wait to fill his water-bottle completely, but snatched it away from the tap half-full and began gulping it down, water dribbling down his chin. He refilled it and drained it twice more before he thought to offer any to her. She took a few sips, then sat down in the shade against the side of the Landcruiser.

'Any food?'

She nodded. 'The cool-box. Go easy at first or you'll make yourself sick,' but Mark was already tearing at the lid.

He sat down beside her, firing staccato questions at her between mouthfuls of food. 'How did you find me? What are you doing here?'

'There are British forces swarming all over As Salman. They tried to turn me back at the fenceline twelve miles north of here. They claimed to have destroyed the plant, but I want to know what's there and why they're trying to keep us away from it.' She paused. 'The Brits told me you were dead. They said you hadn't ejected.'

He nodded, showing no surprise.

She glanced up. The sun was already low over the mountains. She fingered the bruise on the back of her head, then got to her feet. 'Come on, we're going to As Salman.'

He grabbed her arm. 'We can't. I found a report at Porton Down. As Salman's contaminated with chemical agents. It could be toxic for at least ten years.'

'It's all right. I've got a spare NBC suit.'

'You don't understand. That's why I was trying to reach you. An NBC suit may be no protection.'

She froze. 'What did the report say exactly?'

'I can't remember the precise words. Something about NBC suits being of uncertain value.'

'Tell me what else was in it.' She remained motionless as Mark spoke, dredging his memory for every detail of the Vw file, then she squared her shoulders. 'It's a chance we'll have to take. If you don't want to risk it, I'll leave you here, but I'm going in.'

'Then I'm coming with you.'

She pulled the spare NBC suit from the rack behind the cab of the Landcruiser.

'I've been here for two days,' Mark said. 'It's a bit late for that.'

'You haven't been where we're going now.' The fear that the contamination at As Salman might have spread far wider than the complex itself gnawed at her, but she said nothing. She helped Mark into the suit, then steered the Landcruiser around the goatherd's body and drove away from the setting sun.

Dusk was falling as Natalie stopped in the lee of a dune. She checked the GPS again. 'We're only a mile from the site. We'll walk in from here.'

They both ate some food and drank as much water as they could bear, then began moving forward. The sand slipped and trickled away beneath their feet as they scaled each dune and slid down the other side. Ahead of them lights glowed against the darkening sky, and a low murmur of heavy diesel engines carried to them on the wind.

As they crept towards the crest of a large dune, a sudden series of explosions lit the night sky. Natalie threw herself flat and squirmed back down the face of the dune. Mark lay still, then inched forward to peer over the top.

'It's all right,' he whispered. 'Whatever they were firing at, it wasn't us.'

She worked her way up alongside him. The wind whipped grains of sand against her visor as she raised her head. The dune sloped down to the edge of a broad plateau. Perhaps half a mile from their hiding place, two huge armoured bulldozers illuminated by floodlights ground backwards and forwards, pushing mounds of rubble and debris towards a giant pit that had been excavated in the sand. Three Puma helicopters sat some distance away to their right, black and sinister in the half-light, along with the familiar silhouettes of two long-wheelbased Land-rovers, their machine-guns canted towards the sky.

Natalie rolled on to her back and checked the GPS.

'I don't understand,' Mark said. 'What are they doing? Were the Iraqis using it as a SAM site?'

'Then why bulldoze it? Why not just blow it up? Come on.' She slithered down towards the plateau.

They crept forward. The sun-bleached, wind-stripped skeletons of countless dead animals lay around them, and they passed the bones of rats, birds, goats and even a dead man as they moved through what looked like the remains of some encampment. A few tattered fragments of canvas still flapped from a tentpole, the ends frayed by the wind. A wooden table, split and bleached white by the sun, lay on its side, half buried by the sand.

Natalie saw Mark turn towards her, and knew there would be questions in his eyes, but she could give him no answers yet.

They crept on towards the floodlit area where the bulldozers were still gouging at the sand and rock, and lay full length behind a low drift of sand, the last cover available to them. Soldiers in NBC gear moved across the lights. A couple patrolled the perimeter of the site, but the rest were clustered around a group of cylindrical tents.

'Porton liners,' Mark whispered. 'NBC protection tents.'

'I know, we use them too.' Natalie was also whispering, even though the noise of the rising wind and the roar of the bulldozers drowned any noise they could make.

'What do we do now?' Mark said.

'We wait. They can't work all night.'

'Even if they don't, they'll set sentries.'

'Then let's get in there now. What are two more anonymous people in NBC suits?' Despite the bravado, her voice cracked as she spoke.

'But what are we looking for?'

'Whatever it is that your compatriots are trying to bury. Come on, let's just do it.'

They got to their feet. The wind strengthened and a thin mist of sand hung in the air, blurring the outlines of the men and machines. Natalie stared straight ahead as they went, avoiding the temptation to look at the soldier patrolling the perimeter to their right. The soldier's gaze was drawn for a moment by a bulldozer shovelling a mound of debris towards the pit.

At a sudden, deafening blast on a whistle, Natalie froze. She glanced sideways, but the soldier's gaze was now focused on the tents. There was a second blast of the whistle, and he signalled to the driver of the nearest bulldozer, which ground to a halt, headlights extinguished. The other bulldozer stopped and killed its engine, leaving a silence broken only by the wind. The drivers jumped down and moved back towards the Porton liners, joking with the guard as they strode past him.

Natalie heard another shout, and turned her head slowly. The soldier was looking straight at her. He shouted again. 'Ten-minute break.'

Faint with relief, she raised her arm in acknowledgement. Satisfied, he turned away, and Natalie hustled Mark towards the shadow of one of the bulldozers.

'He won't be the only sentry,' Mark said.

'I know. Come on.' She led him towards the edge of the pit.

The sand was strewn with shards of metal. She stooped

down and picked one up, its edge bright and sharp. She found another and another, turning them over in her hands, scrutinising them in the glare of the floodlights. One had a column of stencilled markings. Natalie looked closely at it, deciphering the letters and numbers, then grabbed at Mark's arm.

'What is it?' he said.

Before she could reply, they heard the crackle of the soldiers' radio above the howl of the wind.

There was a sudden flurry of activity. Natalie and Mark stood rooted to the spot as soldiers sprinted from the tents, piled into their vehicles and stormed up the rise past the helicopters towards the hidden Landcruiser, their headlamps blazing in the darkness. Others spilled out of the tents and began fanning out around the perimeter, appearing and disappearing in the swirling sand.

'Let's go.' Mark pulled at her arm, and pointed towards the helicopters.

'The Landcruiser—'

'Forget it. This is our only chance.'

They began to run, slipping and stumbling. Natalie gasped with the effort, the heavy steel casing clutched to her chest.

'What are you doing? Drop it,' Mark said, but she wrapped her arms even tighter around it and hurried on.

Mark ran towards the third of the Pumas, half-hidden from the soldiers by the other two helicopters.

They both stopped dead as a figure stepped from the shadows by the Puma. He was in profile to them, staring towards the commotion around the tents, but it could only be a moment before he shifted his gaze and spotted them.

Mark motioned Natalie towards the guard. She began to saunter towards the man as Mark crouched and ducked away, running behind another of the helicopters.

The soldier turned, saw Natalie and shouted a challenge. She raised an arm in greeting and carried on strolling towards him, but the barrel of his submachine-gun swung up and the safety catch clicked off.

There was a sudden dull thud, then the soldier's knees buckled and he pitched forward. Mark tossed aside the rock and pushed Natalie ahead of him into the cab of the helicopter. He jumped in behind her and pulled the door closed. The sudden quiet was more oppressive than the noise outside. He glanced down at the warning patches on his NBC suit. They glowed blood red. He hesitated and gave a despairing look at Natalie, then began tugging at his hood.

'Mark, you can't do that. You don't know what we may be contaminated with.'

Mark ripped apart the seal. 'I'll have to chance it. I can't fly it without one of these.' He gestured to the flying helmets on the seat, the black stubs of night-vision goggles protruding from them. He pulled one of the helmets over his head and switched on the goggles. A faint whine was followed by the familiar green haze flecked with white points of light.

Natalie put a hand to her own hood, but then withdrew it, leaving the other flying helmet lying on the seat between them. 'How can you fly it anyway?' she said. 'You fly fast-jets, not helicopters.'

'I did a couple of flights in Pumas as part of my initial training.'

'A couple?'

'You don't forget. I hope.'

He flicked the battery switch, and green light showed on the instrument panel. He reached up above his head and gripped two levers among the mass of switches and dials. He hesitated a moment, peering out at the dark shapes moving through the sand, then he set his jaw and pushed the levers to ground idle, feeling the click as they slid forward a notch. He glanced across at Natalie. 'This is where the shit hits the fan. Get down on the floor.'

As he thumbed the left-hand ignition switch, there was a huge explosion from the desert to the west of them. 'There goes our alternative transport.' He pushed the starter. There was an electronic whine above them and the left engine began to turn over. He stared at the RPM gauge, willing it to move faster. When it reached twelve per cent, he pushed the fuel switch. The engine noise grew louder, but he was already firing the right engine.

The temperature needle crawled around the dial. Mark thumped his right hand against the column in frustration, his left hand poised on the rotor break above his head. 'Ground idle,' he muttered pushing the lever forward. The blades began to move, sounding like a windmill creaking in a gale.

As Mark pushed the throttles forward another notch, into flight idle, the rotor began to turn faster, chopping the air and rocking the cabin. The downwash from the blades threw even more sand and dust into the air. Natalie knew it was not enough to protect them. She glimpsed a shadowy figure running towards them, the floodlights glinting on the barrel of his weapon.

The juddering of the Puma slowed as the engine note rose and the blades began to blur. Mark released the parking brake and pushed the cyclic forward, paddling the left rudder pedal to turn the Puma away from the other helicopters. It rumbled forward along the ground.

There was a crack and the Perspex window in his door starred as a round smashed through and exited through the roof. He grabbed at the collective beside his seat but jerked it upwards too quickly. The Puma rose a few feet then tilted forward, its tail rising above it. Mark rammed the collective down again as the desert floor rushed up to meet them. The helicopter righted but crashed back down, bouncing violently on its wheels.

The rattle of punctured metal and the whine of ricochets were audible even above the howl of the rotors, as more shots were fired.

Mark hauled on the collective again and the helicopter bucketed forward. He eased the cyclic column away from him. Through the whirlwind of dust and sand he could see more dark figures dropping into firing positions. He pulled the lever further upwards and felt the helicopter wavering, its weight now on the rotors, not the ground. Another shot smashed through the Perspex, punching a fist-sized hole.

'Come on! Come on!' Natalie shouted.

He snarled a reply, pulled the collective again and dragged the cyclic back. The helicopter rose higher, wavering in the air, then he pushed the cyclic away from him and felt the Puma jerk forward.

Its flight was as ragged as a winged grouse. Every correction he made to the cyclic seemed to make it even more erratic. It lurched and dipped, shaken by the gusting wind. The tail-boom slewed and it hit the rotor of one of the other

Pumas with a grinding crash, sending the broken blades spinning into the darkness. Not daring to breathe, Natalie waited for theirs to follow.

Agonisingly slowly, the helicopter chopped forward into the wind. Shots pursued them, rattling and whining around the Puma's armoured skin. One round smashed its way upwards through the floor of the cab, no more than an inch from Natalie's head.

'Get up on the seat and strap yourself in,' Mark said. 'The floor's no protection now.'

The Puma yawed sideways. As it swung around, Mark caught a last glimpse of the site. Through the night-vision goggles he saw a flicker of green fire as the rotors of the other, undamaged Puma began turning, the light flashing from the blades as they accelerated. 'They're coming after us,' he shouted.

He pushed the stick forward, dropping them towards the desert floor. Natalie felt the straps tighten against her chest as the ground loomed before her, then the helicopter levelled, skimming over the sand and rock.

Mark peered into the darkness. An outcrop reared towards them, showing as a solid green block in his goggles. He twitched the cyclic and paddled the right rudder as hard as he could. The Puma lurched like a drunken man, the flailing rotors missing the rock by inches.

Mark eased the stick back, sending the helicopter higher. 'Keep watching behind,' he shouted.

The wind had strengthened again into a howling storm that battered against the cab as the Puma plunged forward. The strange green vision of the world through his goggles coalesced as dust and sand whirled around them. He was aware of nothing but the narrow tunnel of his vision and the feel of the stick in his hand.

Suddenly Natalie shouted and pointed behind them. He risked a quick glance. The outline of another Puma showed in his goggles, its engine intakes pulsing holes in the green-flecked image.

He switched his gaze back to the onrushing desert, his vision now even more clouded. He rammed the throttles forward as far as they would go and pushed the cyclic forward, easing the Puma even closer to the ground.

Searing flashes of tracer, blinding sparks in his NVGs, zipped past them. Mark switched the Puma right and left, but the other helicopter was still gaining, the fire from its guns slicing through the darkness towards them. He was lost, caught between the rock of the pursuing Puma and the hardest place of all, the solid ground skimming by, only feet below them.

The pursuing helicopter grew larger, steadily gaining on them. Mark bucked and jerked, weaving and dodging over the flat desert floor, but knew there was nowhere to hide. Each time, the lines of tracer slipped away and then returned, homing swiftly on him. The Puma loomed, guns chattering. Rounds ripped into the cab with a smell of burning.

The fury of the rising sandstorm had all but obliterated Mark's forward vision. Suddenly he pulled back on the throttles, telescoping the distance between the two helicopters. Still peering into the green-flecked duststorm ahead, he groped for the toggle switch on the cyclic. As his hand closed around it, his thumb stabbed downwards, holding the switch locked open.

The entire contents of the Puma's flare rack – fifty phosphorus-packed canisters – ejected into the slipstream behind them and ignited in a blinding flash of white light. As he glimpsed the reflected flash, Mark hauled the helicopter to the right, away from a looming ridgeline. Blinded by the full impact of the flare-burst, the other Puma flashed past, guns still chattering. The ghost image in his goggles became a blinding white flash and then dissolved into a mist of shapeless fragments as their pursuer hit the ridge and vapourised.

The smell of burning grew stronger and warning lights flashed on the panel in front of Mark. One engine spluttered, missed, faltered and then caught again, but its beat was as ragged as the breathing of a dying man.

'We'll have to put down.' He pulled the throttles back further but the blizzard of green flecks in his vision grew even more dense as the sandstorm raged towards its peak. He caught a momentary glimpse of parallel lines to one side of them, then pinpoints of light whirled in his eyes.

He eased the cyclic forward, nosing the Puma towards

the ground, but the wind shrieked and battered at them. The engines faltered and the Puma slid sideways and downwards.

Mark threw the switches to cut the engines as the Puma plummeted the last few feet through the storm. It snagged a wire fence, then tore free and smashed into the sand, the rotors flailing and snapping like twigs as they buried themselves in the face of a dune.

The ensuing silence was broken only by the ticking of hot metal, the steady drip of fuel and the howling of the wind.

Mark heard Natalie groan and stir. The smell of burning was still strong. He glanced behind him and saw flames flickering upwards through the floor at the back of the cab. 'We have to get out. It could blow at any second. There's some kind of shelter to the right of us.'

He clambered up the steep-tilted cab and dragged himself out, hanging on until Natalie was safely out, then he dropped to the ground.

The full force of the wind hit them as they came out of the lee of the Puma. Fine sand forced its way through the visor of Mark's flying helmet. He lowered his head, hung on to Natalie's arm, and stumbled through the darkness.

The building was empty and abandoned, its face scarred. They pushed their way in through a door sagging from its hinges, wading over the sand that had drifted yards inside. They groped their way to a far corner and huddled down, their arms around each other, shivering with cold and shock.

Mark sat staring into the darkness, not speaking. Although he knew that the sandstorm would screen them from their pursuers, he started at every noise, every change in the pitch of the wind. At last, bone weary, he closed his eyes.

Chapter 19

It was light when Mark awoke. His eyes were still stinging, his breathing laboured. He hauled himself upright and looked around.

Natalie lay asleep at his side, still clutching the piece of metal. He ached to ease off her NBC hood, brush a tendril of hair away from her mouth and kiss her. Instead he gazed at her through her visor, etching every detail of her sleeping profile on his mind.

They were in a blank, featureless concrete cell, its floor half-buried by drifting sand, the walls cracked and collapsing. The doorway gaped open. The wind had died to a steady breeze that stirred eddies of fine sand in the space beyond. He stood up, stretched the stiffness from his body and walked to the door. From the angle of the sun it was around eight in the morning. Although the storm had abated, a fine mist of sand still hung in the air.

Mark peered cautiously around before stepping into the sunlight. There was no sign of movement. A concrete pillar, once part of a triumphal arch, reared upwards above him, capped with the stone face of Saddam Hussein. He ran back inside.

Natalie was sitting upright.

'We're in the prison where I was held during the war.'

She nodded. 'Then we're still much too close to As Salman. I'll try to call Lars.'

She checked her GPS and fumbled with her radio. 'Cobra, this is Natalie. Cobra, this is Natalie. Emergency Code Red, repeat Code Red. I'm at 379142, heading due north on foot.' The only answer was a hiss of static. She repeated the message, then slipped the radio into her chest pocket, her face a mask.

'No go?' Mark asked.

'I don't know. It's near the limit of its range.' She stepped to the door and peered out. Mark stood at her side, his brow furrowed. She glanced across at him. 'Solved the puzzle yet, Mark?'

'It's as we thought. Saddam used chemical weapons against the Coalition, despite their nuclear threat. When it came down to it, the Coalition just couldn't carry it out. When this gets out, it'll expose the West's nuclear deterrent strategy for what it really is, what it always has been – nothing but a bluff. We've got the weapons, but we'll never use them.'

'Good try, Mark, but there's still one piece missing. This one.' She tossed the shell casing to him. He caught it and turned it over in his hands. 'Notice anything about the markings?' Natalie said.

'They're not in Arabic script.'

'More than that, Mark.' She took it back from him and stabbed her finger down on it. 'Manufacture date 10/90. Loading date 12/90. Just before the Gulf War. Serial number PD 798653. That's a British serial number, from Porton Down. Know what the yellow triangle means?'

'A white triangle means nukes.'

'And a yellow one means chemical or biological weapons. What your countrymen are so desperately trying to bury back there are the remains of British chemical weapons.'

'What? But we don't have any.'

Natalie heard the doubt in his voice. She allowed the silence to build, watching his face as he struggled to come to terms with the enormity of what she had said.

'If the scientists at Porton Down had developed a doomsday weapon,' Natalie said, 'it wouldn't be enough just to test it on the animals and human guinea pigs back home.'

Mark was silent for some time, then he slowly nodded. 'They'd need to test it under battlefield conditions. And what better test-site than an Iraqi chemical weapons plant? If anything went wrong, the Iraqis, not the British, would be blamed.'

Natalie looked at him 'They detonated the new weapon and marched their troops right through the area. Then they collected every available bit of data: chemical agent detector equipment, samples of contaminated soil, sand, fabrics and as many dead bodies – animal and human – as they could get their hands on. That's what all those guys in unmarked fatigues were doing in the Gulf War. The troops – the spearhead troops – were given inoculations and pre-treatments. Among these was Inoculation Scimitar. It was untested, of course, and with unknown and potentially dangerous side-effects, but it was the only effective antidote to the weapon they'd developed.'

She gave a bleak smile. 'You saw the evidence yourself in the file at Porton Down. The unprotected Iraqis died in their hundreds and thousands or simply fled, while the British casualties were entirely acceptable: ten per cent immediately, a further twenty to thirty per cent over the next five years. A good result in military terms.'

'But how could one agent have such differing effects? If it could kill thousands of Iraqis almost instantly, why has it taken Dan and Steve so long to die?'

'Perhaps it isn't just one agent. Saddam regularly uses mixtures of agents against the Kurds. We assumed that the Porton Cocktail was a vaccine, but what if it was a cocktail of chemical and biological agents? A virulent chemical agent would kill instantly over a compact area. A biological agent – perhaps a deliberately modified strain of the AIDS virus—' again she saw his eyes widen in recognition – 'would disperse over a far wider area. It would pass unnoticed, but its longterm effects would be equally fatal.'

'But there's no military point in that.'

'Isn't there? Widescale use of this would cripple any enemy, destabilise any regime.' She tapped the shell casing.

'Look. It's the batch identifier, showing which agent the shell contains.'

Mark glanced at the stencilling. 'Vw,' he said. 'That's the title of that file from Porton Down.'

She shook her head. 'That's not a "w". It's the Greek symbol for omega – the last letter of the alphabet – the end of everything. Your country has developed the most devastating weapon the world has ever seen – V-Omega – and they'll do anything to protect it.

'VX was one of the most potent chemical agents ever developed, tens of times more dangerous than the original Nazi nerve agents. Imagine how many more times more deadly V-Omega must be. Perhaps even deadly enough to penetrate NBC kit.'

Mark fell silent, remembering his stinging eyes and constricted throat and chest on the ranges at Porton.

'With an agent this powerful, you could defend territory simply by spraying it.' Her face hardened, the corners of her mouth twisting down as she spoke. 'But of course its real value isn't defensive. An effective antidote – Inoculation Scimitar – would turn the agent into the ultimate offensive weapon. You could destroy your enemies but leave their weapons and equipment, their buildings and industries intact.'

Mark was silent, staring past her at the mound of sand half-blocking the entrance. The British authorities would do anything to ensure the last skeleton of Desert Storm remained buried. The poisonous secret had tainted everyone it touched. Luther Young and David Isaacs had been killed, and Dan, Steve and Stumps were dying because of it. He and Natalie had barely escaped with their lives.

His thoughts were interrupted by the sound of engines. Natalie peered out through a chink in the wall. He knew from the way her shoulders sagged that the British had found them. She fumbled with something at her belt, then straightened up.

'Come on, Natalie, let's not wait for them to drag us out of here.'

She took his hand and turned to face him. 'No regrets?'

'Only one.' He pressed his forehead against her NBC hood, aching to bridge the gulf that separated them.

They walked outside, blinking in the light. British soldiers had surrounded the buildings, and their snub-nosed guns swung to cover them.

The officer stared at her. 'You should have heeded the warning. It would have kept you alive.'

Natalie fought back the fear. 'But then you'd have got away with it. Now it's too late to bury the evidence. We put it out on the net. The news will be in New York by now.'

'We traced your transmission. All I heard was a Mayday call. Now it really is too late.' The officer stepped forward and ripped her radio set out of her waistband, then ground it beneath the heel of his boot.

Natalie tossed the bomb casing towards him. It stuck upright in the sand. 'You know what this proves, don't you? You're being used to cover up more than a war crime. This is a crime against humanity.'

'It's not my job to worry about that,' the officer said, sliding off the safety catch of his weapon. 'This is my job.'

Mark closed his eyes. He felt the heat of the sun on his head, the breeze stirring the hair on the nape of his neck. A bead of sweat trickled slowly down his cheek and he smelt the faint metallic tang of gun oil.

There was no command, just a sudden burst of rapid fire. He heard the distinct, sharp concussion of each shot, felt their passage through the air, heard the impact of metal on meat.

Mark swayed but did not fall. He opened his eyes. The officer was sprawled several feet from where he had been standing, his body twisted. Two of his men lay twitching in the sand. The others stood frozen. Beyond them, Mark saw the outlines of forty or fifty NBC-suited figures prone in firing position.

'Make your weapons safe, throw them down and raise your arms high above your heads.' The voice was American.

The remaining British soldiers took only a second to weigh up the odds, and dropped their weapons.

A team of American soldiers moved forward. As each man was searched, he was spreadeagled, face down, and bound with plastic handcuffs. When the last one had been secured, the commander spoke a few terse words into his radio, then smiled at Natalie.

'Dr Kennedy, I presume.' He had a friendly open face and a major's badges.

'Hello, Jack. You certainly took your time getting here.'

'Just in time to save your ass again. It's getting to be a habit.'

Mark watched the exchange. 'How—'

'By helicopter.'

'Did the UN contact you?'

Jack shook his head. 'We intercepted your transmission and traced it, just like the Brits. Starting from Dharhan it took us a little longer to get here.'

Mark barely heard him. He was staring at a group of unarmed men dressed in desert fatigues. He could see no names, badges of rank or unit, apart from a yellow scorpion, speared by a lightning bolt.

'Who are those guys?'

The major stared at Mark for a moment, then turned away as the distant thunder of helicopter rotors broke the silence. Five black shapes appeared over the southern horizon. The helicopters – a massive Chinook and four Cobra gunships – swept in and hovered over the site.

Mark clapped his hands to his ears and closed his eyes as the Chinook came in to land, its rotors whipping up a fresh storm. The din subsided as its engines wound down.

Eyes narrowed, Jack glanced at Mark. 'What about him?' he said to Natalie.

'He comes with us.'

'Natalie . . .' Jack hesitated. 'We'll talk about this back at As Salman.'

As they walked towards the helicopter, Natalie stooped to pick up the bomb casing. They left the bodies of the British soldiers where they lay.

Jack met the question in Mark's eyes. 'We've made other arrangements for them.' He turned to Natalie. 'Is your suit still viable?'

She nodded. 'As much as anyone's.'

The helicopter rose into the air and swung away to the south, retracing the route that they had flown through the storm. As they approached As Salman, Mark could see the bulldozers standing immobile, surrounded by US army trucks, Bradley fighting vehicles and chemical detector vans.

As the dust from their landing settled, Mark climbed down from the helicopter and looked around. Lines of men in NBC suits carried boxes and black sacks, trekking backwards and forwards from every corner of the site like columns of ants returning to the nest.

He looked up to meet Natalie's steady gaze. 'Finally worked it out, Mark? You know the real British crime, don't you? They didn't tell the US what they had.'

'So our rescue by the US cavalry was obviously no humanitarian gesture,' Mark said. 'They're all over this place like flies on shit and they're not collecting samples for the UN.'

She nodded. 'V-Omega will be in production at Edgewood Arsenal in the States within a month – strictly for defensive purposes, of course.' There was a note in her voice Mark had never heard before.

He looked from Natalie to Jack. 'So this is going to stay a cosy little secret between Britain and the US. All you care about is getting the weapon for yourselves.'

Jack laughed. 'You'd hardly expect us to hand it to the UN.' He glanced at Natalie. 'Half the UN staff are spies for one country or another. Can you imagine what Iran or Iraq could do with a weapon like this?'

As Mark stared at the shell casing under Natalie's arm, a sick, cold feeling engulfed him. 'Jesus,' he said. 'You're part of this, aren't you?'

'We all have to choose a side, Mark. Whatever the cost.'

'But Dan—'

Her jaw clenched. 'Dan's dying because of what your people did, not mine.' She paused. 'And if there's any hope of a cure being found, the US has the resources to find it.'

'But that's not all, is it?' His eyes bore into her.

'You can't uninvent a weapon, Mark. V-Omega exists and can't be wished away again. All you can do is decide in whose hands you want to leave it. I've made the safest choice.'

At the dull click of a safety-catch, Natalie wheeled around. 'There's no need for that, Jack. He's been in the middle of As Salman without an NBC hood. He's dying anyway.'

'You don't know that. It's been six years. Surface contamination will be minimal by now.'

'But if the ground is disturbed . . .' She gestured to the bulldozers.

'I can't take the chance.' He gave a harsh laugh. 'He might even go to the UN.'

'Jack, don't,' she said, moving towards him.'

He shook his head. 'You've let it get personal, Natalie.' He pushed her away.

Still clutching the shell casing, she raised her head to meet Mark's gaze. Her mouth worked soundlessly, framing words which would not come. The tear in her eye was the last thing Mark ever saw.

There was a burst of gunfire and Mark's body was hurled backwards. He gave a final, convulsive jerk and lay still.

Her face wet with tears, Natalie walked slowly away across the sand.

Afterword

Although this is a work of fiction, it is grounded in some unpalatable truths. Despite the international treaties banning their use, several countries are still developing ever-more toxic biological and chemical warfare agents. Western complicity in Iraq's chemical and biological weapons programmes is also well documented.

Although the plot and main characters of the book are products of my imagination, the case histories of Gulf War Syndrome sufferers are all true, based on the heartbreaking stories of men, women and children, some already dead, many more suffering appalling illnesses and incapacities.

The official evasions, denials and half-truths about Gulf War Syndrome are also accurately reflected. This official indifference to the plight of Gulf War veterans mirrors the disregard for the fate of Porton Down human guinea pigs exposed to chemical agents, and veterans of the nuclear weapons tests following World War Two.

Some have spent decades fighting for recognition of the cause of their disabilities and for compensation for them. It is already too late for many, but we owe it to their memory, and to the survivors and their descendants, to ensure that no more precious time is wasted.

John Nichol, April 1997

Bibliography

BOOKS

Adams, James, *The New Spies*, London, 1994.
Carter, G. B., *Porton Down: 75 Years of Chemical & Biological Research*, HMSO, 1992.
de la Billière, General Sir Peter, *Storm Command*, London 1992.
Harris, Robert and Paxman, Jeremy, *A Higher Form of Killing: The Secret History of Gas and Germ Warfare*, London, 1982.
Hersch, Seymour, *Chemical & Biological Warfare: America's Secret Arsenal*, London, 1968.
MacArthur, Brian (ed.), *Despatches from the Gulf War*, London, 1991.
Parker, John, *The Killing Factory*, London, 1996.
Robinson, Julian Perry, 'The Role of CB Weapons', *The Problem of Chemical and Biological Warfare*, vol. 1, Stockholm International Peace Research Institute, 1970.
Schwarzkopf, General H. Norman, *It Doesn't Take a Hero*, London, 1993.
Smith, Graham, *Weapons of the Gulf War*, London, 1991.

REPORTS

'Abuse of Iraqi Children by Security Forces', Amnesty International, 14 March, 1989.

'Arming Iraq: Biological Agent Exports Prior to the Gulf War', statement of Senator Donald W. Riegle, Jnr., 9 February, 1994.
'British Position on Chemical Agents in the Persian Gulf', file no. 68360155.94d, US Department of Defense, Washington, 1994.
'Diagnosis and Treatment Strategies for Chronic Pyridostigmine Poisoning in Gulf War Veterans,' Lewis M. Routeledge Phd, 5 March, 1995.
'Gulf War Syndrome', House of Commons Defence Committee, 11th Report, 29 October, 1995.
'Health Aspects of Chemical and Biological Weapons', World Health Organisation, 1970.
'Inquiry into the Nature and Scope of Gulf War Syndrome', Report of the US Senate Committee on Banking, Housing & Urban Affairs, chaired by Senator Donald W. Riegle, Jnr., May, 1994.
'Report of the Defense Science Board Task Force on Persian Gulf War Health Effects', Office of the Under-Secretary of Defense for Acquisition and Technology, Department of Defense, Washington, June, 1994.
'Report of the Secretary General on the Status of the Implementation of the Special Commission's Plan for the Ongoing Monitoring and Verification of Iraq's Compliance with Relevant Parts of Section C of Security Council Resolution 687 (1991)', United Nations, 10 April, 1995.
'Resolutions of the United Nations Security Council and Statements by Its President Concerning the Situation Between Iraq and Kuwait', UN Department of Public Information, 1994.
'Tests on Biological Agents in Samples from the Gulf', Report to Senator Riegle from the Lawrence Livermore National Laboratory Forensic Science Center, 15 April, 1994.
'When Science and Politics Collide', James Tuite, Chief Investigator to Senator Riegle, 1995.

PRESS ARTICLES

Adams, James, 'The Red Death', *The Sunday Times*, 23 February, 1994.
Adams, James, 'Russia Develops Genetic Weapons', *The Sunday Times*, 1 October, 1989.
'April 1995 Casualty Report', *Phoenix* (Gulf War Veterans of Georgia, Inc.), April, 1995.

Barry, John, 'Planning a Plague?', *Newsweek*, 1 February, 1993.

Batin, Shyam et al, 'Putting the Genie Back in the Bottle', *Observer*, 8 January, 1989.

Bellamy, Christopher, 'Farewell to Misery of Poison Gas', *Independent*, 19 October, 1996.

'Chemical & Biological Warfare Section', *Phoenix*, September, 1995.

Chetwynd, Phil and Baldwin, Tom, 'Navy Widow's Gulf Anguish', *News* (Southampton), 18 March, 1995.

Cohen, Nick and Wilkie, Tom, 'Gulf Teams Not Told of Risk From Uranium', *Guardian*, 11 February, 1994.

Cole, Peter, 'The Cocktail with a Lasting Hangover', *SSAFA News*, Spring, 1995.

Crossette, Barbara, 'Iraq Admits Germ Warfare Program', *New York Times*, 16 August, 1995.

Doyle, Leonard, 'The Poisoned Legacy', *Independent*, 2 August, 1988.

Friedman, Alan et al, 'Sinister Alchemy', *The Financial Times*, 3 July, 1991.

'Gulf Families Fight Back', *Disability Now*, February, 1995.

Hastings, Chris, 'Tragedy of War Babies', *Journal* (Newcastle) 22 January, 1996.

Hay, Alastair and Dando, Malcolm, 'Iron Curtain Goes Up on Anthrax Offensive', *Guardian*, 24 November, 1994.

'Hebrew University Research Sheds Light on Gulf War Syndrome', undated press release from the Hebrew University of Jerusalem.

Hedges, Stephen J. et al, 'Baghdad's Dirty Secret', *US News & World Report*, 11 September, 1995.

Koenig, Peter, 'Gulf War Syndrome', *GQ*, September, 1994.

Mahnaimi, Uzi and Adams, James, 'Iran Builds Biological Arsenal', *The Sunday Times*, 11 August, 1996.

McFadyean, Melanie, 'Something Nasty in the Gulf', *Independent on Sunday*, 12 February, 1995.

Miller, Russell, 'Children of the Storm', *The Sunday Times*, 14 February, 1996.

'National Unity Conference Report', *Gulf Vet* (newsletter of the Gulf War Veterans of Massachusetts), 16 March, 1995.

'Nerve Damage in Gulf Troops', *Disability Now*, 15 June, 1996.

Nuttall, Sarah, 'Gulf Veterans seek Recognition', *SSAFA News*, Autumn, 1994.

O'Kane, Maggie, 'Baghdad and a Have-a-go Hero', *Guardian*, 19 October, 1996.

Parks, Dave, 'Vets Claim Win in Struggle to Prove Gulf War Disease', *Phoenix*, June/July 1996.
'RAF Doctor Says Gulf Syndrome Does Not Exist', *Evening Advertiser*, 31 January, 1995.
'Rape of the Gulf', *The Sunday Times*, 5 August, 1990.
Sebastian, Tim and Old, Jon, 'Official Cover-up: The Living and Dying Proof', *Daily Mail*, 12 November, 1995.
Sebastian, Tim, 'This Simple Form . . .', *Observer*, 22 September, 1996.
Simpson, John, 'The Night Watchman', *Guardian*, 15 September, 1990.
'The Emperor Has No Clothes', *Phoenix*, October, 1995.
Theodoulou, Michael and Dynes, Michael, 'Baghdad Hails Courage of British Mission', *The Times*, 20 February, 1995.
Tyler, Rodney, 'Are These Britain's Gulf War Babies?', *Mail on Sunday*, 20 August, 1995.
Tyler, Rodney, 'We Must Know Why Our Babies Died', *Mail on Sunday*, 5 March, 1995.
Walker, Martin, 'Lethal Exposure', *Guardian*, 20 June, 1994.
Watkins, Alan, 'Gulf War Heroes Radiation Sickness', *Today*, 23 June, 1993.
Watkins, Alan, 'Our Gulf Fever Agony', *Today*, 6 February, 1995.
Watkins, Alan, 'Shot Down', *Today*, 28 October, 1993.
Watkins, Alan and Fitzmaurice, Eddie, 'My War Will Never End', *Today*, 24 June, 1993.